Maksheyeva issued the [...] Nevada desert a cont[...] gigantic bolt of energy [...] waiting Strategic Defense Initiative battle [...] was split into myriad lightning blasts by the host of perfect mirrors. Lightning erupted on the Central European plain and whole divisions lay ruined.

'Again,' said Rykov, and a great battle group erupted and sank into the depths of the Atlantic.

'Again,' said Rykov, and *Backfire* and *Blinder* strategic bombers tumbled in flight like shot ducks, and SS-18 *Satan* ICBMs melted in their silos.

'They are suing for peace.'

'Unconditionally,' said Rykov, *and the game ended*.

STEALTH BOMBER

Barnaby Williams

Sphere Books Limited

A Sphere Book

First published in Great Britain in 1990 by
Sphere Books Ltd

Photoset in North Wales by
Derek Doyle & Associates, Mold, Clwyd.
Printed and bound in Great Britain by
William Colins, Glasgow.

ISBN 0 7474 0410 0

Sphere Books Ltd
A Division of
Macdonald & Co (Publishers) Ltd
Orbit House
1 New Fetter Lane, London EC4A 1AR

A member of Maxwell Macmillan Pergamon Publishing Corporation

For Anne, with love

ACKNOWLEDGEMENTS

To Richard Coltart at Jane's and Profile Political Relations; Anthony Preston at Navint; Imogen Parker, Linda Shaughnessy and Debra Isaac at A.P. Watt; Barbara Boote, Jane Mason and Nick Webb at Sphere; many thanks.

DefCon V

Lowest level of alert. Peace

THE WHITE HOUSE

Lieutenant-General Ulysses Zachary Coogan was used to having both men and machines trying to make holes in his hide, or separate him into his component parts. As a USAF test-pilot he had coped with the vagaries of beyond-the-state-of-the-art aircraft with unpleasant tendencies to spread themselves and their occupants in small pieces over the countryside, as a combat pilot he had put in his dues for his Uncle to considerable effect. He had handled his career with consummate skill, fighting off the efforts of equally-ambitious rivals to ground him until he sat where he was that day, at the very head of the pyramid, the air force's chief of staff.

Never until then, however, had he endured the experience of being tethered out in the centre of the arena, awaiting the arrival of the High Priest to begin his sacrificial slicing. He found the sensation quite uniquely uncongenial.

Coogan was seated as one of a number around the oval table in the Cabinet Room. The occasion was the first meeting of the Executive Committee, EXCOM of the National Security Council in the new presidential term. Those present represented the nucleus of the nation's command authority. They included the holders of the obvious offices, such as the secretaries of state and defence, the national security adviser, the director of central intelligence. The joint chiefs were there. The brass plaques on the backs of the eighteenth-century-replica armed leather chairs had been changed to bear the names of the new administration's cabinet. As they waited for the President to arrive the powerful men in the room rested their well-polished shoes on the soft grey-green carpet with its embroidered border, and looked out over the wintry Rose Garden, or checked the room to see what changes had been made. President Cord had retained the portraits of Jefferson and Lincoln, and substituted Coolidge and Roosevelt for Eisenhower and Taft. President Nixon's portrait did not hang, but the oval mahogany table bought by him remained. As always, the Presidential flag stood behind the President's chair, and with it, in the position of honour to his right, the national flag of the USA. At least Cord hadn't moved that, Coogan thought cynically.

Reflecting the changes that had taken place within the highest reaches of command since the inaugural meeting chaired by President Kennedy on the eve of the Cuban missile crisis of 1962 was the presence of the directors and deputy-directors of the National Security Agency and the National Reconnaissance Office. The world of human intelligence – HUMINT – of spies and moles and agents had largely given way to that of technical intelligence – TECHINT – covering various arcane specialities as electronic, communication, laser, radar, photographic and signals intelligence, all with appropriate acronyms. Much of the intelligence harvested was processed and analysed by the men and women of the National Security Agency in their vast headquarters in Fort Meade, not far outside the capital. The air force and the National Reconnaissance Office were between them responsible for the exotic aircraft and satellites that gathered the intelligence, and the three great, and powerful organisations coexisted together in what was at best a state of uneasy harmony.

Both the NSA and NRO were 'black' organisations. Each had larger budgets than any other intelligence organisation, including the CIA, and yet were enveloped in secrecy. This policy again went back to the administration of John F. Kennedy, which considered it foolish to boast to one's enemies just how much one knew, and was able to know about them.

For years the inside joke in intelligence circles was that NSA stood for No Such Agency. They had been remarkably successful at maintaining their anonymity. While for years CIA personnel and directors had been making the trip up to Capitol Hill to be grilled by hostile representatives NSA hummed quietly away to itself off the Washington-Baltimore Parkway, just like Br'er Rabbit.

The NRO went one better by not existing at all. While it was clear that *someone* must be responsible for the design, development and procurement of the fabulous satellites that orbited the earth and sucked in the intelligence of NSA to chew, the furthest the ordinary person would get to satisfy his curiosity would be a small sign on a locked door in the Pentagon that said Office of Space Systems.

They were represented at the EXCOM meeting, however, their military directors and civilian deputy-directors being present. Different presidents had differing views on whether military men should wear uniform. Jimmy Carter had preferred that all government employees appear in business suits. Succeeding him Ronald Reagan had quietly suggested at his first EXCOM meeting that it might be appropriate for those in the armed services to wear uniform, so that he might be able to distinguish soldier and civilian. The word travelled fast and the next day the more impressionable Washington citizen might have been forgiven for believing that the Third World War had started, so full were the streets with men and women in uniforms fresh out of their dust protectors.

The habit had stuck, and when President Cord entered the room for the first time in his incumbency men in grey and blue suits rose with those in blue and olive uniform, star and braid of silver and gold. Given the perceived views of the president, it was likely to be their last airing for some time.

11

With Cord was his White House chief of staff, Harrison Taylor, his former campaign manager and the man widely credited by those in the know for his candidate's astonishing success throughout the electoral process. Everyone there made due note that Taylor was being given rank appropriate to his achievement.

Cord greeted them and brought the meeting to order. He had good looks of the order of John Kennedy or a younger Ronald Reagan. They put General Coogan's teeth on edge, who unable to account for the electorate's perverse choice of leader had to attribute it to something. To himself, he wryly, if bitterly admitted that it would be a rare goat, finding itself tethered to the sacrificial marble that could admire the pleasing visage of the approaching executioner in his robes of office.

Cord was positively brutal in the speed with which he came to the point.

'Gentlemen,' he said, smiling. 'I'm sure you're all familiar with the saying that a week is a long time in politics. So it is. It's a long time in all our businesses. It's why we get immersed in the tactical detail of what we are doing, sometimes to the extent of missing the broad principles. It's for that reason that I believe that it would be a good idea for us to agree upon the strategic issues facing this nation over the next four years – maybe longer – and our response to them.'

All of those present saw clearly that they were being invited to agree with the views of a president at the beginning of his term of office, elected by an unexpected majority, and enjoying the support of a Senate and House of Representatives controlled by his own party. They furthermore realized that Cord was sufficiently confident to be already thinking about re-election, and that he had firmly grasped the principle that if yours was an activist government – of whatever hue – you smashed straight ahead and forced through your contentious measures within the first half of your elected term, thus offending all vested interests early, and giving them time to get used to

12

it, and you time to salve whatever wounds needed to be salved before offering yourself to the electorate once more.

'Some of you may be aware that before taking up my present vocation –' Expressions remained frozen at hearing the office of President of the USA described as a vocation, and Cord smiled. '– I was an academic, so I will ask your forgiveness if my presentation comes over like a lecture. Old habits die hard. And yes, vocation, gentlemen. I taught at Yale. Those of you not graduates of Yale may be unaware of it, but the function of the Yale Law School is to train Presidents of the USA. They have not had great success so far, but they're still trying.'

A small ripple of laughter. Cord's election had caught most by surprise, they had to get to know their new master, this unknown quantity.

'I did not teach Law, but History. Like some of you here I acquired a reverence for the iron laws of history while being shot at. There is something quite certain about trajectories, velocities and weight of warhead, especially when they are coming in your direction.'

One for the generals, there. Cord had had not two careers but three. In reverse order, politician, lecturer in History, war hero.

'When I was lecturing I often found a suitable illustration to be worth quite a number of words, so let us begin with a picture.'

A screen for the overhead projection of slides was at one end of the room, and it was illuminated with a cartographic representation of the globe; pocking its surface like a disease was a thick rash of blue stars.

'Would anyone like to tell me what this is?' asked Cord.

Everyone kept their gaze firmly fixed on the screen, and their mouths firmly closed, unwilling to be tempted into indiscretion until they had ascertained the rules of the game.

'General Coogan?' Cord prodded gently.

'It has similarities to a representation of the various defence commitments of the USA on a global basis,' he said

13

crisply. 'However, that is not what it is.'

Cord nodded, with genuine admiration.

'Very good, General. The similarity *is* remarkable. Our present commitments include soldiers in nearly thirty countries, membership of four regional defence alliances and active participation in a fifth, mutual defence treaties with over forty nations, membership of over fifty international organizations, not to mention the furnishing of military and economic aid to nearly one hundred nations world-wide. Put on a map they would look very like that map there.

'However, *that* map is over seventy years old. It is a picture of the various interests undertaken by the British Empire at the height of its strategic overstretch, after the First World War. To observers of the time it seemed the mightiest empire the world had ever seen, adamantine in its strength. So, no doubt, would have the mythical empire of Ozymandias. Carved to his statue were the words, "My name is Ozymandias, king of kings: Look on my works ye mighty, and despair!" If you recall, the traveller from that antique land found the statue, "two vast and trunkless legs of stone," the only edifice for miles around in nothing but desert.

'I take it we are all familiar with Great Britain, former owner of the greatest Empire the world has ever seen? When last heard of, a small island off the coast of Europe. To be sure, she has made some remarkable economic strides recently, and fought an excellent small war in the Falklands some while back but, in essence, Great Britain is today much what she was at the end of the seventeenth century, before a formidable and extraordinary combination of fortuitous circumstances propelled her to her apogee as the world's foremost military and economic power – a small island off the coast of Europe. The British fall from greatness has been precipitous and cataclysmic. An examination of it – indeed of the rise and fall of all Great Powers in history – is instructive for those such as ourselves, who occupy their one-time position of greatness,

14

but wish to avoid emulating their fate.'

Cord paused to sip some water.

'Like the British before us, we have to attempt a *threefold* feat: simultaneously to provide military security for our national interests *and* to satisfy the socioeconomic needs of our citizenry – guns and butter – *and* to ensure sustained growth, this being vital both for affording the guns and butter in the present and for avoiding a relative economic decline which will damage our military and economic security in the future. This is a remarkably difficult task, especially given the uneven pace of technological and commercial change, and the unpredictable nature of world politics. Yet achieving the first two – guns and butter, or even simply guns *or* butter – without sustained economic growth will inevitably lead to relative eclipse in the long term. Do you know what happened to Great Britain, gentlemen? Between 1870 and 1970 her productivity growth lagged but one per cent behind her competitors and she turned in that time from being the world's undisputed industrial leader into the truly mediocre socialist economy of but a few years ago. These years not coincidentally saw her precipitous descent from her apogee as the world's Number One power to obscurity.

'So where, as her successor, do we stand today? In *relative* terms, we are in decline. I say relative, as measured against other powers. After the Second World War we were unquestionably Number One – in 1945 we possessed perhaps forty-five per cent of the wealth and power of the world. Only the presence of the Soviet Union prevented us from being in an unchallenged position rather like Great Britain through much of the nineteenth century after 1815. It was bi-polar world. Now, we are moving back to a multi-polar world, as Europe has recovered, the Pacific economies boom, there is an economic giant out there in Japan, and China possesses perhaps the greatest potential of all to be great. We cannot permanently retain such an advantageous position as we had immediately post-1945.

15

Our problem is that we have truly enormous military commitments, ones acquired when we occupied that uniquely advantageous position. "The weary Titan staggers under the too vast orb of its fate." Our industry is in decline. Our agriculture is suffering from the world-wide competition from newly-greened revolutionary agricultures. The uncompetitiveness of our industrial products abroad and the decline in agricultural exports have led to staggering deficits in visible trade – and these deficits cannot be covered by invisibles. We have gone in but a few years from being the world's largest creditor to the world's largest debtor. Finally, at the bottom of it all has been the budgetary policies of the government. Immense increases in defence expenditure have been coupled with considerable decreases in taxation, *without* any significant reductions in federal spending elsewhere. Continuation of current trends will lead to the US national debt being around $13 *trillion* by the year 2000 – that is fourteen times that of 1980 *in real terms* – and the interest payments on that debt to $1.5 trillion – *twenty-nine* times 1980 in real terms. Historically there is only *one* other example of a Great Power so increasing its indebtedness in *peacetime*, and that is the France of Louis XVI in the 1780s. The fiscal crisis so caused interreacted with the domestic political crisis and directly caused the events of 1789. I take it all of us here are aware of what happened to Louis XVI.

'Unless we get the proportions between defence, consumption and investment back into balance, the future of this nation is bleak. Furthermore, the decisions have to be taken *now*, in the short-term, in order to ensure the long-term viability of the USA.'

All the generals in the room listened with expressionless faces. They knew which side of the national triangle was out of kilter with the others. The years of fat, the years of mega-budget expenditure were coming to a close. It was going to hurt.

'We are militarily top-heavy, gentlemen. While we

devote seven per cent or more of GNP to defence our competitors do not, thus freeing vast funds for the civilian marketplace, plus the scientists and engineers that we employ in defence, plus *commercial* R&D. One per cent less was all it took to put Great Britain at the bottom of the heap. What we are looking at now is a lot more than one per cent. And furthermore, what is happening now is nothing to what is lined up for us in the future, should the military be allowed to have all the systems they currently are asking for. Are we all familiar with the spiralling growth in *real cost* of military systems? Of course we are. British Edwardian statesmen, used to defending their empire on the cheap, were appalled to find that a pre-1914 Dreadnought cost £2.5 million. They would turn in their graves if they knew the British Admiralty now has to pay £120 million for a *frigate*.'

Cord paused to look around the long, oval table.

'I wish our problems were as simple as a few hundred million per ship. Every project coming up has a billion-dollar price tag on it as a result of our military's desire to have the most advanced "state-of-the-art" weaponry to fight absolutely every possible scenario, however implausible. The result is fewer and fewer, more and more expensive weapons. If something is not done, the ultimate end will be as forecast by the cynics, when they point out that on current trends the entire Pentagon budget will be swallowed up producing *one* bomber in the year 2020.

'We're going to reform. We're going to pull back from our strategic overstretch while we still have the strength to recover, not wait until some years from now, when we will be too exhausted to stay, too exhausted to return to vitality. Diplomatically, we will make every effort to persuade our allies and friends to make more effort to protect themselves. The Japanese, for example, have long benefited from the protection of our umbrella that has allowed them to spend almost nothing on defence, while building up their formidable industrial empire which

17

causes us so much trouble. We intend that they, like all our allies, should shoulder more of the burden. This will have the dual advantage of putting a certain brake on their economies while freeing our own.'

Cord paused, his back to the wintry rose garden, where frost still touched the double French windows.

'National psyche is a curious thing, gentlemen. There have been heroic individual Italian soldiers, but as a martial nation the ancient schoolboy joke about their tanks having five gears, four of them reverse has the ring of verisimilitude to it. And what about us? Are we martial? Are we imperial? Why have we shouldered this immense military burden? We entered both World wars this century late, and suffered minimal casualties. We *won* the wars not through military ability but through industrial might. The *British* were a martial, imperial nation, all the way to 1914. *Their* casualties in that war were appalling, and afterwards it was not the same. Had we not been isolationist between the two wars the evidence of their lack of will and strength might have been more obvious than it was. Vietnam was a disaster, an unconventional war we fought as a conventional one and performed badly. If the invasion of Grenada was anything to go by, if our performance against some poorly-armed and badly-trained Caribbean islanders is any guide then we had certainly better avoid taking on the kind of troops likely to fight on the central front in Europe.

'But like the British, who have the Somme and Passchendaele living in their psyche, we have a most dreadful bloodbath that colours our own national memory – the Civil War. I say it made us what we are today – not a warrior nation, but a nation that does business.'

Cord pointed to the portrait of Calvin Coolidge above the fireplace, flanked by the marble busts of George Washington and Benjamin Franklin.

'Silent Cal knew. You may wonder what a Democratic President is doing with a Republican on the wall. He said, "The business of America is business." So it is. Militarily,

18

we are cutting back. It will be short-term hardship for long-term gain. Before we go on, are there any comments?'

'May I, Mr President?'

Cord looked at the neat figure in the blue uniform. The air force general was small, near the minimum height for a pilot, vigilant, alert, appropriately predatory and bird-like in his movements and appearance. Cord nodded politely.

'Go ahead, General.'

Cord had expounded at length. Coogan kept what he had to say short and cogent.

'You have talked about the short-term and the long-term, Mr President. In the long-term we are all dead, but in the short-term, which would become the long-term, I do not wish to see the Gettysburg Address replaced in our schools by selections from the works of Marx and Engels. What you have said would make much sense except for one thing, the very reason for the strength of our armed forces. *What about the Russians?*'

Cord bowed his head in agreement.

'Precisely. What about the Russians. I know that to some of you I may seem to be some kind of reincarnation of George McGovern, risen phoenix-like from some bed of liberal ash, and that what I have outlined this morning is designed to give the USSR world domination on a plate. I assure you that this is not the case, that far from weakening liberal Western values of freedom, what I propose will greatly strengthen them. I hope to convince you that far from being a dove, I am in some ways the ultimate hawk, for it is my belief that it is within our power to win the long contest with the USSR which has been going on now since 1945 – or slightly before – *all without going to war at all*. We will be the victors. The Russians suffer the fate of the Spaniards, Habsburgs, Ottomans, British and all the other great empires that became strategically over-stretched. We all know of your expertise, and depth of knowledge of the Soviets, General. Tell me what you think their response would be to our pulling back?'

'Without doubt they will see it as evidence of weakness,

19

sir, and will seek to capitalize on it.'

'They will try to move into areas formerly influenced by us?'

'Yes. The Soviets may have been willing to relax their grip on the very expensive satellite states in Eastern Europe, but this does not apply to the home republics. No Berlin Walls are coming down at home. They would see benefits, a strengthening of their hold on the internal empire by acquiring third-world assets.'

'You feel that they will try to resume their stalled drive for global influence, if not dominance?'

'*Perestroika* and *glasnost* have neither, in my opinion, altered the driving ideology of world communist domination, which has remained the same since 1917. I cannot see that they would be able to resist the opportunity.'

'*Exactly*,' Cord said triumphantly. 'I am sure that I don't have to point out to anyone here that the problems we may have the Russians have in spades. Their response to our retrenchment will have the exact opposite effect for them as our pull-back will have for us. Their dash for dominance will prove quite fatal. Instead of decreasing their strategic over-stretch, they will increase it. While our economy will be recovering and booming, for a few short years it may seem as though the Russians are becoming masters, but the effort required will so over-strain them as to be crippling. I remind you that the Marxist economy of the USSR is not efficient. Its GNP is far behind that of the USA and the European bloc. It is being overtaken by Japan, and even – if current trends remain – by the radically-governed People's Republic of China. In 1913 Imperial Russia had a real product-per-man-hour three and a half times greater than that of Japan. The Soviet regime has spent all the time seizing power – all its socialist years – in slipping relatively backwards. It is this overstrained, understrength economy that will bear the burden of the Soviets' expansion. By tempting them into terminal strategic over-stretch we will administer the *coup de grace*.'

Coogan stared at Cord in sheer disbelief. The son-of-a-bitch is trying to steal my clothes, he thought.

Cord looked around the room triumphantly.

'We are being offered an opportunity that comes but rarely to leaders of a nation, gentlemen. The chance to finish off our most mortal enemy.'

128, GRANOVSKY STREET, MOSCOW

It was an ordinary room, protected from peeking eyes by thick velvet curtains. Two green, felt-topped tables, fixtures of almost all Soviet institutions, were pushed together, and chairs had been pulled around them for the players to sit at while they read, or made notes or decided what to do next. On the tables were white, lined pads of paper, cleanly-sharpened yellow pencils and opened Global Political-Military Simulation packets, containing a statement on the game's objectives, a schedule, and a wad of closely-typed pages defining the game's scenario. By the wall was a line of computer terminals for the players to summon up information and issue commands, for it was one of the chilling new realities of wargaming that what players saw on a video display during a computerised game were often exactly the same images that would appear on the video display of a commander during a real war. In a combat control centre, commanders saw electronic symbols of far-distant targets, not the targets themselves.

This game was the *Nash* Game – Our Game – taking its title from the name given to the home team. Rykov commanded the others – *Chuzhoi* – the others, the foreigners, the aliens. *Nash* was good, it was ours, it was *rodina*, the motherland. *Chuzhoi* was bad, untrue, foreign. Rykov's *Chuzhois* were the Americans. The *Nash* Game was being played to give some idea what was to happen to the motherland. The home team called themselves the *Nash* team, but Rykov used the American terminology of Red and Blue teams, Ivan and Sam.

The cold coffee cups told the story of the game's progress. In the Red room they had a saffron-coloured metal keg of *kvas*, the malty, fermented peasant drink consumed all over Russia, but Vladimir Rykov insisted that the Blue team think, act and behave like Americans. Americans drank coffee, and on the plates were the crumbs of sandwiches and danish pastries. Polyansky, a KGB general, played the Director of Central Intelligence, Admiral Maksheyeva represented the Joint Chiefs. They had Mikoyan, professor of political science in from the University – Moscow State – to represent the State Department. Rykov was President Cord.

It was the fourth day. The game was reaching its end. They were playing on a ninety-day schedule between moves. A move usually took two to three hours to decide upon. Control brought in a slip of paper with some new information on it.

'The Soviets have had an appalling harvest, worse than usual. Their reserves are down to twenty-three days. Canadian and South American grain harvests were relatively poor this year, but we have a good crop,' Rykov said, reading out the figures.

The Red team were on the ropes. The Soviet Empire was beginning to disintegrate. There was fighting in Latvia, Lithuania and Estonia following their declaration of independence and the arrival of Soviet troops shortly afterwards, effectively announcing the end of *glasnost* and *perestroika*. Polyansky was following up his earlier success in supplying communications equipment, from short-wave radios to photocopying machines to dissident groups, especially nationalist and religious – they had had great effect among the Islamic Asian republics – by full-blown covert military aid to the Baltic provinces. It was beginning to make Afghanistan look like a Sunday picnic.

The Americans were putting the screws on the USSR.

Mikoyan had arranged with the Saudis to cut production by half. Soviet citizens were on rationing, and the number of little licence-built Fiats on the streets were few.

'They want to buy grain,' said Mikoyan.

'Let them starve,' said Rykov.

'They are. The peasants are slaughtering cattle.'

'Food riots too,' said Rykov.

'They've ordered mobilization on the Central European plain,' said Maksheyeva. He looked questioningly at Rykov.

'Trying to export their problems. And blackmail. We'll smash you unless you help us out of this mess.'

'Shall I?' said Maksheyeva.

'Yes. Do it.'

Maksheyeva issued the instructions to Control. In the Nevada desert a controlled nuclear explosion sent a gigantic bolt of energy up into the stratosphere to the waiting Strategic Defense Initiative battle station, where it was split into myriad lightning blasts by the host of perfect mirrors. Lightning erupted on the Central European plain and whole divisions lay ruined.

'Again,' said Rykov, and a great battle group erupted and sank into the depths of the Atlantic.

'Again,' said Rykov, and *Backfire* and *Blinder* strategic bombers tumbled in flight like shot ducks, and SS–18 *Satan* ICBMs melted in their silos.

'They are suing for peace.'

'Unconditionally,' said Rykov, and the game ended.

The post-game critique, the 'hot washup' as Rykov called it, borrowing the terminology from the US Naval War College, where such war games were regularly simulated, was a gloomy affair. Now they were not Red and Blue teams, not Ivan and Sam, but Russians again.

'I was pleased,' Maksheyeva said miserably. 'Joyful as the power in my hand struck them down. But it was *rodina* that I was doing it to, it was our motherland.'

He took off his Dodgers' baseball cap that he had worn during the game and reached for the bottle of Stolichnaya on the table.

'*Nichevo*,' he said. 'Never mind. It was only a game. It will never happen.'

Rykov went down in the lift to the underground car park. There among a handful of Chaikas and Volgas waiting for their chauffeurs, and more boxy, spartan little licence-built Fiats waiting for their proud owners, was a gleaming blue Ford Thunderbird. It did not bear the distinctive white on black coded licence plates issued to all foreigners, it was the property of Rykov. His eyes caressed its flowing, jelly-mould lines lovingly, he had inherited the American's love of fancy automobiles. Slipping into the leather seat he switched on and the shoulder harness automatically whirred forward. The engine started throatily and with a puff of power from the supercharged 3.8 litre V-6 he purred up the ramp and on to the street. It was late afternoon, almost evening, and the winter's night had come early, leaving the city lit by the iridescent bluish glare of the streetlights.

As Rykov went down Granovsky Street, going against the numbers, he paused to make the turn into Kalinin Prospekt, passing two lines of polished black Volgas parked illegally but confidently over the kerbs in defiance of the No Parking signs, their chauffeurs eyeing their mirrors for their charges. As he waited for the lights to turn green a woman came trotting out from No. 2 Granovsky, a drab beige building with its windows painted over. The sign by the door claimed that the building was the 'bureau of passes', and a plaque informed those interested that Vladimir Ilyich Lenin had addressed Red Army commanders there in April 1919, but the woman, smartly dressed in Western clothes, was carrying bulging bags and packages discreetly wrapped in brown paper. Her chauffeur came scurrying to help her, and as Rykov turned left, heading for the Lenin Hills, he saw the woman comfortably ensconced in the rear of the limousine, the chauffeur filling its trunk with the purchases. Rykov was familiar with the procedure. His own wife shopped at the 'bureau of passes'.

24

Rykov lived in an apartment in a modern important yellow-brick building perched on the Lenin Hills overlooking downtown Moscow from across the Moscow River. It was a very select address, one-time Prime Minister Kosygin had lived there. He put the Ford in its parking place beneath the building, and took the lift up to the ninth floor. When he rang the bell he was greeted by his wife, Lena. He kissed his two children, Sasha and Alexei, who were watching Pink Panther cartoons on the VCR. Rykov had racks of Western videos, Walt Disney cartoons for the children, the latest films for he and his wife, ABC, CBS, CNN current affairs programmes for his work.

'I have to write a report, darling,' he apologized. 'Tomorrow I'll be free, and we'll spend time together.' He had been busy almost night and day with the *Nash* Game for weeks.

'That will be lovely,' she said. 'I'll bring you supper on a tray.'

Rykov paused in the kitchen to make a jug of coffee on his West Bend drip-filter. His contemporaries, those who had *blat* usually went for West German Kuppersbusch cookers and refrigerators, and furnished their homes in Finnish modern, but Rykov had chosen Westinghouse equipment, and had ordered his furnishings from Sears. The orders had been swiftly processed, like his request for the latest, top-of-the-line Ford Thunderbird, for Rykov had more *blat*, more privilege, connections and access than most.

The coffee was ready, and he went into his study to pay for that privilege. A comfortable, warm room fitted with wall-to-wall shag-pile carpet, and looking over the river, it was equipped with the tools of his trade. On his oak-and-leather desk rested an IBM electric typewriter, and in one corner there was a computer terminal made by the same company. He had a Hitachi twenty-four-inch television with VCR and a Sony photocopier and Fax machine. On the shelves that lined the walls were complete sets of Jane's reference books, together with bound copies of Jane's *Defence Weekly, Aviation Week* and *Space Technology*, Scientific American *Journal of Electronic Defence, Air Power, Air Force Magazine*; there was every edition of the US Department of Defence's *Soviet Military Power* since 1981, there were monographs such as *US Space System Survivability*, published by the National Defense University, and *Verification and Anti-Satellite (ASAT) Weapons*, published by the Federation of American Scientists. There was *Forbes* magazine, *Time, US News and World Report, the Quarterly Review*.

Rykov took a mug of coffee and sat down at his desk. He rolled a sheet of Croxley Script 100 gm/m^2 A4 paper into the IBM and began to type immediately. He knew what he wanted to say, he did not have to think about it.

He tapped the key for capital letters, and his title appeared boldly across the crisp white paper.

THE CONTRADICTIONS FACING THE USSR.

The wording was deliberately provocative. In Marxist terminology the word 'contradiction' was a very specific, loaded one, and referred to the tensions which – it was argued – inherently existed within the capitalist system of production and would inevitably cause its demise. Rykov was applying it instead to the USSR, the world's first Communist state. It was a dangerous thing to do, but what he was about to suggest was dangerous. It was very dangerous indeed, but only exceeded in level of risk in his view, by doing nothing at all.

He began by drawing attention to, and quoting from the speech of the Secretary-General at the recent Communist Party Congress. There, where Khrushchev had once boasted bombastically how the USSR would overtake the United States economically and 'bury' capitalism, Secretary-General Krilov, Gorbachev's successor and heir to his policies, had confessed to the grievous problems afflicting the Union. Rates of economic growth had declined visibly, even more than in the eighties. Targets had not been met. Lags existed in the material bases of science and education, health, culture, everyday services, in engineering, oil and coal, electricity, ferrous metals, chemicals. None of the targets for the main indicators of efficiency and the improvement of the people's standard of living had been approached.

Rykov was careful to preface his paper with these admissions from the top. *Glasnost* and *perestroika* were not dead letters, they still offered the only chance of the complete re-thinking of scientific socialism – on the lines of the Chinese Communist Party, their neighbour, the People's Republic of China, let it only be whispered – the USSR so desperately required. But for such re-thinking to take place would require time, time to demolish the adamantine bureaucracy and dead-from-the-neck-up thinking of the Soviet state. Rykov was about to offer Secretary-General Krilov that time.

Both Rykov and Krilov knew that things were in fact far bleaker than even Krilov's unprecedented admissions had allowed. The USSR was faced on the one hand with the kind of subtle but explosive high-tech future that was emerging in California and Japan, an industrial revolution of such scope that it threatened to make the gap between those who could do it and old-style industrial states who could not analagous to say, the West Germany of the 1970s and Upper Volta. On the other, conditions within the USSR – its autocratic and bueaucratic habits, the privileges which insulated the party elites from reality, the restrictions upon the free interchange of knowledge, and total lack of a personal-incentive system made the USSR most cruelly ill-fitted to handle such a high-tech future. What made things much worse were the factors only hinted at by Krilov to the Congress, factors that – *if something was not done to alter the USSR's position vis-a-vis the West* – would surely in the fullness of time consign the USSR to an unhappy companionship with the wretched, miserable Africans in their bleak Central African home.

These factors were numerous. Rykov listed them in the knowledge that he need go into none-too-great detail about them for a man like Krilov, whose very dreams were probably made nightmares by them. He began with agriculture, which both started the alphabet and underlay the most illustrative of the Soviet Union's problems. The Americans devoted five per cent of their total investment to agriculture. The Russians thirty per cent. In the USA, it employed two per cent of the labour force. In the USSR over twenty per cent. Each year, the USSR had to pay out billions in difficult-to-find hard currency to buy grain and meat from the capitalist West to make up the shortfall. *And yet* the four per cent of private holdings by peasantry in the USSR produced twenty-five per cent of the total output. Stalin's hideous act of genocide against the rural members of his own people continued its baleful influence over his country over half a century later.

Any school child, let alone graduate of the Harvard Business School, could recommend the correct course of action to take, given those simple figures. Why, all you did was scrap collectivisation, thus saving yourself billions in bureaucracy, and return responsibility and initiative to the individual peasants, whose combined intelligence and knowledge of their profession far outweighed any centralized bureaucracy – even one ideally designed and staffed, which no one with experience of it would claim for the one run in the USSR.

It wasn't going to happen, not yet, not without time, and lots of grease – money – to soothe the vested interests – the urban population and bureaucrats and managers who ran Soviet agriculture, for it would be the final victory of the shade of Bukharin, who had favoured agricultural incentives, and the repayment of the peasantry for the terrible events that had happened to them in the first years of the 1930s.

The 'planned economy', with its malign excess of bureaucratic influence also affected Soviet industry. It had become clear that the great success of the years after 1945 had been achieved at staggering cost, by fixing ambitious targets and then throwing vast quantities of money, energy and manpower at them. And here was the rub – now all three were running out. Hard currency was difficult to find – there was very little the West wanted from the USSR, except peace. Energy was running low – the great reservoirs left were expensive to get, located under the permafrost, and Soviet industry was amazingly inefficient. Rykov quoted the grim statistics, that the USSR required 1500 kilos of coal and 135 kilos of steel to produce $1,000 of GDP, while France required 500 of coal and 42 of steel, and the Swiss only 370 and 26. Finally, the manpower was running out. Not only was the birth-rate among the Russians in the USSR declining, but even more awful, because of the slow erosion in hospital and general health care, because of the fantastic levels of alcoholism, people were living for less long – a man could only expect to live to be sixty-six years less than in the mid-1960s. And the most horrifying, that infant mortality was on the rise – the only historical instance of it happening in an industrialized country. The Soviet authorities were now up against the limits – they had kept men in the labour force in the factories longer to compensate, but they were simply falling dead over their lathes, and there weren't enough children coming up to replace them.

As Rykov knew, behind the majestic stage-setting of the Five-Year-Plans lurked a shambles. The USSR had not one economy but five – defence industry, heavy industry, consumer industry and an illegal counter-economy. Only the first and last performed at all adequately. Underlying all was the fact that the system was such that most people spent great amounts of time and ingenuity not working for the state but against it – by 'slipping through' the rules that bound them in order to pursue their own personal ends. 'Slipping through' was the national pastime. The expert on America, Rykov appreciated how little the Americans understood how *Russian* the USSR was. Obsessed by Communism, they were not aware of the far greater influence of the centuries-old Russian culture upon its people.

He finally came to what was simultaneously the USSR's greatest asset and the reason if something was not done she would in the end fail, like some huge statue whose foundations have been afflicted by rust and rot – the military. Russian leaders, whether Romanov or Marxist had *always* insisted on the possession of armed forces equal to or preferably larger than those of any other power. It had been so with Peter the Great and it was so with the Kremlin of Krilov. Alexander II had emancipated the serfs not from any desire to alleviate their lot but because serfdom was militarily inefficient, as the Crimean War had just shown. Krilov's Russia was still spending on defence at a higher rate than GDP was rising, and something was going to have to give, which inevitably meant the prosperity and health of the people, and the need for fresh capital investment in agriculture and industry, with all the baleful consequences that this implied for the longer-term.

There was a tap on his door and his wife came in with a tray. Tall, hook-nosed, Rykov had a slightly oriental air, but Lena was almond-eyed and had missed the curse of Russian women – the potato nose. When Rykov was working he ate at his task, and she had brought him a grilled fillet steak with baked potato and butter, and a side-salad. After she had left, and as he ate, planning what he was to say next, the old Russian joke of the little girl asking her mother the difference between rich and poor people in Russia came into his mind. The answer was: 'The rich eat tomatoes all year round, but we only eat them in summer.'

Rykov's steak was from Scotland, the butter from Wales, the salad from Spain, the orange for dessert from South Africa. The potato was from Russia. The beer he would drink was from the USA and the cognac *digestif* from France. Rykov was not simply *vlasti*, one of those for whom ordinary people would be removed from their seat on a railroad train, Aeroflot flight, from their hotel room or reserved ticket for the opera, he was *nachalstvo*, one of the bosses. On official business his chauffeur-driven Chaika would sweep down the road, scattering pedestrians like so many chickens, forcing other drivers to the side with an arrogance of a Czarist nobleman's carriage racing along the centre of the highway, spattering the peasants with mud and filth.

If Western society resembled a diamond, with a small number at the top, swelling to a huge middle class before narrowing to a small number at the bottom, Soviet society was like a pyramid, with vast numbers at the bottom, narrowing to a point containing Rykov and others of his ilk. Furthermore, within the upper reaches of this pyramid, a caste system operated. Military families intermarried, as did scientific families, Party families, writers' families and so forth, all using *blat* to rig the system their way. The only ones who could not use *blat* were the great mass of untouchables below. It was a potentially explosive situation. A stroke of genius during the *Nash* Game had Polyansky as the DCI fomenting *class hatred*. The USA did not have a class system. The October revolution, having removed Czarist aristocracy promptly replaced it with one of its own. That aristocracy was now entrenched, dynastic and possessed of an arrogance and disdain greater than the haughtiest rich in the West. It was dangerous, Rykov knew, because of the very *Russian-ness* of the USSR: Russia had a history of peasant rebellion that went back beyond Pugachev to Stenka Razin. Stoic, tough, beast of burden, when finally driven over the line, the Russian peasant was a fearsome enemy, as many a Boyar found when his serfs finally turned. 'Seize them, punish them, hang them, treat in the same way as they, having no Christian feelings in them, oppressed you, the peasants,' Pugachev's exhortation had echoed down the years. It rang in Rykov's ears.

Rykov reflected that the Russians remained Russian. The one chance that they had had to become Russian in a new mould, instead of the old, to become part of Europe in person as well as geography, that extraordinary, roaring, booming industrial revolution that had finally taken off and which would have dragged them westwards had been killed by the events of October 1917 and their repercussions, to be replaced by the kind of industrial revolution that Peter the Great would have readily understood. And the Russians remained just as he would have understood them too.

For Rykov one incident summed it all up – the sailors of the *Pamyat Azova*. The old cruiser – *The Memory of the Azov* – had been awarded the order of St Andreas for its part in the Crimean War, and thenceforth the sailors of any ship bearing its name wore the distinctive gold cap tally as a badge of merit. For their less meritorious role in the events of 1905 – the practice run for 1917 – the order of St Andreas was removed from the ship and its crew by the Czar. And after the revolution, what did the sailors want from their new communist leaders? Their award back! So from that day on, the sailors wore the *Czarist* order of St Andreas, suitably dressed up as the Hero Ship award of the Red Banner Fleet. The incident encapsulated all.

All this had been factored into the *Nash* Game and the results were grim. They were grim anyway, but once the strategy of James Cord, President of the USA was added, and the game played, it was worse. Cord saw correctly that – provided the conflict was economic and not military – the main threat to the pre-eminence of the USA came not from the USSR but from Japan. If Cord was given enough time to curb military expenditure, protect Silicon Valley, pump resources back into the civilian sector then a newly-resurgent USA would emerge, one capable of not only taking on Japan but of holding the USSR's feet to the fire long enough to eliminate her as a military threat as well.

However, time was what Cord required.

'What we are being offered,' wrote Rykov, 'is a brief "window of opportunity", a fleeting time in which our military superiority will be combined with an American administration not only looking the other way – towards

Japan – but thinking economically, and with a new ideological prejudice *against* military involvements. If we seize the time it will, as the proverb has it, lead on to greatness. Fail to grasp our opportunity, and we will stagger and fall under the sheer weight of our own armour and "contradictions".

'There is a different historical model of economic growth which reckons not with the factors that obsess the possessors of Master of Business Administration degrees, and is one not considered by them. It is the model of predation, the model successfully followed by the likes of Napoleon and Hitler – until both overreached themselves. It is possible to increase your assets, increase your growth, provide both guns *and* butter, provide money to facilitate internal reform to be re-born with a dynamic economy, to provide the *time* necessary to facilitate those reforms.

'Physical possession of Saudi Arabia and the Gulf States would grant the USSR the majority of the remaining surplus oil supply of the globe, while denying it to the West. The desirable effect that this will have on the Soviet economy and the adverse one on the economies of the West may be imagined. My plan calls for the Revolutionary Islamic regime of Iran to be used as our agent, and our diplomacy will have to be mobilized to this end. The government of Khalif Hossein of Iran should find the prize attractive; with religious views that can be considered full-blown mania, his brand of Shi'ia Islam finds possession of the Holy city of Mecca by the Whahhabis to be the equivalent of its occupation by Satan. In Christian terms, by Anti-Christ. One has to return to the religious wars of the Middle Ages to fully understand the depth, savagery and immutability of the religious bigotry involved. Possession of Mecca will be a bauble we can easily afford for the chance to suck dry the great underground seas of oil beneath. The election of Cord, an American President anxious for the first time to be looking in a different direction, with a weakened military, will give us our unique opportunity.'

Rykov continued to detail his planning. It was late when he finished. He went through the pages and put them in a dark blue folder. There was but the one copy. General Secretary Krilov was the man who had commissioned it, had demanded that the *Nash* Game be played. In the morning Rykov would summon the KGB aide to collect it and take it to his master. He went out, and to the kitchen. The apartment was quiet, his family asleep. He helped himself to a Michelob from the refrigerator and drank it from the can as he had done as a student at UCLA. Rykov had been destined for the top for a long time. All over the USSR, little children were measured and examined from as young as three and four years old. Thousands of the correct dimensions and aptitude were funnelled into sport, where training and drugs would form them into suitable symbols of Soviet glory, and a tiny handful to strut upon the world stage for an hour. Rykov had a brain; it was special, it saw patterns where others only saw random collections of facts, it saw into the future. He was a seer. No effort had been spared to make him knowledgeable about the Soviet Union's greatest foe, the USA. Rykov was more American than Russian.

Sipping the delicious, prickly, cold beer he went over what he had written in his mind. It was necessary to talk of reform, and for the time to implement, but Rykov knew they were empty words, that *glasnost* and *perestroika* either inevitably led to genuine democracy or they were empty letters, buzz-words with which to dazzle liberals in the West, and in a land which Peter the Great would have had no difficulty in comprehending, whoever imagined democracy could flower? We are still doing what Peter did, thought Rykov, trying to import Western artefacts without Western ways to make them work. Possession of Middle Eastern oil will not *solve* anything, it will merely postpone the evil day. But was that not the essence of conservatism? And was there nowhere more conservative than the USSR at the close of the twentieth century?

As Rykov undressed, listening to his wife's quiet

breathing, he reflected that putting off the the evil day, the day of reckoning for the USSR could only be good. Historically he knew that genuine threat to the Great Power status of a nation inevitably meant war, and that no Great Power *had ever* relinquished its position without having been defeated in a Great Power war, or by being so weakened by Pyrrhic victory, like Great Britain, that imperial withdrawal became inevitable.

Rykov was suddenly anxious, aware that he was putting gigantic, historic pieces of machinery into motion. The Soviet Union could not, *would not* allow herself to fall. What was a little oil between friends, between enemies even, if it meant peace. The Americans would realize the Soviet's position, surely. They must do.

THE WHITE HOUSE

An aide moved around the oval table, slipping identical glossy blue folders in front of each member of the Executive Committee. Cord continued.

'I make my prediction as to the future fall of the USSR through strategic overstretch not simply through academic analysis, although that has played a role, but through rigorous scientific testing by means of the most comprehensive political-military simulation of recent times. Game Sigma took place at the National Defense University earlier this year. It was designed to my specifications by the RAND Corporation. Players included former senior government officials, national corporation CEOs, retired military officers of three- and four-star rank. You will find details of the game – kept top-secret – in the folder. The Soviet Red team was played by foremost political and academic experts on the USSR. The Blue team – the USA – was headed by myself. I played the President.'

All present felt a prickle of apprehension at hearing Cord admit to this. Presidential involvement in political-military simulations – as the wargames were known – was one of the most closely kept secrets there was. The rationale behind this was that knowledge of a President's actual thoughts regarding such issues as nuclear warfare would be one of the greatest secrets an adversary could learn. There were rumours, and occasional hints, such as the photographs of President Johnson peering down at a sand-table model of Khesanh, or Kennedy, his eyes locked on to a plotting-board of US and Soviet ships during the Cuban missile crisis. It was known that Ronald Reagan had been an avid *kibitzer* during the great Ivy league political-military simulation of 1982, that ended with former CIA chief Helms – playing the President – wiping out most of the USSR with the SIOP's – Single Integrated Operation Plan's – Major Attack Option – a massive retaliatory nuclear barrage. Cord was planning something less dramatic, but more effective. All present fingered the folders gingerly.

'All right, gentlemen. Let's move on to what we're going to do. Which is cut the military budget. To my way of thinking, there is considerable evidence that we have for many years now been spending vast amounts of money on conventional systems in order to fight the kind of conventional war that does not now exist, whereas we would do far better to spend money on Special Operational Forces – at far less cost – to fight – far more effectively – the kind of unconventional warfare that is taking place today.'

'We have an SOF Command, Mr President,' murmured Coogan.

'Sure,' Cord said sharply. 'Commanded by a three-star general who has to report to you big-shots in the JCS, who overrule him and steal his funding. I *know* how it's done, General. Let's get on with it. We'll begin with the Air Force.'

36

Over the years the Air Force had fought to consolidate and even increase its share of 'turf' in the defence establishment with a tenacity and skill which if matched in wartime would augur well for the chances of the USA. When the men in the blue suits wanted the latest bombers and ICBMs and fighters they understood clearly that there were two ways of getting them: by demonstrating to the White House and Congress that the Soviets were arming to the teeth, and by passing that chilling message along to the public by judicious leaks to the news media. To do this successfully it was necessary to establish a certain dominance within the intelligence community when preparing National Intelligence Estimates (NIEs) which notionally were prepared under the jurisdiction of the Director of Central Intelligence (the DCI) and which were supposed to reflect a general consensus within the intelligence community with pertinent expertise in the area under examination. Preparation of NIEs traditionally meant fierce infighting between the military and civilians. Martial ardour had historically carried the day. When Eisenhower had sent the U-2s over Russia searching for SS-6 ICBMs the CIA interpreted the evidence available in a manner that concluded the Russians were running into dreadful problems with the vast missile. The Air Force, interpreting every flyspeck on film as a missile, concluded that the Soviets were ready to commence full-scale production of the nuclear-tipped giant. Their campaign was so skilfully run, with the wonderfully emotive catch-phrase of the 'missile gap', that even Eisenhower, who deeply mistrusted them, and wished dearly to separate the blue-suiters from interpretation of their own intelligence, was forced to assent. The squadrons of B-52s and fabulous supersonic B-58 Hustler bombers rolled from the production lines, as did the Atlas missiles.

Over the years the Air Force defended their share of 'turf' and brought home what they needed. They muscled their way into control over their own satellite surveillance systems against the fierce opposition of the CIA and NSA, and if President Carter didn't believe them and cancelled the B-1 bomber President Reagan did, and gave them it back. But far, far more important than that, was the time they got the go-ahead to order the B-2. The Northrop B-2 was also known as the ATB, the Advanced Technology Bomber, or 'Stealth' bomber. It was 'stealthy' because the highly advanced sciences used in its construction were believed to make it invisible to hostile radar and other sensors. The B-2 was the subject of the greatest aircraft development programme of all time, without doubt. So, without doubt, was its cost.

'When I referred to the bomber that will consume the Pentagon's entire budget in the year 2020,' Cord said acidly, 'I must have been thinking of the Son of Stealth. The figures here are that SAC originally contracted to buy 132 B-2s at a total cost of $36.6 billion. The cost has now risen to somewhere over one hundred million *per copy*. One wing of thirty-six aircraft is to become operational at Whiteman AFB. Upwards of a billion is earmarked for improvements at the base, small beer on this scale, I admit. The bomber has less range than the B-1 and thus will require large numbers of new in-flight refuelling tankers. Malmstrom AFB in Montana is to be dedicated as the base for the fleet.'

Cord looked up from his figures and Coogan stared stonily back at him.

'The B-2 is being cancelled, General,' Cord said flatly.

'We've already got it.'

'You have ten of a projected first thirty-six. You're going to park them in the obsolete aircraft facility at Davis-Monthan,' Cord said brutally.

'I do not understand how the Air Force is to defend this nation if we have the only weapon that will do the job taken away from us.'

'You still have your B-1s.'

'The B-1 cannot guarantee to penetrate Soviet defences by itself.'

'You should have told President Reagan that. As I

38

understand it, the B-2 was designed with the mobile SS-20 and SS-24 missiles in mind. Those missiles have been taken out of use following the SALT treaty signed by my predecessor. Not that there were the numbers of them predicted by the Air Force in the first place. Another missile gap?'

'The B-2 carries a number of weapons including the General Dynamics Convair AGM-129A Stealth cruise missile. A future war might not necessarily go nuclear, and furthermore if you read history – I read your book, Mr President – may well be a war of great coalitions in which victory goes to the economically and industrially greater side. In such a war an aircraft which *cannot be detected* and thus may not be shot down is only limited in weight of explosive delivered by the capacity of the magazines at its home base – *which in this case happens to be the productive capacity of the USA*. Given its Stealth, and the extreme accuracy of its weapons, measured in feet, the B-2 has an MOE – a measure of effectiveness – Pk, that is, probability of kill higher than 0.9, that is, a guaranteed successful attack destroying the entire target over ninety per cent of mission. The B-2 is a war-winning weapons system.'

'The only war we are going to fight with the USSR is the economic one I have described, and we are going to win it. The ultimate security of the nation will continue to rest upon MAD, Mutual Assured Destruction. We do not need to have vast arrays of assorted weaponry capable of retaliation at every possible level of escalation. The *Ohio*-class submarines in service with the Navy are at least a decade ahead of both comparable Soviet submarines and more importantly, of Soviet surveillance and recon-naissance ability, whereas we will soon have both the capacity to detect Soviet submarines through the synthetic-aperture radar on the KH-13 satellite, and to kill those submarines with our *Los Angeles* attack submarines. The submarine force is in place, paid for and effective.'

'And remarkable value for money,' murmured Admiral Fulton. 'Or so the official recent Congressional budget hearing ruled.'

Yes, divide and rule, you bastard, Coogan thought savagely. Now he knew what had happened. Fulton was wily, more politician than sailor. The Navy had been remarkably quiet while the projected costs for the B-2 soared out of sight. The Air Force had never been ones much concerned with getting more bang for the buck, they specified the bang and worked on the system to foot the bill. With their labyrinthine specifications, regulations, and horde of 'blue light specialists and red light specialists' that bill was always large, and could be calculated to win a 'Golden Fleece' award from Senator Proxmire somewhere along the line when a pair of washers and a nut costing thirty-eight cents at the hardware store worked itself into a two thousand dollar tag by the time it had gone through the Air Force's spares system and been fitted to the bolt holding a C-130 co-pilot's lunch-tray in place. With the B-2 the whole process had gotten completely out of hand given that the shortcomings of the system had been compounded by the fact that the manufacturers were working with technology that did not exist before the bomber was ordered.

But it worked. To Coogan it did not matter if it cost one hundred million per copy or two, for it was what he said it was, an undetectable, war-winning weapon a whole decade ahead of anything the Soviets had. And it was to be abandoned. For what? *A few submarines.*

But there you had it. If the Air Force had what in Coogan's opinion was the better weapon, the Navy had fought the war better. The Air Force had known early what Congressman Cord's likely views were and had discreetly – they thought – lobbied against him. Fulton had read his military history, he was well aware of Napoleon's dictum that a successful general should never interfere while his enemy is in the process of destroying himself. Coogan glanced across at the army's general Martin. He'd be in on the act. If the budgets were being cut then it had come down to it, dog would have to eat dog. The two older military orders had long resented and envied their upstart young rival, had fought for years for air power to be subordinated to their interests. *That was what was so important about the B-2*. It kept the Air Force strategic. If the *missiles* were aboard the SSBNs, the vast *Ohio* class submarines, and the Air Force's Minutemen were aging, could be bargained away, and the MX and Midgetman were cancelled, and the B-1 soon obsolete what future for the Air Force? Coogan looked at it and it was bleak.

Cord was talking about MAD. Bitter bile rose in Coogan's throat, and he swallowed hard to force it back down. He had never believed in the doctrine of mutual assured destruction. It was a concept dreamed up and supported by a long line of deviants that began somewhere with John F. Kennedy and included all the other liberals like McGeorge Bundy, George McGovern, Jimmy Carter and Cyrus Vance, and had reached its final, dangerous and foetid flowering in the form of James Cord, President of the USA, who was about to gamble away the entire security of the western world through some crack-brained professor's theory.

Coogan *knew* that MAD was false, because it took two to tango, and he had solid, incontrovertible evidence that the Soviets believed that they could, if necessary, fight a nuclear war and win. It was all in the thick file. Fact: every apartment building built in the thirty-nine largest cities of the USSR since 1955 had been constructed with a vast nuclear-bomb shelter in the basement. Fact: the buildings were connected by tunnels containing water and electricity conduits, medical supplies and hospital facilities. Fact: every factory in the thirty-nine cities had its own massive shelter. So the workforce was to be protected. Fact: inside the Moscow beltway, the highway that rings Moscow as the capital Beltway circles Washington, Coogan's intelligence experts found seventy-five enormous underground command posts; vast creations each the size of the Pentagon, sunk deep, deep in the ground, protected

41

by one hundred feet of reinforced concrete and four hundred of earth fill. It provided about three times the strength of the Hoover dam. Coogan's satellites, the Air Force's KH-9 Big Bird orbiters had provided the photographs, and the Air Force intelligence men had applied all their arcane arts to them, manipulating them by applying false colours to bring out hidden details, digitally manipulating the images from radar satellites so that the bunkers, hidden to the naked eye jumped out of the image produced. The great subterranean shelters were provided with vast tanks of fuel and water, with silos of oats, barley, greens and wheat, *bought from America*! The irony of it.

Coogan then had his men perform some very clever detective work, using the satellites to eavesdrop on the Soviets, but he'd needed the assistance of the boys and girls at the NSA here, because it was their field, they could – and did – listen to everything from a Soviet general calling his mistress to arrange a suitable liaison to the Secretary-General talking on his limousine car-phone. They found out that the shelters were for the use of the Politburo, the industrial chiefs, the men in the KGB, the GRU, the top brass. Then when they looked, they found in the provinces, in Leningrad, Vladivostok, Gorki, Novosibirsk, smaller replicas.

All this had been done before Coogan was the Air Force's number-one man, when he was in command of Air Force intelligence, on his way to the top. For him, the evidence he had accumulated all indicated that the leaders of the USSR – those paranoid, chill but wily men – believed what they had always believed, which was that given the proper preparation the people of that empire would in the main be able to ride out a nuclear war, to emerge victorious over a murdered USA and a Europe not merely Finlandized but taken over – a concentration of industrial and technological might that would finally ensure Soviet hegemony over the globe.

Coogan understood his Russians. When he had studied military history at Harvard as a young man he took a minor in learning Russian. Even then he had known it would be useful. He had read Marshal V.D. Sokolovskii's major work *Soviet Military Strategy* – with its emphasis on civil defence as a war-winning measure in a nuclear age – in the original. Coogan had immersed himself so much in the culture and ways of thought of his enemy he sometimes woke up *dreaming* in Russian.

Unfortunately, there were those in positions of power who did not know the Russians as he did, and this had caused them to allow themselves to be hoodwinked by the Soviet leadership. Why, even *before glasnost* and *perestroika*, those liberal buzzwords, there had been so many willing to believe that the Russians no longer desired to inflict a Marxist-Leninist dictatorship upon the world and had settled for coexistence and guaranteeing the safety of the motherland. They existed in droves in places like the CIA and the State Department and they had pursed their lips doubtfully when they saw Coogan's evidence, and explained to Congress that it wasn't really so, that yes, there were bunkers, but that after the experiences of the Second World War it was natural that the leaders of the USSR should think defensively, and anyway, the bunkers wouldn't withstand a nuclear attack, which Coogan knew they would. The problem was that here one entered into the arena of verification, and verification was a word that was *always* politically loaded. In other words, some people only saw what they wanted to see. Like the people in the CIA and State Department, the Kremlin's useful fools who wanted arms control agreements so bad they were willing to suppress hard information provided by the Air Force in order to get them. Traitorous *detentenik* fools the whole lot of them.

They were still at it. Uppermost in Coogan's mind was the great SDI 'Star Wars' facility outside Smolensk, which housed some of the most expensive equipment and finest scientific brains the Soviet Union had. The systems being developed there had the potential to render the USSR invulnerable to nuclear attack, since they would form a space-based ABM anti-ballistic missile system. That, together with the civil defence measures in the USSR were trump cards, and all Coogan's study of military history told him that a nation enjoying such an advantage would be very tempted to use it. But to the men in the CIA and State Department, Brooks Brothers' besuited drones, obsessed with the last SALT agreement, such revelations would have 'perturbed' the negotiations, and they had allowed it to be classified as a 'research' establishment.

Which brought Coogan to the whole vexed problem of space reconnaissance itself. Cord was rabbiting on about NATO, Asia and burden-sharing. Dear Jesus and Mary, how had Cord made it to the presidency? He would have betted the budget for the B-2 bomber itself that the man would never have made it to Super Tuesday, let alone the nomination, and *never* to the top job itself. God, but he'd had the luck of the devil himself. Pits dug for him miraculously filled in as his foot stepped forward over them, political time-bombs left waiting for him were defused, accidents befell his rivals, how they did.

Cord's presence in the White House – in his own words, as some phoenix risen from a bed of liberal ash – meant that control of space reconnaissance had become ever more important. The combination of sheer difficulty of penetrating the USSR in 'mole'-like terms, added to the problems of interpretation of such HUMINT, together with the long-standing American love for and understanding of technology had brought about a situation whereby what the aerial and space-based reconnaissance and surveillance systems saw and heard formed the data-base from which the analysts synthesised their perception of what was happening within the Soviet Union. Since this was so, then whoever had his hands around the choke points through which the information flowed could control that information as his political leanings or convictions dictated. Even the president of the USA could only make decisions based on what he was told.

As a plan of action hardened in Coogan's mind, he heard

Cord winding up the EXCOM meeting.

'Any comments, gentlemen?'

'If I may, Mr President,' murmured Coogan. 'I hope I am not presumptuous to say that I see similarities between us. You have read Soviet history, so have I. You speak Russian as I do. You have played in political-military simulations, as of course I have. And yet we draw different conclusions. With regard to wargaming, I have found it useful, but not for the reasons that you do. A nugget of historical information, sir. The nations that took wargaming most seriously in both World wars this century were the losers. *Their* war games predicted that they would win. *You* believe that this Game Sigma predicts the fall of the USSR. *I* have never found a wargame to *predict* anything. It only identifies *problems* that you have to deal with.'

Cord smiled confidently, brushing Coogan aside.

'I think levels of rigour have moved on somewhat since 1914 or 1941, general. As for accuracy of prediction, I think we'll let the future prove Game Sigma right, shall we?'

Coogan nodded politely. What all games, however multi-factored left out was the human element.

Across the table, not far from the vapidly-smiling portrait of George Washington sat Major-General Calvin Moore, the Director of NSA, and his deputy director, Dr Hamish MacDonald. The lights of the room flowed off the badges of rank of the small soldier opposite them like liquid silver, lit up the blaze of colour of the solid block of medals on his chest, flickered as his pale blue eyes constantly moved, searching for weaknesses, for threats. General Ulysses Zachary Coogan looked at the men from NSA; he leaned back in his hard chair and smiled, like a bird of prey opening its beak.

Upon leaving the EXCOM meeting Hamish MacDonald separated from Moore and had his driver take him the short distance to the Metropolitan Club on H street. When he got out at the pillared entrance to the graceful, four storey granite and brick building at 1700 the gold and blue flag was flying at half-mast. MacDonald was unsurprised, much of the membership of the prestigious club was elderly, the flag spent much of its life half-way up the pole.

'Who's dead, Rogers?' he asked cheerfully, as he passed the doorman.

'Willard Hanks III,' said the servant. 'And Admiral Case.'

'Those on the waiting list will be happy,' observed MacDonald, heading up the broad staircase. The Met was in the same league as New York's Century, Boston's Somerset and Pittsburgh's Duquesne, and its waiting list was filled, like theirs, with the ambitious, the powerful, with blue-bloods and with shakers, all wishing to rub shoulders with those already ensconced.

He found his lunch partner in the second floor bar, amid burnished wood, polished brass and a truly enormous oil painting depicting the Rape of Lucrece. It was often difficult to tell the profession of any of the club members, since all, lawyer or senator, lobbyist or government servant tended to wear the same clothes, dark three-piece suits and English wing-tip shoes from Church's were the club uniform. Those who were unfamiliar with the two old boys making their way up to the fourth floor dining room might have taken them for academics, as MacDonald had been in his time, for both had a scholarly air, but in fact both were long-term, top-level intelligence professionals. MacDonald had been Deputy-DIRNSA for over ten years, and had seen a succession of military directors come and go. The man who sat opposite him over the crisp white linen amid the hum of male voices and clink of sterling silver on imported plate in the columned room was the outgoing Director of Central Intelligence. The nominee of the previous, Republican President Monroe, Francis Townshend had begun planning his retirement the moment the returns had started coming in the previous November.

'So what's the view from the hill?' he asked.

'Grand strategy,' MacDonald said succinctly. A steward in starched beige jacket came to take their order. MacDonald chose green turtle soup amontillado, with broiled swordfish and lemon butter to follow, Townshend lobster bisque and chilled rare roast beef. They drank martinis.

'Cord's thinking in global and historical terms. He's picked up on the "British Empire – fate of – and us" analogy that was beginning to haunt the previous administration and is going to do something about it. We cut back, the Soviets overreach themselves and collapse into a pit of their own making just as our economy, rejuvenated by the transfer of priorities from military to civil, bursts forth to dominate the world once again.'

'Military cutbacks?'

'Across the board. The Air Force most of all. B-2s gone, they can keep the F-117s they have but won't get any more, freeze on SDI, cancellation of the ATV. He even rubbed salt into the wound by saying first that America isn't a martial nation, and that second the JCS have been planning to fight the wrong – conventional – war for decades, at vast and unnecessary cost to the nation, when they should have been planning for the new unconventional war which is the only one they *will* ever get to fight.'

'He's right. Cord's probably too intelligent and too educated to make a good President, but there's nothing wrong with his powers of deduction. I recall when I was DCI and JCS hired an independent outfit to analyse the wars going on in the world. The analysts came back and reported that of the 132 wars only the Iran-Iraq conflict could be considered conventional. The military were so annoyed they refused to accept the report. But let's take the scenario of World War Three. Mention it to the military and the Navy's pushing out the battle groups and the SSNs are massing at GIUK, the Greenland Iceland United Kingdom Gap, the Army's getting the troops and supplies mobilised to go to Europe and by God what a mess *that*'d be, their planning dates from WWII and half the railroad tracks and docks aren't *there* any more, and the Air Force's above the speed of sound which is the only place it likes to be, and they've all forgotten that the whole thing's going to be decided in the ten-day to two-week period of Transition To War, no-peace, no-war, when the special forces will take care of everything. Not *ours, theirs*. *Spetsalnaya Naznacheniya*, the Special Purpose troops. *Spetsnaz* for short. During WWII the military devoted 300,000 men to protect vital installations in the homeland itself. Today, if I recall what the Commander of USREDCOM said, there is not a single soldier, sailor, airman solely dedicated to the security mission within the USA. Our borders are porous. *Spetsnaz* teams could be infiltrated with ease, along with agents-in-place to be targeted against key command and control centres, nuclear capable assets, critical lines of communication and other targets critical to the war effort, not to mention the 1,500-odd priority human targets. Assassinate those key men and women and society being as complex as it is in time of crisis will simply not function.'

Townshend paused to fill up on soup.

'Cord got anything to back him up on his grand strategy or is it his own?'

'Political-military simulation. He ran a big game at the national Defense University.'

Townshend rubbed the lobe of his ear. 'Yeah, that would be it. He's the right type to go for it, it's the scientific and academic thing right now, isn't it? It's a buzz. I had to be involved when I was DCI. You know what bothered me about it all? The scientists, the computer nuts got fed up with *people* being involved. People are slow, they aren't always logical, they have consciences. It's *very* difficult to get them to start a nuclear war. They'll always back away from it. So the computer nuts have done what they do best and transferred the whole thing inside computers. My last year at the campus RSAC had two of them, Ivan and Sam, and they nuclear-war-gamed all the time. I don't like it. I don't like the whole trend away from humans. It's the same with intelligence. The whole slant of US policy has been to supplant HUMINT with TECHINT. When they came up with the plan for Monarch Eagle a while back, to get the HUMINT back it was shot down like that. It's dangerous. But then, aren't we supposed to be a machine-minded people? Wouldn't that be one of Cord's national characteristics? We don't understand people too good, that's for sure. So tell me, how did Coogan react to having his toys taken away from him?'

'He took it. Had no choice, did he? I even saw him smile a couple of times.'

Townshend finished spooning in his soup.

'You had better watch Coogan,' he said quietly.

MacDonald looked up in surprise. 'Why? What have I to do with the blue-suiters? Apart from having to have them every so often as DIRNSA, like Moore, who we have at the moment, for our sins.'

'Who are the most important people in the nation, in terms of forming policy?' Townshend asked rhetorically. 'Are they to be found in the Senate? Are they Congressmen? No. Is the Secretary of State among their ranks, or the Secretary of Defense? No. Did Cord say he would cut back on reconnaissance and surveillance?'

'No.'

'Of course not. He *must* have intelligence. You and I supplied it. You still do. The "assets", the SR-71s, U-2s and TR-1s and RC-130s, the satellites like Rhyolite, Magnum, Big Bird and the KH-11s all bring in the "product". The data gathered are vast. There is so much of it that you have to have an idea what you are looking for, so you 'task' it, you ask the smart people in NSA, CIA, the National Photographic Interpretation Center, to look out for it. We have the very best technology available to help us – always a decade ahead of its civil equivalent. We keep track of each and every military and economic development throughout the world that could have an effect on our country and her allies. It means not only investigating new military equipment but also maintaining an accurate inventory of foreign agricultural and industrial assets, production, needs and potential. Through our assets we are able to verify arms control. The National Technical Means. We are able to act as an alarm system that will be triggered when any of the many indicators that signal a possible attack on the USA or its allies are observed.'

The steward had smoothly gathered in the soup plates and served the two entrees.

'I say "we", but who am I talking about?'

'The top analysts,' said MacDonald. 'GS-18s. The experts at the peak of the pyramid, the new elite of the massive machine we have built.'

'Yes,' said Townshend. '*They* are the most important people in terms of forming policy.'

'What does that have to do with Coogan?'

'I know Coogan, I've worked with him. He is sincere, convinced, and a dedicated patriot. He is a very brave man. He has more combat time than most people have time. If the war starts I would like him to be in the lead bomber. What I don't want is for Lieutenant-General Coogan to decide whether the war will start or not. Coogan is a zealot. He believes that the Soviet Union will abandon its mission of world communist domination the day that Hell freezes over. He may be right. And he may not be.'

No one took any notice of the two men, successful businessmen, college professors, maybe, quietly eating their meal in the alcove.

'The importance of the top analysts in our system is that the decision-makers in the government, the prime-movers, including those on the National Security Council, including the very president of the USA himself, view the world very much according to what these operators of the intelligence establishment tell them is out there. They have no choice. *So whoever controls that establishment in effect makes policy.*

50

'To Coogan, if President Cord believes that the moon is made out of blue cheese, or that the Russians believe in MAD, then it is because men and women who have formed their view of the Russians from a study of the *Washington Post* and the collected works of Dick and Jane have told him so. If you removed these people and replaced them with people who knew what they were about would things not be different? Are the Soviets building a Stealth bomber? Who do you want to tell you, some spotty GS-16 over at the CIA whose experience of aviation is limited to ordering a second martini on the shuttle to New York or a man who's ridden an F-4 into the fire of Saigon? What capability does the new, huge submarine being constructed in Severomorsk have, and what does it indicate about Soviet intentions? Some other GS-16 or a man who has had command of *Los Angeles* and *Ohio* class SSNs and SSBNs? What are the Soviets up to at the SDI complex at Smolensk. Someone over at NSA who spends their weekends watching science-fiction videos or a man who worked in the cold space of the *Challenger*'s bay retrieving and repairing satellites?'

Townshend raised a hand. 'That's Coogan's viewpoint. Personally I would say that not only do our civilians do a great job, but allowing the military to interpret their own intelligence is highly dangerous. Coogan thinks the way I have described. I would point out that he is also a trained and successful fighting soldier, a general whose whole life is the planning and winning of campaigns and battles. A large number of the nation's top analysts work for you out at NSA.'

Townshend cut a good segment of succulent pink beef from Scotland, wrapped it around a new potato and lathered the whole with horseradish sauce before popping the forkful in his mouth.

'Keep an eye out for small, predatory five-star generals working their way around to your rear,' he said indistinctly. 'Me, I am going to cultivate my roses.'

Townshend looked into an uncertain future, his eyes unfocused for a moment.

51

'Then there's the Russians,' he said softly. 'They aren't going to sit still for this one, are they ... You know the ancient Chinese curse, Hamish? "May you live in interesting times".'

Townshend raised what was left of his martini in a toast. 'I think they're here,' he said.

SIGINT CITY: NSA HEADQUARTERS, FORT GEORGE. G. MEADE, MARYLAND

The CIA was the bogeyman of the liberals, for whom 'the turnoff for Langley' had become synonymous with the covert warfare and machiavellian, evil-doing of right-wing presidents. They were glad to see it shackled following the fall of AntiChrist after Watergate, pleased to see its Operations personnel slashed and its wrong-doings dragged out into public view. If there had to be a director of Central Intelligence, a DCI like William Colby, intelligent, liberal, unhampered by any ideological strait-jacket when dealing with the Russians would do.

Unfortunately, neither the CIA nor the DCI were what they seemed. For all its power to bring about nightmares in liberal hearts, the CIA was established by Congress under a public law, the National Security Act of 1947, which set out its legal mandate, and just as importantly, the restrictions on its activities. There was another agency however that had simply been established by presidential decree in 1952 by Harry Truman and to which the only laws that had been passed concerning it were ones prohibiting the release of any information about it. It was the National Security Agency, the lineal descendant of Herbert O. Yardley's Black Chamber. Yardley, poker player and cryptologist of genius had founded America's first official code and cipher agency just after the First World War, known as the Black Chamber after the French Chambre Noir; Noir, or Black because it was *secret*.

Yardley's enterprise had once been small enough to fit into an office in a brownstone on East 38th Street, New York, and had contained a handful of code and cipher experts and a few clerks. The same could not have been said of its grandchild, the National Security Agency, which lived in what was a city in its own building, half way between the capital and Baltimore, and employed more people than all the rest of the intelligence community put together. In one respect, however, nothing had changed and that concerned the quality of those operatives. Yardley had been able to draw upon the help of Theodore W. Richards, his country's first Nobel laureate in Chemistry to head his Secret Ink subsection, and his cryptologists were of equal calibre. The same was true of NSA seventy years later. The Agency wanted the very cream of the scientific and mathematical brains in the country and got them. It was prepared to buy, woo or kidnap people of special talent from industry or the academic world. If it sounded ruthless it was, but then, there were no legal restrictions on its activities at all. Except for anyone releasing information about it.

The Agency's primary task was the collection and analysis of signals intelligence, hence its nickname of SIGINT City, although its top analysts went far beyond that, and made use of all sources available to them, from human intelligence to the digitally processed images produced by NPIC in Washington. Liberals might think that the CIA under its DCI was the most powerful and dangerous intelligence agency in the land, and watch anxiously for signs of the fabulous beast attempting to break its bonds and escape from its cage to work evil in the world again, but they were wrong. The NSA was far larger, had a budget five times the size and was legally unhampered from doing anything it chose. Congress had gone on record to note that far from the DCI controlling over-mighty barons in their intelligence fiefdoms, the truth was that the two most powerful figures in the intelligence community were DIRNSA, the director, and his deputy.

The Agency's power was vested in its awesome technological capacity to eavesdrop. Its ability to listen to almost anyone or anything, anywhere, whenever it chose provided the most important source of intelligence for the free world. Some liberals, aware of its role and capacity were also aware and fearful of the potential of Dr Jekyll to turn into Mr Hyde. Senator Frank Church noted that should the Agency ever turn its capabilities on the American people then 'no American would have any privacy left. There would be no place to hide.'

The turnoff for Fort George G. Meade was half way along the Baltimore-Washington Parkway. Although the agency functioned twenty-four hours a day, the majority of the fifty thousand-odd employees who worked there did so on the regular nine-to-five shift of other office workers, and in the morning going in, and the evening going out the traffic on the Parkway slowed to a crawl. Some lived in and around Baltimore, some in and around the capital. Among those from Washington, where she lived in the elegant Georgetown district, was Ashraf Amran. With the American penchant for shortening names, everyone knew her as Ash. It suited her, her hair was that shade of blonde; although in her mid-thirties with her high cheekbones and grey-green eyes, her looks were exotic, she might have been a model earlier in her life.

The agency did not employ her for her looks, however striking. NSA required that everyone who worked there was special in some way, even the secretaries and clerks were a breed apart, having passed the government's most stringent security checks. At the upper levels there were many GG-17s and above, about 650 GG-15s and above and some 275 super-grades who ran things. Ash was one of these. NSA employed her for her brain, which was special.

Although she had the right kind of academic background to interest the agency's headhunters in the old McCormack Post Office and Court House building in Boston, from whence they emerged to scour the West's universities for the finest talent, having been a Rhodes Scholar with a double-first in History at Lady Margaret Hall, Oxford, she was something of an anomaly within the organisation. They had recruited her in something of a hurry because they needed her talents, and once in, she had proved so useful, so effective that she had never travelled the usual route of the high-flyers, taking time out for a Ph.D, and going through the once-yearly, eighteen-week course at NSA's Cryptological School like the 'cipher brains'.

She was the protégé of Hamish MacDonald, the deputy-director, who had recognised in her the ability that the best historians shared with the best analysts, the posing of the questions: of any given information, was it significant? Was it interesting? Was it true? 'Only connect', was the dictum of E.M. Forster and Ash understood that. She was patient, methodical, curious, knew the value of trivia, of miscellaneous information, with the power of her brain could both process and remember an enormous range of data and assimilate it into a pattern that others might miss, could always see, as if through instinct, the relationship between the parts and the whole.

Brought up in Persia, graduate of the Lycée, she had been to university in Oxford and Paris. NSA employed her as a consultant, suddenly aware that they were woefully short of real expertise on Iran, that they had put all their eggs in one basket in reliance on the Shah, and the CIA's belief that they had SAVAK in their pocket; attached to a Special Collection Element team in the Teheran embassy, whose job it was to electronically eavesdrop, Ash, in her old home town swiftly began writing reports that accurately presaged the downfall of the Shah. Once proven correct MacDonald had had such respect for her ability he decided to employ her full-time. She was head of the Iranian section.

SIGINT City, as it was sometimes called, was surrounded by twin ten-feet-high Cyclone fences making a sandwich of a high-voltage electrical fence. Ash entered through the main gate, where her green identity badge, colour-coded, computer-punched, plastic-laminated, worn around the neck, had been checked by the armed, blue-uniformed Federal Protective Service guard. She parked her VW Golf in the lot reserved for the senior operatives. Her office was in the Headquarters-Operations building, a truly vast affair, simply the biggest government building in the Washington area bar the Pentagon, a nine-storey Headquarters tower flanked by two more modern towers of equal stature, tan in colour, filling the jutting wings of an enormous, boxy, A-shaped operations building on which the precast concrete panels had been faced with sickly green stone chippings. All windows were permanently sealed, the great complex being fully air-conditioned.

On the roofs of the towers a technological forest of antennas had grown. Two huge radomes stood at each end, one with an angular, pocked surface like a great golf ball, the second smooth, as a ping-pong ball. In between there were log-periodic antennas, long-wire antennas, parabolic microwave dishes and a big white satellite dish hidden inside an enormous green shell.

Ashraf Amran made her way into the Operations Building, where she took the escalator up to the third floor operations area, where her office was situated. The Iranian section was situated within the Middle East group, access to which was gained through a heavy steel door off one of the broad hallways where sensors searched for unauthorised, untagged persons, and cameras and loudspeakers waited to interrogate such persons when found. The door bore a round red seal, colour-coded to indicate that the work carried on inside was compartmented, and thus off-limits to anyone without a specific 'need to know'. The red seal had been on the door a long time, and given the turbulence of the region few saw the day when it would be replaced by anything less sensitive. Just in case anyone unauthorised should attempt entry the door was defended by a cipher lock. Ash put her hand into the black box, which contained ten buttons and pressed four in the correct sequence, gaining access. Inside were individual offices such as her own, and also open plan areas where personnel worked at grey, government-issue desks, talked on black telephones for unclassified calls, or grey ones for secure conversations, or scrawled on the green chalk boards that lined the pastel walls. She greeted her colleagues while moving swiftly to her own office. There she collected her documents from her safe and retraced her steps to the Tower lobby, passing by the giant, shimmering mosaic of the Agency seal. Cobalt blue and white cubes of hand-cut Byzantine glass depicted a stern eagle grasping a large skeleton key in its talons – a key to unlock secrets, and keep its own. Ash had always thought it ironically appropriate that the Agency should have chosen Byzantine glass.

In the lobby she passed another armed guard to take the automatic lift. This would have taken her down one floor to the basement, filled from end to end with the most powerful computers in existence, but that day, she went all the way up to the ninth floor executive offices, known in the Agency as Mahogany Row. At the far end of the hall was room 9A197, set behind a bright blue door, and was the office of the director Lt General Calvin Moore of the Air Force, newly installed. Next to it was the office of Dr Hamish MacDonald.

Ash went through the door into the outer office where the executive registry secretaries worked, and was let into the deputy-director's own office. It was unobtrusively comfortable, with a pleasing view over the green, tree- and farm-covered Maryland countryside. The windows were defended from the sun by venetian blinds and a huge globe, intricately painted rested beneath. A few small

watercolours of wild flowers adorned the walls;
MacDonald relaxed from the intellectual stress of his job
by painting, and was a skilful amateur. Two cream leather
armchairs sat in front of the desk facing a sofa, the suite
arranged around a glass-topped coffee table. They sat in
the two chairs and MacDonald poured coffee.

'Ash, my dear,' said MacDonald. 'Have you come to tell
me that the recent welcome peace, that lack of lecturing
mullahs from Iran is about to be broken? Is this the
explanation of your presence?'

'I think it is,' she said.

MacDonald sat back in his chair. 'Then begin.'

A blue file lay on the table, marked with the warnings
HANDLE VIA COMINT CHANNELS ONLY and TOP SECRET
UMBRA. MacDonald was renowned in a bureaucratic
organisation for his preference for hearing intelligence
from the horse's mouth rather than wading through reams
of paper.

'When the Iran/Iraq war finally ground to a close, and
Grand Ayatollah Khomeini was visibly failing, there were
many who hoped that the time had come for an end to the
fundamentalist extremism which had so marked the
Khomeini years, and which had been the main source of
instability within the Middle East during that time
responsible for the realignment of a number of recognised
political arrangements, the second Israeli invasion of
Lebanon to cope with the threat from the Iranian-backed
Hezbollah Party of God, and Saudi and Gulf states support
for Iraq in the war with Iran among other things.

'Within the country there was a great feeling of
war-weariness, and a rejection of the religious fanaticism
that had brought the people little but sorrow. Much of the
infrastructure of government within Iran remained intact.
The legal system, although hijacked by clerical judges like
Khalkali still functioned, as did the *Majlis*, the
parliament. Enough moderate politicians were there to put
into motion moves to open up Iran once more to the
outside world, normalise trade and political life within the

country and ease the stern Islamic diktat of the state in social affairs. There were those of us who felt that given a favourable response from the USA and the West these hopeful moves could lead to the establishment of a working democracy. The Shah, like Reza Shah before him made the mistake of using democracy to strengthen his own power. Unlike his father he had not the will to do the things a despot must do if he wishes to stay as one, and he fell. Now the monarch is gone, and the country has suffered years of hell. We felt that now the poison might be purged, that life might return to normal.'

Ash sipped some coffee before it became cold.

'This happy state of affairs – not unlike the English restoration, when Charles II, his powers somewhat curtailed, came back after the years of instability, civil war, rule by the religiously-motivated Major-Generals – may still come about. But not until Khalif Hossein dies, or is removed from power. It has been Iran's misfortune that one tyrant, Khomeini has been succeeded by another, one even worse. The moderates are either dead, once again in exile or in Evin prison. The grip of Khalif Hossein and his extreme mullahs is tighter on the country than Khomeini's ever was.

'There are one or two things I want to say about the Khalif before I go on to what is worrying me particularly, because it is because he is what he is that I am worried. Firstly, there is the point that the popular view of him here is quite incorrect. He is seen much in the "Mad Mullah" image, a kind of younger, crazier version of Khomeini, in the same black gown like a crow, and same black turban and silver beard, although Khomeini's was white, being an older man. The little that Hossein allows of himself to be seen outside the country, via television, mainly, supports this image, as he usually arranges to be seen in his *rowzeh-khan*, or rabble-rousing preacher role. It is not true. It is an image, arranged mainly for our benefit. It works, in that most people over in the West, including members of Congress think of him in just that way – as a crazy, rag-headed would-be prophet. He isn't. He is a very intelligent, calculating, chill, ruthless man. But he *does* believe that he is *Nabi*. That is, the Emissary of Allah, one of the Prophets who have the right to exercise political and military power on behalf of the Almighty. Do you understand the significance of that? There are plenty of people about who think that they are the Emperor Napoleon, or possibly the King of England, but once it becomes apparent nice men in white coats come along and take them somewhere comfortable until they feel better or die, whichever comes first. Hossein thinks that he is in a line with Jesus Christ and Mahomet. But no one is going to take him to the funny-farm because not only did he win a singularly vicious power-struggle to be Khomeini's successor but his grip on the country is secure.

'There is the point about both his name and his honorific. He is Hossein, named after Imam Hossein, grandson of the Prophet Mohammad and Third of the Duodecimal Imams of Shi'ism. When I was a little girl I remember going to see a *Tazieh* in Teheran – that's the Islamic equivalent of a European mediaeval Passion Play – which told the story of the Imam's struggle for the *Khalifat*, or leadership of the Islamic world in AD 661. Urged on by a large section of the Islamic community Imam Hossein challenged Umayad Khalif Yazid for the *Khalifat*, the contest leading to war and the final battle at Karbala in present-day Iraq where the Imam, abandoned by all those who had supported him except for a few relatives and disciples was ruthlessly put to the sword.

'As with Christ's Passion, the martyrdom of Hossein to this day forms the basis of a vast and complex religio-philosophical edifice extending far beyond its mere historical dimension. Combining elements of Zoroastrianism, Christianity and Judaism it has not only influenced the Persian psyche at a deep, unconscious level but raises questions of the legitimacy of government, separation of temporal and eternal power and so forth. By adopting the honorific of Khalif – Hossein is a Grand

Ayatollah and he could have remained content with that – Hossein is making claims not only to leadership of the Islamic world but also to the mantle of the Third Imam. Indeed, given his habit of occasionally being seen on a white horse, that he may be the reincarnation of Imam Hossein, or Hidden Imam, who will unite the world under Islamic leadership and bring peace.

'No one should be surprised that Iran is under the rule of such a man. Until the evolution of democracy it was not uncommon for people to live under the rule of men who were by most objective standards, mad. This century has seen such figures as Stalin, Hitler, Pol Pot, Idi Amin. What is dangerous about Khalif Hossein is his belief in his destiny.'

MacDonald leaned forward and refilled their cups with hot coffee. Ash sipped a little then resumed her story.

'Like Khomeini, Hossein is fanatically opposed to *Taghut* – Satan – by which he means the USA and the West in general. Hossein hates the USSR too, but as a 'lesser' Satan to the greater *Shaytan Bozorg*. What differentiates Hossein from Khomeini is not only his greater degree of fanaticism, and greater mental powers due to his relative youth, but that many of those close to him share his hatred of the USA but also have experience of it, having lived and trained here during the years of the Shah.

'It is not particularly good news for us that we have a very powerful religious leader, implacably hostile to us and our interests, holding power in one of the most turbulent and sensitive areas of the world, but it is something that I am sure we can live with, especially given the damage to the Iranian economy due to the near-interminable war with Iraq. Iraq, formerly considered a threat to the stability of the region is now brought low due to the damage of the war years and can be discounted for some years to come.

'It was not always so. During the war years both sides made really serious efforts to acquire nuclear weapons

61

technology, something that caused quite a number of people to sit up and take notice. Both sides started with severe drawbacks – mainly lacking the engineers and scientists, and the technological base from which to build such a project – and both sides suffered setbacks. The Israelis, correctly seeing the Iraqi drive to acquire nuclear weaponry as a mortally-dangerous threat to their very existence took out the Osiraq reactor near Baghdad on June 7 1981 by means of an F-16 air strike such as has made their air force famous. It was a hundred per cent successful and effectively put an end to the Iraqi hopes. In turn, towards the end of the Gulf war the Iraqis managed to knock out the Iranian Bushehr 1 reactor, again by means of air strikes.

'By the end of the war both sides were pretty much broken-backed. The oil price is still low and the regime of the Khalif quite naturally has problems reconciling the concept of a modern technological economy with its absolutist Islamic beliefs that reject the whole notion. Indeed, in international political terms there was every reason to hope that Iran would become some horrific, sealed off, paranoid regime rejecting the outside world, on the Albanian model. The people of Iran would suffer greatly, but the poison would be contained.

'Iran's nuclear programme has seemed to be at a halt. While they have resources in terms of yellowcake and so on, and could probably get the materials to irradiate and produce plutonium for weapons they are completely short of the trained nuclear technicians and scientists required for such a project. However, we naturally keep an eye on them to see what is going on, and a couple of months ago I got this.'

Ash opened her file and drew out a photograph. It was an overhead oblique of a wharf with some people on it.

'The latest KH-11 got it going over Khorramshahr, the big port. You see anything?'

MacDonald scrutinised it in detail.

'It's not very clear, but is that man a European?'

62

'You have it,' said Ash. 'He is. The two men either side of him are IRGC guards. I took the images along to the boys at NPIC and asked them to run them through their computers and give me a three-dimensional of his face, and this is what they came up with.'

Ash took out one of the startling images that the supercomputers at the National Photographic Interpretation Center, using digital technology, could produce. Normally bridges over the Volga, smokestacks in Sverdlovsk, SS-19s on the pad at Tyuratam, this one was a man. He was in his early forties, short haired, a small, neat beard, brown greying hair, green eyes.

'Who is he?'

'He is Michael B. Logan,' Ash said carefully. 'And he is dead. Single man, no family, died abroad on holiday. A "colleague" came to identify him. Authorised cremation. That was a month *before* this photograph was taken. Michael Logan worked for Lockheed, he was a guidance engineer, responsible for work on the Trident II D-5 SLBM, the submarine-launched ballistic missile currently fitted to the *Ohio*-class SSBNs.'

The skin around MacDonald's eyes crinkled, taking on an anxious expression as he realised that this was not all.

'I've been running checks. Over the past eighteen months I can find eighteen technicians and scientists who have "vanished". They either cannot be found, were offered very good jobs abroad and have never been heard from since, or have "died". They are all expert in their field; and that field is ballistic missiles. None of them are in the fields necessary to manufacture nuclear weapons. They have training in such areas as solid and fluid mechanics, polymer sciences, metallurgy, electronics and computer sciences, electrical engineering and management and design engineering, and they have put this to use *practically*. All, like Logan, know how to handle, to make, the parts of a ballistic missile. They aren't theoreticians.

'Now, all this is bad, and it gets worse. Following the grounding of the Shuttle after the accident, and the

63

consequent problems with the programme there was a considerable bottleneck in getting satellites into orbit, and all available places on the Atlas rockets were taken up by us or the military, causing commercial interests to look elsewhere for launch vehicles. There's the French Ariane, or you can go to China, they have their own Long March rocket and are keen to get into the aerospace business. The only problem with a US company wanting to send a state-of-the-art satellite up on a Chinese rocket is that the government is extremely unhappy about the idea of such technology leaving the country to go into a potentially hostile power. They feel, with good reason, that the temptation for the Chinese to take it apart and get a quantum jump in technology would be too great. Okay. So, in the spirit of enterprise that has made this country great, a company was formed, SatOrCo, which came up with the very ingenious idea of purchasing Chinese rockets, purchasing surplus oil tankers – there's a glut and they're cheap – marrying up the two in US waters, beaching the tanker to provide a stable platform, and firing off the satellite into orbit. Marvellous. They manage to do it. They purchase six Chinese rockets which they proceed to bring back to the USA in a converted container ship. *It never makes it*. The last report from the vessel has it going down in a storm in the Pacific. Exactly where, one is not sure, but somewhere in about 5000 feet of ocean.'

Ash stared intently at MacDonald.

'Any rocket capable of placing a modern satellite in orbit has the range of an ICBM, and in place of that satellite could be fitted with guidance equipment and a nuclear warhead, if you had the technology to produce MIRVs – Multiple Independently-targetable Re-entry Vehicles. If those rockets are *not* at the bottom of the Pacific, then I say they are in Iran. Do you know something else? SatOrCo is wound up. Okay, so they said they had all their money tied up in the rockets, and once they'd lost them there was no way to stay in business. *But you can't find anyone to do with the company*. They've folded their tents and stolen away in the night. *I* say that SatOrCo was formed *only* to provide a cover for acquiring the rockets. Apart from anything else, the Iranians have a history of trying to get hold of long-range rocketry that predates the rule of Khalif Hossein. During the war with Iraq both sides fired numerous missiles at each other in the "war of the cities" in 1988. These were relatively short-range Soviet Scud-Bs, home grown Oghabs (copies of the Chinese Type 83 artillery rocket) a short-range battlefield weapon, hardly a long-range weapon, and a few home-grown IRAN-130s, which never worked very well. Prior to that in 1985 Rafsanjani – one of those carried out feet-first during the Hossein *putsch* – visited Beijing in China in search of missile technology, and actually wanted to purchase M9 long-range ballistic missiles. Like anyone else, the Chinese couldn't see the necessity for the Iranians having such things, especially when every worthwhile target in Iraq was within 150 kilometre range of the Iranian border.'

MacDonald got up from his seat, and went over to the window. He stood looking out for a few moments, propelling the globe around on its axis with his hand.

'How's your husband?' he asked, without looking around. 'Any news?'

'Afsar is still in Evin prison,' Ash said quietly. 'But still alive. There is still hope.'

'Can you do anything for him?'

'From time to time I manage to get some extra food in, sometimes medicines if he is ill. It is dangerous, for to call attention to him is to invite his death at the hands of some latter-day Khalkhali.'

'I wish we could help,' murmured MacDonald. 'But it is difficult to achieve anything in Iran now …'

'There are two sorts of Muslim. There is the sort we have become used to on our television screens, rabid mullahs and fanatical Ayatollahs, the Khomeinis and Hosseins who would inflict a regime of rituals and prayers to fill any and every man and woman's day, every day of the year, that would banish thought entirely except for focusing attention on the grandeur and majesty of the Creator and the wisdom of his prophets and imams. This kind are in fact in a tiny minority, but not unlike their secular *alter egos*, the fanatical Marxists, their obsession is such that as they think of nothing else, they have managed to take and keep power in the Iran post-Shah, who dug his own grave.

'There is the other sort, the ones who live in and enjoy the benefits of the civilisation that fourteen centuries of evolution has wrought upon the original bare framework created by the genius of the Prophet Muhammad. Muhammad's idea became a religion because of him, then a culture, a way of life and finally a civilisation. Khalif Hossein is symbolic of those who lead the fundamentalist cause. That is the kind of flowering it produces. My own father might be taken as an example of what mature Islam produces. He is dead now, but when he was alive he was *Mujtahid*, a very learned man, a theologian and a philosopher, an *Aref*, a Sufi. He held the Chair of Philosophy at the Royal Academy. One of his tasks was to find words for the new concepts, scientific expressions, technological terms that were entering the language. Although a muslim, my father was mindful that Persia had not always been an Islamic or Shi'ite land, and he helped cleanse the Persian language of both unnecessary foreign imports and of all the Arabic formulae introduced by the mullahs in order to obfuscate and mystify their flocks.

'He was a wise man, those unsure of what to do would come to our house to seek his advice. They were many: prime ministers, parliamentarians, academics, generals, students from the university and ordinary humble folk. They all left happier and richer than when they came, for mature Islam is a practical religion, it recognises the fact that men are weak and seeks to help them, not force their minds into a hideous ideological prison of endless ritual.

'My father is gone, and great is his loss. In his place we have Khalif Hossein and his kind. Hossein and the fundamentalists are afraid of the modern world, both Islamic and otherwise. They fear its power, and turn to find safety and protection in a past world that did not exist as they imagine it. They seek to reject fourteen centuries of evolution and maturation of Islam, and reduce it once more to the embryonic form it once was. The world will be a grim place should they ever succeed.'

There was silence for a few moments.

'Is there any SIGINT to indicate that the technicians, the Chinese rockets are inside Iran?' asked MacDonald.

'None,' said Ash precisely. 'As I mentioned, Hossein and his advisers are familiar with the West. They hate us, but they know us. It is my belief that they are fully aware that here –' she waved a hand in a circular motion to indicate the vast NSA complex '– we have the capability to crack codes in nano-seconds, the ability to eavesdrop on any electronic emission anywhere in the world, whether it be telephone, microwave, radio, whatever. I believe that everything will have been done by men meeting in offices, in mosques, in corridors and under trees, and exchanging quiet words.'

'You make them seem formidable.'

'They *are*. Don't let the fact that they are, if you like, marching to a different drummer mislead you into thinking that they are ineffective. Within the narrow and bleak confines of their cause they have a belief, a certainty of victory that makes my belief that the sun will rise tomorrow look like self-doubt.'

'So what is your conclusion? Why the technicians, why the rockets?'

'It all adds up to only one thing. If Hossein was restarting his nuclear programme he would require theoretical scientists. The technicians I believe he has kidnapped are not that kind, but practical men capable of working on ICBMs. He would need a reactor. He hasn't got one. He would need specialised equipment, like a "hot box" for handling the radioactive materials. I cannot find any evidence that any of these rare and exotic pieces of equipment are within Iran. It all points to only one thing.'

Ash paused.

'I do not know when, or how or where, but Khalif Hossein must be planning to acquire, buy, hijack, steal intact nuclear devices, warheads suitable for fitting to ballistic missiles.'

TEHRAN

They came for Jane Payton in the night. Their knocking on her door was not aggressive, but insistent. When she opened it two IRGC soldiers were outside, accompanied by a cleric, a mullah dressed all in black from the *na'alayn* simple slippers on his feet to the carefully wound turban on his head. He was a man of about forty, with his beard dyed with henna in the old style.

'I am Judge Motahari,' he said. He spoke in English, with a slight American accent. She was English, and could not place it. 'We have heard that you have things here contrary to the wishes of God, and we have come to see for ourselves.'

'There is nothing illegal here,' she said fearfully.

'You will let us in.'

'Whose authority do you have for this?' she cried as the soldiers pushed past her.

'We have the authority of the Lord we serve,' he said certainly. 'And need no other.'

He knew where to go, and opened her case of supplies, taking out two clear bottles.

'You see, we were right to come.' He held the bottles up. 'Alcohol.'

'I'm a *nurse*. I *work* here, that is medicinal alcohol. You don't drink it, you use it to cleanse. Even you must know that.'

He shook his head. 'Alcohol. Strictly forbidden in the

68

Qur'an, the Lord's book. You will come with us.'

'I'm under contract here!' she protested. 'I'm due to go back to London. Look, check with your department, I have done nothing wrong.'

He simply held up the bottles mockingly, and they hustled her out of her apartment in her nightgown, taking her downstairs to where a sand-coloured van was waiting. They put her inside and shut the doors. The interior of the van was hot, and dimly lit by a small bulb behind a wire grille in the roof. Plank seats ran along each side and on one of them sat a tall, thin man in a tan lightweight suit, rather dishevelled. He saw that she was European.

'Hi,' he said. He was American.

It was a relief to find someone of your own kind.

'Where are they taking us?' she said.

'I don't know,' he said. 'I'm Chuck McCaid, they arrested me last afternoon, came for me in the cell about an hour ago, put me here.'

The van was grinding along the road. It was full of bumps and holes, and the interior soon became filled with airborne dust, that stuck to the sweat on their faces and bodies.

'Why did they arrest you?'

'I sell machine tools. The Iranians need them for their war effort. My company's been doing business with them for three years now. I was with Khonsari in the Ministry of Supply yesterday, he's the guy who handles it. Now he's usually a fairly reasonable guy, considering, compared to some of the nuts they got here. Suddenly he accuses me of charging them interest on money owed. Now, I ain't that dumb, I know usury is against their code. Sure, our costs are all figured to account for interest back home, but usury, no. Anyhow, he doesn't listen to a word I say, there's two goons waiting and a religious rag-head calling himself a judge, they pronounce verdict on the spot, one Chuck McCaid, guilty as charged, and here I am. Hell, my wife told me not to do business out here. I shoulda listened to her.'

Jane told him what had befallen her and the lines of worry on his face tightened. The van stopped again, and once more the rear doors were opened to allow another man to be pushed in. He had clearly paused to dress before answering the door. He wore polished black shoes, grey suit trousers and a white shirt. He was middle-aged, short-haired with rimless glasses, efficient. He also had a grip on himself, despite the lateness of the hour and abruptness of his arrest, he had an air of authority, and Jane's hopes rose. They introduced themselves. He nodded formally at them both.

'I am Per Larsson,' he said. 'Swedish envoy to this benighted country. I am one of the few left, I represent everyone else.'

'Why have they taken you?' the girl asked.

'I am supposed to be in the pay of the devil,' he said, and his face crinkled slightly at the absurdity of it all.

'Satan?' said McCaid.

'His representative here on earth,' Larsson said drily. 'The CIA.'

'Where are they taking us?'

'I would say, we are to be deported.'

'They'll just put us on a plane?'

'I would assume there will be a show trial. This must all be *pour encourager les autres*, after all,' he sighed. 'I have had to deal with irrational people before. I was in the Lebanon.'

The van drove for over an hour. When it stopped, and they were let out they were taken into a building. Inside, they could see that it was a mosque. Six others were already there, under guard. One was an older man, dressed all in white, white slippers, white gown, white turban. He sat cross-legged at his devotions. Two Iranians sat on chairs by the wall, in Western dress. Squatting close by on the floor was a poor peasant, bewildered and fearful. Two Jews, man and wife like the Iranians stood nearby.

Per Larsson recognised the man praying.

'He is Shaikh Khósrow Hussein,' he said, in

puzzlement. 'He is a member of the government. What is he doing here?'

Larsson went over to him and attempted to talk to him, but Hussein continued to pray, as if he was not there, and a guard pushed him away.

The Iranian couple were expatriates who had fled Fundamentalist Iran to seek refuge in Kuwait. They had been kidnapped. The Jewish man was assessing the situation, and did not like it.

'He is Zoroastrian,' he said, pointing to the peasant. 'So here we have the people of the head tax. Clearly, we are all *aghyar* in some way, we are the "others", those outside true Islam, even the cleric there. Perhaps he is *munafaqeen*, a hypocrite, and we all know what is thought of them.'

'I don't,' said McCaid.

' "Killing a hypocrite is more worthy than a thousand prayers," ' the Jew quoted grimly.

'Son of a bitch.'

Judge Motahari appeared, he waited until Hussein had completed his devotions, then went up to him, and greeted him respectfully. They murmured together, then Motahari knelt in front of Hussein, who seemed to give him a blessing. The judge then came over to them with a guard carrying a sheaf of white gowns over his arm.

'You have been tried in the eyes of God and found guilty,' he said. 'Take off your clothes and wear these.'

Chuck McCaid was a brave man. He picked up one of the coarse cotton shifts and looked at Larsson.

'I wouldn't say this was good news, would you, Mr Larsson?'

Larsson frowned angrily.

'This is preposterous.' He called to Motahari. 'I wish to speak to someone in authority.'

Motohari spread his palms expressively. 'You did not speak to the Lord when you had the chance. His authority was all you needed. Now he has spoken to you.'

When they were changed, bare-legged and naked

71

beneath the shifts, the guards took them outside, leaving their clothes heaped upon the tiled floor behind them. They emerged into a great courtyard of beaten earth. It was dawn, the sky a pale blue, and as they walked out the courtyard seemed to emit a high-pitched, savage sigh of anticipation. Peering fearfully around her Jane Payton saw that all around the walls of the courtyard were waiting people. As they were prodded to the middle they passed piles of faggots, sticky and tarred. In the middle nine holes had been dug in the ground, they were made to get in, when they stood there earth was piled around them, so that they were buried up to their waists. The men and women around the mud-brick walls started closing in. At the side of the mosque a raised platform had been constructed, on it a technician operated a television camera. As the people crowded closer to them they left a wide passageway leading from the shrine to the killing-ground. Frantically, irrationally, Jane Payton wondered what her parents would do when she did not arrive at Heathrow, whether they would wait for another aircraft to come.

Light flickered all around. The torches in the people's hands crackled as the flames caught hold. The crowd parted to make a human passageway from the shrine. A shining white figure on a white horse came riding slowly towards them, a flaming brand held high.

'It's fuckin' Hossein himself,' McCaid muttered hoarsely.

The Khalif stopped in front of the circle of sacrifice. The courtyard was silent but for the frantic breathing of the victims in their holes and the crackling of the torches. In the distance Jane Payton saw the cameraman focus in on the shot. Hossein made a very slight motion towards the cleric, praying calmly at his post, and then threw the first brand.

The sky was filled with fire.

NSA HEADQUARTERS

Ashraf Amran hit the freeze on the VCR and just the image of the Khalif remained, staring full into the camera, fanatical, denunciatory, a figure out of an age that people who watched television had never known existed.

'Are you still sure he isn't simply barking mad?' said MacDonald. 'A head of state instigates and participates in mass murder and broadcasts it to the world on live television. Even Idi Amin never did that.'

'It was done for a reason. If the survival of the Faith requires the shedding of blood then Khalif Hossein will be there to perform his duty, you may be sure. There is no evidence that he enjoys the act of killing, or of torture, as did Amin, however. Amin took it to the lengths of ritual cannibalism of various victims. Hossein is a very chill, calculating man. This was done for a purpose. The choreography of the murder is easy to understand. The use of fire and the number of victims being nine is simply a re-enactment of an ancient Muslim story from the Qur'an, in which nine emissaries from the Byzantine emperor were burned to death before being able to harm the Prophet Muhammad. The killing of the nine at Qom indicates to all believers that the tale has come true again, and that, clearly, Hossein is more than even an Imam, if Allah has protected him in this manner. Hossein also took the trouble to appear on a white charger, thus reinforcing his claim to be the Hidden Imam.

'The underlying motive must be that it has cleared Iran of foreigners. They have all left, just as fast as they could get on to the jets. With the country locked up tight it makes it so much more difficult to get anyone in, to find out what is going on. About rockets, yes? And nuclear warheads?'

'It's almost impossible to conduct espionage in a hermetically-sealed environment,' agreed MacDonald. 'After the Second World War we tried to set up networks in the East, and in Russia itself, but it was a great failure. They can do it to us with ease, because we are an open society, but it's not the same in reverse. It's one of the reasons we rely so much on TECHINT.'

'Is anyone thinking on the lines of taking Hossein out?' murmured Ash.

MacDonald looked slightly alarmed. 'Assassination? I would doubt it. "Kings do not kill kings." Cord doesn't seem the kind to authorise such a thing.'

' "When there are no rules of the game clubs are trumps." Hossein isn't playing by the rules. What do *you* think he wants nuclear weapons for? To join in MAD? Hardly. "We give law to hares and deer ... but it was never accounted either cruelty or foul play to knock foxes and wolves on the head as they can be found, because they be beasts of prey". St John knew what he was talking about. Strafford was a beast of prey, he was Charles I's "Man of Blood", the parliamentarians knew it. So they took him out and had him made shorter by a head before he could do it to them. Some three centuries later a British diplomat in Berlin prophesied that Adolf Hitler would bring about general war within a few years, and asked his superiors for permission to shoot him from a window that overlooked the Nazi podium where marches were reviewed. They didn't let him.'

'Assassination's a very tricky area,' MacDonald said again. 'There's an awful lot can go wrong, for a start.'

'Would it not have been better had it been done? The Nazis would have been like headless chickens. There would have been no war. And who is talking of CIA hitmen, or special teams?' Ash waved a hand around to

74

indicate the vast amounts of machinery and electronics all around them. 'This stuff is good for more than just listening to Russian generals making appointments for assignations with their mistresses.'

She leaned forward. 'Hossein could be killed from this very room.'

'I think we'd better steer around it, Ash,' said MacDonald carefully. 'NSA is in the intelligence business. James Bond never worked here.'

'Intelligence is there only in order to facilitate the making of decisions. Someone will have to decide what to do about Hossein. I hope it is done *before* he does something with his nuclear devices.'

MacDonald got up to leave. 'Well, he hasn't got them yet. We'll know if he does.'

Ash looked up at him quizzically. 'You haven't mentioned the most important thing about that,' she said, pointing at the screen that had so recently held pictures of horror.

'Hossein murdered a little English nurse, which was quite shrewd, because it sickens the liberals, who might otherwise go along with his anti-American line. He wants no allies here, not even "useful fools"; he and his men will do all this by themselves, for the glory of God, or fall trying. He killed an American businessman to indicate his hatred for us. He killed a Swedish diplomat to put himself beyond the pale. Three Christians – "Cross-worshippers". Two Jews, one Zoroastrian. An unfortunate, taken from the tiny population of that religion simply to make up the quota of *ahl al-dhimma*, or the people of the head tax. Two expatriate Iranians who had taken refuge and made new lives, to represent the *munafeqeen* – the hypocrites among the *aghyar*, the others. That made the numbers up to eight. And then he called for a martyr, without which the act would not be complete, for Hossein's Islam is Motahari's Islam, the religion of agitation, revolution, blood, liberation and martyrdom. That was Shaikh Hashemi, "accused" of working for the CIA. That would have the effect of "encouraging" the others, of keeping everything water-tight. That is important if, as I say it will, a plan is to take effect to acquire nuclear weapons. Did you notice, Hossein genuflected to Hashemi, he inclined his head very slightly just before he threw the first flaming brand, acknowledging the man who was going on to the finest rooms in Paradise.'

'So what did I miss?' asked MacDonald. 'What is the important thing?'

'Hossein's Islam believes that it is opposed by a "monster with four heads". The first and principal head is the Jew, "the eternal schemer against God", the second is symbolised by the Cross of the Christian "Crusaders", the third, secularism – those Muslims who advocate separation of mosque and state and fourth, atheism, whose contemporary manifestation is communism.

'So did Hossein not murder two Jews? Three Christian "Crusaders"? Two expatriate Iranians, secularists? And a poor Zoroastrian and a martyr for good measure.'

Ash stared intently at MacDonald. *Where was the communist?* The Russians are at least the "lesser Satan". He didn't kill a Russian. *He should have done.*'

DAVIS-MONTHAN AFB, ARIZONA

A lot of different outfits called the vast, sprawling desert air force base home. The National Air Guard's weekend fliers trained in their ground-attack A-10 'warthogs' there, the 868th Tactical Missile Training Group trained Air Force personnel in the management of the Ground Launched Cruise Missile system. The 41st Electronic Combat Squadron flew EC-130Hs out of there, and more National Guardsmen, men who held down civilian jobs that ranged from corporate pilots to corporate lawyers, crop dusters to engineers, flew F-16s and from time to time demonstrated their expertise by beating the regular Air Force in competition, much to the latter's chagrin. Those who ran the base called the various outfits their 'tenants'.

The biggest, in terms of numbers of aircraft and of acreage, was the Aerospace Maintenance and Regeneration Center, and its aircraft did not fly. Only rarely did an intact aircraft taxi out from AMARC and its pilot get the words 'cleared for take off' in his headphones. AMARC aircraft were cleared to land. Old and tired, they were ferried in from their army, air force, navy and coast guard commands, and parked out in the desert in long silent rows. With intakes and nozzles sealed, canopies and radomes sprayed with white vinyl plastic Spraylat that kept the interior cool even in summer, resting on the alkaline soil, and in the dry air of Tucson, where it hardly ever rained, the aircraft could last almost forever.

Bearing the marks of their service, some 2500 aircraft stood out on AMARC's 2,300 acres, surrounded by thirteen miles of perimeter fence. Birds perched up on their canopies and tail fins, dirt dobbers began the process of sealing up hydraulic nozzles and pitot tubes with nests of mud and fibre for the incubation of their children, spiders spread nets across landing-gear struts like fishermen of the air; in season, coyote pups chased each other over the caliche, darting in and out of the slowly deflating tyres. From time to time AMARC workers arrived to begin the process of cannibalisation, for the aircraft were a useful source of spare parts for others still in service. They acted as a kind of organ bank. When there was nothing left that anyone wanted, like old workhorses they were delivered up to the knacker, Southwestern Alloys of Tucson, who chopped them brutally into pieces, and boiled them up in the smelter to begin new lives as wrappings for beer and dog food.

The military shared the duties in the tall, boxy control tower above Base Operations with the civilian controllers of the FAA, who manned the five area surveillance radars and directed all IFR traffic in the Tucson area. The Air Force personnel manned the precision approach radars of the base itself. The captain on duty that day had little doubt that the aircraft on long final for the active runway, although arriving to visit AMARC, would be leaving under its own power. He could see it on his radar scope, but also, if he chose, by looking out of the window through the crystal clear desert air, a gleaming, pure-white dot that metamorphosed into a shining, polished F-16. This little fighter had many more flight-hours left in it, it was the cosseted executive transport of an important man, destined never to be shot at. The white, single-engined General Dynamics jet was famous within the service; it bore the person of the chief of staff, Lieutenant General Coogan about his great domain.

When the F-16 taxied in to the ramp Colonel Travis, commander of AMARC was waiting for it. A sergeant wearing ear defenders guided Coogan to his parking point with bats, once in place he drew a hand across his throat in the sign-language between ground-crew and pilot, meaning 'kill it', and the Pratt & Whitney F-100 spooled down in a long-drawn-out metal sigh. The man who climbed out of the cockpit in his olive-drab nomex was as lean and agile as any of the young men who normally flew the fighter; only when he removed the large bone-dome, scratched and chipped from years of use did the silver hair and thousands of hair-fine crinkles that time spent high in a sun-filled sky give a man become visible.

''Morning, Travis,' said Coogan.

'Good morning, sir.' Travis was out of the mould too. He still looked like an air force jock. The covetous glance he gave the F-16 confirmed it, Travis felt about aircraft the way some men felt about women.

'Pretty bird,' he volunteered, seeing Coogan notice his gaze.

'She's a good little scooter,' agreed Coogan. 'And I like to stay current. Though I'm a bomber man by training. You too, isn't that right?'

'I was, sir,' Travis said easily. He had gotten used to hiding the deep reservoir of his disappointment. 'I'm in charge of the old folks' home now, you might say.'

'Yeah …' Coogan looked at Travis thoughtfully. 'The museum open?'

'Sure is, sir. The car's waiting for us.'

The two officers got into the blue Air Force Ford and the driver took them from the north ramp past the main gate, where Colonel Olds' famous Phantom sat by a row of spindly palms, still bearing its four red stars, on to Quijota Boulevard, where they went through all the residential housing of the base. The driver slowed to 15 mph in the school zone of the Frank Borman elementary school and then speeded up on Wilmot, travelling around the edge of the base. On the southern flank they turned into the Pima Air Museum, where more than 130 aircraft representatives of America's aviation history were displayed in the open air.

The museum had full-scale mock-ups of the Wright Flyer and the supersonic X-15, as well as genuine examples of everything from a WWII B-17 to a Teledyne-Ryan reconnaissance drone that flew in Vietnam, but Coogan had come to see only one aircraft.

The two men strolled across the red-brown caliche with the various displays high above, casting long shadows in the early light. Coogan stopped some way off to get a good look. Just under one hundred feet long from the tip of the barber-pole pitot boom to the muzzle of the 20mm General Electric cannon in the tail, delta-winged, four long turbojets, the giant underbelly bomb pod and the thrusting fuselage itself all combined to produce an effect that was still futuristic over thirty years after it was built. Made to carry nuclear weapons at 60,000 feet and mach. 2.2, or 100 feet and mach. 0.9 the B-58 Hustler had been way ahead of its time.

'It's been a while,' Coogan said slowly. 'I'd forgotten how beautiful she was. Unstoppable. There was a quantum jump in warfare, if you want it. We could have gone all the way to Red Square with thermonuclear devices on board and there was nothing the Soviets could do about it. Too high and too fast. The missiles couldn't get up there and the fighters flamed out trying. It ain't too often you get a complete lock on the enemy, Travis, but that jewel there was such a thing. LeMay was still into that box-formation-to-Berlin thing, that's why he liked the B-52. Me, I was always a believer in the highest technology you could get.'

Coogan stood looking at the fabulous, drooping-winged beast, its hand-polished aluminium skin gleaming in the sunlight, slightly nose-down on its famous stalky landing gear, one of the most beautiful aircraft ever made.

He rubbed his face in memory. 'Makes me ache,' he confessed. 'There's a price to be paid for beyond-the-state-of-the-art technology. We lost more than a few. I was a part of the flight test programme. We were out of Carswell one morning, 28,000 feet and 450 knots when the number three engine shrapnelised. Took out the number four, and with full rudder on we yawed to fifteen degrees to the right. The vertical fin disintegrated and I initiated the ejection sequence. We all three punched out about a half-second before the entire aircraft came to pieces. We had the SAC seat in the early stages of the programme, it was before the encapsulated seat, and the airblast didn't do us much good. I was in hospital four months, and it was near a year before I flew again. But then we were lucky, there were a lot of boys who didn't make it at all.'

Coogan turned away from the widowmaker.

'You flew F-4s in Vietnam.'

'Yes, sir. Two tours.'

'Yeah … the SAMs could get at us then, couldn't they.'

'Yes, sir, they came up like telegraph poles.'

'Now, with the B-2, with Northrop's ATB that's not a problem.' Coogan said. 'The Soviets can't see it. Their little radars can scan all they want, *but they can't see it*, so they can't fire their little missiles at it. Which means we can go bomb them back to the Stone Age and there is nothing they can do about it. We got the B-58 Hustler back, Travis. We have that quantum jump.'

He turned to the colonel, and the smile died from his face, leaving it chill.

'Or, we did have. The B-2 is cancelled. Did you know that?'

'Yes sir, I did.'

'Yes sir, you do,' Coogan agreed. 'You do, because the ten we have are due to come here, aren't they. The President has ordered them stored here with the old Phantoms and Vigilantes and Starfighters. And if my guess is right, not long after that you will get a quiet telephone call from President Cord himself, ordering you to have your men take a torch to them. Do you think that you'll save one, to put here in the museum next to its illustrious ancestor?'

'I'll try, sir.'

Coogan's pale blue eyes were like chips of flint.

'Like hell you will, mister,' he whispered. 'I'll tell you what's going to happen. I'm going to ask you to do something illegal, but if you love your country you'll do it. If you do it I'll get you an operational posting again. If you won't I'll have you transferred somewhere less salubrious than here.'

Travis smiled wryly. 'I'm an operational flier, sir. Looking after retired airplanes is about as bad a posting as I could get.'

Coogan stared intently at him. 'No, it isn't, Colonel. I do assure you I can find many worse things for you to do.'

Travis swallowed. 'I'm sure you can, sir. What is it you want me to do?'

'Tomorrow I am sending a team to you here. I want you to provide sufficient hangar space for ten B-2s. My team will bring with it the materials to construct replicas of the bombers, suitably clad in protective materials. Shortly afterwards our ten B-2s will fly in from Whiteman AFB. They will be parked here as they would be for storage.

This base is somewhere off the beaten track as far as Soviet surveillance satellites are concerned, however, for this they will undoubtedly send a *Cosmos* overhead to get images of the B-2s here. Once they have done so, and have moved the satellite's orbit once again, we will fly the B-2s back to Whiteman, where they will rest inside their purpose-built hangars. In their place here we will put the replicas. A lot of work has gone into them to make them give the same characteristics should the Soviets run infra-red and other sensors over them. We had to get real parts from Northrop. They're *almost* the real thing. They just won't fly. I will need you to firstly inform the President that the B-2s have arrived. Then when you get his call to put the torch to them I will need you to inform him subsequently that it has been done. Will you do it?'

'I will, sir,' Travis said quietly.

'Good. Let's get back to the base then.'

They retraced their steps to their car. The first few visitors were trickling in, they looked curiously at Coogan in his flight suit.

Back on the north ramp they had Coogan's F-16 refuelled and ready to go. He looked up at Travis, who was some six inches or more taller.

'You couldn't have got in the B-58,' he said. 'Room was scarce, we picked for size.'

'I heard that, sir. It wasn't a problem in the F-4.'

'It's not a problem in the B-2 either,' said Coogan. 'When they leave here you're going too. You'll join the team at Whiteman. You were a fine pilot, you had your problems since the war, that's why they put you out here. You're a fighting soldier. I need the very best for the B-2.'

Coogan looked out over the serried ranks of retired aircraft to the greenish blue of the Santa Rita mountains.

'Get sharp,' he said quietly. 'The president has some very funny ideas about defence, and the Soviets are going to try us out. The B-2s may be going into Russia sooner than you might think.'

MOSCOW

The polished black Zil limousine hissed along the wet, salted highway, carrying its sole passenger, Rykov. The closest almost any Soviet citizen got to a Zil was to get out of its way as it passed imperiously by, for they were rare, and the perquisite of the very elite. It was in the gift of General Secretary Krilov. Had he been in it it would have been a part of a four- or five-car motorcade, for Krilov was no less nervous of assassination than his predecessors. Brezhnev had mixed his cars up, using Zils, his Rolls Royce, Mercedes or Cadillac, following the January morning in 1969 when an Army Lieutenant loosed off at him coming out of the Kremlin's Borovitsky Gate, and Krilov, although less obsessed by Western automobiles than he, had retained the practice, as had his predecessor, Gorbachev.

Most Soviet citizens would have relished the opportunity to sit on the hand-tooled vinyl, rest their feet on the carpet, enjoy the warmth of the heating system, or air-conditioning in summer, and generally admire the radio-telephone and other gadgets aboard, but travelling in it depressed Rykov. To him, it epitomised what was wrong with his country. Not unlike an elongated sixties Lincoln Continental, the Zil was hand-built. In technological terms it was out of the Ark.

Rykov's Thunderbird contained a small on-board computer that continually monitored rpm, torque and speed, and adjusted fuel flows, timing and exhaust emission for maximum performance and economy. It informed him when it was due for a service and if something was wrong with it. It reminded him to do up his seat belt and to switch out the lights if he was leaving it. He could operate the locks from his key-ring when a hundred yards away and play orchestral-quality music through quadraphonic speakers via its on-board compact disc system. In terms of technology, however, it was not near state-of-the-art. The American fighters that repeatedly blew their Soviet counterparts from the sky when piloted by Israelis against Syrians and Libyans in the surrogate battle of the Middle East were closer to it, with their superb avionics, radar, miniaturised guidance systems and so forth.

Ever since the days of Peter the Great Russia had enjoyed its greatest military advantage in comparison to the West when the pace of weapons technology had slowed sufficiently to allow standardisation of equipment and therefore of fighting units and tactics, as in the eighteenth century infantry column or mid-twentieth century armoured division. Whenever the pace of technology placed emphasis on quality rather than quantity the Russian advantage had diminished.

The kind of accelerating pace of technology embodied in the products of Silicon Valley and Japan, and the super-computers of NSA threatened to consign the Soviet military to the dark ages. The technology of SDI was a case in point. Born in the Reagan administration the Strategic Defense Initiative might not really make the USA completely invulnerable to nuclear attack, but the protection it offered to US air bases and missile sites placed appalling strain on the Soviet economy in terms of the increased number of rockets and warheads needed to swamp the system, and furthermore, while most commentators thought in nuclear terms even more worrying to the Soviets were the implications of SDI for *conventional* war, in which a superior US SDI system might simply be able to take out much of the USSR's conventionally armed aircraft, tanks and ships.

It was a prospect not lost on the Soviet military, who enjoyed unrivalled access to the scientific and productive resources of the state, and had their own vast SDI complex outside Sverdlovsk. Even if President Cord had – as the latest SIGINT indicated – cancelled the truly remarkable B-2 Advanced Technology bomber for domestic political reasons, if he could get away with his military cutbacks and transfer American resources back into the domestic sector in a few years the economy would have grown to such an extent, and the cutting edge of the new technology be so sharp, that the USSR could never catch up, or even be able to deploy her military forces at all, since they would have become roughly equivalent to the nineteenth century Polish cavalry that attacked German machine-guns and barbed-wire fortifications at the beginning of the First World War – an irrelevance, to be ignored, or swatted like a fly if they became a nuisance.

Rykov returned from his dark musings to the interior of the Zil. It was not that the Soviet Union could not produce vehicles that worked properly – some of their fighters and Armoured Fighting Vehicles were excellent – it was that the system could not produce consumer goods *and* fighters and Armoured Fighting vehicles. The Soviet people had been bought off for decades – regarded by their leaders as producers, not consumers – by the fact that things did, *very slowly*, get better. The average man or woman living in what to Western eyes was a horribly cramped little apartment in a high-rise block in one of the big cities could comfort themselves that they were living better than their parents, who had had only an *izba*, a small wooden house in the countryside with no conveniences. But things were changing. The younger people were more impatient, were fussy about shopping, were aware that in the *West*, the improvement in the quality of life was *accelerating*, they couldn't remember the Great Patriotic War. The Soviet leadership had shrewdly played on the patriotism of the Russian people for decades – Russia, *rodina*, the Motherland, something that had to be done with considerable delicacy and skill because of the ancient enmities between ethnic Russians and all the other nationalities, like Georgians, Armenians, Lithuanians, Uzbeks. Rykov wondered how long the balancing act could be kept up. Saudi Arabian oil would do it, black gold would buy the leadership more time, would sate the desires of the people for a while.

Rykov was well-familiar with the route the KGB driver was taking. They had headed west out of Moscow. Here the gently-rolling hills contained the dachas of the *nachalstvos*. Rykov had his own modern dacha in Nikolina Gora, set in the beautiful forest, along with the other academicians, journalists, writers and top government officials. Nikolina Gora, along with Peredelinko, the writers' colony were close by Zhukovka, the very heart of dacha country, where of a summer morning it was possible to see anyone who was among the high and mighty of Soviet politics, science, culture. The USA had Detroit as the capital of the automobile industry, Hollywood for movies, Washington for government, New York for finance, publishing, television, Silicon Valley for the second industrial revolution, but the USSR had Moscow, the Big Apple for everything.

They passed by the large, low cement-block village store complex where in the good weather Rykov and his family did their shopping. Set in the heart of the picturesque village it contained anything the dacha-dwellers might want or need, from a new Italian suit to a microwave. It had been built for them by Nikita Krushchev, and while now Krushchev was a non-person, he lived on in lore, for the elite dryly called his creation 'Krushchev's store'.

They went through the wintry village, for they were headed for the most exclusive mansion of all, two hamlets on, opposite the settlement of Usovo. Here was the enclave of the politburo, and here Krilov lived, in the dacha of Krushchev and Brezhnev, set in lovely grounds on the bank of the slow-moving Moscow river, with marble stairs going down to the water.

The Zil halted at the guard-house at the beginning of the drive. The driver had taken off his dark blue raincoat in the warmth of the car and folded it on the seat behind him, but retained the flat, short-brimmed fedora, his badge of office. He nodded at the similarly-dressed plainclothesman who allowed them in, whom he probably knew.

The grounds were shrouded in snow, but it was warm inside. An aide showed Rykov into a large room overlooking the gardens. It was a Russian room, a big fire burned in the grate, and it was decorated in the colours of the *ancien regime*, in red and blue and gold, and the *parketnye* flooring wore rugs, and furniture stood waiting, that had been used by the Czar and his nobility. It gave the lie to Krilov's immaculate western suit, crisp white shirt and regimental-style tie. Krilov was of medium height, balding, trim, sharp of eye and mind, very like his mentor, Gorbachev.

'Sit down,' he said to Rykov, pointing to a carved, leather-seated armchair. Both men were in western dress; Soviet rulers and elite had come a long way from the coarseness of a Krushchev, and not just in terms of baggy serge. Like Gorbachev, Krilov understood that there were better ways of manipulating the West than taking off his Italian loafer and beating it on his desk at the UN.

'Your analysis is excellent,' said Krilov.

'Thank you.'

'Your plan has been accepted by the politburo,' said Krilov. In fact, it had not. More important than the members of that body were the top military men, whose forces would play a vital part in implementing Rykov's operation, and the members of the extra-ordinary Group *Nord*, the chiefs of all the KGB's operational divisions, who met at least once a month to co-ordinate the efforts of all the KGB's States. Gorbachev had reduced the old-time conservative politburo members to the status of a group of rubber stamps, and Krilov had kept it that way. When they were required to approve Rykov's plan they would do so.

'The Iranians will provide what we need – plausible

deniability – while our own special forces will strike at the truly vital targets. Our involvement will be hidden by the fog of war until it will be too late for the Americans to do anything about it anyway. It will be a *fait accompli*.'

'Afghanistan was a superb operational laboratory. The Americans never learned from Vietnam. They are still training to fight a conventional war, whereas *our* troops have several years' worth of honing their skills in the new fashion of warfare. It is my estimate that the Saudis will collapse totally in under five days. Their entire leadership amounts to no more than two hundred and fifty key figures. With them removed and vital communications destroyed, plus the "new government" calling upon the "assistance" of Khalif Hossein we should have total command of Saudi Arabia and be mopping up the Gulf states in under a week.'

'That is our opinion also.'

'It will be necessary to test the resolve of President Cord first. However, he will be expecting our strategic overstretch, so I do not anticipate any problems. It would be as well to be sure, however, we need to receive the right signals to be sure we are not instead starting the Third World War. If the US reacted fast and seriously opposed us we would have to back down or go to war. It could be 1962 and Cuba again.'

Krilov nodded seriously. His predecessor, Khrushchev had paid with his job for miscalculating both the strength of will of the young president, John F. Kennedy and the sophistication of the still-young US overhead surveillance and reconnaissance system, and their associated analytical intelligence operatives.

'Something should be chosen that is in the American backyard, in the area they have traditionally thought to be theirs. Central America or the Caribbean. If President Cord's administration will swallow that wedded as they are to their new plans of non-intervention, then the way will be clear.'

'It is underway,' said Krilov.

Something was puzzling Rykov.

'Everything has moved very fast,' he ventured. 'I had presumed a delay of a year to eighteen months for negotiations with Khalif Hossein to succeed.'

Krilov looked at Rykov, thoughtfully, curiously.

'You always thought he would agree?' he asked.

'Yes. The notion is very attractive to him. But I imagined it would take some time to build bridges with so paranoid a regime.'

'Yes,' Krilov said softly. 'That is the curious thing. *We* did not approach them. *They* approached us.'

MARYLAND

General Coogan lived in a small farm house about thirty miles outside Washington, not far from the little town of Norbeck. He was separated from his wife, a once-slim and effervescent girl to whom a life spent living on military bases and commands around the globe married to a man who was never there had given a gin voice and a bridge habit. She lived in Boston, near their only child, a grown-up daughter. It was another disappointment. When she had married the quick-witted, ambitious young air force lieutenant they had agreed that a large family was the only thing. As she had bitterly pointed out, more than twenty-years later, a man could have five children around him or five stars on his shoulders, but not both, because either took most of your time.

Coogan's home was handy for going in to Washington, since the chief of staff could not afford to be far from the seat of power, and was pleasant, in that it reminded him of his rural Kentucky upbringing. He was there one evening when his telephone rang.

'Coogan.'

'Good evening, General.' It was someone on a car

phone. 'You don't know me, my name is Riva. Gulio Riva. I'm on Harrison Taylor's research staff in the White House.'

'Yes?'

'There's something I want to talk to you about. Could we meet, do you think?'

'What is it you want? If you need to see me, or the President wants you to give me a message, go through regular channels.'

'It's not that, General … this isn't official … I need to talk to you …'

'What about?'

'It's about some things in the administration …' the young man's voice said hesitantly. 'I'm worried … I'm not sure what I should do. I need advice.'

Years of being shot at by people of hostile intent, whether his country's enemies or rivals on the ladder of success had given Coogan the ability to make decisions instantly.

'Okay,' he said. 'Come round. Are you nearby?'

'Yes … I'm in Norbeck. But I don't think we should be seen … I don't think I should come to your house in case anyone is watching.'

'Then I'll meet you. There's a parking lot outside the seven-eleven. Be there in fifteen minutes.'

Coogan slipped on a windbreaker and went through his ranch house to the garage, where his dark blue Cadillac was waiting. He felt no alarm at going out in the night to meet someone he had never met. Armed combat had never worried him overly. Coogan was a warrior, he came from a line of them. He had an ancestor who had charged towards the grape-shot at Bull Run and had lived to talk about it. Coogan was bred for it, like a bird-dog.

He drove through the dark into town. Parking outside the seven-eleven he got out. From a blue Ford close by someone waved, and he went over, and got in.

'I'm Coogan,' he said. 'Are you Riva?'

The young man, only in his twenties, nodded

nervously. He was dark-haired and olive-skinned, of Latin appearance.

'Okay,' said Coogan. 'I'm here.'

Riva's eyes darted about, and he licked his lips as he looked at the air force general. Although Coogan rarely felt fear himself he could recognise it in others. He reached across and patted Riva on the shoulder. Despite only having one child he had a good way with young people, he had always been able to inspire great loyalty in the young men and women of his flight.

'Let's take our time,' he said avuncularly. 'I'm glad you called, if I had to sit through one more episode of *MASH* I think I'd have lost my mind.'

The only television Coogan ever watched was real-time surveillance transmitted digitally from overhead satellites, but he realised that a lot of people didn't have enough to do, and sat getting square eyes and softening of the brain in the evenings.

'Let's have a swallow of something cold to get acquainted,' he said. He got out and walked across the parking lot to the small liquor store on the far side, where he purchased a six-pack of Bud and a couple of small air-line bottles of Wild Turkey. He took the brown bag back to the car and passed one of the little bottles and a chill red white and blue can across to Riva, who took them gratefully. Informers needed a belt before they could spill, Coogan thought coldly.

The fiery liquor was chased down the young man's throat by the clean beer, and Riva gasped in appreciation. Coogan kept the second bottle in his jacket pocket in case it was needed, and pulled the tab off a can to show willing. He drank only sparingly. He had seen careers ruined and lives lost by a desire for alcohol.

'Okay, General. Let me explain who I am. As I said, I work for Harrison Taylor who is as you know the president's chief of staff in the White House. I got the job because I was on the campaign team, right from the word go. I finished my law degree, the elections were coming up, I'd always been interested in politics and I thought, hell, I'll spend six or nine months working on a campaign before I go into practice, it'll be exciting, a lot of fun and could be good for my career too. I picked Cord because he was from my home state, and because, well, he didn't really have a chance, did he, but I liked his ideas, he was an exciting candidate. Because no one thought he could win, he didn't have a big staff, and that meant I could get aboard real easy, and probably get a crack at something difficult along the way. Campaigns are *always* short of talent. If you ever wrote an essay in high school and have any kind of special knowledge or interest you can bet *somewhere* along the line you'll get the chance to write a campaign speech. You do a good job, and you're on the way.'

Coogan nodded.

'I was looking at it from the point of view of getting experience this time to go on *next* time in a position of authority. It's a good route. It's a well-known route. John Ehrlichman was a baggage-handler for Richard Nixon in 1960. His organisational ability was such that he became one of President Nixon's two top aides. Gary Hart was doing something similar for George McGovern, and in 87/8 ran for the presidency himself. And what's more – and I know Ehrlichman went to jail – if Hart had kept his pants zipped aboard the Monkey Business he would have been president too, given the way it all went. Okay, I've picked a couple of guys who fell at the last fence, but Jerry Brown, Phil Friedman, Richard Nixon, George McGovern, Orville Freeman – guys like these all made it by getting on in what seemed like a no-hoper job.'

'That's sound,' said Coogan, while Riva took a slurp of his beer. 'It's more difficult in the military, but it can be done.'

'What's more, that's what Cord was thinking of doing. *He* was running in order to establish impeccable radical credentials for *next* time. Cord was thinking of eight years later. He and his men had it worked out. He was a young,

92

successful Congressman. Okay. But Congressmen don't get elected to the presidency any more, the public's got sophisticated, they think Congressmen are a bunch of lightweights whose secretaries can't spell and spend most of their time kneeling under the Congressman's desk. The public like proven competence in government, which is why a governorship is the best route. Jimmy Carter, Reagan, Dukakis, yes? Cord was going for the state governorship, which was probably up for grabs given Huggins' problems. Probably *is* up for grabs, we'll see. So Cord goes into the presidential race with this long term haul in mind, and what happens? He steamrollers the opposition in New Hampshire. From that moment he's on the way. Now all the qualities they were planning to use on the road to the governorship and the next election bar one come alight. Cord was a Forward Air Controller in Vietnam – not only can nobody point the finger and say he Quayled at the thought of combat the guy is a *hero*. He's been a college professor with good, solid books published – the guy has a brain. He's been in politics; he knows his way around. And all of that said, he should have been long gone by Super Tuesday. He didn't have the backing, he was up against some heavyweights, men who knew where the bodies were buried.'

'Cord is President,' observed Coogan. 'So how did he make it, Mr Riva?'

'The history of American politics is filled with early stars reduced to nothing by the meat-grinder of the primary system. It didn't happen to Cord. Potholes miraculously filled themselves in in front of his feet, man-traps dug for him by his rivals succeeded only in ensnaring their builders. From early, early on Cord had some remarkable talent working for him. What about that extraordinary piece of intelligence that blew Jenkins out of the water and gave Cord the nomination? Jenkins had that buried deeper than a coal mine. And what about the hostages in the Lebanon? Who told Cord it would be worth while going at all? And above all, how did Cord get them released?'

'Who did all this for him?'

'At the back of it all is Harrison Taylor, then Campaign manager, and now chief of staff. Taylor was a crack ad-man in California. What the hell was he doing attaching himself to an outfit like Cord's? But he was there right from the start. It was Taylor who had some of the star talent wheeled in so early on. There were some awful rumours floating about early, about what he was doing … It amounted to blackmail, and extortion, what he did, but then as Cord's rise seemed unstoppable, everyone forgot about it. But to take an example, *one* of the reasons Cord won New Hampshire was because he could spend money like water on the really smart advertising campaign they ran. That money came from a series of concerts put on by the rock promoter J.J. Haan. I don't know if you know it, General, but the electoral reforms have had an unintended side-effect. The true value of a contributor is not counted, in that if you get a big rock star filling an arena with 50,000 people, each of whom have paid $25 for their ticket, it is not counted as one contribution of $1,250,000, but as 50,000 contributions of $25. J.J. Haan's rock concerts kept Cord alive through New Hampshire, Florida and Pennsylvania. Now *why* did Haan do it?'

'Okay,' said Coogan. 'So it was an exceptionally dirty campaign, behind the scenes. I doubt if that reality would surprise most people with even a nodding acquaintance-ship of the world of politics.'

'Sure,' said Riva. 'Dirty tricks and politics have been bedfellows since Cain slew Abel. But there's more to it. It's what happening now Cord's president. The run-down of our defences is too much, too fast. I'm a patriot, sir, my father found refuge in America, for me it *is* home of the brave, land of the free. I think what the President is doing is so wrong as to be lethal. The Russians are going to get the better of us.'

'Cord is an elected president, he has a mandate from the people,' Coogan said softly. 'Who are we to say he is wrong?'

'But that's it, General. That's where all the funny stuff that went on during the election comes in. It was just *too much*. Too much power, too much knowledge. Harrison Taylor *always* had a better hand to play, he could always pull out a trump when he needed it. Cord didn't know what was going on, or if he suspected he ignored it. Why should he have? He was winning. But Taylor still has great power over him, even now he's president. *So who is Taylor working for?* Who had enough power to get the hostages released? Just in time for the election? So that Cord won?'

An appalling notion had been forming in Coogan's brain as the young White House staffer was relating his story. It had long been Soviet policy to acquire control over certain men and women in the West. Always in positions of power, whether journalists, politicians, trades union officials, television executives, businessmen, these people were known as Agents of Influence, and were normally recruited and controlled by KGB officers of the First Chief Directorate from the Soviet embassy within that country, whether France or Britain, Japan or the USA itself. Agents of Influence could vary in both motivation and awareness of what was happening, from those who were conscious, controlled agents who knew precisely what they were doing and did as they were bid, through those who understood that they were collaborating with the Soviets and getting paid for their services, to those who would not have wittingly done anything to harm their country, but who were used subtly, without their knowledge. In influence operations, whether someone was witting or unwitting did not matter that much. To the KGB and the men who controlled them, all that mattered were the results.

What was causing Coogan's pulse rate to rise, for adrenalin to heighten his awareness, was the concept that the USSR might have been able to acquire the President of the USA, James Cord, as an Agent of Influence. He would be unwitting, but with the crypto-Soviet, Harrison Taylor always at his elbow. *Look at what he had already done to the country's defences*. Dear Jesus and Mary in Heaven, did it not fit?

'Why have you come to me?' he asked quietly.

'You're a patriot too, General. And Harrison Taylor wants you fired. I thought to myself, with General Coogan gone, where will we find someone to stand up against all this?'

'Will you help me find out what's happening?'

Gulio Riva's eyes shone in the light of the neon outside the store.

'That's why I called you, sir.'

AMELIA ISLAND, FLORIDA

Hank Sultani had been born Hosain, and a long way from either Amelia Island, just on the Florida-Georgia border, with its smart resort town of Fernandina Beach, where he lived, or the pretty Georgia port of Savannah, where he had his business. He and his father, Hosain Sr., had been successful entrepreneurs in the petro-booming Iran of the Shah. Seeking to expand their business they had formed an offshoot in the Iranian middle-class' favourite nation, the USA, and it was to this business in the picturesque, historical coastal city of Savannah that Hank fled when the king of kings was toppled by an obscure religious zealot called Ruhollah Khomeini. He had become a local success-story. Sultan Electronics occupied the entire block on the industrial park that had contained their original small office.

Hank was unmarried, though enough pretty girls from Atlanta and the university of Athens spent the weekends at his luxury home for any doubts as to his proclivities to be allayed, an important factor among the locals for whom the country boy's motto of 'ain't no queahs roun' heah' held good. He commuted to work in the company's Hughes 500 turbine helicopter. Hank held both fixed and rotor-wing licences, and flew his company's Cessna Citation executive jet out of the airstrip they owned a few miles out in the Georgia boondocks west of I-17 and the great submarine base of Kings Bay just north of Fernandina Beach.

He liked to mix business with pleasure and would seal a deal on the golf course, or at the country club. He was popular, and most people had even forgotten that he had originally come from Iran, so successful had he been in adopting the identity and mores of his new environment. In fact, they were proud of him, and when, hailing Georgia as the new home of the sunrise industries he would say 'Ah don't see why all them kooks and nuts over in California should have a mo-nopoly on high-tech.' His fellow businessmen at the nineteenth hole would say, 'Bah God, ole Hank's all right', to each other and call for another Canadian Club and ice for the boy.

Hank was in his mid-forties and kept fit with swimming and tennis, which was an important factor in his success, for he kept a punishing schedule, spending more than two weeks in most months flying his Citation coast to coast arranging business for his firm. There were few cities in any way involved with the high technology of the 'Second Industrial Revolution' that he had not visited and acquired useful connections. He was fanatical about acquiring the very latest equipment for his firm, all of it ultra-sophisticated. He appeared to some to be like a little boy collecting toys, for while Sultan Electronics had ample need for such things as semi-conductor manufacturing equipment, and high-pressure oxidation systems for use in the conversion of silicon into wafer or chip in the manufacture of integrated circuits, the list of other things that had made their way through the Savannah plant was long, and his workers would occasionally reminisce about the time when the water-cooled, ultra-smooth laser mirrors were ordered, together with their pulsed power sources, and laser range-finders. Someone might cap that with the time that about three million dollars' worth of the very latest microwave receiving and antenna systems, designed to intercept communications, came in. Or the intertial guidance components, with their miniature and laser gyros, instrumentation systems, precision cine-theodolites and low-light-level television systems.

But, by God, you had to admit that ole Hank was a salesman beyond compare as well as an entrepreneur and businessman, for none of the equipment stayed long, and it was all moved on at a profit. Sultan Electronics' healthy cash flow provided for a remarkable turnover in equipment, for Hank would have nothing but the best, and if something new, something a fraction closer to the cutting-edge of technology was produced then out would go the old complete systems, the hardware and software, and manufacturing machinery, and in the new. And yet, Hank still saw to it that his firm lost little, for he found buyers for the old in Europe, in Germany and Britain, and had them shipped out.

'Back in the old days,' he would say, confidently, 'the Brits used to ship us their old lathes and spinning jennies, when they was slap wore out, well, now we're repaying the favour!' They'd all laugh merrily at the prospect of the limeys getting reamed by the good ol' boys in the South, and few would remember that by any standard the equipment was still ultra-modern, and hardly used.

Savannah's air- and seaport facilities were useful in expediting the export of the equipment, as was Hank Sultani's reputation in the area. In running his business he delegated anything unimportant, and nothing at all that was vital. This included both the export of technology and his latest venture, which involved the setting up of shadow plants in South Korea. 'Jes' takin' advantage of the wages they pay those little brown folk over there,' he'd say. He had recently acquired from an inventor of genius but businessman of mediocrity an entire factory specialising in the production of laser mirrors. The erstwhile producer had come up with a process of polishing the mirrors that was some years ahead of anything currently in production. Because a high-power laser was big and cumbersome, the beam that it produced had to be reflected off a mirror that could be aimed easily and precisely. If the mirror was not perfectly smooth, the beam and the energy it contained would be scattered, and its effectiveness impaired. Lasers were used to perform precision surgery, for controlling industrial robots and in light shows for rock-and-roll performers. They were also used by the military to designate targets for bombs and missiles with cross-hair accuracy, and in research of the kind involved in the Strategic Defense Initiative, with the intent of being able to destroy missiles such as ICBMs in flight. Hank Sultani had had the equipment in his laser-mirror factory duplicated, and was in the process of having it shipped out to his shadow factory in South Korea.

Assisting Sultani in this, as with the export of all the other technology was Victor Anton. Like Hank, Victor spoke three languages fluently, and while Hank had acquired his business expertise on the job, Victor had an MBA. The two men always met at night, at the Amelia Island home of the expatriate Iranian. The few neighbours that could see the approach to his home were familiar with the habits of the hard-working businessman, and when cars came and went during the evening they excited no comment.

The two men talked in detail for some three hours, continuing their discussion while they enjoyed a good meal of cold cuts, baked potatoes and salad, washed down with the sweet iced tea so favoured by the Georgians and Floridians and which Sultani had adopted along with the rest of his persona since arriving in the Deep South. When the talking was done they celebrated with a hefty shot of Jack Daniel's No.9 whiskey each, for the acquisition of the laser-mirror technology represented a most amazing *coup*, one that could not possibly have been carried off by anyone other than a man like Sultani, who had his ear so closely attuned to the high technology world burgeoning within the USA.

Like any businessman having had a drink at the end of the day and preparing to drive his automobile Victor Anton brushed his teeth and took a shot of Gold Spot before getting into his Chevrolet hire car and driving over the bridge and taking the road through Yulee to Jacksonville International Airport. He arrived in time for the Eastern flight to New York, a seemingly-typical young, ambitious executive putting in the miles and hours needed to succeed within any US corporation. When he arrived he took a cab to his Queen's apartment, getting to bed after midnight.

Despite his late night he was up early, checking in at his place of work overlooking the East River. There were many of his countrymen there, along with representatives from most of the other countries in the world. Viktor Antonov worked for the United Nations Secretariat. Some 330 Soviet personnel were employed there, of whom about forty per cent were KGB or GRU officers. Viktor, who anglicised his name when away from the UN, was a Major in Directorate T, which was the Scientific and Technical Directorate of the KGB. Of all the arms of the KGB, Directorate T was the most productive. Its job was to acquire, by any means at all, the advanced technology that the Soviet Union was unable to produce by dint of its own efforts. Its success was such that through looting, theft, bribery, deception and blackmail within the open societies of the West, and especially the USA and Japan, the value of the data acquired was far greater than the entire cost of operating the whole of the KGB.

Having checked in, Antonov left to deliver his report and receive instructions from the Soviet residency on East 67th Street. There were many advantages to working for the UN. Soviet diplomats were restricted to travel within a twenty-five mile radius of New York, a stipulation that did not apply to those working for the UN. Antonov spent little time at his official post, which mattered little; the organisation was as thoroughly penetrated by the Soviets as blue cheese with mould, and work rules so lax that it was easy for Antonov to spend his days diligently attending to his real tasks.

The laser mirrors and the machinery and polishing equipment to make them would soon be travelling on their way out of Savannah and the USA. They would not arrive at Hank Sultani's Korean shadow factory, nor did he intend that they should. Like much of the rest of the advanced technology he had looted from the USA in his stupendously successful career they were destined for the USSR. His Western microchips guided Soviet air-to-air missiles, mainframe computers acquired by him co-ordinated troop movements in Eastern Germany. At the flight range in Vladimirovka Red Air Force pilots in the Soviet's best heavyweight fighter, the Su-27 practised shooting down cruise missiles using radar technology Sultani had stolen from the USA. At Zeleenograd, a city twenty-five miles north of Moscow that 'did not exist' components for nuclear missiles were manufactured on machines bearing the label 'made in the USA'.

The laser mirrors, however, like the bulk of Sultani's acquired state-of-the-art technology was destined for one place only, the great Soviet Strategic Defense Initiative research establishment outside Smolensk.

NASHVILLE, TENNESSEE

J.J. Haan had been in the music business all his adult life. He made it as a performer, he was lead guitarist and then lead singer with The Purple Alternative, just when the Beatles had made it A.O.K. to be druggie and psychedelic, and sang songs about having a hole in your head where the rain came in, and my God, J.J. Haan knew plenty like that. The Purple Alternative had quite a cult following for a while, purple was such a with-it word then, and alternative, why, of *course*, that was what it was *all* about, man.

There were five of them, Droog, who knew Lou Reed and would have made a great punk fifteen years later, sang and could sing under the influence of whatever mind-altering substance he had got a hold of that day, which was every day. The fans were all ripped to the wide themselves, so it was a meeting of like minds, when the P.A. did a gig for their faithful followers. If you had no money except the price of your ticket you could go in and get high on the marijuana fumes from everyone else. There was 'Cool Hand' Collins, who was as black as the ace of spades and played the sax with fingers of genius, fingers that could unhook a girl's bra or produce pure liquid gold from his instrument with equal ease. There was Ratfish Jones, the drummer, who beat those skins to death, because you didn't belong in music unless you had an ego that could fill Sheay Stadium, and quarter-hour guitar and drum solos were mandatory. The fans loved it; it seemed like five seconds or five hours, depending on what they had circulating in their blood, and equally pleasing. There was their lady, Cindy Speedbird, who played pretty bad bass guitar but had tits and ass that didn't stop, and a face like a fallen angel.

The P.A. were a fast-lane outfit, nothing was more certain than that they would burn out, but in the peculiar ethos of the times, when the gleam of rotting pork was mistaken for style, all concerned viewed the prospect without misgiving. They lived for the day, if not the moment.

You took acid too much it altered your mind, and stopped doing the good things anyway, J.J. Haan found that out before his own went, but early on when they were experimenting it was different. They were in the hotel one night after the show, they were tripping, and they had Droog's gun, a Ruger .44 Magnum the colour of 'Cool Hand' Collins' skin and the size of his dick, and they began playing Russian Roulette. They put one huge shell in the revolving chamber, spun it, and gave it to the person on the left, who put it up against your chest, right where your heart was pounding, and slowly ... slowly ... squeezed the trigger. It could seem like a month waiting ... in the flickering candlelight and smoke from the joss sticks.

Because nothing happened, they put in another great shell, it seemed perfectly logical at the time, and then another ... Cindy Speedbird held it tight against J.J. Haan's chest, her eyes were frantic with excitement, the black serrated hook of the hammer rose, J.J. was peculiar, he was uninterested in the myriad groupies, sex played little part in his life, unlike 'Cool Hand' and Ratfish, who were racing each other to 1000, and spreading various types of sexually transmitted diseases among the nation as they did so, but as the hammer rose and Cindy Speedbird's sexual panting filled his ears he realised that he was as hard as the barrel of the gun at his chest.

When the pin smacked down to find only emptiness in the chamber he remained aroused. When Droog took the gun, he murmured 'Another.' And Droog agreed, slipping another shell into the chamber.

'Another.'

All his life, J.J. Haan remembered the click of the shell sliding into its receptacle, the scent of the gun oil.

'Another.'

They felt they were receiving communion.

As the shell ignited, pushing the enormous piece of soft lead down the rifling of the barrel, J.J. Haan exploded. His orgasm seemed to him to last forever, as it died away he was just faintly surprised to see Droog somersaulting backwards across the room, blood spraying in vast gouts from the hole blasted through his chest.

He had the sense to take the gun from his own hand and put the warm, lifeless fingers around it before allowing it to drop.

That a stoned rock singer should blow himself away

playing with a gun came as no surprise to anyone, certainly not the hard-faced Southern Sheriff who investigated the incident and quite openly asked the rest of the band to follow suit, if they would care to. They left town, and never went back.

J.J. Haan found the flattened bullet, and took it away with him. He had it cast into an ornament, with gold, to hang around his chest. You would never know what it was. He knew.

J.J. Haan quit performing while he was ahead. He took no more drugs, left the life of three hundred days on the road, because he knew there was far more money to be made in organisation. He became rich, a millionaire.

The other members of the band did not fare so well. 'Cool Hand' Collins died in bed, shot to death by the enraged husband of its owner. Ratfish Jones and Cindy Speedbird were married, but descended into a pit of drug-addiction. They emerged years later, thin, and lined, with Cindy Speedbird's fabulous looks entirely consumed by the quantities of toxic substances she had taken. They were saved by religion, converted to Islam, J.J. Haan heard, and spent their days in an endless round of prayer and ritual.

J.J. Haan continued to get rich.

A man came to see him one day, a fast-track advertising executive from the coast. He was faintly tanned, although maybe that was his skin colour, for it was fashionable to be pale, such was the fear of skin cancer. He was fit, with no trace of the running nose of cocaine; he was formidable. He smiled.

'The election's due,' he said. 'The candidates will be up and running soon.'

He said he was campaign manager for his candidate, and named him, a no-hope Congressman nobody had ever heard of from a state most had forgotten.

'We'd like you to help,' he said.

J.J. Haan smiled in amusement at the man's presumption.

'How?'

'We'd like you to put on a series of rock concerts with your biggest stars, for our campaign.'

Haan's smile grew broader.

'I'll bet you would,' he chuckled. 'And what will you do for me in return?'

Harrison Taylor, campaign manager for Congressman James Cord smiled back.

'I like your jewellery,' he said, looking at the ornament around Haan's neck. Haan's pleasure suddenly chilled.

'What will we do for you? We'll see to it we don't have you prosecuted for murder.'

ALBUQUERQUE, NEW MEXICO

The Senator had agreed to meet Harrison Taylor privately. It would have been difficult for him not to, since Taylor represented one of the front-runners in the race, albeit of the other party. The Senator had survived through a long political career by keeping his senses alert to changes in the wind, new smells, the noise of predators moving quietly into position. People were beginning to hear a lot about Congressman James Cord, but it was what Harrison Taylor wanted them to hear. About the campaign manager himself people knew little, but uneasy rumours were beginning to break through the oily surface, for those really in the know. The Senator decided to meet with him, when asked to.

The former advertising executive came to the point quickly, as was his wont.

'The debate's coming up, Senator,' he said. 'It is very important that Congressman Cord be seen to decisively defeat Governor Davis.'

'Vital,' Senator Mason said succinctly. 'Whoever wins the debate will go on to the convention, where he will be defeated by Governor Jenkins, who has it all wrapped up anyway. If you've come here for advice I'd say, ya'll start looking for new jobs as soon as you can.'

'Well, you let us worry about defeating Governor Jenkins,' Taylor said easily. 'The important thing is to get to the convention to do it, which is why the debate is so vital. We are perfectly confident as to our candidate's ability to perform well in the debate. However, as you yourself know well, as a political veteran of some standing, to *win* the debate you have to win the interpretation, the post-debate debate. Now what we are looking for here is for a heavyweight political figure, whose endorsement we have secured already, but not made public, to call by telephone on the set a few minutes after the debate has ended, while the press is still swarming about the candidates looking for reactions. Having been notified of the call by an aide, Congressman Cord will grab the telephone nearest the press corps and accept the congratulations with the modesty that befits a graceful winner. The next morning this endorsement will be followed up by a press conference, at which Mr Big will formally declare for our candidate. When the press asks why, he will simply say, "Did you see the debate last night? After that exchange I could not stay silent." '

'Sound political strategy,' agreed Mason. 'Provided you can get a political figure of sufficient *gravitas*.'

'Or bottom, as the Brits say. Oh, yes, we can. We thought that it would carry even greater impact, and be of use further into the campaign if this man, this Mr Big is of the opposing party.'

'Damn right,' said Mason. 'On the lines of "Democrats for Nixon" in 1972. That worked like a dream.'

'It would continue to work once our man has the Democratic nomination, and goes into the final campaign. To have a senior Republican organising support for our candidate, making the heaviest attacks on the Republican candidate, would simultaneously weaken him and give Congressman Cord even more credibility on the lines of your-own-man-says-so, that if people in his own camp can't support the Republican candidate then there must be a deep flaw in his character or his positions.'

'Mr Taylor,' Mason said heavily. 'I am in full agreement with your political theorising. However, you are overlooking two factors. Firstly that you will be unable to get any senior Republican to commit political suicide in such a manner, and that even if you did, all of this is academic, since there is no doubt that this is the year of a Republican victory. The Democrats have as much chance this time as our Barry Goldwater did back then against Johnson.'

'Well, you leave the battle for the presidency itself to us,' Taylor said easily again. 'It's the nomination that concerns us at the moment. We would like to formally extend our invitation to you to be that senior Republican figure, our Mr Big who will endorse Congressman Cord after the debate. And you would not necessarily be committing political suicide. We would be suitably grateful, and offer you a position within the administration after we win.'

Senator Mason choked over the cigar he was lighting.

'Mr Taylor, you and your candidate have as much chance of getting to the White House as a pair of high-school students organising a raffle. I have been Senator for this state for fifteen years now. I represent the interests of its people as faithfully now as I did when I was first elected, and I would not betray those interests in the manner that you have shamefully suggested.'

'Oh, right.' Taylor got up out of his chair. 'We *know* who you represent, Senator.'

He headed for the door, and Mason watched him in amazement.

'Is that it?' he asked. Taylor turned with his hand on the knob.

'Sure,' he seemed surprised that Mason should have to ask. 'I've told you what we want you to do. I'm sure I don't have to go through it in detail for a man of your background and experience.'

He paused in the doorway and looked back at the silver-haired politico behind the desk. Mason was ideal for the job, he reflected.

'Senator.'

'Yes?'

'Watch the news,' he said.

LAS VEGAS, NEW MEXICO

Once a year the Fanucci Family met to review *in toto* the activities of their business. Not everyone present was related, for the Fanuccis were Mafiosi, but the business, which had a cash-flow which if revealed would have put it into *Fortune*'s Top One Hundred, took its name from the patriarch, Don Gianni, and his three sons. When they held their audit each year, it was at the family mansion, set in an artificially-watered oasis some fifteen miles into the desert from the garish gambling city which contained most of the family's assets.

On hand at the meeting were the four Fanuccis, the *capos* of their three *regimes*, the *consigliori*, the managers of their five hotels and their associated casinos. Also available were the second-rank of their officers and management. The grounds of the mansion were guarded by armed rank-and-file, or *soldati*. Good food and drink was available, served by pretty waitresses from the casinos, for such was their success as a Family, that it was always an occasion to celebrate, even when as on occasion happened, someone had been found cheating in some way on the Family, and would be brought in front of the assembled mobsters to confess their guilt before being taken out into the desert to be executed in some imaginative fashion, for Don Gianni had a belief in the punishment fitting the crime that would have won the admiration of Pooh-Bah.

Living burial except for the hand, glued to which would be five aces, was standard for employees caught diverting profits rightfully belonging to the Family into their own pockets, although once the word got round, this happened but rarely, thus increasing the pleasure with which the accounts were greeted during the once-yearly audit. Drugs contributed mightily to the booming Fanucci economy. Here, offenders merely got a month's free supply of high grade crack administered to them, at the end of which they were turned loose, hopeless, ruined and gibbering.

The Fanuccis could pay for protection, all the way to the top.

When the police came at the end of the Fanuccis' special day, they were mystified as to how entry had been effected, for the mansion was ringed with Cyclone fencing, and guarded both by electronic means and by men with guns. The electronics they found working; the men they found dead, with their guns in their hands. When the Las Vegas Forensic team began its long task it found, upon opening the corpses that the outer ring, the guards had been shot with professional accuracy by a person or more likely persons unknown using Gudunov sniping rifles. Furthermore, that they had been killed by these persons when they, the killers, were *inside* the mansion.

When they started looking efficiently enough to pull things apart they found that the killers had entered the grounds through a *tunnel*, a professionally-dug affair that led from a culvert a quarter of a mile away, smooth-floored, timbered and roofed, and built as much as two years before the mass-killings took place. And mass they had been. The intruders slipped quietly into the building, one team taking over the top floor, where they silently knifed to death the youngest Fanucci, who was enjoying the company of one of the waitresses before going downstairs. Once they were in position with their rifles, a second team entered the kitchens, where they butchered all present as the third team threw fragmentation grenades into the reception rooms. Once the small bombs had exploded, and the soldiers guarding the grounds outside were jerking and tumbling like tin ducks in a fairground shoot, they went in and executed all the wounded with a bullet through the forehead.

With their task done, the killers assembled, and carrying their weapons jog-trotted back into their tunnel. They were seen by the sole survivor of the massacre, a young waitress, poor white trash from Alabama, who had come to Vegas to make her fortune and made a living waiting and part-time hooking. She saw the tanned, fit young men, all from a mould, and believed she had seen a rival gang of mobsters.

It was the opinion of the police too, the little they cared, so overjoyed were they to have such a sizeable proportion of the state's senior criminals removed at a stroke.

ALBUQUERQUE, NEW MEXICO

Senator Mason was still seated, transfixed with horror in front of his television when the telephone rang.

'Good evening, Senator,' Harrison Taylor said quietly. 'The interests you represent have undergone a change.'

Mason could not speak, and Taylor continued.

'What they knew, we know,' he said.

Everyone agreed that the debate was a *tour-de-force*. Cord was excellent, as was to be expected, and his campaign aides had little need to adopt that finely calculated sense of restrained celebration – the kind that indicated they realised it was bad form to uncork the champagne bottles on the set of the television station. Their pleasure was real, and noted by the press. What hopes Governor Davis' team had of salvaging victory with hysterical demands to run it again were obliterated by the mega-ton impact of Senator Mason's telephone call.

Everyone agreed that that was what sent Cord inevitably through to the convention, to fight it out with Governor Jenkins for the nomination.

On the television, Mason saw Cord hang up the 'phone, and he put his own back into its cradle. On stiff legs, he staggered the short distance to the discreet toilet off his office. His legs buckled and he fell forward, vomiting until there was nothing but strings of mucus in his mouth. The devil of organised crime he had known, his new masters he did not.

MARYLAND

Coogan switched off the reading light that pointed down at the slim file on his lap and they sat in the dark of the country road on the black leather of the Cadillac's rear seat.

'How'd you get this stuff?' he said.

'Legwork,' said Gulio Riva. 'What I heard in the campaign. Going and talking to people. I did a black-bag job to get those two documents photographed.'

'You're an enterprising young man,' Coogan said dryly. 'I don't suppose you ever heard of Gordon Liddy? A little before your time.'

'There's not enough to make a cast-iron case, not by a long way. But there's two things, straws in the wind if you like. Firstly, Harrison Taylor got a lock on J.J. Haan through the two surviving members of his original band, the Purple Alternative, the drummer, Jones, and the girl guitarist, Speedbird. The *interesting* thing about that is that they went through years of drug-addiction, which they eventually conquered. However, their experiences left them somewhat altered in mind, and they joined some far-left, animal-rights, vegetarian, socialist, Trotskyite outfit. Now that would be where the Soviets would have picked up the information, right?'

'Sure,' said Coogan. 'The KGB is always fishing for information with which to blackmail interesting or important people in the free world. They have an entire department in the First Directorate turned over to it.'

'The second thing was the evidence from the only survivor of the Fanucci massacre, the young waitress from Alabama. The whole way the operation was run points to military training, and crack troops at that. A bunch of second-generation Italian mobsters *could not* organise such a precision operation, whatever the Las Vegas PD thought. But the girl, who had been sent out to a storeroom to get some supplies, hid as she heard the explosions and gunfire. She caught a glimpse of the troops as they filed back into their tunnel, making good their escape. They had transport waiting in the culvert, and no trace of them has ever been found. It was surmised that they probably had an aircraft come in to land on one of the desert roads, and were spirited away.

'But the troops. The girl said they were all of a type. They wore fatigues, they were young, fit and disciplined. But they were the same to look at. The same race, facially similar. The girl didn't have a very high I.Q., she made most of her money with her body, and they had trouble getting her to make a lot of sense. But there, see in the transcript –'

Coogan illuminated the page with his pilot's pencil light, designed to hang around the neck and light up a chart or approach plate without ruining night vision.

'There. She says "They was tough-looking guys. White guys. They looked, you know, not like us. Like they was Swedish or sump'n. Yeah, Nordic, whatever that is." '

'Slavic,' said Coogan. 'Spetsnaz troops. The crack forces of the Soviet Union are entirely manned by Russians. They leave the support roles and cannon-fodder to be filled by the Asian republics. Where is this girl now?'

'That's the other interesting thing. She was found dead

a week later. A drug overdose. But one of her acquaintances, another part-time hooker said she saw her going off with a young guy.'

'Swedish?'

'You got it. The acquaintance said she noted it because she wondered why the young guy would need to pay for sex. She said he was good-looking, fit, strong. She said he could have got as much free action as he wanted just hanging around a beach or at the country club. Men who pay hookers only get it free with blow-up rubber dolls.'

'Tidying up the ends,' said Coogan. 'We need to know more about Cord's campaign in the presidential contest itself. The Senator from New Mexico was right, the Republicans should have had it sewn up. We need to know more about the hostages in the Lebanon. How *did* Cord get them released?'

'I'm working on it,' Riva assured him. 'What gets me is the amount of effort, of commitment put into this.'

'To get the president of the USA as an Agent of Influence, even an unwitting one, the Soviets would spend the entire GNP of the empire, for a year.'

Coogan stared out into the blackness of the forest.

'The ultimate aim of the Soviet state has remained the same since November 7 1917. World domination under Soviet Communist rule. There are some people who have forgotten that,' he said quietly.

'I have not.'

NAVAL SUBMARINE BASE
KINGS BAY, GEORGIA

The symbol chosen to represent the Kings Bay base was a circle enclosing a Neptune's Trident, the silhouette of a nuclear submarine and a ballistic missile. Earlier eras might have had prancing unicorns supporting an emblazoned shield. Kings Bay housed, supported and trained all the elements of the USA's most powerful naval deterrent, the Trident II (D5) fleet ballistic missile equipped *Ohio* class SSBN nuclear submarines.

The vast base was home to submarine squadron sixteen, whose nine submarines made up one third of the navy's deterrent; it was the newest, most expensive and with the Pacific port of Bangor, Washington, the most important naval submarine base in the USA. On Kings Bay itself, the channel that led through Cumberland Sound out to the Atlantic, on the waterfront were all the facilities for berthing and maintaining the submarines from the tender that carried everything from paperclips for the captain to the missiles themselves, the auxiliary repair drydock, the industrial facilities needed during refit following the 65-day cruises of the craft, to the tenant that all the submariners were glad existed, but hoped would never be needed – the Loss/Disaster mission with its *Pigeon* class submarine rescue ship, DSRV (Deep Sea Rescue Vehicle) that was built to dock with the hatch of a disabled submarine and take off the crew, and Meerestchnik four-man midget search submarine. Both the DSRV and Meerestechnik were air-portable to provide a quick-reaction world-wide rescue service should an emergency arise.

The waterfront, together with the industrial and magnetic silencing area and Defensive Ordnance Support facilities made up the Trident refit facility, which was one of the two major elements of the Kings bay complex. The other was the Trident Training Facility. Located at the opposite end of the base to the waterfront, close by the Benjamin Franklin Gate on state route 40, it was an enormous building occupied by some 450 permanent staff, including instructors, and up to 1200 students at any one time. The students were prospective and off-patrol *Ohio* class submariners, and the building in which they trained was in effect a complete Trident II *Ohio* class submarine, complete with missile system, broken up and formed into a classroom and laboratory training complex. The building had cost the taxpayer some $50,000,000 to build, and the components in it a cool billion. The size of several large shopping malls, it was laconically known on the base as the 'little red schoolhouse'. It was the biggest and most complex military training facility in the free world.

The officers and enlisted men who studied there were all intensively drilled in their specialised tasks. Like aviators, they benefited from the extensive use of computer-generated simulators which enabled them to tackle the many arduous and potentially hazardous situations that might arise on a cruise – especially one that might be a wartime one – without having to pay the price for getting it wrong the first time. The training of the men was especially important, as unlike some navies, and perhaps incongruously for a military arm of such a technologically-oriented nation, the US Navy largely eschewed automation, they preferred two-man operation, considering humans more reliable than machines.

The crews were trained in the operation of strategic and defensive weapons, in navigation, operations and engineering, according to speciality. Part of the operations course featured a series of lectures on offensive and defensive operations, and for the young officers who might one day expect to command SSN and SSBN – the nuclear hunter-killer and ballistic missile submarines – these were very popular, for the same reason that medical students always packed out the classes on pathology, where they were shown what lethal diseases had done to patients, because it was the real thing, there was the enemy that you had come to fight.

Another reason that the classes were popular was the choice of lecturer. Commander Jack Kowalski knew of what he spoke. Kowalski had been deep inside Soviet territorial waters, had conducted espionage, placed and retrieved listening and recording devices on Soviet underwater communications cables, had (so it was rumoured) tangled with Soviet ASW, both aerial, surface and hunter-killer while engaged in this covert activity, and had lived to tell the tale. In a peace-time world, Kowalski was as close as you got to a war-time veteran, and his students revered him. Kowalski was the son of a White Russian refugee who had escaped Trotsky's Red Army with his parents in 1919, and had arrived finally in New York after long and hard travels. His students felt that his blood gave him that extra insight into the Russian psyche; he had outwitted his Soviet attackers in the deep dark water because he understood them, and submarine warfare was most definitely associated with an understanding of psychology.

Kowalski held down two jobs at the base, he commanded the Loss/Disaster mission as well as lecturing on his chosen subject. American nuclear submarines were very reliable, and while the mission maintained its own level of training and readiness, Kowalski had time left over which he employed to pass on his knowledge.

When he entered the classroom on the fourth level his students were waiting, young men in Lieutenant's uniform. As he set himself up at the front the door opened and an older man with the four rings of a Captain on his sleeve slipped in to sit at the back.

'Hi, Mark,' Kowalski murmured, and Mark Ross, commanding officer of the *Maine* smiled and gave a little wave.

'Good morning, gentlemen,' said Kowalski, a tall, straight figure at the head of the class, grey at the temples, the creases around his eyes indicating his Slavic ancestry. His voice, however, was New York. Like many immigrants, his grandparents had travelled thousands of arduous miles to sit down with relief a few miles from the docks and set up home once they had entered the promised land.

'Today I am going to lecture on Stealth. This is very much the buzzword of the moment, mainly due to the activities of our aerial cousins, who are so delighted with their new-found ability to fly about without anyone knowing where they are that they have adopted it for their own. Indeed, listening to the trumpetings of some aviators one might be forgiven for believing that they had invented the concept.'

Kowalski looked wryly over his class.

'They seem to have forgotten that stealth has been the essence of naval strategy for many centuries. It is still very difficult to find even a large surface vessel on the vastness of the ocean. It is incomparably more difficult to find a submarine, which is the stealthiest of modern weapons systems, and whose tactics tend to be dominated by the need to maintain stealth. It is not always so, of course, as we shall see, and stealth can, and sometimes has to be abandoned for limited periods.

'Paradoxically, the submarine commander must shed his cloak of invisibility in order to perform most of his missions. In peacetime stealth and invisibility appear all-important, and anti-submarine – ASW – forces count upon a submarine being contained if it is detected. It may not be so in any future war, just as the manner in which pre-war stealthy training was routinely abandoned in World War Two in order to successfully attack targets shocked most of the pre-war experts. This may be a pointer to the future.

'Of course, the experiences of the Second World War are not necessarily the best guide with which to approach tactics for a future war, if only that for both sides, the submarine used is a different animal. As you know, all modern submarines are descendants of the Walter-designed German Type XXI of 1944, which introduced two radically new features. Firstly, it could manoeuvre and attack entirely submerged, on account of its high sustained underwater speed, and secondly its snorkel enabled it to operate entirely submerged. It had a number of other attributes which have been followed up in the years since – its underwater speed was such that it was capable of outrunning surface ASW vessels, something the

Soviets seem to value if the production of their titanium-hulled *Alfa* class is anything to go by; an *Alfa* is capable of forty-two knots submerged, and has also picked up on another attribute of the Type XXI – it can dive deep, manoeuvering violently as it does so. The Type XXI could operate at least at slow speed, at 600-800 feet, which was below wartime sonar, and make full use of the thermal layer. The *Alfas* can go to 3000 feet, again beyond the reach of most Western weapons.

'The Soviets have the largest submarine programme in the world, with eight major classes underway, and appear to be pursuing this line of thought, if the large titanium-hulled *Mike* and the *Sierra* classes are anything to go by. It is worth noting that such submarines require the most advanced technology in terms of hull construction and for computers as they are very largely automated. It is generally believed that the KGB plays a considerable role in acquiring such technologies from the West.

'The Type XXI had two other qualities which enabled it to defeat the ASW of the day: because of its streamlining it presented a much smaller sonar target than the physically smaller Type VIIC *and* it was quiet. Submerged at fifteen knots it was equal to the quietest US Fleet submarine at eight knots. On its special motor it was so quiet that it merged with background noise as it could then be measured, still travelling at 5 knots, and was able to detect and get a bearing on a 16 knot destroyer at many times the range the destroyer was able to detect it.

'Largely, this is the avenue down which US naval practice has travelled. We have substituted nuclear power for the snorkel and have made our submarines very, very quiet. They are also very difficult to detect by means other than passive sonar. The reasons for the differing emphases between us and the Soviets are not hard to find, and in turn, have led to different appreciations of strategy and tactics. For example, the best Soviet submarines are very good indeed, but this is because their construction is considered of sufficient national importance to merit special industrial attention. As there are only so many skilled craftsmen to go around, this has a very bad effect on the rest of the submarine fleet, and exacerbates the awful effects of the Soviet's rigidity in their centrally-planned economy, run by Gosplan, something that *glasnost* and *perestroika* have had very little effect upon. Making a truly silent boat requires dedication and skill bordering on the fanatical, and limited-run high-quality equipment. The USA can supply these, whereas the Soviets find it extremely difficult. This in turn affects the way that tactics are planned, although the Soviet lack of stealth may not, curiously enough, prove as disastrous as is usually thought.

'For example, in theory, a US attack submarine would use its acoustic superiority to get into position to attack a Soviet craft, and then fire a Mk 48 torpedo. This is the point at which the US commander has abandoned his cloak of stealth in order to perform his mission. It is the beginning of "warning time" for the Soviet commander, since the Mk 48 is a noisy weapon and he can hear it from the moment of launch. Since he knows that the 48 is a wire-guided weapon it makes counter-attack most attractive, and his most likely option is to fire two torpedoes back down the line of bearing defined by the Mk 48, switch on his own active sonar and close in, not unlike a World War One dog-fight. Under such circumstances, the US preoccupation with stealth turns into a marked disadvantage.

'The Soviets, since they cannot compete with us to the same extent in terms of stealth because of the limitations of their economy, do appear to be more willing to abandon it on occasion. Although they remain wedded to long-range stand-off attack in order to preserve the craft – they can't turn out massive numbers of new aircraft or submarines in wartime – they have also adopted the tactics of "sprint and drift", and appear to be willing to trade stealth for aggressiveness, numbers and speed to attack and then to evade. Such tactics look like being very effective especially if the submarine commander makes use of alternative quiet-speed modes, varying operation between bursts of very high and noisy speed and lower but very quiet speed, then he may well be able to avoid attack by staying one step ahead of the opposing ASW command and control system. It requires great coolness on his part, and a sophisticated understanding of the opposing force *plus* a submarine fast enough in the quiet mode. I cannot answer for the Soviet commander, but certainly the latest Soviet attack submarines seem ideally suited for such a role.

'Before I finish this preliminary sketch of the uses of stealth in submarine operation I might mention one area not normally considered by either side, which is relatively shallow water.'

Glancing over his students, Kowalski saw Mark Ross, commander of the *Maine* smile faintly.

'Since the Second World War both the USA and the USSR have displayed little interest in shallow-water operations, probably because both sides expect to fight primarily in the deep waters of the Atlantic. However, it should be noted that inshore operations have proved remarkably successful, for example the relative freedom with which German U-boats with snorkels operated in British coastal waters right to the end of World War Two. Shallow water is attractive because sonar pulses reflect off the bottom, and because the sea bed is covered with so much debris. Shallow-water reverberation reportedly explained the apparent failure of British ASW in the Falklands, when the Royal Navy expended many lightweight homing torpedoes without effect. They heard a number of explosions, which turned out to be the torpedoes hitting the shallow sea bed. From the point of view of the submarine, given the limited quantity of modern weaponry carried aboard ASW ships or aircraft, if of greater power than in the past, the commander of a submarine under attack in shallow water would seem to have a very good chance simply by lying on the sea bed with engines stopped and blending in with the debris all around, and later, quietly, quietly creeping away.

'I have indicated that there are major differences in terms of strategy and tactics between us and the Soviets. For example, Soviet strategy is defensive-minded. This is one reason they build so many submarines is in order to deny the sea approaches to the Soviet Union to Westerners. In principle this defensiveness derives from Soviet ideology, which sees the USSR as the centre of world revolution, and thus always threatened by, and hence must deter, a West determined to destroy that revolution before it is itself brought down. Most of us in the West would describe the Soviet position as paranoid. Furthermore, it is an attitude of mind profoundly dangerous, in that it can engender violently offensive actions, as the Soviets choose to pre-empt a non-existent Western threat.

'During your careers you will take part in many peacetime wargames, although one hopes not wartime ones. You will find that the human factor is always missing. I have always thought it a great mistake. Should another major war ever occur it will probably bear as much resemblance to the one we are training to fight as did the two major wars early this century to the ones their combatants trained to fight.'

Kowalski pushed the papers of his preliminary lecture together and looked over the class.

'Furthermore,' he said, 'if it comes about it will be because men believed in theories that left out the human factor.'

As the students left the room for their next class Mark Ross, the commander of the *Maine* paused in the corridor to talk to Kowalski.

'I enjoyed the lecture,' he said.

'It's just an introduction to the course. We get technical later.'

'I saw you touched on shallow-water operations. You'll have to work up a whole lecture on that.'

121

'I got it in mind,' Kowalski said with a smile. 'The refit done?'

'All done,' confirmed Ross. 'I guess they'll try us out somewhere soon.'

Ross was commander of the 'Blue' crew of the submarine. His crew alternated with the 'Gold' crew, the names chosen from the navy's traditional colours. When the submarine returned from a cruise it was met by the new crew, bussed down from Charleston South Carolina, where the submarines were homeported, and the crews and families lived. The two crews spent four days turning over, following which the offgoing crew went back to Charleston for off-duty rest, and the new crew worked extended hours to bring the submarine to readiness for its new patrol. The *Maine* had had an extensive refit in the ARDM drydock, and was now ready to go to sea.

As the two officers talked in the corridor another man came by, a tall commander. He paused on his way.

'Hi, guys,' he said. 'You must be off soon, Mark.'

' 'Morning, Cy,' said Ross. 'At the end of the week.'

Commander Cyrus T. Sanders was in communications. Having stopped to say hullo, he seemed anxious to get moving again. He smiled, and the skin pulled tight over his face.

'Better be going,' he said. 'Have a good cruise.'

'Sure,' said Ross.

'Cy's not looking too good,' observed Kowalski.

'Wasn't there some bad divorce there a little while back?' said Ross. 'He's a good man at his job. You never know what goes on in some people's private lives. I thank God for Mary and the kids.'

'Yeah. Me too. I'm lecturing on the era of the submersible 1900–1945, the rest of this week, if you want to drop in.'

'May do, if I can. I love all that historical stuff. You know, they were brave sons of bitches, who went out in some of those things.'

' "Intelligent mines" is what Admiral Doenitz called

them.'

'You got any favourites?' Ross said inquisitively.

'Oh, surely. In the chamber of horrors, of Boats I Am Glad I Never Served In, the British steam-powered "K" class of the First World War has to be high on the list. For ideas ahead of their time, the French "Surcouf" with its twin 8-inch guns and the British "M" class with its 12-inch gun both foreshadowed current cruise missile concepts, in the 1920s and 1930s. What about the Japanese I-401s? *Submarine aircraft carriers* 3530 tons and 400 feet overall. Biggest submarines ever built until ballistic missile craft. For Submariners I Would Have Been, that has to be the first of us all, doesn't it, Sergeant Ezra Lee floating down the Hudson River in 1776 to attack the flagship of the British fleet at anchor. There was courage. The *Turtle* was wooden-hulled, hand-propelled and Ezra had to try to screw a time-fuzed charge to the *Eagle*. Even though the weapon failed, the effect of submarine warfare worked. The blockade was relaxed because the ships were compelled to shift berth, and thenceforth all warships were vulnerable at their weakest points, under the waterline.'

'You lecture really well. Do you ever miss going out and doing it?'

'Any of your boys get it wrong out there and I'll be doing it again in the DSRV,' Kowalski said with a smile. 'No, I don't miss it, Mark. I did it enough. After the last time I decided the Lord was trying to tell me something.'

'You hit a "Whiskey" didn't you?'

'Yes. There were two. I took out the second with two Mk 48s. We got away in the confusion. They thought it was us, breaking up down there.'

'Any of the other commanders drop by your lectures?'

'Some.'

'You're a talisman,' said Ross. 'You went out and came back. Maybe we're superstitious.'

They laughed, and Kowalski went about his business as

Ross headed for the waterfront. At the end of the corridor, Cyrus T. Sanders took the lift to communications.

Three expert submariners.

Two with but days to live.

DefCon IV

**Strategic Air Command
lowest level of alert. Peace**

AMELIA ISLAND, FLORIDA

Hank Sultani flew his Hughes 500 from the airport at Savannah down the coast. In the late afternoon's clear winter air the beaches and myriad curling inland waterways were spread out like a map, with the occasional white scars of fishing boats moving across the water. In the summer the haze could be almost as thick as mist and force him to use his VORs, but that day he could almost see his destination from the moment he climbed up to 3500 feet.

With the great submarine base visible to his left he let down and made his approach to the hangar along the line of the runway at his private company airstrip out in the Georgia forest, cut out of the pines. He landed on the waiting wooden pad, handling collective and cyclic smoothly, putting it down on the beckoning cross. The hangar was very large, for the number of aircraft it contained; there was ample room for as many again. Rolling back the doors the Citation was visible inside, he pressed the switch and the pad, complete with its helicopter began moving into the hangar on its rails. When all was safely stowed away he got into his Cadillac and drove home.

Sultani stood by his window watching the dusk turn into night. Acquisition of the laser technology was probably his greatest feat, but it was unimportant compared with the events he was about to initiate. The man he was waiting for knew better than to arrive before it was dark, but Sultani was certain that he would be unable to delay long. He was right. It was barely dark when the green Pontiac slowed on the road outside, and turned in, its tyres crunching on the gravel. Sultani went to the door, deliberately leaving the porch light out. The driver came quickly inside, a tall figure in the gloom, Sultani shut the door behind him and they went into the living room, where the curtains were drawn.

Commander Cyrus T. Sanders put a folder down on the table, the kind of bag in which an artist carries samples of his work.

'I have something for you,' he said.

'That's marvellous,' Sultani said softly. He stood beside his drinks cabinet and extended a hand. 'Care for something?'

Sanders shook his head impatiently. 'No. What I have for you is important.'

Sanders' eyes were inward-looking, his impatience, the movement of his hand that beat a tattoo on the bag, almost a tremor, all betrayed the increasing severity of his addiction. Sultani's face was smooth, expressionless, but inside he was exultant. He had waited a long time for Sanders to arrive at this point.

'Tell me, please,' he said, and sat opposite the naval officer.

'The KH-13 satellites being built now at TRW's plant at Redondo Beach are going to have the capacity to identify Soviet submarines at all operational depths. The KH-13 has an imaging system consisting of four essential parts: the mirror telescope, which is approximately ten times as powerful as that on the KH-11, which was fabulous anyway, an infra red scanner, separate sensor electronics package, containing photomultiplier tube, thematic mapper, multispectral scanner and so forth, and an array of charge coupled devices, arranged in a mosaic. As you know, CCDs collect radiation. The ones in the KH-13 are made by Texas Instruments, and once again are an advance on those in the KH-11. They contain 800 by 800 pixels – the miniature receptors – a total of 640,000, and yet again are only one quarter of an inch square.'

Sultani did the sums in his head. The KH-13 would have real-time capability and astonishingly good resolution. The pixels worked like buckets arranged in even rows to make a square, collecting rain in a field. The 'rain' was incident radiation (photons, electrons, neutrons, protons) and the CCD thus worked as a tiny, extremely precise light meter able to capture radiated energy transmissions across the visible and invisible bands of the spectrum so that they could be amplified and turned into pictures. Furthermore, unlike earlier reconnaissance cameras, the CCDs did not 'stop the action' but kept recording it in real time.

Sanders could see that Sultani had worked out the possibilities.

'Right,' he nodded. 'The CCDs are somewhere around 500 times as efficient as standard film cameras at collecting visible light. However, to make use of that you need a very good telescope. The KH-13 has it. The primary mirror is a bit larger than that on the Space Telescope, 102.5 inches. The telescope itself is plugged into a two-position zoom lens to give it both area-surveillance and close-look capability. For the close-look mode, the primary mirror has been made to be a "rubber" type, the surface can be computer-adjusted to compensate for atmospheric distortion. The active optics will detect curved light waves hitting the mirror and will adjust for them, flatten them out by making very subtle adjustments in the shape of the mirror itself. They're using a shearing infermometer to look at the whole wave front to find the slope errors.'

Sultani nodded. The American reconnaissance satellites, hand-crafted in small numbers, employing arcane and fabulously expensive technology, made the Soviet mass-produced, assembly-line Cosmoses seem like relics from the first industrial revolution.

'The KH-13s will be able to find Soviet submarines at any depth,' Sanders said brutally. 'Once found, the satellite will "tag" the submarine with a laser, and to all intents and purposes, the submarine will have as much freedom of action as a hound on a leash. In the event of war, the US could take out any and all it chose.'

It was all what the Soviet leaders feared. Their entire military effort reduced to the status of Polish cavalrymen floundering in the mud, transfixed by barbed wire, picked off at will by superior technology, unable to fight back, their brightly polished swords thrashing the air, just so much decoration.

'While the US Navy naturally finds this state of affairs most acceptable, they would like to make it even better. They would like their own SSNs and SSBNs to remain invulnerable to Soviet overhead surveillance systems, and in fact, would like to increase their "stealthiness" to the extent of having them be able to move undetected even in relatively shallow waters, thus making effective anti-submarine warfare practically impossible for the Soviet Navy.'

Sanders reached over and undid the buckle of his artist's bag. He pulled out a dark grey-green tile, light but rigid, about eighteen inches by twenty four.

'That's what's going to do it,' he said, putting it down on the table. 'Sonar-absorbent, sound-absorbent, radiation-absorbent. It wasn't supposed to exist until the twenty-first century.'

The two men looked at the tile.

'The pace of change of technology is *accelerating*,' Sanders said quietly. 'It won't be long before you won't recognise the world from year to year, let alone decades.'

You will in the USSR, thought Sultani. The pace of change there is glacial.

Sanders looked up at Sultani for the first time. His lips were dry, he licked them; the beat of his hand had become a tremor. His addiction was terminal, burning, consuming. The skin over his skull had become tight as though a disease was eating him away. It was, it was there inside, in his brain.

'How much is it worth?' he whispered.

'How much do you need?' Sultani asked softly.

130

'A quarter of a million.'

His habit had grown, now it required vast amounts of fuel.

'I need it *now*.'

'You shall have it,' Sultani promised. He got up and left the room. In his basement he opened his safe, and withdrew blocks of new $100 bills. He put them in a box and went back upstairs. Sanders was where he had left him. He did not look at the pile. Sultani put the box of money into the artist's bag, and did up the strap. Sanders took it, unable to control himself any longer.

'I must go,' he whispered.

'Good luck,' said Sultani.

Sanders smiled brilliantly, for the first time. It was frightening. It illuminated the full extent of his madness.

'I don't need luck.'

He turned at the door before going out into the dark.

'How can I lose?' he said exultantly.

LAS VEGAS, NEW MEXICO

The whore sat on the edge of the bed, feet and knees together, demurely. With her styled hair, puffball dress and young good looks she could have been taken for a girl waiting for her date to arrive. He had done. She was sitting quietly, carefully watching the man she knew as Mr Morgan, standing by the window of the hotel room, staring out into the neon-lit darkness, letting the coruscating lights below fill his eyes like a boulevard on a circle of Hell. He was tall, thin, his skin stretched tight over his bones, dressed for the part in immaculate white shark-skin tux. His disease had worsened since he had last been with her. She would have to take every opportunity to pick up largesse in the form of *gratis* chips from his winnings. His judgement had been consumed, leaving only raging desire behind. She remained confident that she could skim ten to fifteen thousand before it vanished. In her short working life she had received a brutal education in human nature that had left her expert in various types of manipulation. She was like the driver of a hugely powerful racing car, dependent solely on her wits, reflexes and skill to survive the run down a precipitous descent lined by rock walls on the one side and chasms on the other. She neither drank nor smoked, and never touched drugs. She aimed to retire worth a million before she was thirty. If she could survive.

The man took in some deep breaths. He was trembling slightly.

'Now,' he said.

She slipped forward off the bed and went lightly across the room. Her smooth, nylon-clad knees kissed the carpet by his feet; she flicked the zip of his trousers open expertly and leaned forward. He was ready, and gained relief in seconds. She knew his excitement had nothing to do with her attractions; it was the city, the casino, the business. She came free with the hotel suite. When you played for stakes like he did, it was a pleasure to offer the man such facilities. The hotel and its casino had once been owned by some Italian-American mobsters called Fanucci, they were dead now, their investment had been picked up by a rival outfit whose founder had come from a Sicilian village a few miles from the descendants of the Fanuccis, they had been overjoyed with their luck and had picked it up for a song. High-rollers like Mr Morgan could contribute fifty, a hundred, two hundred thousand in a night or two. Few hoteliers could charge or receive such sums for the provision of a luxury suite and a pretty flint-hearted whore with a body like a gymnast and a mind like a computer.

They went downstairs and Commander Cyrus T. Sanders, USN breathed in the febrile, charged air like the drug it was.

'Let's play,' he whispered.

The whore watched from a distance as Sanders pushed out the last pile of red chips, and the croupier spun the wheel. She had calculated on something over twenty-four hours, and had been correct. It was nearing midnight the next day. Sanders had left the casino only to relieve himself, and twice, to take amphetamine tablets to keep going. $500 were riding on the spin of the wheel out on the table, $28,000 lay tucked into the flat silk body-belt she wore under her puffball dress, $171,500 had made their way into the coffers of the casino.

She stood beside the lobby telephone and dialled the number the man had given her. She had played her part as hired to, she had assisted in the ruin of the man called Morgan, she was making the call to confirm that she had done what she had been paid to do.

'Yes,' said the man.

'He's through,' she said.

The telephone went down without comment.

Across the floor Sanders was getting up from the table, his bet scooped away by the croupier's rake. The whore knew about addiction, there was addiction to booze, to pills or cocaine, to women, but worst of all was the addiction to gambling, for which there was no cure except death. Sanders' addiction had consumed every dollar he had brought with him, leaving him with only a return airline-ticket home. He shambled across the floor of the man-made hell, limbs loose, eyes vacant.

'Come on, honey,' she said, taking him by the elbow, as one would a man suffering from shock, from the effects of an accident. 'Let's go up to the room.'

Sanders allowed himself to be led. His trained mind was dazed, unable to comprehend what had happened to him. The girl took him up in the lift, and quietly let him into the room. The curtains were drawn, and just a bedside light cast illumination. Sanders stumbled in, and she slipped aside into the bathroom as the man had ordered her to.

Sanders paused, focusing in surprise at the figure sitting in a chair by the window.

'Hullo, Cy,' Sultani said softly. 'Come and sit down.'

Sanders stared wonderingly at Sultani.

'What are you doing here?' he whispered.

Sultani patted the chair next to him. 'Sit down,' he said. 'I came to see how you were getting on.'

Sanders folded into the chair like a child's puppet.

'I lost …' he said in bewilderment. 'I lost it all …'

'Your luck was out,' Sultani said comfortingly. 'You'll win next time.'

'I have no money …'

'You'll have money, Cy.'

Sanders looked at Sultani with the beginnings of hope.

'How's your head? Can you discuss some technical things?'

Sanders nodded. His was a trained mind, he was a naval officer, he had experience of long hours putting that training to use, often under pressure, and Sultani could see him drawing in the strands, tightening his grip.

'Yes. I can talk.'

'The *USS Maine*. The *Ohio* class ballistic missile submarine that has been retrofitted with the sonar/noise/radiation-absorbent tiles. It's getting ready for its first cruise, right?'

'Yes. It's in King's Bay now, under the care of the "Blue" crew. Its cruise will be the normal seventy days, at which point it will return to King's Bay for a thirty-two day refit, following which it will return to sea under the command of its "Gold" crew.'

'Once at sea, how are communications between the submarine and those who control her affected?'

'COMSUBLANT. COMSUBLANT Operations in Nor- folk will control the *Maine*'s movements. They can communicate with their submarines via Atlantic Fleet Communications and *vice-versa*. If the sub commander has something to say he can come up to periscope depth, and poke up a laser transmitter. This locks on to the carrier wave signal of the Atlantic SSIX, the Navy's satellite there, and the commander can then send a high-density

134

transmission without revealing his location to the Soviets. It's sent in a fraction of a second, the satellite picks it up and shoots it back through UHF to Atlantic Fleet Communications.'

'What if COMSUBLANT wants to communicate with the *Maine* when she's dived?'

'He can use ELF radio. That's Extremely-Low Frequency. All nuc's trail a long wire antenna to pick up the signals. ELF has a very narrow data band width, and it makes for slow transmission, one character about every thirty seconds. The message is sent in three-character groups, each group standing for a pre-selected word or phrase. It's a cipher, and the communications officer on the submarine has a "one-time-pad" code book that he uses to turn the three-letter groups into the message sent.'

'The books are published every six months, isn't that right?'

'Right. They're distributed to every nuclear submarine.'

'Yes,' Sultani said softly. 'That is our understanding of the situation.'

In the bathroom, the whore heard the murmur of voices, and wondered what they were talking about. She felt no urge to eavesdrop, however. There were many things in life, she knew, which you were better off not knowing about.

'Cy, we want to explore the possibility of substituting a code-book of our own for the official code-book. We want to see whether it is possible to move a US nuclear submarine from where COMSUBLANT intends it to be to somewhere *we* want it to be.'

Sanders could see the possibilities instantly. If you could move a submarine by altering the message and giving it *your* orders then instead of trying to *find* the stealthy creature *it came to you*. Where you were waiting with your full ASW complement to send it to the bottom. In a nuclear-war fighting scenario it was a trump card.

'The books are due to be changed soon, aren't they?'

'Next week. Just before the *Maine* sails.'

'We want you to substitute our book for the real one.'

'*Jesus*,' Sanders exploded. 'I *can't*.'

'You can,' Sultani said softly. 'It is a trial run, that is all. Nothing will happen to the *Maine*, apart from taking a different route to her patrol station. The subterfuge may even not be discovered. If it is, there are a number of explanations, from administrative incompetence to espionage, and even if the authorities plump for espionage, there will be nothing to tie *you* to the substitution.'

It was flannel, Sanders knew, but he had seen a small shoe-box by Sultani's chair. It must have money in it.

'How much?' he whispered.

'$250,000. $50,000 now, to recover your luck, $200,000 once you have made the substitution and the *Maine* is at sea.'

Sanders closed his eyes for a few moments. At times he knew how ill he was. He had had his disease a long time, but for years it had been under control. Slowly, slowly, like the alcoholic who began with a social drink and progressed into addiction with a drink here and there, and then one in the morning, on the way to work, it had taken him over, ruined his marriage, his career, his life. He was quite unable to fight it.

'All right,' he said, opening his eyes.

'Good,' said Sultani. 'The code book will be in your desk, in your house, when you return. Here is a little something for your luck.'

He passed over the shoe-box, and it had crisp blocks of one-hundred dollar bills inside. Sanders felt the elation flow in his veins like a shot of whiskey.

'I think I'll take a shower,' he said unsteadily. 'I've been up a while.'

He wanted to wash off the bad luck, to begin anew.

He went across the room to the bathroom. As he came in, the whore slipped out. He closed the door, and she heard the hiss of the water in the tub. She padded through into the dimly-lit room on silent feet. Sultani was standing

136

by the window, very still. She could hear him murmur, saw him bend his neck slightly, his hands move. He caught the change in light from the corner of his eye, and turned to look at her. This one's dangerous, she thought.

'I didn't mean to disturb you. Have I done what you wanted?'

Sultani nodded. 'You have.'

'I didn't know you were Arabic.'

Sultani stared at her for several seconds.

'My family comes from the Middle East,' he said. 'But I live here. What made you say that?'

'You were praying,' she explained. 'I knew. I have an eye for that kind of thing, it's the job.'

'You're very observant. But it will be to your advantage to keep your observations to yourself.'

There was menace in the soft voice with its acquired Southern accent, and she nodded hastily, regretting the exposure of her skills.

'I never talk about clients,' she assured him.

'Good,' he said. He went out, and she felt better for his absence, even though he had enriched her by several thousand dollars. The door to the bathroom opened, and Sanders came out. His hair was wet and combed back, his pupils narrowed from the stimulants he had taken. He shrugged himself into his jacket and beamed his crazy, insane grin at her. It wouldn't take long to separate him from his money, she thought. She had been up a while, over a full day, but she was strong, she had stamina, it was one of the all-time good paydays.

'*Are you ready?*' he cackled.

'Honey,' she whooped. '*Let's play.*'

DAVIS-MONTHAN AFB, ARIZONA

On the third Tuesday of the month, a number of similar men filtered into Tucson on scheduled airline flights, hidden away among the other passengers. Although in age they varied from twenty five to forty five, they had characteristics in common. All were fit, with no overweight. None wore glasses. The faces of the older ones were marked by the fine mesh of wrinkles caused by exposure to the sun's radiation at high altitude. They were calm, took no advantage of the hospitality trolley on their flights, carried soft athletic bags and dressed rather badly. Military officers were notorious for their lack of style out of uniform, most of them resembling tourists from Terre Haute on day three of a European coach holiday. There were twenty of them, two for each of the B-2 bombers waiting at the base.

The advanced technology, stealthy aircraft had been at Davis-Monthan nearly six weeks, parked in an even row all by themselves, jarringly out of place among the carcasses of old fighters and cargo aircraft, so evident was their newness, and the difference in the materials from which they were made. The USSR had paid them the compliment, even in death, of sending a *Cosmos* satellite swooping overhead in low orbit, to take their photograph.

They were parked at the west end of the base, in front of a row of six large hangars, close by the threshold of runway 24. Inside the hangars, under total security, stood the ten replicas ordered by General Coogan, and prepared by his crack ground crews. The art of military replicas had come a long way. Both the army and air force had invested large sums in purchasing replica tanks, trucks and fighters for use in Europe and South Korea. The dummies looked real, and were fitted with small internal generators to produce an authentic thermal signature, and plastic overlays to make items like headlights, windows and canopies to glitter in the sunlight. The aim was in wartime to draw costly fire from an enemy, which would give his position away as well as saving the US a lot of money with $3500-worth of dummy M-1 tank going up as against $2.5 million for the real thing, or $15,000 for a carbon copy F-15, as against the $40 million original.

Such dummies were perfectly adequate for battlefield-level sensors, but were exposed for what they really were any time they were examined by a surveillance satellite. Two methods of analysis used could determine the composition of anything imaged by the satellite. Multispectral scanning and thematic mapping lenses and cameras measured the image from earth in bands of the visible, and infra-red, near through far, sectors of the electromagnetic spectrum and converted it into digital numbers, producing a picture that was made up from as many as three hundred million digits – a rich and detailed portrait that would reveal painted wood and canvas for what it was – a fake.

Coogan's dummy B-2s were very largely made from real components for this reason. They would appear real, to a *Cosmos*.

Despite the sophistication of their sensor systems, satellites were in some ways dumb, and only as clever as the people operating them. The people who controlled the low-flying reconnaissance satellites had to have the abilities and reflexes of fighter pilots in order to keep the satellite stabilised and pointing where it was supposed to point. Computers not withstanding, the number of precise and highly integrated manoeuvres and other operations that were required to operate the attitude control systems and prevent the super-sophisticated, but dumb, machine

139

from wandering off and peering at acres of blank ocean, or square miles of black space, when it was meant to be making a precision pass over the target could drive its operator nearly frantic. Furthermore, the accelerating pace of technological change operated in this military arena just as much as all others. It was possible, if you had the kind of super-computers that could draw the correct SIGINT out of the vast quantities of information produced by the 'vacuum-cleaner' approach to intelligence gathering, if you knew the correct frequencies, codes and transmission sequences, then you, rather than its makers and masters could control what a satellite did, or did not do, saw or did not see. Such advanced electronic warfare was known in the arcane circles to which it was restricted as 'spoofing', and was the most insidious – and by far the 'blackest' or most secret – of ways in which to make a satellite dysfunctional, reducing such devices as the F-15 air-launched anti-satellite missile to the level of crudity of the caveman's club.

Automobiles and a Chevy van owned by Colonel Travis collected the aviators in suitably bland and stealthy fashion, transporting them in batches from the airport to the air force base. By late afternoon all had arrived. They changed into their flight suits and settled down to wait. It was a public holiday, AMARC was deserted except for security.

The flight from Arizona across the United States to Missouri was a simple one, a mere ferry flight with a cruising altitude of 35,000 feet, off airways. The ten bombers would take off at a pre-arranged hour, and land at a pre-arranged hour. Where the flight was unusual was that it would be made in total radio silence.

The reason for this was that people were listening.

The National Security Agency was the biggest electronic eavesdropping concern in the world bar one. That one was its equivalent in the USSR. NSA was by far the most sophisticated, but the Soviets compensated with more manpower and allocation of resources. Collection of electronic emissions was mainly performed by satellites known as 'ferrets', an apt name for a relentless hunter of rats and other rodents. While the fabulous imaging satellites remained the most glamorous of the orbiting spacecraft, it was the more numerous SIGINT ferrets that performed the everyday work of technical collection. Ferrets outnumbered their PHOTINT cousins by almost four-to-one, and thus if each was to have its own booster, $100 million for a Titan 4, the cost quickly became numbing even by government standards. The Americans through the National Reconnaissance Office had adapted by pressing on with the very latest technology, building miniaturised, highly sensitive receivers, small, very powerful transmitters, and lightweight, folding, large antennas, all packed into a satellite small enough and light enough to be squeezed in on top of the booster along with a bigger satellite such as one of the Keyhole or KH series. They were known as 'piggyback' satellites.

The USSR simply kept its production line open for both satellites and boosters, and blasted off as many as it felt was required. Cosmoses of varying descriptions and giant A-2s were stacked in rows at Plesetsk. For the military, the account was always open-ended, filled up by the People.

While the USSR's SIGINT platforms were less sophisticated than those of the USA, they were always there. If the pilots of the B-2s spoke a word over the radio before start-up, while taxiing out, during the flight or upon landing at Whiteman AFB, Missouri they might just as well have sent a telegram to the Kremlin announcing the fact that the B-2 ATB Stealth bomber was not mothballed, awaiting conversion to low-visibility advanced alloy beer cans, but was snug in its series of specially built hangars, back at its home base, like an unsheathed weapon waiting to be used. Entirely because of a hard-nosed, knowledgeable, hawkish Air Force Chief of Staff.

At midnight, like a formation of giant black bats, the

ten bombers moved out along the taxiway. One after the other read quiet. The bombers used four General Electric F118-GE-100s, uprated but non-augmented versions of the F110 fighter engine. The largest composite aircraft ever built they were so curved and rounded as to seem organic rather than mechanical, an impression heightened by their very precise, almost live surface finish and bat-like shape. The B-2s were flying wings, wider at 172 feet of wingspan than they were long, only 69 feet. Even with the naked eye they were hard to see as they lined up, so well did they blend with their environment. The on-board sensors, data-processing and display sub-systems were the most sophisticated ever fitted to a warplane. One after the other, the pilots moved their three-position 'master mode' switches to 'Takeoff'. The mission data tapes were transferred. Performance data were presented. Radios came on, the communications parts of which the pilots deleted. Flight controls went into takeoff mode. One after the other, they hissed down the runway, and vanished into their natural element. On the vacated ramp area, the ground crews rolled out the replicas into the spaces they had left behind.

USAF SATELLITE CONTROL FACILITY, SUNNYVALE, CALIFORNIA

The Air Force owned it, and the SCF, an hour's drive south from San Francisco was the place from which all the military satellites of the USA were controlled. It was useful to have it there, close to Vandenberg, their own Special Projects Office in El Segundo, and Silicon Valley, for while some of the staff at the Control Facility were blue-suiters, and sent there, many were civilian employees of the contractors who built the array of communication, navigation, meteorological, mapping and data-relay satellites, as well as the family of surveillance and reconnaissance types, and it was helpful to have them close by where they lived, for civilians were notorious for not wanting to move, unlike the military transients. However, since the SCF, or Big Blue Cube as it was sometimes known sat slap over a geological fault considered ripe for earthquake, and had thoughtlessly been built within infantry-portable missile range of a main highway, the Air Force, back in the good old days when budgets were open-ended had covered themselves by creating their Air Force Space Command Consolidated Space Operations Center in Colorado Springs, which was designed to have satellite control facility. Until the day Soviet *Spetsnaz* troops opened up with *Sagger* missiles from passing Toyotas, or California fell off into the ocean, the SCF remained the place of primary importance for the controlling of satellites. American ones, usually.

General Coogan was there as his B-2 bombers were taxiing out for take off in the dark Arizona desert night. He was there, rather than with the machines, because it was the place for him to be, to exert control over events if things went wrong. They did.

The first Coogan knew of it was shortly after the B-2s had taken off. The Facility was manned twenty-four hours a day by teams of blue-suiters and shirt-sleeved civilians, and while inside the operations area it might be day or night, it made no difference to those controlling the satellites, which listened and watched all the time, and whose charges needed constant care. The brigadier in charge, Temson, who was one of the small band of officers who knew the truth about the B-2s, came quietly but quickly up to where Coogan was watching.

'We got a problem, General,' he murmured. 'The Soviets have just moved a *Cosmos*. It's going to go close to Whiteman.'

He took Coogan to a computer display terminal, where the path of a satellite was visible, shown on a map of the world. Because of the Mercator-style projection of the map, the path of the satellite appeared to be in an S-shape, the letter lying on its side, that alone indicated that it was a Soviet craft. Polar orbits were superior for reconnaissance purposes, but it was more difficult to get satellites there. Since the earth spun from west to east, launching a spacecraft as far in that direction as possible reduced the amount of thrust required per pound of payload, since the momentum of the planet itself helped get the rocket off the ground. Launching a satellite to the north or south, as the Americans did, required extra thrust. Being at right angles to the motion of the earth, half of the effect of that motion had to be overcome. A KH-11 or -13 launch was inclined at nearly 97 degrees, which actually went against the movement of the earth, and required even more thrust, but the Americans did it, because the whole philosophy of their reconnaissance programme, which was mission-oriented, called for perfection. Polar orbits were superior not for geographical coverage, since there was little but ice, penguins and polar bears there, but because near-polar orbits were sun-synchronous. With the sun in the same place every time the satellite flew over a certain spot, shadows and other lighting conditions remained constant, thus greatly facilitating photo interpretation.

The information alongside the map told Coogan about the satellite. It gave its *Cosmos* number – now up in the thousands – time and place of launch, type, orbit 73 degrees and so forth. It was an imaging satellite, and they had moved it. It was going to go by Whiteman.

'Is there anything sinister in them moving it now?'

'I don't think so, sir. I think they just got unlucky. They're looking at Whiteman because it's there, and they want to know what we're doing with it now the B-2s are gone. Or supposed to be gone,' he murmured. 'Ellis says the Soviet admirals have got to the top of the ladder and it's their turn, they want to look at the Navy's new layout in Bangor, Washington. They know same as we do that you risk point failure of the satellite each time you move it, so they're trying to get as much coverage as they can.'

Coogan looked at his watch. The B-2s were in the air,

and could not be stopped. Once they had landed, and had taxied in to their special hangars, they would be hidden away. He made a quick calculation, tapping in the time of arrival, and was reassured to find that the Cosmos would be off the coast of Australia at the time, so actual pictures of the bombers, caught red-handed, would not be taken. However, it was little comfort, since on its next pass the satellite would go by, and while its camera would record nothing but a base asleep, its infra-red imaging equipment would pick up the heat trails of the bombers from runway to hangar, heat trails that might just as well write in words of flame for all to see: B-2 Bombers Live Here.

They were supposed to be mothballed in Arizona.

'We'll have to spoof it, if we can,' said Coogan. 'Who's your best man?'

'Ellis,' Temson said, without hesitation. 'He has a doctorate from MIT. I think he's only with us so he can start his own company selling us his ideas when he leaves.'

'Let's go to him.'

They found Major Randy Ellis at his computer display terminal, where he was fishing for more information about the *Cosmos*.

'We have some things going on at Whiteman AFB we do not want that bird to image,' Coogan said crisply. He glanced at his watch. The B-2s were destined to be in the air for just over one hour and twenty-two minutes. 'If you can spoof it so that it cannot see you can walk out of here a Lieutenant-Colonel.'

Randy Ellis grinned. He was unfazed at the proximity of the Chief of Staff. Temson was right, he planned to use the multitude of contacts he had made working in the USAF satellite programme, and start his own electronics company. It was a tried and tested way to your fortune, known ever since a bunch of former Naval officers, who had become familiar with cryptography and SIGINT during the Second World War, banded together to form Engineering Research Associates, Inc, which then proceeded to take on naval security's most complex assignments, beginning with the SIGINT world's first computer, Atlas, delivered by ERA in 1950. Work for naval security led to work for NSA, the biggest SIGINT customer in the free world. What Randy Ellis would take with him from SCF into the marketplace would make him a million-aire near-overnight. So he grinned at his superior officer. Besides, he was smarter than General Coogan, whom he regarded as a species of cunning, if dangerous, dinosaur.

'Sounds good to me, General,' he said cheerfully.

'You got just on one hour,' said Coogan.

'Just one question, sir. Is it necessary that the Soviets not know that their *Cosmos* has been interfered with?'

'Essential,' Coogan said succinctly. Jesus, thought Ellis, it's the goddamn B-2. Coogan must have some there. Immediately the thought surfaced in his mind he suppressed it, and kept with the job in hand. Any indication that he had knowledge of Coogan's deception would be a certain ticket to an interesting, career-long job clearing penguin guano from runways on Baffin island.

'Okay,' he said. 'That rules out some of the more obvious ploys like firing the manoeuvring engines about over the Pacific coast. You do that the satellite becomes disoriented and lost. If you keep it up it burns all its fuel and is useless. But they've just moved it, and point failure is a not-unknown consequence of playing with your bird in this way. It would be best if this one developed a glitch of some kind … Maybe ultimately fatal, eh General?'

'Certainly,' Coogan responded. The destruction of Soviet hardware was always a pleasing notion.

Ellis had the mark of the real professional in any business; he could talk fluently while he went about his difficult task, and he kept up a flow of interesting information as his fingers danced on his computer keyboard, drawing out the facts he needed.

'Well, now, look at that. They've given it a 7-degree tilt. That's smart, that means when it rotates you get a much bigger arc of surveillance. We've only been doing it these past ten years.' He sighed. 'They ain't bright, but they stumble on it in the end.'

146

Ellis had the intellectual's genial contempt for those he considered his mental inferiors.

'Okay. It'll take a little finessing, but what I intend to do, General, is to try to convice old Boris over in Plesetsk that the on-board attitude system needs adjusting when in fact it does not. Here we go then.'

Ellis began tapping in the series of codes, frequencies and transmission sequences that NSA's giant computers in Maryland had sieved out of their SIGINT for him. They watched the computer display as the *Cosmos* arced away over the tip of Greenland, to Scandinavia and into the USSR. Alongside the display new information began printing. Ellis chuckled gleefully.

'Got him got him. Too much vodka last night, *tovarich*. Boris has bitten, General. He thinks the Cosmos needed adjustment, so he's done it. In fact, it was dead steady, but I fed him disinformation. Now it *is* tumbling. Let's make things worse, shall we?'

As Ellis resumed his high-tech warfare Coogan glanced at his watch. The B-2s had just touched down. The *Cosmos*, now rocking and rolling uncontrollably, was coming across the Pacific. Ellis had performed his task just in time.

'Well done, Colonel,' he said, and Ellis nodded with a smile, accepting the compliment. He tapped in some more disinformation and leaned back.

'If Boris swallows that, it'll de-orbit.'

Coogan stayed to see the acknowledgement of victory printed out on Ellis' computer display, writ as large for him as the final score on the electronic board at the Super Bowl.

'Poor bastards,' Ellis said dismissively. 'They still think it's 1945. You can play them like fish.'

Coogan left the SCF with the pale light of dawn on the horizon. Despite his lack of sleep he felt elated. There was nothing to compare with defeating the Russians in combat. Nothing at all.

LAS VEGAS, NEW MEXICO

The whore had a hunter's eye, she could detect and snare fast-moving prey in seconds; she would have made an excellent skeet shot had she been able to see profit in hitting something not flesh.

It was her day off, too, she gave herself a free day every week, to enjoy herself, relax, go shopping. She was in the pleasing cool of the air-conditioned mall, where children could skate on the ice of the rink, sit in the atrium, when outside in summer it might be over one hundred degrees, when she spotted him.

He was young, no more than twenty two, good-looking, tall and dark haired, expensive casual clothes, silk shirt, Sea Island cotton slacks, Italian Gucci loafers, gold and the Rolex – *Arab*. In Las Vegas. Her finger squeezed the trigger as the bobbing little rabbit came into range and her lovely smile gleamed at him, a demure but exciting smile that said she was a lady, but one prepared to be wooed by such a handsome and virile man as he. She had such confidence in her abilities, I could drive a Bishop crazy, she would sometimes think, adding her stocks and bonds, watching the interest rise at the bank, and laugh to herself.

It took but a few minutes before they were seated in the French-style sidewalk cafe taking a mineral water and coffee. He was Ali. It was his first time in the USA.

'I felt I had to see Las Vegas,' he said winningly. 'But now I am here I do not know where to go. Everything is so large ...'

He looked about in the vast, multi-storey mall, filled

148

with anything and everything people could want to buy.

'Are you yourself a native of this city ...' he enquired tentatively.

'I've been here since Mama had me baptised in the church down the street. We lived in Los Alamos for a while. Daddy was an engineer, you see. But once I was out of high school I came to work here.'

'What is it that you do?'

'I'm an airline stewardess,' she said. 'With Pan Am.'

The whore was the daughter of a construction worker and his wife who had rowed since the day they were married, the girl had left home when she was sixteen and had never been back to Arkansas since. The being a stewardess was always a good touch, she felt, a lot of men still thought the 'coffee, tea or me' image came with it. It was enticing.

Ali looked at her ingenuously. 'It would be too much to ask if you would show me around?'

'Why,' she said, shooting a glance at him from under her eyelashes. 'I don't know what to say.'

He smiled, showing excellent white teeth under his combed moustache.

'Take pity on this poor stranger,' he said, and they both laughed.

They went out and her predatory instincts had not betrayed her, an immaculate silver Mercedes Coupe was waiting outside, not a cent under $500 a day to hire, her trained valuer's eyes told her. They got in, and let the garish neon of the road wash over them.

'Do you like to play cards, or throw dice, Ali?' she said, pretending to be tentative.

'Oh, yes,' he said enthusiastically. 'I love to gamble.'

She laughed delightedly, and delightfully.

'Well, let's *play*.'

There were three or four casinos where she had a deal with the management, when she went in she caught the pit boss' eye, he nodded, ever so slightly, and they knew she would be around the next day, to collect her percentage.

There was admiration in the man's acknowledgement. *Where* did you hook that one, it said, so ripe for the plucking.

And so it proved, Ali dropped nearly fifty thousand in a few hours, and twelve of that made its way into the flat silk body belt. It seemed not to bother him at all.

'We will take a break before beginning afresh,' he announced. 'My luck will then be better. A little drive, I think. Some clean desert air, the stars …'

Okay, she thought. She knew how johns operated. A fuck and it's back to the tables. She estimated she could keep him going into the small hours, when his judgement would be shot. Oh, baby, she said to herself, let's wring this one while its got water still in it.

She giggled charmingly. 'Come on then,' she said promisingly.

The desert air was crisp and fresh after the artificial variety pumped through the gambling-chamber.

'You are so pretty,' he murmured, as he unpeeled her. The chill air made her nipples rise, as if with desire. An old trick but a good one, she thought, as he entered her. He lay for a moment or two, breathing deeply after the pleasure. His weight was pinning her to the blanket they had spread on the sand. He took his hands, large and capable, from the intimate parts of her body that they had enjoyed, and slipped them around her neck. They were soldier's hands, trained and strong, they snapped her slim neck almost before she realised that it had gone wrong, that someone had placed oil in the path of the powerful racing car she had so confidently piloted down the lethal course. She died, incredulous that her skill had let her down.

The assassin left her where she lay. He stopped a mile or so down the road, and buried all his clothes, gold watch, neck chain in the desert, changing into fresh casual gear from a bag. He drove to the airport where he checked in in time to catch the late flight home.

His was one of the last flights into Washington, he

collected his car from the multi-storey park and drove home. If he looked tired the next day, if one of the White House secretaries commented he'd just flash his boyish grin and say: When we party, we party hearty, and they'd all laugh.

Gulio Riva knelt, and said the last of his prayers to his maker.

The sun crept over the edge of the horizon, bringing light to the hard desert. In the still air a buzzard circled. Its eyes registered food, and it lost altitude, coming to rest by the still figure on the blanket. Cautious, it waited for signs of life before taking a first, stabbing thrust. The flesh remained inert. In the sky above other birds were flying. The buzzard hopped forward, tearing at the soft parts of the dead thing with its hooked beak.

KINGS BAY, GEORGIA

Commander Cyrus T. Sanders lived in a pleasant brick house in the unspoilt Georgia countryside a short way up I-96 from the submarine base, overlooking the Satilla river. A twenty-foot fibreglass boat was tied up at a wood jetty, a little low in the water, slimy green algae coating her bottom, a relic of the days when the naval officer had had hobbies that interested him. His house was on a slope overlooking the river, with a front yard off the red-dirt road, and a sun-deck jutting out over the slope behind, secluded among the pines.

He parked his car in the yard and went into the house in the gloom of the evening. He stumbled slightly as he went over the step, moving like a blind man in unfamiliar territory. A light was on inside, he paused, and slowly looked around, momentarily leaving the object of obsession inside his head. Hank Sultani sat in a chair, and two men stood silently in the shadows behind him.

'Hey, boy,' Sultani said quietly, in the soft southern drawl he had acquired. 'We been waitin' on you.'

He got up, and eased Sanders into a chair by the table. A bottle of Canadian Club stood there, with a tumbler, and Sultani poured a hefty shot for him.

'You need a drink,' he said. Sanders took the glass, and let the fire burn within him. When he put it down, his voice was husky from the raw liquor.

'The *Maine*'s missing,' he whispered.

'Yeah, I know.'

'Your people have an arms build-up in Nicaragua ... you've taken out an SSBN close to home ... we think you're seeing how much crow Cord'll eat. They're preparing a report for the PDB now ...'

He poured another shot of Club himself.

'It was me,' he said, and acknowledged the enormity of his crime for the first time.

'Yeah,' said Sultani. 'It was you.'

'What's going to happen?' Sanders whispered.

'They're going to get you,' Sultani said directly. 'Put you away for ever, and ever, Cy.'

'What am I to do? Can I defect?'

'You wouldn't like Moscow, Cy. No casinos there.'

'No ...' Sanders was confused, he was losing the ability to concentrate his thoughts.

'Besides,' said Sultani, 'you're ill, aren't you, Cy? You've been ill a long, long time.'

Sanders nodded hopelessly.

'You're never getting better, Cy,' Sultani continued softly. 'And it hurts, doesn't it? Nothing takes away the pain any more ... not the booze, not the money, not the little girl ... because you lose, Cy ... you always lose.'

'Yes ... yes.' Tears began running down his tight face, like a skull crying.

'Nothing works any more, does it?'

'No ...'

'Nothing takes away the pain ...' Sultani whispered, his

mouth close by Sanders' ear. He looked across at the men standing by the curtains and nodded, and one quietly switched off the light, so that they were in semi-darkness.

'Nothing works ... it's never going to get better, they're going to put you in a place with padded walls and rubber spoons, and you'll have to live the rest of your life, forever and ever with the rat gnawing at your brain, right there in your skull, minute after minute, hour after hour, day after day ... you'll be raving, Cy, but it'll make no difference ...'

Sanders sat sobbing at the table.

'What have I done ...'

'Best to end it ...' Sultani said softly, kindly. 'Put an end to the pain while you can.'

'Yes.'

'Come on ...' He helped Sanders get up, and they went out into the dimly-lit sun deck. Beneath the brown boards the river bank sloped away, ten feet under them. There was a wooden picnic table and benches, long disused. By the heavy rail, something white lay coiled, attached to the rail.

'It won't hurt,' Sultani said gently. 'The pain will be all gone.'

Sanders stood in a daze as they slipped the noose around his neck.

'Stand on the bench. There. You can get your legs over the railing.'

As Sanders sat on the rail with the drop beneath him his mind cleared and he understood all that had happened to him. He turned to look at Sultani, standing just behind him.

'It was *you*,' he accused. 'All along it was you. You did this to me, made me the way I am.'

'It was the will of God,' Sultani said, and pushed.

NSA HEADQUARTERS

The office of the director, DIRNSA was not dissimilar to that of his deputy next door. To see either man a visitor went through the bright blue door, set in a matching wall, with the Agency's proud seal upon it, past the outer office of executive registry secretaries and through a polished wood door. Inside, both offices were comfortable, with polished desks, leather armchairs and sofas, large painted globes. It was the occupants who differed. No matter which two men held the two top posts in the agency, they came from different backgrounds and had different training. They were subject to differing external pressures which might cause them to wish to take different decisions. This dissimilarity stemmed directly from the fact that the director was always a military general or admiral there in a managerial capacity for a limited tour before moving on to collect another star, and the deputy was a long-term intelligence professional, and a civilian.

The marriage could work well, as the tours of such directors as Major General Canine, the agency's first head, or Vice-Admiral Bobby Inman, the youngest DIRNSA in the agency's history indicated. However, when the two sides were not seeing eye to eye, and most especially when the military felt it had an axe to grind, it could be a different story.

MacDonald had been deputy director for over ten years, and always felt that a good pointer to future relations between a new director and his civilians lay in the choice of decoration. Everyone liked to bring something of their own to a new job, to decorate their office, to make it seem familiar. MacDonald chose to display some of the watercolours he painted to relax from the strain of his job. The personnel histories of those deeply involved in intelligence were littered with the damaged minds of those who had allowed their work to become obsession, and to maim them.

When Admiral Inman had arrived as DIRNSA, he had brought a pleasing wooden model of a schooner with him, which rested on a ledge. MacDonald had felt it a good omen, and so it turned out.

General Calvin Moore, the new director, had brought a model with him too, and it rested on his desk. It was a beautifully-crafted one-fifth-scale F-4E McDonnell Douglas Phantom II, complete with AIM-7E Sparrow missiles, CBU-39 Gravelmine pods in SUU-41 dispensers and KB-18 strike camera. The modeller had hand-decorated the craft with a red-and-gold dragon in front and below the cockpit, two MiG symbols and the name of the crew, Major J. Herbert, the back-seater, and Colonel C. Moore, aircraft commander. General Moore kept it there to remind him of where he had been.

Practice of warfare had given Moore ample experience of what was known as collateral damage. Collateral damage was the military euphemism for the number of women and children you killed when you were attempting to do something else.

Sometimes those you maimed or killed were on your side.

He had summoned Ashraf Amran to see him that morning. She could see on his desk the model Phantom fighter-bomber and a copy of her report on the Iranian nuclear weapons programme. However, Moore looked at neither but at her.

'We've had a complaint about you, Mrs Amran,' he said.

'Someone's unhappy with my work?' she said, in surprise. 'They think I'm not doing a good job?'

'Not exactly,' Moore said dryly. 'More that you do too good a job.'

'I don't understand. Perhaps you would explain, General.'

'Certainly. A few months ago you took part in Game Tau at the National Defense University, where you led the Iranian team. You were chosen for your specialised knowledge, expertise and understanding of the country and its leaders.'

'Yes,' said Ash.

'Your principal opponent was Major-General Curtiss, of Special Operations Forces. Game Tau was meant to demonstrate the new-found expertise of SOF in a place like Iran, scene of debacle for the USA in the past.'

'Right.'

'You dicked Curtiss about nine ways from Sunday,' Moore said crudely. 'For four days you tricked him, ambushed him, beat him up and, in short, comprehensively defeated the SOF capability of the USA.'

'It was easy,' said Ash. 'The US military has no real understanding of SOF as it should be conducted. Curtiss is regular Army to his bootstraps, he goes by the book. The book happens to be the Field Manual. If it isn't in the FM then no matter how good an idea it is or how much you need to do it, you won't. Curtiss didn't. He doesn't understand that you need to keep everything in your head. If you aren't smart enough to keep it there then go get your hat and find some other, less demanding line of work.'

'Well, old Curtiss may be doing just that after the Tau Game,' Moore said, not without a certain amount of malicious pleasure at seeing the Army fall on its face in the mud. 'However, Curtiss was so mad at the way you reamed him out that he made an official complaint, claiming that no real American could be so convincing as a wily bad Iranian, that you had to be just that. The complaint arrived here, naturally, as we are your employers, and so we had you checked out.'

Moore smiled amiably at Ash. 'We found some funny things. In fact, I'm not sure why we employed you after all.'

'You employ me because I am expert at my job,' Ash said equably. 'I am better and know more about it than anyone else you could possibly find. That's why I work here, General.'

'Is it? Is it?' mused Moore. 'We'll see. And are you the best? You don't even have a PhD. Anyone of weight here has a doctorate.'

'Any academic worth two *Qarans* in old money can get a DPhil. or a PhD.,' Ash said icily. '*I* have a Double-First from Oxford University.'

Moore smiled faintly. He liked spirit. Recognising that this was very poor ground on which a non-academic should choose to fight he moved on.

'This report, in which you claim the Iranian government is planning to acquire nuclear weapons. It's pure conjecture, unbacked by hard SIGINT of any kind.'

'You will find in the report that I consider Khalif Hossein and his advisers to be familiar with the West in general and the USA in particular. It is my definite belief that they know our capabilities regarding the acquisition of TECHINT of any kind, and for this reason have taken great pains not to transmit any part of their plan electronically. I have HUMINT sources within Iran that give credence to this view.'

'This is the National Security Agency,' Moore expostulated, throwing up his arms. 'Most large corporations measure their computer capacities in square feet. We measure it in acres. Our capacity to extract *hard* information is unrivalled. HUMINT belongs to the past, it exists in James Bond movies and novels by John Le Carré. It's gone, Miss. We use high-technology because our computers and sensors have never been shown to lie for purposes of expediency, or because they don't work for the opposition, because they never have lapses of memory or become confused. They do not drink, take drugs, need sex or have ego problems.'

'Equally, machines cannot read minds, guess intentions or see through the roofs of buildings,' Ash murmured. 'Even so, if the opposition is deliberately not committing anything to SIGINT channels –'

'So you suppose.'

'So I *know*. Then you make use of whatever methods you can. Furthermore, I have hard evidence that Michael Logan, a guidance engineer working on Trident II missiles for Lockheed is inside Iran, apparently a prisoner, and that seventeen other rocketry specialists are missing under peculiar circumstances.'

'Hold on now. You have one picture put together by the boys at En-Pick. I personally think that they could make Yogi Bear look like the president if they wanted to.'

'You cannot have it both ways, General,' Ash said mildly. 'Either computer-driven technology is the be-all and end-all of late twentieth-century intelligence or it isn't. I have no doubts in my mind at all. Khalif Hossein is planning to acquire nuclear weaponry, and I personally cannot imagine anything more dangerous for world peace than that.'

Moore looked quizzically at the analyst.

'You hint in the report that it would be beneficial for everyone were Khalif Hossein to meet with a fatal accident.'

'Surely. Is it not always beneficial for the citizens of a country for a tyrant to die? The Romans recognised that by his actions a tyrant had made himself a legitimate target. They defined legitimate tyrannicide.'

'I can see that,' said Moore. 'Though assassination is not, and never has been this agency's speciality. Is that all there is to it?'

Ash looked blankly at him.

'Is that all there is to what?'

'I'm talking about you, Mrs Amram. It is my opinion that you are not necessarily all you seem. I accept that you know a great deal about Iran, and that you have a trained, and first-class mind. That said I would still not hunt for a chocolate egg at Easter-time on the strength of this report.

'What worries me is that you seem to have extra-curricular activities. You know and keep in touch with a number of influential Iranian exiles. We know that you have been seen talking to former members of SAVAK, and of the Imperial Guard, and other branches of the Shah's military and intelligence.'

'I'm an *analyst*, General. What would you expect me to do?'

'Most of your analysts do it from the "take". They rely on TECHINT.'

'*Your* analysts told President Carter the Shah wasn't in the trouble he was. *I* was among the people in Tehran when I was attached to the embassy, and *my* reports were prescient to a degree.' Ash retorted.

'You *do* know a great deal about Iran. Is that why you were there just after Grand Ayatollah Khomeini died?'

'It isn't a crime to go home,' she said quietly.

'You went with your husband. Wasn't he in the newspaper business under the late Shah?'

'My husband is a talented journalist. He was Editor of *Kayhan* which was a big daily newspaper. That was before the revolution.'

'He came to America with you once Khomeini was in power. Where is he now?'

'You know quite well where he is. He is in a dreadful place called Evin prison.'

'Put there by Khalif Hossein as an enemy of the revolution.'

'Put there with many other good men and women for trying to give the Persian people democracy.'

'And these extracurricular activities of yours, these people you see, might they have anything to do with getting him out? With attempts at overthrowing Khalif Hossein?'

'As I said, sir, I am but an analyst. Matters of policy are formed high above my head.'

'Don't pretend to be naive with me, Mrs Amram,' Moore said softly. 'You know well that those who form policy can only do so from what they are told. *By top analysts like you.*'

Moore had clear, unblinking, fighter-pilot's vision. In his fifties, he still did not require glasses. He stared at the woman opposite him.

'I'm suspending you from duty. I want to have you investigated further. That's all.'

As Ash went out through the offices and into the corridor of Mahogany Row a secretary was waiting by the door that led to the deputy-director.

'Dr MacDonald wants a word,' she said with a smile.

MacDonald was spending his lunch hour painting a small vase of spring flowers.

'Sit down, Ash,' he said from his easel. 'Moore put you on suspension?'

She nodded, still with her breath taken away by Moore's action.

'Well you're not,' said MacDonald. 'I'm going to transfer you to other duties while I get all this sorted out. Let me tell you what's going on. This place used to be a regular battleground between the military and the civilians over "turf". We have always tended to have more civilians than military among the higher grades. Sometimes the military would win. I recall the rule of Army Major General Wolff. He used to be described as a "wheels-up, ballsy character, a tough-ass." ' MacDonald's face crinkled at the memory, as if at a bad smell. 'When he arrived he decorated his office wall with a chrome-plated machine gun and announced that he ate civilians alive.'

MacDonald put down his fine hair paint-brush.

'None of it helps the work of the Agency. President Cord's policies have had the effect of re-opening the old battles for power here. In the past month I have lost two heads of section, good people. You are the third. All of you have been fired or suspended under very marginal conditions. In each case, General Moore has a blue-suiter lined up to take over. It is not just the Director, but his own superior officer, Chief of Staff Coogan. Coogan wishes to control not only access to intelligence, but also the interpretation of it. That is where real power lies, and the General has not been slow to realise it.'

MacDonald sighed. It was always a bad sign for him when he needed to paint in his lunch-hour.

'Coogan will take some stopping. In the meantime I am not going to lose you. It is my belief that you understand all that is going on in Iran better than anyone in the Agency, or indeed within the intelligence community. Pack a bag and catch the plane down to Jacksonville Florida. You're going to the big Kings Bay submarine base. You'll liaise with a Commander Jack Kowalski there.'

'Why?'

'The Navy has lost one of its submarines. They don't know where it is. The agency may be able to help them find it.'

'It's gone down?'

MacDonald shrugged. 'They don't know. It failed to report when they sent it an ELF message.'

'What kind of sub is it?'

'The *Maine*. It's an *Ohio* class ballistic missile submarine. The Navy are frantic. The fact that it's missing is Top Secret Umbra.'

'That's a Trident II submarine,' Ash said softly. Her heart was beating very fast.

'The latest,' MacDonald said unhappily. 'I hope to God it's simply had an accident. The Soviets have been pulling Cord's tail in Central America. I hope like hell they haven't sunk it just to see how far they can go without him reacting.'

Ash swallowed, for her mouth was very dry.

'It's not the Russians,' she said. 'It's Khalif Hossein.'

KINGS BAY, GEORGIA

'We know that something must have happened to her,' said Kowalski, 'but unfortunately we don't know where she is. Submarines are stealthy systems, if they let home base know where they are all the time then the enemy knows where they are too.'

'Has she got buoys, or something to release if she's trapped on the bottom?' asked Ash.

'In the past submarines have had such signal buoys but they create problems. They tend to be noisy, and the major fear of the crew is that in a combat situation they could become dislodged by ASW weapons, thus giving the enemy the precise location of the craft. In World War Two they were welded down, and modern submarines like the *Maine* don't have them. However, if she's immobilised on the bottom it's possible for the crew to release an antenna from within through either the escape hatch or a torpedo tube. This she hasn't done. Equally, if she was disabled in relatively shallow water the crew could escape making use of the Mommsen Lung escape equipment on board. Once again, this they have not done. We have a craft known as a Deep Sea Rescue Vehicle which will attach to the hatch of a disabled craft and get the crew off – it was designed and built following the *Thresher* disaster in 1963, when it was recognised that we had no way of getting a crew out from depth. That's on its mother ship right now, the *Pigeon*, together with divers, and a midget submarine we use as well. She's out in the Atlantic in the area. The *Coral Sea*'s out there, if anything happens I'm getting in a Navy fighter and it's going to take me out there. They'll helicopter me on to the *Pigeon*. Our problem is that, roughly speaking, she could be almost anywhere in her patrol area. Underwater navigation isn't tremendously precise, so the craft are assigned individual patrol areas. Since we don't know *when* whatever happened to her took place because it was *days* before we knew the *Scorpion* was missing in 1968, we don't know where she might be.'

'Could they still be alive?'

Kowalski hesitated. 'The *Scorpion* was lost with all hands. Western submarine designers tend to assume that penetration of the pressure hull at any substantial depth will be fatal. Ballast tank volume is limited in the interests of speed, so the ability to surface despite damage is limited as well. No modern Western submarine has even a one-compartment standard of survival.'

'You seem to be assuming that that is what has happened to the *Maine*.'

'The evidence points that way. No contact, no survivors. And something else. I should be with the *Pigeon*, as commander of the Loss/Disaster outfit here. I'm *not*, because a commander in communications here didn't turn up for work a couple of days ago. Someone went round to see him and found him hanging by a rope from his sun deck. We very much fear sabotage.'

Ash was fitting pieces together in her mind. She was very much aware of MacDonald's warning not even to mention her theory that the Iranians were behind whatever had happened to the ballistic missile craft. 'They will think you mad,' he had warned. 'If it was anyone but you who had such a theory I would think them mad too.'

'I've been sent down to do anything NSA can do. If you need anything we can provide, just ask.'

'Thanks,' said Kowalski. 'We will.'

'I did check one thing before I left Fort Meade. I was told that the *Maine* was missing. I was given the dates. I ran a check to see if *anything else* had happened in the broad region then, over the ocean, or on it. I came up with one thing on the 29th. During the morning, a twin engined Cessna 421 executive aircraft vanished on a flight from Trinidad to Puerto Rico. Took off from Port of Spain bright and early and no one ever heard any more about it.'

Kowalski ran his finger along the map on the wall.

'The *Maine* shouldn't have been anywhere near there. Trinidad … Puerto Rico, a big twin, could be drugs, yes?'

Ash shrugged. 'Maybe. You know what James Bond said. "Once is happenstance. Twice coincidence. Three times enemy action." Perhaps we'll get some third thing to make it enemy action.'

'Maybe,' agreed Kowalski. 'It's something to remember.'

'Can I help at all while I'm here?'

'Could you mind the store?' Kowalski said eagerly. 'With everyone gone I'm short-staffed and I'm busy with the boys from the Defense Investigative Service about Commander Sanders – that's the guy found on the end of the rope.'

'I'll be happy to,' promised Ash.

That afternoon, the telephone rang.

'Hallo?' enquired a little old voice. 'May I speak to someone regarding poor Commander Sanders?'

Ash had never been in the South before. It was an education to her how in lightly-populated Georgia well-to-do folk stuck to the traditions of their forebears and lived in comfortable houses stuck out of town down red-dirt roads. Making her way to where Sanders had lived she was struck by the number of large, expensive pick-up trucks liberally decorated with colourful stickers bearing such slogans as The South Shall Rise Again, and offerings from the NRA informing the public that when it was criminal to bear arms only criminals would bear arms. The pick-up truckers bore arms. They had them on racks in their rear windows. Ash suspected she was out of place. She was driving Kowalski's Ford Thunderbird, which

164

bore a sticker that said 'Money Isn't Everything. (But It Keeps the Kids in Touch.)' The ever-polite Georgians with whom she had come into contact since arriving in the state might not have been exactly sure where she came from, but she had the feeling they had summed her up in a nano-second or two. After all, if you weren't a good ol' boy or gal, then what were you? A DamYankee.

She propelled the Ford down the dirt road that led to Cyrus Sanders' house. A number of dwellings were built along it, spaced at suitable distances from one another, nestling quietly among the big Southern pines. She turned in the driveway of the house next door, a single-storey brick building with a well-tended front yard, and clean paintwork on the wood. She got out, and her shoes scrunched gently on the layer of pine needles.

At the side of the house, the big central air-conditioning unit sat silent, awaiting the shocking heat of the Georgian summer. Ash rang the bell and it played a selection. She thought she recognised something about the Land of Cotton, then the door opened.

Mrs Nobles wasn't that old, but she had the fussy old lady's air that some of the southern women could acquire at almost any age. Her hair was suitably hennaed and coiffed and she was smartly dressed in skirt and blouse.

'Mrs Nobles,' Ash said. 'I'm Ashraf Amran from the naval base. You called us.'

'Oh, my Lord,' she said. 'I didn't realise the Navy employed such pretty young gals. Come in, my dear.'

'I'm attached temporarily,' she said, going into the hallway with its polished wood floor. 'To investigate Commander Sanders' death.'

The other woman winced slightly at the reminder, then brightened.

'Oh, so you're FBI,' she said happily, and Ash nodded, as if in agreement. NSA employees absorbed the Agency's policy of practically not admitting its own existence from their first days there, as if by osmosis from the air around them.

'My boy wanted to be in the FBI when he was little, he saw all those TV shows about G-men, wasn't that it? He's in real-estate down in Florida, Vero Beach. Of course, he couldn't have been in the FBI anyway, don't you have to be a lawyer or an accountant, you're far too pretty to be an accountant, honey, so you must be a lawyer.'

Ash smiled guilelessly and nodded again.

Mrs Nobles ushered her into the living room, which was spotlessly clean, and Ash sat on the sofa, while the older woman settled herself in what was clearly her favourite chair, nearby the window. On a low table were some photographs of a married couple, and their children.

'My boy Alfred, and his wife Connie,' she explained. My, but they can talk down here, thought Ash. 'Their little ones, Al. Jr., and Harriet Lee. She's from South Carolina,' she confided. 'But at least he had the sense to marry a Southern gal.'

Ouch, thought Ash.

Having stuck a knife into the pretty Northern gal, in the nicest possible way, Mrs Nobles got closer to the subject of her deceased neighbour.

'That's why I only just heard,' she explained, shifting her eyes towards the next door house about two hundred feet away, and looking suitably solemn. 'You see, on the night that ... that ...'

'He died.'

'He *passed on*,' Mrs Nobles corrected, reprovingly. 'On that night, I was getting myself ready to go to see my son and grandchildren. I left real early the next morning to catch the airplane from Jacksonville, and I've only just heard, I only got back yesterday and Mrs Jones, where I do my shopping told me, I met her in the mall. So it is true what she said then?'

'It appears that Commander Sanders took his own life, yes.'

'Oh ... Lord ...' She sat in her chair, twisting her hands together. 'Why would anyone want to do that ...'

'From our investigations, Commander Sanders had

large gambling debts. Once uncovered, they would have led to the end of his naval career.'

'Gambling ... it's the devil's work ... my uncle would gamble, he became an addict, playing poker, he lost the family farm in a poker game.'

The old lady was more distressed than the mere act of her neighbour's suicide seemed to warrant.

'Is there anything you can tell me about him, Mrs Nobles?'

She shook her head to and fro, worrying.

'There is, honey. You see, he had visitors that night. The night he ...'

'Took his life.'

Mrs Nobles nodded, as if grateful that the Northerner had managed not to spell out the details of how Sanders had been found suspended from nylon cord from his own sun deck.

'I like to keep an eye out for things around here. Three men came to his house before the Commander came home from the naval base. They went in, and maybe twenty minutes after he came home they left. I didn't give it any mind, you see ... not until now.'

Ash leaned forward. 'What did they look like? Did you get a good view?'

'Well, the two men with him were big. Tough young men.'

'With who?'

'With Mr Sultani. The electronics manufacturer.'

As she pulled out on to the blacktop from the dirt road, Ash thought: I'm going to need a gun. If Sultani had killed Sanders he was certainly capable of killing her. It never occurred to her to get in touch with the FBI, or police. Any contact and this Sultani would be off, and she would get no credit. She knew full well she was living on borrowed time, that General Moore, DIRNSA, intended to get rid of her, in order to fill her place with a blue-suiter. To prevent him from carrying this out she needed kudos. Capturing the man who had manipulated Sanders, and who was responsible for the destruction of the *Maine* would do it.

She took 25 on to route 17 to get to Amelia Island and in White Oak stopped outside a sporting goods store full of fishing rods, reels, lines, an earthy smell from a hatch where bait lived, large knives and stuffed bass on the wall, alongside stuffed deer heads. There were dinghys, outboard motors and tackle boxes. There were bows, crossbows, arrows and bolts. There were firearms.

The proprietor, a weathered individual for whom business was clearly pleasure also looked up from arranging a line of Case knives as she entered.

'Hi,' she said. 'I need a gun.'

'Why, sure you do, ma'am,' replied the old country boy. 'Ever'body needs a gun. Now what kind were you looking for?'

Ash knew nothing about guns at all.

'Something … for defence. In case of burglars.'

'Sure,' he said jovially, his creased face lighting up with approval. 'Something for around the house. Let's see, now.'

He opened the back of a glass cabinet and took out a large, shiny, blue-black revolver.

'A Smith & Wesson .357 Magnum. That's as good a revolver as you'll find.'

'Lovely,' said Ash nervously.

'Takes .38 rounds too, but .357's best.'

'It is?'

'Why sure, ma'am. With this by your side, you wake up one night and see some low-life slimeball crawling towards you you just reach over, shout "Hallelujah!" and ventilate him in the name of the Lord. He won't get up, I can tell you.'

'Fine,' Ash said, rather weakly. 'I'd better have ammunition too.'

He produced a green and yellow box.

'Fifty magnum semi-jacketed hollow-points.'

'How do you load it?'

He thumbed the catch and the cylinder swung out from the frame on its crane in a well-oiled, precise manner. He fed five shiny, silver-and-copper shells into the magazine, leaving one empty under the hammer.

'I'll take it.'

She paid some four hundred dollars and left. It was a very solid, heavy piece of machinery. She was surprised at how heavy it was.

Mrs Nobles knew Sultani because they had been introduced. She had wealthy friends who lived out on Amelia Island, who were acquainted with the electronics manufacturer, and would occasionally share a round of Tom Collinses with him at the country club. Mrs Nobles had been visiting one weekend and had been invited to join them; she had a proudly-posed photograph to commemorate the event. She collected celebrities and enjoyed boasting about them to her friends. She had given Ash a copy of the photograph, and a promise to give evidence for the FBI at the trial, should there be one. She'll dine out on this for the rest of her life thought Ash, as she passed the turnoff for 40 to the submarine base and went over the Georgia/Florida border with its souvenir shops. The next turnoff was for Amelia Island. She wondered why her mouth was dry.

Driving over the bridge the water of the intracoastal waterway was grey and chill in the fading light. She stopped at a convenience store and bought a map of the island; Mrs Nobles had taken care to acquire Sultani's address. She located his house and made her way through the streets to it. She parked the Ford a little way off, and switched out the lights. Access to any property was easy in the South she had noted, the front yards of the houses commonly ran up to the road, and were unfenced. She was aware that practically everyone in the deep south, man, woman or dog, owned some piece of lethal ordnance and kept it in their house, and supposed that this gave them confidence to make their dwellings so accessible. It wasn't so in Georgetown, she thought. She gripped her own newly-acquired weapon, concealing it behind her handbag, and slipped out into the dark. The houses on the road were large, and quite well hidden. Sultani's was masked by a screen of shrubs and trees, which provided perfect cover for her as she approached.

Two cars were parked outside, a silver Cadillac Seville and a blue Ford from Avis. Her shoes made no sound on the short, tough grass, and she was able to come right up close to the house. From the first window she peered into she could see the living room, large and open-plan, across a hallway. It was lit, and she padded softly around the perimeter of the house to see in.

The curtains were only partly drawn. Staying away from the light illuminating the lawn, she could see two men inside, seated at a table in conversation. One she recognised from the photograph as Sultani. He was of medium height, strongly built, with dark eyes and hooked nose. He radiated competence and power. He was clearly a prime-mover, even seen at a distance through glass.

The second man was aged thirty-seven, had been born in Leningrad, was a career officer in the KGB, currently working for Directorate T, the Scientific and Technical arm of that organisation. His name was Viktor Antonov, and he was one of the 330-odd Soviet personnel 'working' for the UN Secretariat in New York. Ash knew all this and more about him because her brain had near-total recall, and when she had headed up the NSA Special Collection Element team in Tehran one of their targets, successfully acquired, had been the Soviets operating in the city, one of whom had been Antonov.

She made the decision to go in, and moved around to the back of the house. Testing a wood-and-glass door under a porchway, the handle moved smoothly, oiled, as were the hinges, and she slipped inside the house. She put down her handbag on a table and gripping the heavy pistol in both hands crept forward. Peeping around a door-jamb in the hallway she could see the men sitting at the table. A dark grey-green tile was between them; Sultani was describing its qualities, it appeared to be part of a US nuclear submarine. She stepped forward through the doorway and stood with her feet apart, some fifteen feet away from them, the gun firmly pointed in their direction. Both turned sharply in alarm.

'I am a government officer,' she said loudly. 'Stay right where you are.'

Sultani's face had clouded with annoyance. He rose quickly to his feet.

'Now, see here, little lady –'

He pushed his chair to one side and advanced, coming around the table, as Antonov also got to his feet. With both hands around the chequerboarded wood grips of the gun she heaved with both forefingers at the heavy, curved metal trigger. The pull required was large. Suddenly the trigger came all the way back with a click that was drowned by the shocking blast of the gun going off. A large section of the roof above Sultani's head vanished, and pulverised plasterboard rained down around the two men like snow. The gun flew back in Ash's hands, striking her hard on the nose. Blood spattered over her face, and began to run down on to her dress.

'I said to stay right there,' she yelled, her ears singing from the explosion. Taking a firmer grip of the weapon she pulled the trigger again, there was another tremendous roar and the middle of the french windows vanished in a cacophony of destroyed wood and shattering glass.

'Jesus, lady ...' Sultani whispered. Both men were completely still, frozen where they stood. A strange recollection of having watched a television show came into Ash's mind, a terrible time waiting to know if her husband was alive or whether he had been killed in Khalif Hossein's Iran, waiting for a telephone call and allowing a banal cop show featuring two women detectives to anaesthetise her brain. They had loud voices and the one who drank had confronted the robbers while the fat one with the frightful voice had come up behind and yelled at them to get up against the wall, it came to her and she used it.

'Up against the wall,' she shrieked, and a tiny part of her noticed that she had used the New York cop's awful accent. 'Hands high and feet apart.'

The two men obeyed with alacrity.

'Make one fuckin' move and I'll blow your balls off,' she promised.

The gun was now waving about in her hands like a piece of asparagus and she doubted her ability to hit the side of the room with it, but the two men watched TV too, and were faithfully planted against the wall in proper suspect manner, and unable to see. She picked up Sultani's telephone and tapped out Kowalski's number. She was aware of feeling weak, and of a strong desire to visit the bathroom.

'Hullo, Jack. I want you to send some men. I'm on Amelia Island. I have the men who sank your ship. They're Soviets.'

The doctor in the medical and dental clinic not far from where the USS Daniel Webster Road followed the west edge of the restricted area forming the strategic weapons facility had examined Ash's nose, and pronounced that although cut and bruised, it was not broken. It would be swollen for a week or so, and she would sport two lovely black eyes where the blood had pooled in the soft tissues.

'I still feel like a boxer,' she lamented to Kowalski. 'One of the less good ones who went three rounds with Mr Tyson, or someone like that.'

'You are one brave lady,' Kowalski said admiringly. 'If slightly foolhardy. I didn't know NSA trained its personnel in the use of firearms.'

'They don't.'

Kowalski raised his eyebrows. 'So?'

'Water pistols.' said Ash. 'When I was about six.'

Kowalski shook his head.

'I had to do it. When I saw Antonov with him I realised I had to get them together, red-handed. Any hint of investigations and Sultani could have been long gone.'

'Well, the Navy is suitably, and extremely, grateful to you. I'm sure that some admiral or other will write you a very fulsome letter you can have framed if you want to. In the meantime, I'm afraid the Navy would like to ask you to do it another favour.'

'I have to shoot at someone again?'

Kowalski smiled. 'No. Just go and talk to someone.'

'Who?'

'You speak Arabic, don't you?'

'Yes, of course. I spoke Farsi as a little girl, but learned Arabic as well, as my father was a scholar. I learned English and French at the lycée.'

'We have received a garbled report that some Arab playboy is claiming he saw a jet fighter dropping bombs in the Caribbean. That's nowhere near the *Maine*'s patrol area, but we think we should check it out.'

'Of course.'

'He says the fighter was marked with stars. Red stars.'

'That makes three,' said Ash. 'Once is happenstance. Twice is coincidence. Three times is enemy action.'

MAMORA BAY, ANTIGUA

The long white motor yacht lay anchored in the crystal-clear blue water about a half-mile from the brilliant white, palm-fringed beach. In the distance wealthy tourists lounged, swam and sailed about the luxury St James' Club hotel. Ash arrived with the lunch aboard the hotel's tender.

As the Antiguan waiter brought cold-boxes up the gangway Shaikh Nasir Khan greeted Ash and seated her under a giant sunshade set up on the foredeck of the yacht. From there there was a pleasing view over the sea, and to the west, Boggy Peak rising up out of the hills. The Shaikh was in his thirties, dressed in casual Western clothes, liberally bedecked with gold and reeked of money.

'What a joy,' he said. 'When the American government called and asked if a representative might see me I never imagined a lovely young lady.'

'I was sent because I speak Arabic, but I can see you speak perfect English. Shall I leave and ask them to send someone from the FBI?'

The Shaikh beamed. 'No, no. We will speak Arabic if you wish.'

The waiter laid out a simple meal of asparagus, lobster, salad, fruit and chilled champagne in a silver bucket. Nasir Kahn personally removed the cork and poured Dom Perignon into flutes.

'It is so civilised to park the boat close by such a good hotel,' he said. 'They bring anything one wants, and one can go to the nightclub or discotheque in the evening.'

'I take it you weren't near here when you saw the fighter jet.'

'No, no,' Nasir said animatedly. 'We were cruising from Curaçao, we were in mid-sea, the *Jumping Jack* here can travel the deep seas, when we saw the aircraft in the distance. It was low, one does not expect to see aircraft circling low over the sea.'

'Can you tell me what happened?'

'I can do better than that. I can show you.'

Nasir Khan called out an order and a crewman wheeled a television and VCR on a trolley on to the deck.

'Movie photography is a hobby of mine, I have video equipment on board, when we saw the jet I thought it might be an interesting subject, there is little to watch in mid-ocean. However, when we saw what it was doing we headed away fast, I can tell you.'

He put a cassette into the machine and in a few moments the picture came to life. As a rich man he had invested only in the best equipment, and what they saw was clear and of good quality.

A muddy-green and brown aircraft was flying away

from them at an angle, its wings level, at about five hundred feet. Ash was no expert on aeroplanes, but she was able to see from the configuration that it was a military jet, a single-seat fighter of some description. Large tubular, bulbous objects, bombs or tanks hung under its wings. As they watched, one dropped away. An orange parachute retarded its fall. It splashed into the water, and the cloth remained floating behind like a stain. The jet went out of picture as the cameraman kept his vision on the area in which the object had vanished. Seconds ticked away, thirty, thirty five, and then the sea boiled.

'A bomb,' Nasir said excitedly. 'A depth-charge. I did not know what the aircraft was bombing and I did not *want* to know. I only wished to go away before it started to bomb *me*. We headed rapidly away, but as we did so the jet came by close on its way back to its target. It took no notice of us, but I was able to capture it more clearly on film. Here it is now.'

The jet came back, large in the zoom lens.

'There.' Nasir hit the freeze-frame and it hung in the middle of the screen awful, deadly. 'Red stars on its wings, a red star on its tail. A Russian jet. What was it doing there? The captain of the *Jumping Jack* knows his trade, these are international waters, there is no bombing range here.'

Ash stared at the picture of the attack aircraft. Red and white numbers stood out clear behind the air intakes. NPIC would have no trouble identifying it.

Nasir ran the film on again, and once more, hit the freeze.

'See,' he said. 'The jet was accompanied by a helicopter. Look it has some missiles or torpedoes, hanging under it.'

Ash got up and peered closely at the screen. And what was that, she mused. There was something that looked like a fly-speck in the distance. Or a twin-engined aircraft, attracted by the spectacle below.

'When did this happen?'

'January the twenty-ninth.'

Five days into the *Maine*'s cruise. Ash made a quick mental computation. The submarine could quite easily have travelled that far.

'I don't suppose you know exactly where you were when you filmed this?'

'But of course,' Nasir said in surprise. 'The *Jumping Jack* has the very latest in navigational equipment, we use the satellites.'

He got up and pulled a map off the television.

'The captain, he wrote it down for me after we were clear. Here, see.'

He pointed to a neat pencil cross in mid-sea, miles from anywhere. From the colour of the map it was relatively shallow water.

'14 degrees 28 minutes of latitude, 63 degrees 43 minutes of longitude.'

14°28′ × 63°43′

The first indication that something might be wrong came from one of the electronic warfare specialists, David 'Locker' Jones, seated with headphones on at his console in the control room. Uneasy at traversing relatively shallow water in his craft the captain, Mark Ross had placed the crew on defense station.

'Sir,' he called.

'What is it, Locker,' said Ross, walking over by him.

'I think I'm picking something up, sir,' the young sailor said, and Ross felt a stab of alarm, for Jones was manning the electronic support measures – ESM – of the boat that listened, through passive, mast-mounted sensors for the pulses of airborne radars and submariners feared helicopters and maritime patrol aircraft – MPAs – almost above all else, for they were both spies, pointing out the hiding craft to other armed vessels and aircraft, and assassins, carrying homing torpedoes themselves.

'Here, sir,' said Jones. He adjusted his controls, and very faintly through the speaker there came the thudding beat of a low-flying helicopter's blades under load. The submarine had in addition to ESM the latest in passive sonar, able to detect the downbeat of helicopter rotors on the water. It was a measure of the equipment's sophistication that it could do so, gliding 120 feet under the surface at 12 knots.

'Defense station 1,' Ross said abruptly, and men hurried to their action stations. 'Prepare for attack.'

For them to have detected the helicopter, it had to be both large and low, and for such a machine to be at such altitude and slow over the ocean, in the neighbourhood of an SSBN did not to Ross smack of coincidence.

'Any idea of type?' he murmured to Jones.

'I would guess at a MiL, sir. MiL-14, the ASW version. It's behind us on a bearing of 160 degrees.'

A sonarman on the other side of the room jerked suddenly.

'We're under attack,' he said crisply. 'One hundred yards, bearing 025 degrees.'

Ross pushed the *Maine* into a steep diving turn away from the sinking charge and everyone waited as the seconds ticked away. When it came, the explosion was heavy enough to jar their teeth, and almost immediately came the call for two more bracketing the boat. This time it was worse, shaking the entire hull and all in it, breaking bulbs.

'This is to get our attention,' Ross called calmly. 'Wait for the torpedo.'

Ross understood well that the primary problem for ASW forces in attacking a submarine was classification, the determination that a certain echo or sound really did represent a submarine. By throwing depth charges at the perceived target they stood the chance of getting it to take evasive action, accelerate, change depth and course, and

177

the opportunity to receive the doppler shift between the outgoing and returning sonar 'pings' that indicated target motion. Now they could hear the grating sounds like being lashed by a chain of active sonar. It was not of sufficiently low frequency to be emitted from a large sonar so Ross discounted a ship. The helicopter was using sonobuoys. And the depth charges? An airplane, thought Ross. They're working as a team.

'Prepare to deploy bubble targets,' ordered Ross.

'Torpedo in the water.'

Ross held an earphone up and could hear the singing of a high-speed propeller in the water, just like a sewing machine.

'Lightweight torpedo, sir. It's searching.'

Soviet 400mm lightweight electrical torpedo, thought Ross. In the 'dead time' between the fire control adjustment given to the torpedo by the operator aboard the helicopter and its arrival at the estimated position of the submarine the submarine had moved, and it had to search. Its entry into the water gave the commander of the submarine 'warning time', time in which to take evasive measures. Ross was confident of his ability to outwit the torpedo. Torpedoes, like missiles, were only intelligent in a very narrow area. It was certainly possible to fool them into thinking something else was the target they sought.

'Deploy bubble targets,' he ordered, and within seconds the canisters were being ejected from the dispensers. Submarine bubble targets dated from the *Pilenwerfers* of the Second World War, and if they had got more sophisticated, they were still most effective at sending disinformation to the small brain of a torpedo that was using active sonar. When the chemical in the canisters came into contact with sea water they fizzed like giant alka-seltzers, providing false echoes for the seeking sonar that the torpedo switched on once it had reached the estimated position of the submarine. As they glided away from the bubble targets Ross could hear the noise of the torpedo screw overlain by its short-range 'pinging'.

'Take her down,' he said. 'We're going to the bottom.'

It was the classic defence measure for a submarine in shallow water, where the debris of the ocean floor masked its presence.

'Prepare to deploy a noisemaker.'

The great nuclear craft settled gently and quietly on the ocean floor, some one hundred and sixty feet down. Ross could hear the noise of the torpedo dying away as it searched aimlessly, attacking the bubble targets until it ran out of power.'

'Deploy the noisemaker,' he said.

The noisemaker was a decoy. Although small, it was smart. The anechoic or echo deadening covering of the *Maine* reduced the apparent size that it represented to active sonars, and thus made the use of the decoy more effective. The noisemaker could do a number of things. It emitted the same sound as the *Maine*. It was able to record incoming sonar pings and return them in amplified form to make itself appear the size of its mother craft, or to give itself the appearance of motion, via the Doppler effect. It could run, change direction and hang quietly in the water, just like a real submarine evading detection and attack.

The noisemaker left the countermeasures tube and Ross, listening through his headphones could hear it heading away from the submarine. Shortly afterwards they heard the blast of depth charges once more in the distance, and then the singing of a second torpedo.

Everyone smiled broadly in silence. It was the submariners' equivalent of the home crowd's reaction to a ninety yard touchdown in the last seconds of a hung game. Now they just had to sit tight, and wait, just like submariners had always waited, for the ASW forces to convince themselves that they had really been successful, and go home.

The sensors aboard the *Maine* could do a lot of things, but they could not detect the array of passive devices, acoustic and magnetic, that dotted the bottom of the ocean floor.

The information that they collected they sent by fibre-optic cable up to buoys, which transmitted it to the ASW forces above. The *Maine* had entered a giant, laid trap. She was in a killing-ground.

The MiL followed up the attack by the MiG-27 with depth bombs on the noisemaker with its own torpedo attack. With this done, the pilot swung back towards the position of the concealed submarine. The sensors on the bottom had transmitted the information to the helicopter, and at his station behind the cockpit the offensive systems operator programmed the next 400mm torpedo. Slowing down low over the water, the Mil dipped it into the ocean and released. Armed and active, but with its motor not yet switched on, and operating on the fire control information given to it by the offensive systems operator the torpedo swam downwards. When its small brain told it that it was close to the target it switched on its active sonar. There, illuminated as if in a searchlight beam was the submarine. The torpedo 'profiled' the target to identify the control room, and accelerating to 45 knots performed its pre-programmed last-second manoeuvre to bring it on a course at 90 degrees to the submarine hull.

In the last seconds of his life, with the rising whine of the approaching torpedo filling his ears, immobile, unable to run, bubble makers rising ineffectually from the countermeasures dispenser, ignored by the locked-on weapon, Ross realised that he had been tricked, that all had been a play for his benefit, to get him to rest his craft on the ocean floor.

The torpedo slammed into the hull, and exploded.

When those responsible for its death finally left the wreck, having completed what they came to do, with its parts spread about over the ocean floor, the hulk became the home of fishes and of crustaceans, its state-of-the-art anechoic tiling the resting ground of algae and of molluscs. Finally another of its kind swam into view, small, unarmed, its slight crew observers, not fighters. It hung in the water, surveying the tomb through its television cameras and ports. It was the *Squab*.

'Jesus and Mary,' Kowalski whispered in horror, surveying the gaping holes in the top of the hull, the empty spaces below. 'They've taken the missiles out.'

NSA HEADQUARTERS

'Welcome home,' said MacDonald. 'And well done.'

'Thank you,' said Ash.

The deputy-director looked at Ash's face, where the swelling of her nose was subsiding, and the black eyes had turned yellow.

'And at what stage of the proceedings did all this happen?' he asked, so Ash described her citizen's arrest of Sultani and Antonov.

'My ... and where is the piece of artillery now?'

'I left it with Jack Kowalski in Georgia. Their gun laws are somewhat more liberal than ours. I might get a licence for it, bring it up here as a memento.'

'Hell,' MacDonald chuckled. 'Keep it unregistered, and write a column for the *Washington Post*. That or chrome-plate it and hang it on your wall. Old iron-drawers next door might like that. We could tell him you eat the military alive for breakfast, along with Soviet agents.'

'How did he take my re-instatement?' Ash smiled.

'He didn't object. You gained his respect. I think he felt in his hawkish way that if you as a woman and civilian couldn't have flown Route Package VIA to Hanoi then taking on desperate Soviet agents was a fair substitute.'

'Where is Sultani now?'

'The Navy and the Air Force got together, and they're conducting joint interrogation, with the Air Force looking after him. Coogan wanted it that way.'

'What about the CIA or FBI?'

'Civilian.' said MacDonald.

'Does the military star shine bright in our sky?'

'It does. The activities of Sultani have given them a stick to beat Cord with. You did better than you knew. Sultani was the Soviet Illegal Resident.'

Ash sat quiet for a moment.

'It makes sense,' she agreed. 'He did a marvellous job of embedding himself into society. He became the archetypal American success story. The immigrant who does well, embraces all the capitalist virtues. With his electronics company and his jet he was well placed to move about the country openly pursuing his business interests. I suppose he got an enormous amount of high-technology, and shipped it out.'

'He seems to have been responsible for supplying technology from the titanium-welding equipment and computers for the *Alfa*-class submarine to half the SDI equipment they have at their great research establishment in Smolensk.'

'The little I saw of him he seemed to be the right type. Powerful, motivated, very strong-willed.'

'He is. You have to be,' agreed MacDonald. 'When you look at the history of the Soviet Illegal residents here; the ones we caught were all extraordinary men. They have to be, the extraordinary is demanded of them all the time. Each one must enter and live here, under a fictitious identity, eternally dissembling and deceiving, hiding his true self, his real thoughts, making contacts and friendships always with the intent to manipulate and exploit. He must, like Sultani, become successful in his own right, which takes great effort, while simultaneously working just as hard at his secret job. He is cut off from his own language, culture and relatives, he has to adapt to our very attractive way of life without succumbing to the appeal of it as other immigrants do. Quite the opposite, he has to remain totally committed to its very destruction.'

MacDonald sat musing for a few moments. The world

of human spies and agents was the one he had been brought up with, before the advent and victory of machines and technical intelligence. Because it concerned people, it was a world that exerted continuing fascination.

'Human agents of this kind are still necessary. But to get the right man ... the task inevitably subjects him to unremitting stress and anxiety, and yet at all times and in all situations he has to retain emotional and mental stability over *years*. He can only rely upon himself, and his inner faith. He must be very intelligent, possessed of great physical stamina, have an ability to deal with people from all backgrounds and social levels, must have courage, determination, initiative and imagination. And if all that is not enough, he must have an invincible loyalty to the Soviet Communist cause, must be prepared to lay down his life for it if necessary. Men like that are very rare. The last we caught, Rudi Hermann was such a one. That was nearly twenty years ago, the Soviets found him in the early 1950s. Now this Sultani is another.'

'Is he ...' mused Ash. She sounded worried. 'Is he?'

'We know he is,' said MacDonald.

'I know ... there is such proof. But the *Maine*'s Trident II missiles were removed, and my thesis that the Iranians were planning to acquire nuclear warheads has not gone away.'

'You aren't saying the Iranians managed such an operation?'

'*Why not*? It fits the facts.'

'Except Sultani is a Soviet agent.'

'*One brought up in Iran*. And who today believes in communism in the manner you describe, to have such burning belief to be able to be the Illegal Resident. Communism is a secular faith and as such has burned out. Who believes in it? A handful of cranks on the fringes of European politics and universities. No real prime-movers like Sultani.'

'You mustn't under-estimate the appeal of communism,' MacDonald admonished. 'It's a very powerful driving force.'

'Was ... was,' Ash said distractedly. 'You Americans have been so frightened of the communists for so long you can't realise the enemy's dying. Cord's right, all you have to do is hang on and the Soviet military threat will over-reach itself. The ideological threat has gone. Gone, gone gone.'

She sat thinking.

'I want to talk to Sultani,' she said, after a while. 'Can it be arranged?'

'Sure,' said MacDonald. 'You know, when Moore had you investigated, and he turned up what he called "extra-curricular activities", I didn't know you knew so many of the Iranian expatriates.'

'It helps to keep in touch,' Ash said blandly, 'in my job.'

'Yes ...' mused MacDonald. 'Why *did* you go back to Iran with your husband after the Grand Ayatollah died?'

'It was my duty. Women's liberation has not advanced so far among Persian women as over here, doctor. When my husband required me with him, I had to obey.'

'I wish you'd talk to my wife about that,' chuckled MacDonald. 'But that's not one of your best lines, Ash. I wouldn't use it if you have to see Moore again. I read your files after he suspended you. There were some things there I'd forgotten. You were President of the Oxford Union when you were at University in England. Like another, beautiful young woman of powerful Islamic parents?'

'Benazir Bhutto,' said Ash. 'She was at LMH a year or two before me.'

'Did you ever meet Aung San Suu Kyi when you were there?'

'The Burmese politician? No, I think she was before my time.'

'The Burmese *lady* politician. The Pakistani *lady* politician. Is our Ashraf a nascent Persian lady politician? You seem to know all the right people.'

'Of course I know those sorts of people. My father was an influential political figure. They all remember his little girl.'

184

'Muslim and Buddhist cultures offer special reverence to the daughters and widows of murdered popular political figures, isn't that right?'

'Yes, that's so.'

'General Zia hanged Benazir's father, the former ruler of Pakistan. Aung San, Suu Kyi's father, was gunned down on the eve of Burmese independence by Ne Win, who went on to take personal power himself. Your father was murdered in the turmoil of Khomeini's seizure of power.'

'Our common misfortunes do not mean I have any political ambitions, Dr MacDonald.'

'We're in a business that looks for patterns.'

'That's right. Do I get to see Sultani?'

'Yes. I'll get you to see him.'

'My mother used to tell me that Satan had many faces, when I was a little girl. If he abandoned one face, you had to look out for him in another. If he has abandoned communism, and left it an empty shell, where has he gone now?'

PATUXENT RIVER, MARYLAND

The United States Air Force had a budget bigger than the GNP of most third-world nations and owned more property than all the heads of the Organisation of African Unity put together; it made the task of squirreling away a Soviet agent for interrogation that much easier. Coogan had the use of a pretty little manor house overlooking the Patuxent river, under an hour's drive from the capital, it was sometimes used to entertain visiting colleagues or dignitaries, and was suitably equipped and guarded. He had Hank Sultani installed there.

Sultani was an important man, Coogan acknowledged the fact by dealing with him personally.

'It sure was a mine of information you had back there at your house,' he said jovially. 'We're still going through it.'

'It is an unfortunate necessity that records have to be kept, even in espionage,' Sultani agreed.

'I would say,' Coogan observed, with slightly more of an edge to his voice, 'that purely on the charges of industrial espionage that we can bring, that the judge would give you forty years without remission. Public opinion is somewhat hot on foreign nations stealing the fruits of American enterprise and know-how these days.'

'I am sure you are correct.'

'That is not bringing into account the charge of murdering Commander Sanders.'

'You could not prove that I had anything to do with killing him.'

'Don't you believe it,' Coogan assured him. 'The Air Force has its own pathologists, just as does the Navy, I am damned sure we can find evidence linking you to his death if we so choose.'

Sultani remained silent.

'On *that* charge you'll get life, or, if we prefer, you'll go to death row. The death penalty is in operation here.'

Sultani still said nothing.

'A little different from the life you've been leading here. It ain't so bad in the land of the free, is it? You did all right. Private jet, successful business, the best food and drink in the world, Mercedes car, big house and pretty college gals from Athens to play with in your jacuzzi. Pretty good, hey?'

'It has been most pleasant,' Sultani agreed.

'Ain't got any of it in the Soviet Union,' Coogan pointed out. 'Ain't even got deodorant over there. Ain't nothing going to change either, you get out in forty years time and we fly you home it'll be the same or worse. Ain't no one going to be interested in some relic of the Cold War. They stick you in some old folk's home in Vladivostock, you won't survive the first winter, not on beet soup.'

Coogan sat back, and the two men looked at each other.

'So what's it going to be? Do you want to stay here with a new name, new address, same good life, same pretty gals, or do you want the other?'

Sultani got up, and looked out of the window at the river sparkling in the distance. It was a beautiful day. All he had to do was play his cards right. 'Bring me some paper, and a pen,' he said. 'I know how it is done. I will write down a short history of my life, and we can go from there. It will take a while, to tell what I know.'

They had given him an upstairs room, large, with a double bed, a bathroom en-suite, and a reproduction roll-top desk. He had his own drip-filter coffee-maker. He poured himself a cup and sat down to write.

'I am Hosain Sultani, although I called myself Hank once I came to live in Georgia. My father was called Mohammed. My story must begin with my father because it is through him that I am what I am today, that I have come to be here, and have done the things I have.

'My father became a communist as a young man, a student at Tehran university. The teachings of Marx, Engels, Lenin and Stalin he absorbed like food; they helped him to believe, to have faith in the ultimate victory of the proletariat over their oppressors. When the British and Russians occupied Iran in the Second World War, my father went to the north, where because of his background he proved to be of great worth to the Russians. When the Russians brought freedom to the people there by setting up the People's Republic of Azerbaijan and the Kurdish People's Republic he worked tirelessly with their Soviet mentors, educating them to the true faith of Marxism.

'It was a great personal blow to my father when the two northern republics of the people were overthrown by the machinations of the imperialist powers only the next year; rather than live among the wreckage of his dreams, my father went across the border, and to Moscow, to learn how to renew the struggle. The sight of Moscow after the war, the capital of world communism came as a shock, long lines of poorly-dressed people queuing for hours before near-empty shops, the buildings in bad repair, patients leaving clinics with bandages seeping blood – it could have been a mediaeval city, not the future of the world. The sight of it made my father realise the sacrifices the Russian people had made in winning the war against the Nazi threat, and it made him redouble his efforts to help them defeat all the other forces in the world ranged against them.

'My father was a very talented man, and this was recognised by his Russian hosts. He was taken on and educated in many ways. At his training centre he met another Iranian, a beautiful, dedicated communist girl, Fakhr. They were soon married. The Russians who were training them decided that they were ideally suited to return to Iran to continue the struggle there. They were given new identities, and the Russians prepared excellent legends for them to learn about their new selves. The recent war had made it easy for agents to be inserted among the refugees and migrants, the dispossessed seeking to settle down again.

'So it was. My parents returned to Iran. They had funds, and my father was to set up as a businessman – a manufacturer of electrical goods. It was a far-sighted step, in that we were well-placed in the end to move in with the new industries of electronics. While I was growing up my father, based in Shiraz, built up his business, while simultaneously working for the good of the Cause. He acquired status, poise and the ability to move in the upper echelons of Iranian society, all qualities of inestimable worth as the Shah began his 'White Revolution' to modernise his mediaeval country within his own lifetime. My father took the opportunity to increase his business – and incidentally his power and influence – while increasing his contacts, *and* his power and influence in the other sphere in which he operated, the political. I, as a child was brought up from the beginning to be familiar with his ambivalence, to be able to appear one thing, but beneath, be another. It is second-nature to me, it is my way of life.

'My father's abilities were such that he became Illegal Resident within Iran. As I was in my teens, he realised that I, too, was possessed of considerable talents – I did well at school, always at the top of the class, I had a gift for languages and he had trained me himself as a Marxist. He suggested that I be groomed for a similar role, but perhaps in the USA, where on the suggestion of our Russian allies we had begun a small electronics firm – which was to blossom as Sultan Electronics.

'The Shah's *massachuseti* – those foreign-educated – often at MIT from which their name was derived – planners did their work better than they knew. In their zeal for change they succeeded in alienating the Shah from his true source of support, the conservative peasantry. In attacking tribal diversity, local patriarchs, family cohesion, provincial accents and tongues, regional dress and in fact anything that offered alternative centres of influence to the state, the Shah was preparing a revolution that would turn against himself. That it was the radical clerics under Khomeini who benefited, and not the People, led by the vanguard fighters like my father is outside the scope of this short character-history.

'My father remained in Iran, and was executed in the 1982 purge of the pro-Soviet Tudeh party. In the pressures of revolution and war, his true loyalties and identity had become revealed. He died a true hero of the October Revolution. I, however, had been in the USA for a while, building up Sultan electronics.

'The outlines of my career here are known to you. My primary role was in the gathering of the very latest technology for the Soviet Union, and in this task I can claim to have been very successful. As I was able to travel throughout the USA in my company jet, and legitimately go anywhere on business for my company I was ideally suited to take over responsibilities such as readiness to maintain control and communication between the networks within the USA and Center in Moscow, should the Soviet legal Residency be closed – the duties of the Illegal Resident.

'There is much that you will want to ask me, many names for you to give to the FBI. This short history will serve as a place to begin.'

Hank Sultani put down his pen, and got up from the desk. It was easy to write, his legend was easy to recall, for nearly all of it was true. He had Coogan hooked, it was just time to reel him in. Coogan wanted to hear what he had to tell him, and it would nearly all be absolute truth. And Coogan did not know the questions to ask, to uncover what was not.

PATUXENT RIVER, MARYLAND

'Good morning,' said Ash.

Hank Sultani rose from the table set in the garden of the manor house, where he had eaten breakfast. It was a fine morning, the remains of rolls, butter, jam, fruit juice and coffee were on the dishes set on the cloths. Ash had spent half an hour watching him from the house through binoculars.

'Good morning,' he said courteously. 'It is the young lady who arrested me. At the time I did not realise how pretty you are. You are far more attractive when not seen behind a very large gun.'

'Why, thank you.'

'Would you care for some coffee? It is still hot.'

'I'd love some.'

She sat down at the table and Sultani poured coffee.

'I thought I'd drop by, see how you were getting on.'

Sultani inclined his head. 'I am being very well treated, thank you. General Coogan is taking care of his valuable property,' he said wryly. 'Tell me, then, what assistance can I render the FBI?'

I won't tell him I'm NSA, she thought. That would put

him on his guard.

'It's not so much official business as personal curiosity,' she said blandly. 'I read the personal history you wrote. I know these military men and economic warfare experts are going over everything with you – what you've been doing since you came to the USA and started Sultan Electronics. I was more interested in your earlier days – when you were in Iran.'

Sultani raised his eyebrows politely. 'Oh?'

'You were brought up in Iran – the Iran of the Shah.'

'Yes.'

'So was I,' she said, and smiled pleasantly. Way back in his eyes she felt she saw a gleam of alarm.

'Well, now ain't that something,' he said, reverting into his good ol' boy cover, and she thought to herself: he's got something to hide. I'm right.

'I was brought up in Tehran, but left before you did – before Khomeini's overthrow of the Shah. Although you travelled here to college, didn't you?'

'Yes. They were preparing me for my role here as a businessman.'

'I went to Oxford myself. Have you ever been there?'

'No.'

'Lovely place. Wonderful.'

She sipped coffee. 'I remember your father, you know.'

'You do?' he said in surprise.

'Only by name. Our Iran was quite a small world, wasn't it, if you were near the top. My father was a learned man, he knew very many people.

'Your father has had a great effect on you. Isn't that what you say in your history? One's parents do. I was a very fortunate little girl, I was much loved and protected, far more than I ever knew. My mother was loving while being firm, she was practical, she ran our house and managed to sustain the way of life of a *grand seigneur*; we kept open house and provided unstinted hospitality, and all on a professor's salary. My father was wise, warm and affectionate, he was like a god, someone who one could always count upon and rely upon.

'And would you believe I gave it all up! I was surrounded by so much love it never occurred to me that the world might be cold outside and that I might never find such warmth again. It was expected of me that I would be like other Persian women, marry young and have children, perform my mother's role, so, so secure was I that I upped and went, so confident, so filled with arrogance in my own intellectual abilities, so sure I could go back to that world whenever I chose, and I could not have been more wrong. "That is the land of lost content, I see it shining plain, the happy highways where I went and cannot come again."

'The air that kills that blew into my heart back then was rebellion, wasn't it? Like a lot of children I thought to myself, my parents think only this of me, I shall be different. And I did it from a very loving background. Your background was different of course. Your father seems to have been a very strict, intellectually rigorous man. I imagine that you too, would have rebelled against that.'

Sultani appeared to give it some thought. 'No,' he said. 'I cannot say I did. I have been a committed Marxist for as long as I can remember. I was grateful to my father for showing me the true way.'

'If your belief is so strong, why are you co-operating?'

Sultani shrugged. 'I have been captured. My usefulness to the Soviet Union is at an end. General Coogan has promised that unless I co-operate I will at the least spend the majority of the rest of my life in some very nasty jail, or possibly be executed. I believe the General. He is a fighting soldier, a man who keeps his promises, and keeps his threats. At this point it makes no sense to hold out. Is that not the maxim they teach all intelligence agents in case they are caught? "When all else fails, tell everything".'

'But that's pragmatism. That is being reasonable, and seeing sense. Sense and reason are not qualities that Marxists have been noted for.'

There was some ice in Sultani's jovial southern smile. 'Clearly my faith is not as strong as I had thought. But whose is? Did not Jesus Christ himself on the cross ask for his suffering to be taken from him?'

'Religion, yes,' murmured Ash. I'm going to have to do it now, she thought. Sultani is too quick, if I give him much more time he's going to see what I'm up to. I will only know if I can take him by surprise.

'I was looking out from the house while you were waiting for your breakfast,' she said. 'The way you were sitting, you seemed very calm, serene. As if you were meditating.'

'But I was,' Sultani said immediately. 'My life has been one of great strain, I have sought, and have found, relief in a form of meditation. A type of yoga.'

'Yoga. Then you must have a mantra.'

'Yes,' he said, and the word hung still in the air.

'*lā ilāha illa-llāh*,' she said. 'There is no god but God. The first *rukn*, the first pillar of Islam. Is that not your mantra?'

Sultani had gone white, and his pupils narrowed for a few moments almost to pinpricks. He regained control of himself, and when he spoke his voice was level.

'Women,' he said, musingly. 'Why women? No, that is not my mantra. Religion may be the opium of the people, but I am not one of them, I remain a Marxist.'

Coming from the house Ash could see Colonel Frost, the air force intelligence officer in charge of interrogating Sultani. She pushed back her chair, and got up.

'I see your work is about to begin,' she said cheerfully. 'I shall have to leave you and get on with mine.'

Sultani was once again in complete command of himself. I won't get him again, she thought. But I saw it, I know, I was right.

'It is a pity you cannot stay,' he said courteously, rising too. 'Colonel Frost is nowhere near as pleasing to look upon as you, and demands incessantly that we discuss the past.'

Ash walked away across the lawn, pausing to speak with Frost. Slim, pretty in her light frock she was an attractive sight. As Sultani stood patiently by his breakfast table, watching her, in his eye was the expression of a farmer, observing a predator, sharp of tooth and claw, approaching his herd, and reaching quietly, purposefully for his gun.

NSA HEADQUARTERS

Ash watched with certain amazement as MacDonald swept his office for electronic listening devices. When he was through she raised her eyebrows questioningly.

'Bugs? Soviets?'

MacDonald shook his head and pointed to the wall. 'DIRNSA,' he said. 'The military are up and charging. Possession of Sultani is proving a trump card.'

He put the equipment back down on his desk.

'I used to have to do this when I was in the field, I never thought I'd have to do it here.' He smiled wryly. 'Carried a gun sometimes, too. The way things are going I'd better draw one from stores. So how did your meeting with Sultani go?'

'Sultani is a dedicated Shi'ia Muslim,' she said flatly.

There was silence for a few moments, then MacDonald waved at the electronics on his desk.

'That's why I have to be certain we're not being listened to. That's all Moore would need to have you removed. He is convinced that you have become obsessed with Khalif Hossein and the Shi'ites. It does happen to intelligence professionals. It's not unknown. If I say a word in your defence at this point I can go take up Harvard's offer of a chair in modern political science sooner than I had planned. However. If you say he is a Muslim you must have solid grounds for doing so.'

'I have no hard SIGINT or TECHINT of any kind. Nothing but my own judgement. But you must remember that I know them because I was one of them. Here I am in America. I do not look how people here think of as someone from the Middle East. I have my mother's looks, she was from Shiraz, where women are famed for their beauty and intoxicating accent. Yet I was brought up as a little Muslim girl, in the house of my father, who was *Mujtahid*, a very high ranking mullah, a very learned theologian.'

MacDonald glanced at the carved agate prayer-ring that decorated her right hand.

'And are you still a Muslim?'

'I believe, as all people should believe, that there is but one God, and all else is quibbling over trifles. Unfortunately it is the trifles that have caused so much misery in the world and are about to again, if what I believe will happen does happen.'

She too glanced at her hand. 'The ring was my mother's, she gave it to me the very last time I saw her. I wear it in memory of another better time.'

'Sultani did not fit the mould,' she said, reverting to the theme of the discussion. 'He has in abundance all those qualities we talked about before, all those characteristics necessary for a man to function successfully as an in-depth double-agent. I fully understand why General Coogan is convinced that he is what he appears to be – a dedicated Marxist, devoted to the overthrow of the West and the triumph of godless communism. This is an article of faith for Coogan, and he cannot think otherwise.'

'But Sultani *was*, without question of doubt the Soviets' Illegal Resident. It is fact that he was responsible for industrial espionage on a gigantic scale. Almost single-handed he equipped the Soviets' SDI complex outside Sverdlovsk. He was captured – by you – in the company of Major Antonov of the KGB. It is impossible to say that he was not working for the Soviet Union, because he was.'

'I know that. My thesis is that Sultani is what he says he

is, but with a twist. Nearly everything he says is true. It has to be, because it has had, and does have to check out under examination by both his KGB controllers and ourselves. He is as he says he is, a man trained from birth to be able to live two lives. A man trained in espionage. But his will, his belief is too strong. I cannot comprehend him being a second-generation Marxist with such strength of will. All his characteristics are those of the convert. If this was 1925, or 1935, I could buy it, for men were converted to communism then. Not now. Islam has revived, seeks out for men's souls. It caught Sultani, it has him today. I hit him with it when I went to see him, I caught him by surprise, and I got the physiological responses that gave me confirmation. He recovered in seconds, and is now on his guard, but I caught him.'

'He has told Colonel Frost that he does not wish to be bothered with you again, that if he is to talk it must be with seasoned intelligence professionals, not amateur female detectives.'

'That's wonderful,' said Ash. 'That's more proof.'

'The Air Force is delighted, of course,' MacDonald said dryly. 'It strengthens their hand.'

'He's a smart operator. My thesis is that Sultani rebelled against the rigidity of his father's Marxist views, probably in his late teens, when children are very susceptible to the acquisition of new and burningly important ideology. All the best fanatics begin young. Because of his upbringing, Sultani would have had to acquire something equally rigid in outlook, but totally different in content, and Khalif Hossein's Shi'ia Islam fits the bill perfectly. Communism, a secular religion is a poor substitute for genuine mysticism. Both are proselytising orders, but communism a fading ember, Islam banked coals with new fuel provided. And he was in the right place at the right time. My thesis is that Sultani is, indeed a double-agent, but the people he is betraying are not us, but supposedly his masters, the Soviets. His real loyalty is to Islam.'

They paused, and then Ash picked up the thrust of her

argument.

'It makes far more sense of the facts. At the moment those who know believe that the attack and gutting of the *Maine* was planned and committed by the Soviets with the intention of testing the will of president Cord. But haven't they done that already by their arms build-up in Central America? Wasn't Central America supposed to be our "front yard"? Isn't that provocation enough? And Cord *hasn't* reacted, he's staying with his grand game-plan of allowing the Soviets to over-extend themselves. Fatally, he hopes. In these circumstances, *the attack on Maine is too much*. The Soviets have already ascertained that Cord is going to give them about as much rope as they want. Gutting the *Maine* only gives hard-liners like Coogan an axe to hit them with.

'But if it was Hossein's Iranians it makes sense. It follows from the massacre of the innocents at Qom, which effectively sealed off the country, and made it very difficult for us to insert anything like Special Collection Elements to eavesdrop and ascertain what is going on. It makes sense of the missing nuclear technicians and scientists. They aren't there to get a nuclear-weapons programme on line, *they're there to restore the stolen Trident missiles to working order.*'

'Are they up to it? Isn't that the question. To actually sink an SSBN, and in the right place, to be able to remove the missiles implies organisational skills of a very high order. Do the Iranians have them?'

'You mustn't think of them as a bunch of rag-heads. Don't be taken in by Hossein's *rowzeh-khan* rabble-rousing "mad mullah" act. It's for our benefit. The best Iranian soldiers are well trained, very highly motivated, very skilled. Don't forget, the war has not been over that long. The Iranians are in practice. They have fighter pilots who are very good indeed. The crack troops of the IRGC are top rate. If you are talking about assassins, then Niaravan in Manzarieh Park, just outside Tehran turns out small numbers of very highly trained, very dedicated

197

men and women ready to kill and die for Allah, in the name of the Khalif.'

'Are they all hard-line Muslims of the Khalif's kind?'

'The assassins, yes. I would say most of the others, no. They are not party to his plans, but are patriots. They would do their best for their country, not for Khalif Hossein. But their best might be very good indeed.'

MacDonald nodded. 'Very well then. At the moment, you have no evidence to support your thesis. If you advance it you will be accused of the analyst's ultimate crime, massaging the facts to fit a theory.'

He spread his hands wide. 'We have in this country a reconnaissance and surveillance intelligence capability that is so expensive no one is able to tell to within a few hundred billion just how much it has cost. The only problem with it is that it produces so much raw intelligence. Our own computers in the basement have to be programmed to pick out key words when they examine the SIGINT. It's how we filter things, a net for catching the fish we want. So much more goes unseen, because we haven't looked for it. If Khalif Hossein *was* responsible for the attack on the *Maine* then somewhere, we have the evidence. Somewhere there. The raw "take" is the haystack, Khalif Hossein's involvement the needle.'

MacDonald went over to the window, and stood looking out. His hand pushed the globe around on its axis.

'That's all you have to do, Mrs Amran,' he said quietly. 'Find the needle.'

NATIONAL PHOTOGRAPHIC INTERPRETATION CENTER, WASHINGTON

Ash began by going into town, to NPIC, known as En-Pick, where primary analysis of reconnaissance imagery took place. Federal Building 213 stood on the corner of M and First streets close by the Old Washington Navy Yard on the banks of the Anacostia River. It was a seedy area unlikely to attract any visitor from out of town, which was why it had been chosen. The building itself looked like a big, bricked-in, beige, government warehouse. The only indications that it was otherwise were the barbed-wire-topped Cyclone fence that surrounded it and the gigantic air-conditioners, almost eighty feet long, and nearly as high as the building, on the side. These huge coolers were necessary to cool the supercomputers inside which scanned the torrent of incoming imagery twenty-four hours a day. They stored the billions of bits of information that went into the data base to be used for comparison against fresh intelligence. Without the capacity and capability of the giant computers and their enormous data banks, the flood of digital imagery which had issued from the first KH-11 satellite in January 1977 would have been totally unmanageable. That flood had never ceased from that day on, only increased in volume. There were few customers on the face of the globe in the market for such monster computers as the CRAY series, but NSA was one, and NPIC another.

The computers were taught to compare new imagery with old, ignoring what had not changed, and calling the interpreter's attention to that which had. Fed recognition data from a truly enormous strategic list of objects ranging from uranium ore through railroad spurs for mobile SS-21 missiles to the type of smoke leaving a factory stack, the computer could not only alert its interpreter, often a highly specialised engineer with years in his or her own trade, to the presence of SLBMs (submarine-launched-ballistic-missiles) coming off a production line, it was capable of analysing multispectrally the smoke coming out of the stack from the furnace and know what was being burned inside. A rise in the production of titanium could forecast the building of super-strong hulls for a deeper-diving submarine, production of ammonium perchlorate indicate that fuel was being prepared for the Soviet Union's own orbiter.

The photo interpreters had to have, like Ash herself, minds capable of making assumptions based on association and orders of probability. It was rarely easy, deducing change and its significance was based on multiple relationships occasionally obvious, and more usually highly complex. Fortunately for the interpreter, analysing imagery and predicting the consequence of what it showed was aided by the fact that all command organisations followed sets of very defined, carefully established procedures. It had been so since the time of Alexander the Great and before. Not to do so was to invite chaos, which in turn could lead to being on the receiving end of the Battle of Cannae. The Cuban missile crisis of 1962 had begun the moment Colonel John R. Wright Jr. looked at photographs taken by a U-2 over San Cristobal in early September. He saw that Soviet-built SA-2 anti-aircraft missiles were being set up there in the shape of trapezoids. Such missiles set up in that matter were used for only one thing, to protect long-range ballistic missiles.

Analysing imagery had come a very long way since those days, with the assistance of the giant computers. There was one area where the computers still required a lot of human input, and that was with people. It was difficult for the computer to recognise someone. Unfortunately, it was sometimes very important to do so. Who was doing what with which to whom could matter. For this task NPIC had people who were experts on people. The Iranian section to which Ash went and was a frequent visitor employed a woman like herself, an expatriate, an exile following the fall of the Shah, and rise of Khomeini. She had been the wife of one of the King of Kings' generals. He had sent her out of the country as the turbulence increased, promising to follow. His loyalty to his monarch had led him to stay too long, and to his death by firing squad on the roof of the makeshift courthouse of the Refah school. His widow was a woman with encyclopaedic recognition of the top layer of Iranian society, from mullah to arms manufacturer. Possessed of an absolute loathing for the clerics who had taken over her country she was pleased to fill her days working at NPIC, driving into the seedy neighbourhood from her smart house in the development in the old Nelson Rockefeller estate off Foxhall Road in northwest Washington.

The two women got on well. Although in her land of exile she was by far Ash's inferior in the intelligence world, Ash continued to treat her with the respect she might have been accorded, had they been in Iran, and she still a high-society woman, intimate of royalty, wife of one of its generals.

'Mrs Madani,' Ash said, after they had exchanged pleasantries. 'This man.'

She produced the small sheaf that was all the historical photographs they had of Hank Sultani. Mrs Madani studied them.

'His name?' she asked.

'Sultani. Hosain Sultani.'

The older woman looked at him with an eagle eye, riffling through the card index of her mind.

'He must be the son of the manufacturer. The one who was executed. Mohammad.'

'That is he.'

She nodded, pleased at her accuracy.

'He came to no good,' she said with satisfaction. 'If you are interested in the boy he must be of the same mould.'

'This is him now,' Ash said. 'And here, the earliest we have, when he was twenty-five. But I am looking for him within Iran, between seven and four years before that.'

'A spread of three years, within all Iran. I do not imagine we have more than ten or fifteen million photographs covering that period,' she said dryly. 'Is it possible that you can narrow the field a little for me?'

'I am looking for him in the company of Khalif Hossein, who was back then simply Shaikh Hossein at the beginning of the period, or Hojat-al-Islam Hossein at the end. Him, or any of his circle of advisers of the period.'

'The *Mufsed fel-Ardh* himself,' she said with venom. 'This fouler of the earth is involved?'

'Yes.'

'It is important, that you find this Sultani, so many years ago?'

'Very,' said Ash. 'It could bring harm to Hossein if I do.'

She was armed with a priority request from MacDonald, but did not wish to insult the old aristocrat by using it.

'Will you find him for me?'

'I shall not rest. It will be as the raising of stones, to see what lurks in the slime beneath,' she said with satisfaction. 'But all the more pleasurable to know that once found, soon crushed. Leave it with me, my dear.'

With her search for a young Sultani under way, Ash moved on to the hardware. She went to see Jim Dalgetti, a middle-aged man who had spent most of his working life in the cargo business. Marrying for the second time he had realised the importance of being able to spend time with his wife and new young family, and had looked for work in the neighbourhood of Washington, his wife's home town. Going through the Help Wanted ads he spotted one for "experts in the field of cargo/shipping/freight, to assess

Soviet, Warsaw Pact, PRC (People's Republic of China) and other foreign nations' efforts in these fields.' Starting salaries ranged from $28,385 to $58,986 and the work was in Washington. At NPIC. Dalgetti applied, was accepted at a rate of pay high up the scale and after some training in his new business found that he was what was known as a 'crate-ologist'. The art of crate-ology was a unique method of determining the content of the large crates seen by KH-series satellites on Soviet railroad cars, or on board the decks of freighters, seen being loaded into military jet transports or awaiting shipment on ramp areas or quaysides. A crate-ologist soon acquired an almost mystical feel for the big boxes, but once he or she had factored in information regarding a ship's embarkation point, or used radio transmissions from a jet transport to acquire its flight plan, put in military production schedules, economic calculations regarding the growth or otherwise within the country, and within particular branches of industry, added information gleaned from NSA regarding personnel movements, promotions, hirings and firings, then the contents of almost any box could be deduced.

Dalgetti was a large, cheerful man with an outgoing manner that had proved successful in keeping wheels greased, and schedules on time when he had been in the business.

'Hullo, Ash,' he said. 'What do we have this time? More guys in turbans making missile parts in Miami?'

He was referring to a successful operation they had conducted to track down the source of electronic parts used in missiles and guidance systems generally. Ash had spotted them coming into Iran to support their war effort, and had acquired evidence that they were coming from the USA. With the help of Dalgetti's expertise in crate-ology they had tracked them back to an industrial complex in Miami, where the Iranians had set up a plant to 'reverse-engineer' what they needed.

'A bit bigger, this time, Jim. One Soviet MiL Mi-14

anti-submarine helicopter with towed magnetic anomaly detection and a MiG-27 swing-wing fighter with long-range tanks and *Otter* torpedoes.'

Dalgetti raised bushy black eyebrows.

'Going from Iran?'

'Yes. Probably Khorramshahr. As to when, I'm not sure. It *might* be any time last year, but most likely towards the end.'

'To?'

'Here,' Ash said flatly.

'*Here?*'

'Here,' she said firmly.

Dalgetti knew as well as anyone else in the business that intelligence was strictly run on a 'need to know' basis. Knowledge was very largely kept compartmentalised, and those like Ash with multiple clearances and certifications usually rare, and at the top of their particular tree.

'Okay,' he said. 'Then we'd better go downstairs. Have you got any priority on this? Then we can jump the queue.'

'I have it,' she said.

The greatest concentration of computers ever seen in the world was back at Fort Meade, where they stretched for city blocks, but the capability of those at NPIC was still fabulous. In the yellow-walled, gold-carpeted basement Jim Dalgetti sat down on a black-vinyl upholstered bench-type seat that surrounded four and a half feet wide, six and a half feet tall hollow semi-circle of narrow gold and deep green panels. All around in the hall were computers, front-end interfaces and mass storage units.

'The world's most expensive love-seat,' he joked, getting himself comfortable. He was seated in front of a CRAY-1 computer, which had stood NPIC in at $15 million. It weighed five tons and was a compact seventy square feet. It contained more than 200,000 integrated circuits the size of a thumbnail, three thousand four hundred printed circuit boards and sixty miles of wire. It generated enough heat per cubic inch to reduce itself to a molten mass in seconds were it not cooled, hence its unique Freon cooling system that used vertical aluminium and stainless steel cooling bars to line the wall of the computer chassis.

The remarkable computer was the creation of Seymour Cray, an electrical engineering genius who had began his career with Engineering Research Associates, the ex-Naval cryptographers turned computer manufacturers. His number-cruncher built in Chippewa Falls, Minnesota had the capacity of six IBM 370/195s put together. NSA had one, and with random access semiconductor memory it could transfer up to 320 million words per second, or the equivalent of two thousand five hundred 300-page books. NPIC used theirs to sort through the digitally transmitted bits of information transmitted from the KH-series satellites.

'Okay,' he said. 'Let's tell it what we want.'

He began tapping out the information, and soon results began to appear on the VDU on the console.

'Well, no problem on both birds. They have a MiG-27 squadron at Safar, about a hundred and fifty miles from the border with Iraq. Trans-sonic at low altitude, effective ground-attack aircraft. Swing-wing, good loiter time, no reason why it shouldn't be used to attack a submarine if fitted with the right weapons. Since they've had them, they have lost five known to ground fire during the war. Plus one just listed as "missing".'

'When was it listed as "missing"?'

'August twenty two.'

'Find a suitable crate around that time.'

Dalgetti fed in the request and in a moment the CRAY signalled that it was ready. He asked for the first and the image appeared on the screen. To the uninitiated, it was simply a featureless aerial landscape shot. The most one might tell about it was that for some reason it had been taken early in the morning, for high areas of the parched landscape gleamed white in the flat sunlight. A bent scratch ran from eleven o'clock to six across the image, casting black shadows along its path.

'When is this?'

Dalgetti read the information printed by the image.

'Just after six am, twenty one August. It's fourteen miles out from Safar, on the road to Khorramshahr.'

'Ahh …' breathed Ash.

'Let's go in. This was taken from a KH-11 No. 5513 on August twenty one, its 993rd day in orbit.'

Dalgetti had the CRAY zoom in on the target. The scratch became a road, a whitish streak a cigarette butt, a toy truck, a tractor-trailer unit.

'Let's have it re-image that from the other shots it has.'

Within seconds an astonishing three-dimensional image of the tractor-trailer appeared.

'That's an M.A.N. tractor diesel. Its markings and numberings indicate that it is the property of the 23rd Air Wing, operating the MiG-27s at Safar. The large crate on the flat-bed it is towing contains, without a doubt, your missing MiG-27, dissembled for transport.'

'And where did it go. To Khorramshahr?'

Dalgetti moved on to the next picture.

'Yup. August twenty four, here it is, being loaded on to a freighter. The *SS City of Flanders*, Liberian flag.'

Within a few more minutes, Dalgetti and the CRAY had tracked down the MiL Mi-14, which had been based some fifty miles down the coast from the port. On 24 August, it too was in a crate, being loaded on to the freighter.

'But where did it go? The *City of Flanders*.'

The CRAY didn't know. No one had been interested in the 5,000 ton cargo vessel, and apart from one shot of her leaving the Gulf, there was no more.

'If she docked over here, it'll be recorded.'

'She won't have,' said Ash.

'What you need is some imagery from someone who looks at us. We don't, the Soviets do.'

He grinned. 'If you want to find your *City of Flanders* you'd better ask the Soviets for some images from one of their Cosmoses!'

'Yes,' said Ash smiling. 'So I should.'

NSA HEADQUARTERS

Ash returned to Fort Meade, and went to her own section on the third floor. There she made her way to the office of James 'Jake' Kirby, her chief communications signals analyst. Kirby was a part of the Office of Signals Intelligence Operations, which given the nature of NSA's mission was always considered first among equals of the four operational organisations and their five staff and support groups, and single training unit. It employed a veritable army of eavesdroppers, codebreakers, linguists, traffic and signals analysts, all of whom made up the single largest group within the agency. They were allied to huge numbers of scientists, engineers and mathematicians who occupied themselves with the exotic business of signals analysis, which included ELINT, RADINT, telemetry analysis and signals conversion, which attempted to locate signals that were being hidden by such means as spectrum-spreading, where the signal vanished into the 'noise' and frequency-hopping.

Ash's request was to be quite simple, however. What she was looking for was simple, uncrypted, single-frequency, un-jammed, un-spread, un-hopped air-to-air or air-to-ground communication.

'I'm looking for a pilot in the Iranian Air Force, Jake,' she said. 'Someone very good, very experienced. He must have time in MiG-27 ground-attack aircraft. And for some time last year or early this he must have been missing from his unit. Most definitely, he must have been out of Iran the last week in January.'

'Okay,' said Kirby. 'Let's track him down.'

They took the lift down into the basement. The agency owned over ten acres of computers down there. It made the impressive array at NPIC look like a country-cousin operation. Here was the brain of NSA, and like a human one, it was divided into right and left hemispheres, code-named Carillon and Loadstone. Carillon consisted of four gigantic IBM 303s linked together, and attached to three IBM 22,000-line-per-minute page-printers. Loadstone had once been the more-powerful CRAY-1, but this had now been replaced by the greatest number-crunchers of all, the CRAY-YMP and CRAY-2. NSA required such capabilities in part through being the 'host environment' for the biggest world-wide computer network in the world, in which fifty-two separate computer systems from such agencies as the British SIGINT organisation GCHQ were linked together. Foreseeing the day when even greater capability would be required, the agencies engineers were researching such arcane technologies as analog optical computing and light-sound interaction and charge-transfer devices in order to achieve multiplications of the order of one quadrillion per second.

Jake Kirby set about instructing the computer to search for Ashraf Amran's missing pilot. The information it would examine comprised all the Iranian air force communications for the period involved. These were picked up, like the similar communications of Soviet pilots and controllers, communiques from embassies to their home governments, the telephone conversations of merchants, businessmen, policemen and criminals, husbands, wives and lovers, by NSA's SPINTCOM system, which stood for special intelligence communications. The electronic vacuum-cleaner that sucked up all these electronic emissions was a huge, squat, cylindrical satellite named Rhyolite. It was about five feet long and weighed three quarters of a ton. Its main dish antenna was over seventy feet across. It had been blasted into space on top of an Atlas Agena-D on 6 March 1985, to sit in geosynchronous orbit 22,175 miles over Borneo, and had been eavesdropping on half the world ever since. What it heard it beamed down to a pair of giant dish antennas hidden in woods behind the Headquarters/Operations building. From there the information travelled through an underground cable past the antenna control facility into the COMM Center where the communications, recorded on magnetic tape were then turned into print by row after row of crypto machines, beating out the world's secrets on multi-coloured, six-ply carbon paper, all bearing the word CLASSIFIED on one side, and warnings against disclosure on the other, to be distributed to the analysts, linguists and codebreakers.

To examine the transmissions of the Iranian air force for the period involved the computer took advantage of a number of attached accessories. One was a unit called Tractor, which located the magnetic tape required from the library, mounted, positioned and threaded it, then transferred the information contained at an amazing 1,128,000 characters per second. To do so NSA had had to make magnetic tape capable of containing three thousand characters per inch as opposed to the normal one hundred, and whip them past the reading heads at 235 inches per second.

Within minutes the IBM had come up with a list of five pilots who might fit the bill. The list came with a percentage recommendation of accuracy; given the list of qualifications it considered one of the candidates ninety per cent certain to be the man Ash was looking for.

'He's an ace,' she said, reading from the print-out. 'Full Colonel, thirty eight years old, 3400 combat hours, mostly in F-15s. Missing from his command from December 20 to February 7. Did a familiarisation course on the MiG-27 from December 5 to 11. No hint at all as to where he went in the missing period. His name's Khosrow Parsa. He trained over here when he was but a Lieutenant in the Air Force of the Shah. He's probably the best pilot they have.'

'Yes,' she said quietly. 'I think he's the one. Thank you, Jake, thank you very much.'

She went to see MacDonald.

'I have what I consider to be the MiG-27 and the Mil helicopter. I have a pilot for the MiG. Jake Kirby is checking on a crew for the Mil, but it's the MiG pilot who is more important, since I believe that he must have been in this country in the weeks before the attack on the *Maine*. The helicopter, being a relatively slow and short-range aircraft would have been deployed from a ship, probably the salvage vessel, in the immediate vicinity of the attack. The MiG, however, would require a runway, and I believe that it was landed in one of the inlets off the Georgia coast and taken to Sultan Electronics' private air strip, where it was put together pending the attack. The strip is out in the boondocks, amid square miles of pine. Nobody goes there, the military have enormous great practice areas to the west. Georgia's really underpopulated. Anyone hearing a jet leaving the strip would think nothing of it. Given the time of the attack on the *Maine* the fighter would have taken off while it was still dark.'

'So what happened to the MiG after the attack? It isn't back at the Sultan air strip.'

'I'll tell you what I think. I think that after the mission was over the pilot, Colonel Khosrow Parsa, if it is he, either landed it on the sea, if you can do such a thing or ejected. Either way, it's somewhere at the bottom of the ocean.'

'This is all very good detective work, Ash,' said MacDonald. 'But you still haven't got anything concrete.'

'There's reams and reams, yards and yards of magnetic tape with his voice on, down in the basement. All coming from Iran. He was here, in this country, I'm sure of it. We listen to and record everyone else's electronic transmissions. The guys in ADVA are always guffawing about how they've heard some Soviet general or party boss talking dirty with his mistress over the 'phone. I'll bet old Khosrow used the 'phone when he was here. If only we recorded all US telephone calls I'd be able to find him.

210

That would be some concrete proof.'

MacDonald stared at her for some moments in silence.

'We do,' he said finally. 'But we don't tell anyone about it.'

'We'd better clear you for RAMPART,' MacDonald said. 'As you know, the CIA is forbidden by its charter from monitoring domestic telephone conversations. We are not. Even the 1968 Crime Control and Safe Streets Act contains a loophole specifically giving us exemption from the act. In the late 1960s and early seventies we worked hand in hand with the Bureau of Narcotics and Dangerous Drugs to provide them with intelligence regarding the activities of drug barons, Mafiosi and Cuban/South Americans. This programme was a part of a wider one the Agency inherited, called MINARET, which was a civil disturbance watch list – basically antiwar and civil rights groups. MINARET was ultra-sensitive because without doubt it bordered on the illegal. Our work with the BNDD was very successful. By monitoring a few cities that are transit points we were able to provide hard international narcotics intelligence. For example, simply by monitoring one New York-South American city link we could pick up calls from other South American cities to other cities in the USA. We became extremely good at it, it wasn't even a very high budget item, but we provided the BNDD with information that led to some quite spectacular drug busts. I recall we tipped them off once about a Cadillac that came in so lined with cocaine – millions and millions of dollars worth – that the drug smugglers had actually built the automobile around the drug. But even that was quite small-time, because we were beginning to put the barons themselves away. We could have cleaned up the country, without doubt, but the anti-drug programme fell foul of the wider implications of MINARET towards the mid-seventies. It was the time of congressional witch-hunts, the uncovering of govern-

211

mental wrong-doing and covert activities, the CIA was being gutted, for sure, if it had got out Woodward and Bernstein would have been beating on our door wanting to write another damn book about us and MINARET, so the whole domestic snooping programme was quietly buried.'

MacDonald got up, to stretch his legs, and went over to the big globe by the window, spinning it on its axis with his fingers.

'Meanwhile, the drug problems and all the related crime, and re-investment of the profits simply began to boom once again. President Monroe, President Cord's predecessor came into office on something of a law-and-order, make America great again ticket, and he revived the counter-crime element that we had in MINARET. The technology had moved on since the seventies, and we now have the capability to monitor all international telephone calls or messages to or from anyone in the USA. As you know, this is because calls are now transmitted through microwave signals, via satellites like those owned by COMSAT. All you really need to intercept COMSAT signals is an equivalent-sized satellite antenna.'

MacDonald smiled wryly. 'We have plenty of those.'

The agency did. COMSAT, the Communication Satellite Corporation handled nearly all nongovernmental international satellite communications; telephone calls, telegrams, telexes, computers talking business with other computers from its four earth stations in West Virginia, Maine, Washington and California. As if by chance, NSA had listening-posts, the right sized satellite antennas, in Sugar Grove, Virginia; Winter Harbor, Maine; Yakima, Washington; Two Rock Ranch, California.

'What most people haven't noticed is that domestic telecommunications have also now moved from the wire to the wavelength. Everyone's used to seeing small, grey, cone-shaped microwave antennas now. They're everywhere, on city roofs, hanging off obscure towers, on hills and in fields. In addition, there is a rapidly growing domestic satellite system. At this point what you don't get from the satellites you can get by situating a microwave tower in the right location and tying it into the local telephone company circuits, which are interconnected with the domestic coast-to-coast microwave telephone system of AT&T. If you look at a microwave routing map you'll see the occasional little circle with several lines entering it, indicating a microwave tower, and the letters RCV, meaning Receive Only Station.'

The globe was slowing on its axle, and MacDonald gave it another spin.

'They're ours,' he said laconically. 'We record all international and domestic microwave transmissions. It is this capability that lies at the bottom of RAMPART, which forms the main thrust of President Monroe's anti-crime programme. However, it is also a capability straight out of the pages of *1984*, and is something that most of the world's despots would gladly give their left testicle to have. It is potentially anti-democratic and the domestic equivalent of nuclear weaponry. For this reason, it is legally considered that although recorded, it may not be examined without legal authority. Have you heard of FISA, the Foreign Intelligence Surveillance Act, and the Foreign Intelligence Surveillance Court?'

'Surely,' said Ash.

FISA and its super-secret federal court, located behind a cipher-locked door in a windowless room on the top floor of the Justice Department building were creations out of Franz Kafka. Only known of and used by the inner circle of US intelligence officers, the court sat in secret session, held no adversary hearings and issued no public opinions or reports. It was not even listed in the *Government Organisation Manual* or the *United States Court Directory*. Its task was to grant permission to US intelligence agencies to snoop, eavesdrop or conduct surreptitious entries – black bag jobs – on or into the persons or property of foreign powers within the USA itself.

'There is also a *Domestic* Intelligence Surveillance

Court,' MacDonald said quietly. 'Set up by presidential decree. It is directly responsible, because of our eavesdropping technology, for the spectacular decrease in crime. We *know* who the bad guys are. The existence of DISC is one of the best-kept secrets of the decade.'

The globe had ceased to spin. MacDonald stood looking down at a point somewhere in mid-Pacific.

'I'm going to clear you for RAMPART,' he said. 'If Colonel Khosrow Parsa came into this country and spoke on a telephone then we'll have him on tape. Then you'll just have to find him.'

It wasn't that easy. As Jeremiah Jones, the Signals Collection Officer for RAMPART explained.

'We get a request through the Domestic Intelligence Surveillance Court from the FBI or DEA or whoever, to get evidence on whatever group of hoods we're concerned with, then we got telephone numbers, and it's easy to programme the computer to recognise a particular number being dialled and give us a print-out of what's said. The latest model here can listen to clear voice and translate or transcribe. What you're asking for is more difficult. We're looking for a *voice*. We can do it if we have some target words for the computer to flag.'

'Let's try Sultan Electronic's telephones, and Sultani's home number to begin with. Try target words of Khosrow, Parsa, MiG, Maine, MiL, Iran. For a start. I'll think of some more.'

The result was a blank. Nothing.

'What we want,' said Jeremiah, 'is a specific word, something we *know* is associated with your man.'

'I'm going to go and dig up some history on Colonel Parsa,' said Ash. 'I'll be back, Jeremiah.'

'Okay,' said the black man, with a smile. 'We'll be here. We ain't going nowhere.'

THREEFORK, ARKANSAS

The fields stretched for miles. Close by the airstrip a large green John Deere tractor was ploughing in the stubble of winter wheat in preparation for planting soybeans. The moist earth glistened as it left the moldboard. On the ramp area outside the hangar a large, bright yellow aircraft sat with its tail on the ground, a silver alloy spreader clutched underneath it like a fan. It smelled agricultural. The middle-aged man in chinos and brushed cotton plaid L.L. Bean shirt squirted a stream of evilly-coloured tobacco juice at a point somewhere short of the large main gear tyre.

'Ol' Khosrow. Yes ma'am, I remember him well. I was in charge of the primary jet instruction for the Iranian pilots back then. Used T-33s. Shooting Stars. I was with Khosrow one night doing touch and go's. Just staying in the pattern about eight of us. Khosrow had it set up on final, pulled the power back to flight idle, and down we come. Yo Yo Four ahead of us makes a real thumper of a landing, stalls it in from ten feet and blows both main tyres. Sits there, blocking the runway. So the guy in the control tower gets on to us. "Yo Yo One, Go around. Yo Yo One." Khosrow acknowledges, and pushes the power back on. Only with those early turbines, it took forever and an age for them to spool back up and start turning cold air to hot again. So down we come.

' "Yo Yo One, Go around. Yo Yo One," says Khosrow, real calm like. Still nothing. If I recall, it was something like thirteen seconds to get the power back. Down we

215

come, and Yo Yo Four is getting bigger all the time. "*Yo Yo One, Go around.*" "Yes, sir," says Khosrow, real polite. "We're trying." '

Former USAF major Chuck Kaman, fighter pilot turned agricultural aviator guffawed happily and tobacco juice squirted over the ramp.

'Heeee ... "We're trying." We just skated by. Man, some of those early jet trainers were no fun at night. Sitting in the back you couldn't see sh – ah, see sugah from Shironah. The boys had to be signed off to do solo night touch and go's, they had to do eight under instruction. I remember, they'd often say to me "What do we have to do to pass, Major?" 'n I'd say "Just get me round without breaking my butt, son, and you pass." The other question they'd always ask was what to do if the engine quit at night. I'd say, "Get down to about five hundred feet and turn on the landing light." "Uhuh?" they'd say. "You don't like what you see," I'd say, "Turn it off." '

Tobacco juice narrowly missed Ash's soft Italian leather loafer.

'What was Khosrow like?'

'Good pilot,' said Kaman, sobering up. 'Real sharp.'

'He's a Colonel now. An ace.'

'Yeah ... that wouldn't surprise me at all. He was a natural, even back then. He was real religious of course.'

'That makes a difference?'

'Yeah ... I think so ... a lot of us in 'nam believed strongly in the Lord. It just seemed natural.'

He looked at Ash almost shyly. 'But that's so throughout history. I don't know if you know that. I'm a bit of a military history buff, like to read about that kind of thing. Men who were very highly motivated in a religious manner make real good soldiers. I just been reading over the winter, all about the New Model Army, 'n how they whipped the Royalists. Rode with a sword in one hand and a bible in the other. I was reading about the battle of Naseby, when the war was won, and one of Cromwell's colonels, as the Royalists broke and ran, on a blazing hot, dusty day, he just broke into paeans of praise for the Lord.'

Kaman removed his tobacco wad, a sinister-looking object, and deciding it had outlived its usefulness tossed it into a nearby fifty-five gallon drum wastebin.

'File thirteen,' he said. 'Khosrow was like that. His belief gave him strength to do his job. I ain't surprised at all he's a big-time Colonel ace.'

'Was he a very serious character then?'

'He was real serious about his religion, and about his flying. But he wasn't a wet blanket, he liked to laugh and have a good time too. He was a good guy. Good sense of humour, and loved a party. Not liquor, of course, but the opposite sex, certainly.'

'Women?'

'Why yes, sir. That boy sure loved pu – ah, he was real fond of the ladies.' Kaman corrected himself. 'The number of times I heard him get back down from the day's training and he'd be on the 'phone to some gal or other. "Hey, honeychild," he'd says. "Whatchoodoin' tonight." Chances were, ending up in ol'Khosrow's bed. And then there he'd be, bright and ready in the morning, prayers said, ablutions done, prayer mat rolled, and ready to go practise blowing someone out of the sky.'

As the day warmed up, the pungent smell of agricultural fertilisers and chemicals emanating from the mixing rig, the large turbine-engined aircraft and sink pit it was resting by seemed to increase. Kaman noticed Ash rub her nose, which was itching slightly.

'It ain't Chanel No. 5, is it?' he said jovially.

'It is quite strong.'

'Yes ma'am,' he said happily. 'That's the smell of money.'

'Honeychild,' said Ash.

Kaman reached in his hip pocket for his pouch of leaf. It bore the emblem of a rushing train, and the stamp Chattanooga Chew.

'Yes ma'am. Honeychild. Always honeychild.'

NSA HEADQUARTERS

Voice analysis indicated that the man flying McDonnell Douglas F-15 Kilo Alpha 72 on December 2, and Mikoyan Gurevich 27 Foxtrot Quebec 33 on December 10 was the same man talking on a payphone in Savannah on the 18th of the following month. Colonel Khosrow Parsa of the Iranian air force.

'Got him,' Jeremiah Jones said with satisfaction. He loved successfully to hunt down a criminal. 'We got him on the eighteenth, and again two days later. The number he was calling is that of a Miss Jennifer Riley. Blonde haired and blue-eyed, I'll bet. Sounds like it was a casual pick up.'

'Yes,' said Ash. 'We'll have a word with her, but I don't think she'll be able to tell us much more than Khosrow's taste in underwear. Thanks Jeremiah.'

'My pleasure,' he said.

Ash went to see MacDonald with her new evidence.

'We found Colonel Parsa,' she said. 'Two telephone calls in January, shortly before the attack on the *Maine* took place. We can prove he was here.'

'Well done,' he said quietly. The Deputy Director was looking increasingly tired, and showing his age, with deep lines running from his nose to the corners of his mouth. 'That's very good. Unfortunately it isn't enough. Coogan could say that it was purely circumstantial. Colonel Parsa taking a surreptitious holiday in the USA where he was so happy.'

Ash looked at him in astonishment. 'Well, you know

that can't possibly be so. And what has Coogan got to do with it anyway?'

'Everything,' MacDonald said sombrely. 'It looks as though Coogan is going to be the next Chief of the General Staff very shortly, and he is almost out of control. Sultani is singing like a bird, and what he is saying makes it look as though President Cord's astonishing victory in the polls was no accident, that he had a quite enormous amount of covert help. All the evidence is stacking up, and Coogan intends to prove that Cord has been the object of a massive Soviet programme aimed at having the president of the USA as an unwitting Agent of Influence. If Coogan can prove this, Cord's position will be very weak, and he will be unable to control Coogan. The general is arguing that with Cord as a president with a non-interventionist, military-cutback, retrenching policy, both the military build-up in Central America and the sinking of the *Maine* have been aimed at testing Cord's will, that if the USA does not respond then the Soviets will move decisively elsewhere in the world. Coogan is planning some kind of retaliatory tit-for-tat attack, to demonstrate that US resolve to stand up to the Soviets remains undiminished. Coogan is assembling hard evidence to support his case; in the scales, your finding of Khosrow Parsa in Savannah will be but a feather. At the moment we cannot even mention that we have a theory that Sultani is an Islamic double-agent, for DIRNSA, Coogan's henchman, would remove both of us from office immediately. We *have* to have solid evidence.'

MacDonald took off his glasses and rubbed his eyes.

'You do realise what you're saying, don't you, Ash? If Sultani is working for the Iranians, if he is committed to the cause of Shi'ia Islam then the campaign to get Cord elected, the attack on the *Maine* was organised not by the Soviets but by the Iranians. The organisation, the planning would be astonishing, the skill of subterfuge practically super-human. I know I have said it before, but are you sure they're up to it?'

'You have the question turned around the wrong way,' Ash said quietly, but firmly. '*We* are the ones who aren't up to it. If one is talking of subterfuge, of sheer multi-layered sophistication and subtlety of thought in manipulating the pieces in games of power then the mullahs have, for some centuries, been plus-two players. They would not regard anyone in the West as being able to compete in the same league at all. They might allow the British as having a twenty-four handicap, but as for the Americans, we are double-bogey duffers. And we insist on playing the game by their rules. We're like some simple farm-boy sitting down at the table at Monty's Place to play seven-card-stud against a man who has done nothing else since he was knee-high to a grasshopper, being taught by *his* father, and who has in consequence a mathematically trained mind capable of calculating the odds on *any* hand within a nano-second of each card being dealt. The farm boy has trouble adding up his change after he's brought a sack of corn.

'Unfortunately, the American "can do" philosophy always reaches first for a hardware solution to a threat instead of careful selection and training of people, the right people. It doesn't work against a culture like that of the mullahs. What we should do, but don't, is to refuse to play that game. Not enter that kind of arena. The farm boy is big and strong. He works hard and obeys the law. The gambler is small, dishonest and slippery as an eel. He can strip the farmboy of everything he owns if the farm boy plays his game. The farm boy should stick to his strengths. We should. The only way to deal with them.'

Ash stood up, and walked over to the window, looking over the lush countryside. It was so very different to her childhood, she thought. Spring flowers were lighting up the woods. Spring had been over before you could bat an eyelid there, bringing the stifling, waterless heat in its trail.

'I say we, doctor, because I live here, I work for the agency. But I'm not really an American. I was brought up an Iranian. I understand them. I'm the only one you've got who does.'

'Then get me hard evidence, Ash. We have to have a smoking gun. We have to be able to tie your *Iranian* MiG-27, your *Iranian* Colonel Parsa to Sultani. We have to prove Sultani is what *you* say he is, not what Coogan says he is.'

'I have some vacation time owing. I'm going to take three weeks off. I might travel a little. Go to Europe.'

'Okay,' MacDonald said slowly.

'I'll need to pack a few things in my bag. Bucket and spade. A few trinkets for the natives. Something from Research and Engineering. A snippet or two from ADVA.'

'I'll see to it.'

'Thank you.'

Ash got up to leave. As she was on her way to the door MacDonald called after her.

'I'll be leaving here soon. If we win I'll retire next year. If we lose I'll be gone before that. We can't afford to lose. It's more than just missing out on one's pension.'

'I know,' she said. 'I'll try to come back with the goods.'

In her office, she called Kowalski in Georgia.

'Jack, it's Ashraf. I'm going away for a little while. Would you do something for me? Check on Shaikh Nasir Khan the Saudi playboy who took the video of the MiG-27. Check on Mrs Nobles, the old lady who fingered Sultani.'

'Okay. Anything particular?'

'Yes. I think you'll find they've vanished. Try to get background on them. I think there won't be any.'

'Will do,' he said with alacrity. 'I'll get on to it right away. I've got to come up to Washington in a week or two. You want me to bring the big pistol with me?'

'Why not,' she laughed. 'Be something to show the grandchildren.'

Armed with MacDonald's authority, she paid visits to the Office of Research and Engineering, and to ADVA and GENS, in the office of Signals Intelligence Operations. At R and E the scientists and engineers strove to maintain the goal of NSA to maintain a near-decade advantage over anyone else in the fields of technology devoted to eavesdropping, from making electronic components so small they required a scanning electron miscroscope to examine them to designing a dish-shaped antenna big enough to hold two football fields end to end, the better to hear what the Russians were whispering about. There she collected something towards the smaller end of the scale, packed neatly away in foam rubber, fitted inside a small silver Halliburton suitcase, like a photographer's. Over in Signals Intelligence she called on Advanced Soviet and General Soviet. ADVA dealt with high-level Soviet cipher problems and specialised in developing new methods of attack. General Soviet worked the lower- and medium-level systems and concentrated on exploitation. From both, she collected items of COMINT.

This done, she returned to her office, where she prepared two messages. Both were secure from cryptanalytical attack in that they required the use of 'one-time' pads by sender and receiver alike. When they were prepared, she had them transmitted, using Super High Frequency. The higher the frequency, the greater amount of information that could be carried in a limited amount of time. This useful piece of knowledge had been discovered by the German U-boat arm during the Second World War, suffering because its long-range HF communications were being intercepted, direction found by the Allied forces, with brutal consequences for the boats, who found long-range Liberators and destroyers armed with a wide selection of anti-submarine devices overhead shortly afterwards. One solution adopted was burst or squirt transmission, *Kurier*, in which the message was compressed for very rapid transmission, thus drastically reducing exposure.

Ash's SHF transmission was a direct descendant of *Kurier*. SHF came into being with the advent of satellites, and had the advantage of tight beams, which were difficult to intercept, high information capacity and channel capacity which permitted the satellite to carry many separate messages simultaneously.

The Satellite Data System satellite 'hanging' in its highly elliptical orbit, ready to relay information did just that. Both 'squirt' messages were received simultaneously, and separately. They were passed back down to their recipients. There was no way for those listening in Iran or the USSR to know what the messages meant, or for whom they were intended. In Tehran, an antenna built into the roof of a house collected the message, and passed it into a regular answering-machine attached to the telephone. Hearing the bleep, Sayyed Kashk picked up the receiver.

In Moscow, on the Lenin Hills, a modem murmured to itself. On the screen, a small code-word appeared, as if at random. A man got up from his desk. His heart was pounding, and he felt sick with anticipation. Before typing in the code words which would release the message he locked his door nervously. He sat at the terminal, and tapped the keys. He would need his one-time pad, concealed in his house. He was Vladimir Rykov.

NORBECK, MARYLAND

Gulio Riva didn't need the booze any more to talk; the act of betrayal was over, the deed done, he was an enthusiastic collaborator. Coogan was not entirely sold on Riva's protestations of patriotism, he felt that there were other motives there – a book maybe? Woodward and Bernstein had got rich, so could Riva. For sure, another president was on the way out. It was only correct, Coogan thought coldly. Without Soviet help Cord would never have been foisted on an unsuspecting electorate at all.

Seeing the glitter in Riva's eyes his mother's words came unbidden into his mind. 'Vice is a monster of so frightful mien, As to be hated needs but to be seen; yet seen too oft, familiar with her face, We first endure, then pity, then

223

embrace.' His mother had been a church-going, upright woman who had brought up her children to honour God, their parents and their country, and never to do wrong. For a second Coogan wondered what his mother would have said, had she been able to see his machiavellian machinations, all aimed at subverting the wishes of his elected president. As quickly as he thought of it he pushed the notion away. There were things in the world that his mother had not known of, things that had to be done, and if the doer ended up with blood or dirt on his hands, so be it.

'I got some stuff here on Dr Hallows,' said Riva. The lights of Norbeck lit up the sky further down the road. It was warm and comfortable in the Cadillac.

'Hallows was the guy who put the steel to Jenkins. It gave the nomination to Cord. It makes interesting reading,' he said, giving a folder to the air force general. 'It's quite a nasty story. Hallows was ruined anyway; Jenkins was a "favourite son" in his state, people wouldn't have minded him being president at all. His practice was ruined, they about rode him out of town on a rail. His widow's hiding out in a little town in Missouri where no one knows who she is. I reckon she'd be willing to talk if she thought we were getting ready to hang Harrison Taylor.'

'I'll go talk to her,' said Coogan. He fingered the slim file; Riva was proving extraordinarily useful. The young White House aide looked across inquiringly.

'Have you captured some kind of Soviet spy?' he asked, tentatively.

'How would you know if we had?' Coogan replied quietly.

'I overheard Harrison Taylor talking. The president was asking where they had got an item of intelligence listed on the PDB, the Daily Brief, and Linkovsky, the National-Security Adviser said NSA had caught a top-level Soviet agent. Taylor knew about it. It was a funny thing, he almost sounded uneasy. Can I ask, who is the agent? What's his name?'

'Sultani. Hank Sultani. He ran an electronics firm in

Savannah.'

Coogan saw no reason for Riva not to know. The *Soviets* knew their man was gone. They'd had to let Antonov go, because of his diplomatic immunity. It wasn't how Coogan would have run things; he would have strung him up by the nuts and left him to turn in the wind.

'Sultani ... Sultani,' Riva mused. 'What's he look like? Have you a photo?'

'Yes,' said Coogan slowly. 'I have one.'

He reached in his briefcase and took out an 8″ by 10″ black and white still of Sultani and handed it to Riva. He stared at it for some moments and then nodded several times, quickly and positively.

'Yes. That's him. It is.'

'Who?'

'The man I saw Harrison Taylor with, during the campaign. I knew the name was familiar.'

The implications almost took Coogan's breath away.

'I put it to Sultani that Cord's election was a Soviet operation. He denied any knowledge, and there was nothing we had to tie him to it. He's been talking about ... other things.'

The destruction of the *Maine* was completely 'black'. When they admitted to it, as they would have to once the families expected their men back, it would be accident. Not an act of war. When the USA struck back at the USSR no one was going to say anything either.

'Is he dedicated?' said Riva.

'Totally. A genuine, dyed-in-the-wool communist.'

'There you are. He's talking about whatever you've got on him, and hiding something even bigger.'

Coogan nodded. He could admire someone like Sultani. It was a pity he had been trained on the wrong side. He would have made a great American.

'Let me see him face-to-face,' urged Riva. 'I can confront him, and then he'll know we have him red-handed. He'll have to talk then.'

The idea appealed mightily to Coogan.

'We have him at a manor house we own, on the Patuxent River. He has his breakfast out on the lawn when it's fine. Come tomorrow morning early. I'll be there. We'll do it then.'

Coogan fired up the huge V-8. For him, American cars had lost all style once they moved away from eight cylinders and 400-plus cubic inches. It was an attitude he admitted was ambivalent, since where his professional judgements were concerned, with aircraft, only the very latest technology would do. But then, he had learned to fly in an ag-pilot's old Piper Cub at sixteen, before he could ever drive a car. He crashed his first car, he had trouble realising you had to slow down for corners. Why? You didn't in an aircraft.

The Cadillac rolled smoothly into town and Coogan chuckled with pleasure at the prospect of real, hard evidence on Cord and his Soviet sponsors in the morning.

'Well, well,' Riva looked at him as the city lights gave illumination to the interior of the car. His sharp features looked even more like those of a bird of prey than usual.

'We're cooking with oil now,' Coogan said triumphantly.

PATUXENT RIVER, MARYLAND

Hank Sultani had finished eating breakfast and was sitting at his table sipping the last of his coffee when he saw Gulio Riva coming across the lawn towards him.

'Some coffee?' he enquired courteously. 'Do have a seat.'

'Thank you,' said Gulio. Sultani poured a cup and the two men stared expressionlessly at each other for a moment.

'You are the second unannounced guest I have had at breakfast time recently,' Sultani said. 'A young lady came to drink coffee with me a short time ago. A very pretty

226

young lady.'

'How nice for you.'

'Not really,' said Sultani. 'She is a young lady of exceptional intelligence and intuition. Her name is Ashraf Amram and she works for one of the intelligence agencies. She was brought up in Iran. As a muslim, although I would say that her faith has lapsed. Her perception is quite acute. Rather more so than my military gaolers.'

'Will she be coming to see you again?'

'I hope not. In fact, I would much prefer she took no further interest in me.'

'I'm sure she won't,' Riva murmured.

'That's good,' said Sultani.

Riva looked up and saw Coogan leaving the house to cross the lawn to them.

'Your gaoler-in-chief is coming,' he said.

Coogan was in full five-star-general fig. He beamed at Sultani as he sat down.

'Mr Sultani and I have met before,' said Riva. 'We were just comparing notes. During the election campaign, wasn't it, Hank?'

'I do not recall that we were introduced,' said Sultani.

'But you were there, with Taylor, and so was I.'

'Hank, ol' buddy,' said Coogan, adopting Sultani's own good ol' boy persona. 'You been holding out on us. Now, do you want to tell the story from the beginning and go to the end, or start at the end and work back?'

Sultani bowed his head in defeat. 'It shall be as you say,' he said.

NASHVILLE, TENNESSEE

Personal transport, mused the air traffic controller in the tower at the Metropolitan airport, came in all shapes and sizes. For the never-ending stream of musical hopefuls that came to the country music capital of the world it was a thumb on the roadside or a Greyhound ticket and the shoes on their feet with which to tramp the endless round of record companies, offices and agents. For most, it was the same thumb or ticket that took them away again, to a job singing medleys of Waylon Jennings songs in Harry's Bar and Grill. Straight from Nashville. For a few, with a hit under their belt, it was a Cadillac, because for country boys anything else lacked style, even a Lincoln Continental. For a select, tiny group of superstars, it was executive jet transport. The controller was familiar with Kenny's Jetstar, with the chartered 737 taking Willie Nelson on tour. He had seen Ray Charles come by in his turboprop Britannia. He was less familiar with men who arrived in their own F-16 jet fighter.

The pure white single-seater came in over Priest Lake and kissed the threshold on the numbers. It taxied over to the jet park, where the pilot got out. He wore a simple olive drab flight suit without insignia. But for his silver hair he looked the standard-model fighter jock, medium build, slim, fit, eyes like a hawk.

Pulling on a plaid wool jacket as a concession to civilian taste and taking a bag with him, Coogan took the courtesy car to the cab rank, where he changed vehicle and instructed the driver to take him in to Broadway. Outside the offices, he requested that he wait.

'I'll not be long,' he said.

J.J. Haan looked both ill and ill-at-ease. He had been sick that morning, when a voice on the 'phone told him that a man would be coming to see him, courtesy of Harrison Taylor.

'Mr Coogan,' he said. 'Harrison Taylor sent you?'

Coogan sat down, and for a moment the two men stared at each other like differing species of rare tropical fish. Haan's hair was in a ponytail, gold and silver discs hung on the walls of his office together with photographs of Haan together with any number of his artistes, most of whom looked under the influence of hallucinogens, to Coogan's jaundiced eye. Coogan had just come from flying his jet fighter at 500 knots IFR, and the tautness of body and spirit that such endeavours gave a man had accentuated his naturally savage demeanour. His jacket did not go with his flying clothes, and was in bad taste.

'Not exactly,' he said. 'But I want to talk about him. More to the point, I want *you* to talk about him. I have here a recorder. Tell me, if you will, the full story of your relationship with him.'

Haan swallowed hard.

'Why should I do that?' he whispered.

'Why? Well let me see. By the way, I like your jewellery,' Coogan said brutally, looking at the ornament around the music impresario's neck. 'Why? Well, for beginners, I won't have you prosecuted for murder. We can go on from there, if you wish.'

VICHY, MISSOURI

In the fighter it was but a short hop to the north-west into the neighbouring state. The weather cleared as Coogan went through the front and he was able to enjoy a fine view of the Mark Twain forest in the crystal clear air as he let down towards Rolla. Seeing the land spread out in front of him, the country that it had been his life's duty to defend he felt an almost physical joy.

Landing at the National airport he taxied into the Fixed Base Operation, where he shut down. The operator came strolling over, looking admiringly at the jet.

'Now ain't she pretty,' he said. He cast a curious eye at Coogan, in his unmarked flight suit. 'I flew in Korea, in eighty-sixes, and I always thought that was the prettiest jet fighter ever made, but this one sure runs her close.'

'The Sabre was a fine aircraft,' agreed Coogan. 'War-winning.'

'You ever fly one, sir?' The old air force Lieutenant had not lost the ability to recognise top brass when he came into contact with them.

'No, I was a bomber man. B-58s.'

The operator sucked in his breath respectfully. 'Now, there, sir, is an aircraft you would not have got me in. Ahead of its time, and paid for it.'

Coogan nodded amiably. You had to have the right stuff to survive in B-58s.

'So what can I do for you, sir?'

'You got a car I can rent?'

'You want me to fill this one up? We got Jet-A.'

'Yes. Top her off.'

'In that case, take my truck.'

'Thank you.'

Coogan shrugged on his plaid jacket and reached in his billfold for his air force fuel card. He collected a map from the operator and drove off in the yellow Ford pick up. The Korean war vet went inside the building, to collect the keys to his fuel tender, and gave the card to his wife, to make out the bill.

'Ain't too often we get five-star generals through here,' he said laconically.

Coogan crossed over 68 on the way to the University of Missouri, but turned off the road through town in Vichy. Using the map, he found his way into a quiet, respectable part of town, with single-storey houses set in carefully tended, green yards. He checked the number of the house against a card he had written on, and parked carefully by the kerb. The front door opened as he came up the path, someone had been waiting for him.

She was grey-haired, but seemed prematurely so, and moved in the manner of a woman older than her years. There was a smell of polish and cleaner in the house, it was very tidy, obsessively so. Coogan sat down at her invitation on a stiffly-cushioned sofa, and when he spoke there was no trace of the manner in which he had dealt with J.J. Haan in Tennessee.

'Mrs Hallows,' he said kindly. 'It's so good of you to see me.'

'It's about my husband,' she said anxiously. 'Isn't it?'

'Yes. I think that we may be able to clear his name.'

Her eyes closed, and through the lids some tears leaked. Her hands were clasped tightly in her lap. Coogan handed her a clean handkerchief, and she dabbed.

'It was your husband who volunteered the information that destroyed the electoral chances of Governor Jenkins, wasn't it?'

She nodded painfully. 'Yes,' she whispered. She cleared her throat, and attempted to speak more clearly. 'My husband, Dr Hallows was a psychiatrist. He was older than I, I was in my early thirties when we married, I had begun to think I had been left on the vine. My husband had a successful practice. I was in many ways an innocent woman, I spent my youth looking after my mother, who was ill, it was only after she died that I could contemplate marriage. I was very flattered to have attention paid me by my future husband … I did not then realise that there are those who enter psychiatry in order to attempt a cure for their own problems …'

The woman stared backwards into a vista of pain, then visibly brought her mind back to where she had left off.

'One day, while the primary elections were still being held, a man came to see my husband. Later, much later, he told me what had happened. Governor Jenkins, as a young man, had been treated by my husband. He had always been a very ambitious, hard-working man, and the strain of political life had brought about attacks of anxiety and depression. This had been a very long time ago, and neither my husband nor he had mentioned it ever after. As far as anyone else was concerned, it was completely buried. My husband admired the governor, he certainly had no plans to bring it up.

'This man, who came to see my husband informed him that he knew of Governor Jenkins' psychiatric treatment.'

'How did he know that?'

'My husband believed that surreptitious entry must have been made, to gain access to his records. He informed my husband that he wished this information to be made public with the alteration that my husband give his professional opinion that what Governor Jenkins had been suffering from and by implication still was – was paranoid schizophrenia. My husband was to make this announcement "in the public interest", as such a man was clearly unfitted to be president. He then informed my husband just how he would destroy him if he was unwilling to co-operate. He had … photographs.'

Once again, she closed her eyes. Coogan took a

photograph of his own from his bag.

'Would you look at this?' he said gently. 'Is this the man?'

Mrs Hallows opened her eyes and looked. Her face contorted as she saw the author of her troubles.

'Yes,' she whispered. 'That is the man.'

'Harrison Taylor. The campaign manager for Cord.'

'Yes.'

'Would you be willing to testify? It will be safe, I promise you. He has no power to harm you now.'

'He has done all the harm he could,' she said bitterly. 'Yes, sir, I will.'

'I will send a man. It will not bring back your husband, but you will have retribution.'

'My husband is dead … I did not know what problems he had, so many years ago. I had hoped for children, my husband hoped that by marrying a woman he might be freed from his other desires but it was not to be for either of us … The shame of destroying Governor Jenkins was as bad as having the photographs released, after I found him in the garage that morning the verdict was suicide while the balance of his mind was disturbed. But it had been disturbed for years, General. It took that man to push him over the edge.'

At the door, Coogan turned again.

'Thank you,' he said. 'Your reputation will in some measure be restored.'

'When I was young, my mama used to say, "You have to eat a peck of dirt before you die",' she said sadly. 'But Lord, I've taken more than that.'

ÎLE ST LOUIS, PARIS

A *Comte* had had the elegant little mansion built to house his family while he worked assiduously to insert himself ever-closer into the writhing mass of French aristocracy that surrounded the personage of the *Roi du Soleil* at Versailles. Although successful, his descendant who held the title just one hundred years later lost it together with his head, which fell into a bloody basket close by the gaggle of *tricoteuses* gathered to enjoy the scene. After a number of different incarnations in the years in between, in the 1950s it had been converted into an elegant small hotel.

Ashraf Amran's room looked out over the inner courtyard where *actinidia* vines were beginning to show their pink- and cream-tipped leaves, and tall, slender *Mme Gregoire Staechlin* roses soared upwards displaying their copper-coloured buds. They were matched with the shorter *Mme Seltzer* – white, like the fizzing tablets – both thoughtfully thornless lest the happy guest reach out for a moment's support against the wall on his way to his room. Ash loved to come to Paris, there was so much of her blood and culture that came from ancient civilisations. When she was here, or in London, or Oxford, when she had been in Tehran, she realised just how young was the most powerful nation in the world, the place she had made home.

Her room was furnished with Provençal fabric, a table was set close by the window and the early-evening sun shone on the glasses and silverware. A wine bucket glistened with condensation; a dark-green bottle of champagne and a fresh green bottle of Sancerre nestled in the ice. She wore a silk Pucci dress, and simple gold jewellery at neck and wrist. She looked lovely. She was nervous.

A soft knock came on the door. She went and opened it, and Vladimir Rykov stood outside.

'Come in,' she said. 'Come in.'

She shut the door behind him, and they stood looking at each other for a moment, smiling with great pleasure, but almost shyly.

'Darling,' she said. 'Open the champagne. It's so good to see you, I want to celebrate.'

Rykov bowed in agreement, and went over to the bucket.

'Laurent Perrier,' he said. 'We had that the last time.'

'Of course. It's *our* champagne.' They laughed. Rykov eased the cork out with a pop and filled the tall flutes.

'Here's to us,' she said. 'And your family.'

'And to yours,' he responded. They sipped on the lovely buttery bubbles.

'How is your husband?' said Rykov.

'Afsar is in Evin prison still. But alive, Vladimir, alive. We will be reunited.'

'You will.'

'Is your family well?' Ash said brightly, determinedly. 'You have your dacha out at Nokolina Gora now, don't you?'

'How do you know?' said Rykov, then allowed his eyebrows to sink back down. 'What a stupid thing to say,' he said in amusement. 'To you of all people. You could listen to me calling Lena to tell her I was on my way home for supper if you wanted.'

'I *could*,' said Ash. 'But I don't.'

'Yes, we have the dacha. And live in Lenin Hills.'

'Well done. Now you're an aristocrat.'

Rykov bowed his head in acknowledgement. 'It's true. Russia has a class-structure again.'

'About three thousand aristocratic families?'

'Perhaps slightly more. They are passing on their possessions, their houses to their childrne. It is becoming hereditary. The son can inherit the father's position, his title.'

'And as an aristocrat,' she said with slightly malicious amusement, 'where are you staying?'

'The Lancaster. On the rue du Berri.'

'Now there was an aristocrat,' said Ash. 'They don't make them like the *Duc* these days. Nice in the Lancaster, is it?'

'Very.'

'Not quite like staying in the Hotel Gorki?'

Rykov grinned. 'I will not be baited, Ash.'

'No,' she said. She filled up their glasses. 'I have asked for our meal to be brought up to us. I did not think that it would be wise for us to be seen in public. I have taken the liberty of ordering, I hope you don't mind.'

'Of course not.' Rykov took a pull at the champagne. 'Ash,' he said quietly. 'What is it? What has made you require my presence so urgently?'

'Some things have happened. Some things *are* happening. Very powerful people think that you, the Soviet Union is responsible. I do not. I am, however, a small figure, crying out with a feeble voice against a stentor. I do not have enough evidence to prove myself right. I want you to help me get it.'

There was a knock at the door and a young waiter arrived with a covered tray. He lit tall yellow candles and removing the cover served two large golden scallop shells. Pouring two glasses of green Sancerre with courteous efficiency he wished them *bon appetit* and ushered himself out. They took red and blue patterned provençal napkins from beside their plates and prepared to eat.

Rykov tapped the upper shell of the scallop.

'How does one enter this?' he enquired.

'The upper shell is pastry, made to look real,' Ash explained. 'It's *Coquille St-Jaques en Feuillete*.'

They cut into the light flaky pastry to reveal the white and

236

orange scallops inside.

'It's delicious,' said Rykov.

'We've lost a missile submarine. An SSBN,' Ash said.

'The *Maine*. We have noted that it seems to be missing.'

'We've found it. It was sunk by enemy action.'

Rykov looked across the table at her in alarm.

'The Trident missiles have been taken out of it. We think you did it.'

Rykov's expression changed to one of outright horror.

'There's a *lot* of evidence linking you to the attack. Is it possible? Might you have done it?'

'I would never have advocated something so provocative,' Rykov said worriedly. The fragrant steam wisped up past his face from the plate. 'We certainly have wished to test President Cord's resolve. My reading of Cord is that he is by training and instinct an historian, and believes in the broad scope of history. He believes, correctly, that American power and status has been adversely affected by its strategic commitments, and is seeking to restore US fortunes by cutting back before it is too late. In so doing he believes, perhaps also correctly, that the USSR will be tempted into the kind of strategic over-stretch that the USA is drawing back from, and that this will bring about our ultimate decline. From our point of view, we certainly wish to test the water, so to speak, to see if Cord will stick to his beliefs, but I would have said that we have done that by our arms build-up in Central America, to which he has not reacted. To sink a missile submarine smacks of insanity … it is too much, I cannot see that he would have any option but to strike back.'

Rykov picked up his fork again and recommenced eating.

'That is my opinion also,' Ash said.

'If *we* didn't do it,' said Rykov, 'then who did?'

'The Iran of Khalif Hossein. I will explain.'

While they finished their seafood she recounted the story of her long-term fears and suspicion of the Iranian drive for nuclear weapons. As she was coming to the end the waiter reappeared, bearing another tray. Clearing the empty scallop shells he replaced them with white plates, embossed around the rim, that each bore a work of art.

'*Medaillon de Veau et ses Beatilles,*' he said proudly. '*La specialité de la maison.*'

The gold medallions of veal were served with Madeira sauce and garnished with sweetbread, brains and veal marrow, together with green asparagus spears, chopped white truffle, fresh chervil and parsley. They looked and smelled wonderful. Ash poured lightly chilled red Chinon from the Loire into glasses.

'Better than borscht soup?' she enquired mischievously.

'Better than hamburger,' retorted Rykov.

The food tasted as good as it looked.

'Sultani is your man,' Ash continued. 'A long-term undercover agent, dedicated, talented, phenomenally productive for the USSR. This is what everyone sees. I see a different kind of double-agent. I see a man certain of his belief beyond any secular force. I see the servant of Allah.'

'And only you see this?'

'Yes.'

'Ash … maybe they are right,' Rykov said gently. 'Maybe we *did* do it. I would not know about it. There are certainly enough hawks in the military willing to squeeze the testicles of the USA, and Krilov has to listen to them just as Gorbachev did, because he has to have their support, he cannot alienate them. Could the Iranians organise such a thing? It would require incredible organisation, total single-mindedness.'

'You have summed up the Shi'ia philosophy of Khalif Hossein. Like the quintessential poker player, Hossein is concentrating on only one subject, considered by him to be of overriding importance, to the exclusion of all others. He has his agenda, and it matters not to him whether the young men of Iran die in thousands or in millions, whether the country is plunged into bankruptcy, whether by his actions the rest of the civilised world consider Iran an international pariah. If any of it brings forward by one day

238

that extension of Islamic power over the planet it is all worth it.'

'So what do you want from me?'

'Proof. We do not make overhead surveillance of the USA. You do. I want the digital data from your *Cosmoses* for the last two weeks of January. If I have it I can find the MiG-27 and MiL helicopter that conducted the attack.'

'Is that all?' Rykov asked, with slight sarcasm.

'No. If I do not succeed in convincing those more powerful than I that I am right and they are wrong then the USA is going to make some kind of military strike against the USSR in retaliation for the sinking of the *Maine*. If it happens then there will at least be one high-placed intelligence officer who knows the truth, and who can impart that truth to Krilov and the high command. For the US and the USSR won't be talking. And what do you think will happen if you *didn't* sink the *Maine* and we sink the *Kirov* say?'

'We'll retaliate.'

'Yes,' Ash said sombrely. She surveyed the remains of the work of art on her plate. 'And where will *that* lead?'

'How do you propose I get the digital data for the weeks you have mentioned?'

'I have some tools that will do it.'

She waited until the young man had removed the plates, bringing with him champagne sorbet in chilled glasses, garnished with wild strawberries.

'In your archives is a man called Alexei Rudenko, who is in a position to provide you with copies of the data you require. You can make friends with him *ty mne i ya tebe*.'

' "You for me and me for you." And how am I to scratch his back?'

'Rudenko loves to read. He cannot obtain the kind of books that interest him in the Soviet Union, for obvious reasons. But *po blatu*, by connections, he could get a regular supply. From you. Bring him some choice items *na levo* and he'll provide you with what I need. He likes biography and history. Make sure you include a

Solzhenitsyn and something by Medvedev. Irina Ratushinskaya too.'

'I'm beginning to see his taste in literature,' Rykov said dryly.

'To make sure your grip on him is secure you'll need a stick to beat him with should you so choose. Here it is. Rudenko, a family man, wants his children to do well. He has a boy and a girl. They are intelligent and he hopes that they will go to Moscow State. To this end he is paying for private tutoring – maths, English and biology. He and his wife drive a near-new Zhiguli. He isn't doing all this on his salary.'

'We have a saying in Russia – if you're really mad at someone – "let him live on his salary". It's a curse. Everyone's in on *vzyatka* of some kind. What brand is Rudenko's?'

'On his days off you may find Rudenko in a small Moscow park, near the statue of Ivan Fyodorov. He's big in the black market for books. In the archives he has access to a photo-copying machine. He does not have to seek KGB permission to use it. Being a man of enterprise he has fixed the machine so it does not register the copies he makes, and ensures that sufficient boxes of paper are suitably 'spoiled' in delivery, *po blatu* with the supplier. He does well. Last month he was selling three-volume editions of the complete poetry of Anna Akhmatova for three hundred rubles. Plenty of buyers, so I was told. Some of his customers call him up, and slip around to his house of an evening. I'm sure OBKhSS in the Ministry of Internal Security would be suitably interested. That's the stick. But I'm sure you can make it work *ty mne i ya tebe*. Rudenko's a businessman.'

'How will I get the data to you, once I receive it from this literary entrepreneur?'

Ash got up and fetched the silver Halliburton suitcase.

'With this. You'll send the data in a squirt transmission on SHF. I'll give you the frequency. Do you remember the old "cheesebox"? If you were an agent, needing to confer with your confederates on some vital matter you rented an apartment, with two telephones. These you connected together through the electronic "cheesebox". One telephone number was known by the confederates, the second only by the agent. The agent dialled through from a distant place, and stalking countermeasures crews would arrive, if at all, at the empty apartment. The equipment in here will do the same job to shield your transmission. There is no way for it to be traced to you.'

Rykov poured small balloons of *marc*. It was fully dark outside, the candle light made pools on the windows.

'I'll have it done,' he said.

'Thank you. In the folder in the suitcase there are some choice pieces of intelligence. They may aid you in your job, make you appear even more of a prophet than you already are.'

'Thank you,' said Rykov, in his turn.

Ash sipped the *marc*.

'Do you want to come over?' she said casually. 'We could get you all out.'

Rykov shook his head. 'I am too old. Too set.'

'You'll be like a Ruritanian princeling soon, out of some long-distant past. Enterprising Jews in Manhattan will run tours to mediaeval Russia, and there you'll be.'

'I'll take care to wear my comic-opera uniform.'

Rykov tossed back the liquor. 'I must go,' he said. 'And take the trinkets for the natives with me.'

He picked up the silver suitcase.

'Thank you for a lovely meal,' he said.

'You have access to Krilov, don't you?' Ash said suddenly, anxious.

'Yes. I can see him.'

'That's almost more important than the data. If it goes wrong. Tell Krilov the truth.'

'I will,' he promised. He raised his suitcase slightly. 'I have my helping of "grease", little Ashraf. Have you no stick to beat me with?'

'I don't need any stick. I would not use it if I had. We

241

both know what will happen if our respective employers find out about us. We will both lose.'

'Yes,' Rykov said dryly. 'You your job, me my head.'

'Take care.'

'Yes, you too.'

'I love you,' she said.

'I love you.'

With him gone, she was suddenly afflicted by a terrible sense of foreboding. She drained the glass of *marc*, but it would not go away.

BEIRUT

The Switzerland of the Middle East was a war-zone. Ash was met by four men at the airport, former soldiers of Khosrow's Airborne Paratroopers, three sergeants and a major. They were armed with Heckler and Koch type 53 sub-machine guns – 'Hocklers' – the favoured weapon of professional bodyguards, or 'bullet catchers' as they called themselves. Ash stayed in Beirut for three days, and they were with her night and day. For anyone of importance to venture into such a land of banditry and war-lords without solid protection was to invite capture and months of imprisonment in a box. Congressman Cord would not come to save Ash, if she were held, but she had come to find why Cord had come, and had produced American hostages like a conjurer.

As the 'principal', Ash followed the rules, and did as her team of guards said. Misfortune came to a guarded target who would not do as his or her protectors asked. Sometimes it was difficult to do so, the demands of the job could not marry up with the needs of total security. For those in such a position, fatalism was the answer. 'If your name is on the bullet,' said the Prince of Wales, 'there is nothing you can do.'

Ash had no need to be seen, and she stayed in the apartment provided for her. Discreetly, certain men came to meet her there. On the third day, she greeted Sayyed Saddam Kashk. The mullah sat down on a sofa and puffed, out of breath by his climb up the stairs. He was big, a fat man. A guard brought cold lemonade and coffee, and some biscuits.

'I received your message,' said Kashk, 'and came as quickly as I could.'

'Thank you,' said Ash. 'Did you encounter any problems?'

'I am my father's son ...' he said. 'For me, and others like me, travel is still possible. Especially here.'

'Hizbollah.'

'Yes.'

'Hizbollah – the Party of Allah. The shoots are here, but the roots remain in Iran. And yet these were the people who held the hostages, and released them to Congressman Cord. Why did they do that, do you think?'

'I think it must be as the-now-President Cord said, "We talked and we realised that there was just one God, whom we worshipped in our different ways," ' Kashk said solemnly.

'I'm not Colonel North, Saddam,' Ash said sharply.

'No, of course,' Kashk said, admonished and unrepentant. 'Clearly, Khalif Hossein wished Cord to win the election.'

'Not the Russians.'

'The Russians? Why should the Russians want Cord elected?'

'I could introduce you to a man who could give you that answer in detail, but he is not here. I have talked with people here, those who know. I can find no evidence of Russian involvement in either kidnappings or releases. Only Hizbollah. All the hostages were seized at the same time. They were kept with some care, husbanded for the day they would be needed. And used, to ensure the election of Cord to the Presidency. Why?'

'I do not know. I could ask my father, who might.'

'Is your father well?'

'He is in Qom, away from the excesses in Tehran.'

'His support remains firm?'

'He has the allegiance of most of the Friday prayer-leaders. He is capable of mobilising millions of people in the name of Islam. Even Khalif Hossein dare not move against him.'

'Good. You will send my respect?'

'I will.'

'Have you seen any Europeans in Iran?'

'Not since Hossein burned the martyrs.'

'They're there. Eighteen. Technicians.'

'I shall ask.'

When Kashk had gone Ash turned to the team leader of her guards, former Airborne Major Ghaffari.

'That was the last. I shall be leaving on tonight's airplane. I want to thank you and your men. You came highly recommended, but Colonel Araki did not exaggerate your skills.'

'The colonel is very kind. It was he who helped us to become bodyguards. Our commander, General Khosrowdad was murdered at the Refah school, but some of us escaped into exile.'

'There were many who died there, and elsewhere. And the killing still goes on. But it will be a different story one day. We have all had to take up new lines of work since we were exiled. Why bodyguarding?'

'We were soldiers, we understood the Middle East. We reasoned that for such as we there would always be well-paid work, and so it has proved.'

'How did you get your start?'

'We went to the colonel – Colonel Araki, our former commander. He had connections, he was able to get us on to the selection course of the training centre of the best bodyguards in the world – the British Royal Military Police. We qualified for the course. We already knew how

244

to use weapons, but they taught us anew, and better, with Browning pistols and Hockler sub-machine guns. Unarmed combat we were familiar with, but they taught us differently. An assassin is usually close to the principal when he makes his attack. When you see him, when you see the hands, you use Kempo Katzu Mo, which is a martial arts composite technique to punch or kick the assassin, while you thrust the principal out of the firing line. Then you draw and start shooting into the assassin.'

'Is your work mostly defending VIPs against assassination?'

'If we were in America, our work would largely be protection of such against "celebrity killers". Here, we protect powerful men and women from their enemies, who would have them killed or kidnapped. The techniques are somewhat different, but of course the principle remains the same.'

'You said "the hands",' Ash said curiously. ' "When you see the hands". What does that mean?'

'That's the motto of all bullet catchers. That sums it all up. If you have not been able to prevent the assassin from getting close to the principal, if he has penetrated your security screen, if the job of "the man" requires that he be exposed in public, then you watch for the hands. The hands give the assassin away. They may contain a gun, or a knife, or a bomb. He may simply be flexing them in the moment before the attack. If you watch for the hands you have that extra moment to save your charge.'

'I'll remember that, if someone ever has a go at me,' Ash said, with a faint smile.

Ghaffari hesitated. 'The Colonel advised us that you were most special, a very important person indeed. I wondered to begin with how this was so. Then I saw the men who came here. I knew them. Men of power. They treated you with respect, as an equal, I thought. Then I looked closer, and I saw that it was more than that, that they were taking out insurance, against the day you would be more powerful than they. I do not know what it is you

245

will be doing, but I and my men, we would be your men. If you need us, we will serve you.'

Ash inclined her head gracefully in assent.

'When the job is mine to give, it shall be yours,' she said, and Ghaffari bowed low.

THE WHITE HOUSE

The President saw Coogan in the Oval Office. With him was his chief of staff, Harrison Taylor. The meeting was at the request of the air force general, who had specified that Cord's former campaign manager be present. Coogan came in full uniform, his stars like liquid silver, the awards for courage in battle and success in career blazing on his chest. Cord felt a spasm of physical rage at thus seeing his wishes regarding the dress of military officers so flouted, having reversed the old Reagan edict that had had unwary Washingtonians believing the next war had started. However, he decided to wait until Coogan had had his say before reducing him to size. Coogan was not long for his job, Cord promised himself.

'Thank you for seeing me, Mr President,' Coogan said formally.

Cord nodded. He was seated in his round-backed leather chair, framed by the two great flags of office that stood behind him. Taylor sat by one of the tall windows overlooking the Rose Garden; Cord kept Coogan standing in front of the big, polished and carved oak desk, a gift from Queen Victoria to President Hayes, made from the timbers of the obsolescent battleship, H.M.S. *Resolute*. All was contained by the vast pale gold, rosette-decorated oval rug that flowed across the room.

Coogan was carrying a blue dossier tied with scarlet tape. Printed across it in matching letters were the words

246

FOR THE EYES OF THE PRESIDENT ONLY.

'I have here, sir, a complete history of the most successful undercover operation ever mounted by the Soviet Union within this country, aimed at securing the services of an Agent of Influence.'

'I thought the job of the air force was flying fighters and bombers, and firing missiles, not catching spies,' Cord said acidly.

'Our job is the defence of this country,' Coogan retorted mildly. 'We do not care how we do it. Our Intelligence is as good as anyone else's. In this case better.'

Coogan's paranoid about the reds, thought Cord. He's got to go. We need to be free from all that Cold War stuff.

'And who is this so-called agent of influence?' he said wearily.

'The Soviet operation was aimed at promoting the interests of a candidate in the presidential elections that they considered would, if elected, put into effect policies beneficial to them. The Agent of Influence would be an unwitting one, but no less valuable for all that.'

Cord looked at him in irritable bewilderment.

'What in hell are you talking about, General. The election's over. Everyone else lost, I won.'

'Yes, sir,' Coogan said with enormous, and only barely concealed satisfaction. 'You are the Agent of Influence.'

The President went white with fury.

'Hand me what you have there. Let me see what you have invented and when you leave this room it will be as a civilian.'

'Very good, sir,' said Coogan calmly, and handed the dossier across the desk. 'With your permission, it might be advantageous for Mr Taylor to see the sheets after you.'

Cord was a speed reader, a talent acquired while sifting through mounds of primary sources as a historian. He had the ability to devour very large amounts of information, and as president, did so. It took him very little time to crunch through the first few pages, and as he did so, his expression altered. He looked up at Coogan uncertainly, and went back to the beginning. He paused, and without a word, began passing the evidence over to his chief of staff, his one-time campaign manager. Without being asked, Coogan pulled up a chair and sat down.

Harrison Taylor looked briefly at the first few pages, then merely accepted the sheets as they came, allowing them to pile in his lap. He looked across the lovely Seymour card table behind Cord, into the rose garden, at the height of its beauty, his eyes unseeing, and Coogan smiled.

When Cord came to the end, his eyes had gone blank.

'One of you has betrayed his country, his president,' he said.

'No, sir,' said Coogan. '*His* country is the USSR.'

Harrison Taylor stood up, and placed the pile of paper on the desk.

'I'll go and write a letter of resignation,' he said casually. 'Reasons of health, that sort of thing. We may as well stick to the formalities.'

Cord was still having trouble accepting what had happened. He was like a survivor of an air crash.

'It's true …?'

Taylor shrugged. 'You didn't imagine you were elected for your boyish smile, did you?'

'You're under arrest,' said Cord. 'The FBI …'

'Mr President, that may not be such a good idea,' said Coogan. He was firm, in command. 'If we charge him, it'll all come out. You would have to resign.'

Cord nodded, accepting Coogan's planning.

'Let him go. He's no danger now.'

He looked up at Taylor. 'Don't bother clearing out your desk, boy. There's a man waiting outside to show you out.'

Taylor nodded, and without a word, left.

'What am I to do …' said Cord.

'You must prove the Soviet Union wrong, sir,' said Coogan, like iron. 'They believed that you would not support the interests of this country. They were wrong.

You are a patriot. You fought for your country in the war. They misunderstood what you really stood for. They have committed three acts of war against this great nation. They interfered with our free elections, they have poured arms into our front yard, Central America, they have sunk the *Maine*, a ballistic missile submarine. Now we must demonstrate our resolve to defend freedom. We must strike back.'

Cord was very pale. He got to his feet, and with quick steps, went to the bathroom discreetly off the office. He was gone some minutes, and Coogan spent the time enjoyably, admiring Dumaresque's oil 'The Signing of the Declaration of Independence' which hung over the fireplace. He did not know anything about art, but he knew something he liked when he saw it. When Cord returned he had some colour in his cheeks, and traces of moisture where he had washed his face and mouth, cleaning himself of vomit.

'So what do we do, General Coogan?' he asked formally.

'We do two things. We re-start the programme you cancelled to get our SDI capability into orbit. The work was well advanced, all the hardware is available, it's only a question of getting the teams back on the job. Two, we take out their principal threat to our security. We destroy their SDI complex outside Smolensk, and kill the technicians, engineers and scientists. It will put them back a decade.'

'What with?' Cord said bewilderedly.

'With our B-2 bombers.'

'I don't understand. The B-2s are destroyed. I ordered them cut up.'

'Through an administrative oversight, your orders were not carried out. I have had the officer concerned transferred to other duties. The bombers are in place, and ready to accomplish the mission.'

'What about Congress? They'll never support such a thing.'

'You don't have to tell them, sir. All you have to do is make a "finding".'

Coogan reached over, and took a sheet of presidential

paper from a pile, and placed it in front of the stricken
president.

'Here you are, sir,' he said. 'I'll tell you what to say.'

Cord stared blankly at the sheet of crisp paper. While he
was doing so, his telephone rang. On reflex, he picked it up.
A voice on the other end spoke agitatedly, and he put it
down without reply a few seconds later.

'Harrison Taylor is dead,' he whispered. 'He died in an
automobile accident leaving here.'

'No doubt overcome with remorse for his actions,' said
Coogan.

'You *killed* him.'

'He can't talk now,' Coogan said coldly. He picked up a
pen and gave it to Cord. 'Now, sir. Write this, please. "On
this day, I find that in the interests of national security …" '

When Cord had written, Coogan reached over, and took
the paper.

'Thank you, Mr President,' he said. 'The Air Force is
proud to carry out your command.'

RAF MILDENHALL, ENGLAND

Lieutenant Colonel Robert Nelson and Major Brad Davis
were aware of the existence of General Coogan much in the
same manner as a pair of highly talented and valued
technicians in a great corporation might be aware of the
existence of the chairman of the board; it still came as a
surprise to find him large as life inside your laboratory,
interesting himself in your business. Nelson and Davis'
'business' was operating the Lockheed SR-71 supersonic
strategic reconnaissance aircraft. Nelson, the pilot, and
Davis, the reconnaissance systems officer, were a part of
the 9th Strategic Reconnaissance Wing of SAC, operating
on detachment from their home base of Beale, California.

From Beale, Mildenhall and Kadena in Okinawa, SR-71s flew operations throughout Asia, the Middle East, the Soviet Arctic as well as central and Southern America.

While much of the US surveillance system depended upon their exotic and fabulously expensive satellites, it nevertheless required the use of manned aircraft as well. Despite their multi-layered abilities, satellites had disadvantages. Principal of these was the fact that they were restricted to orbits, which made them predictable to those not wishing to be spied upon. An aircraft, however, could change speed at a moment's notice, fly wherever it chose, drop under clouds with cameras whirring, return to a target as often as it wished, even hang about until the opportunity to gather intelligence offered itself. Further-more, they were cheap. An SR-71 cost a bargain $19.6 million when the last one had been delivered, and the air force still had nineteen of the thirty five bought left. A photoreconnaissance satellite cost $250 million to put into orbit, and a geosynchronous SIGINT Rhyolite even more than that. Coogan's predecessor as chief of staff had proposed to mothball the SR-17s. Coogan, who liked to have his quiver full, had rescinded the order upon taking command, and the fabulous black fleet remained in service.

Nelson and Davis had prepared for their mission the day before. It was flight-planned by computer, and they familiarised themselves with it. Most of the actions the aircraft would have to perform during the supersonic phase of the mission were pre-programmed on to tapes, which were loaded into the aircraft's central computer. Both pilot and RSO were veterans of many missions, they had flown over the Kola Peninsula, peering down at the Soviet Northern fleet, they had dashed from Beale to capture Soviet freighters off-loading weapons and ordnance in Nicaragua, they had flown out of Okinawa, home of the venomous black snake, the habu, that so resembled the cobra-like frontal silhouette of the SR, flown along the coast of North Korea and dodged one of the near-thousand SAMs that had been fired at SR-71s in the course of its career, none of them with success.

Every mission was special for the very-highly-trained, very experienced crews that flew the SRs, but this one was a little different, in that the timing was vital. They had but seconds to be in the right place, to capture on film a group of people, walking across an airport ramp.

Nelson and Davis had begun their day early, about three hours before they were due to fly, going to Base Ops, filing their flight plan and meeting the tanker crews to go over the details of the individual rendezvous. After the tanker men left to get themselves into position the two 'crew dogs' as the SR operators were known went over to Physiological Support Division for breakfast. There they were unexpectedly joined by Coogan, and all three had a meal of steak and eggs, with orange juice, low residue-high protein for energy, as they would not be eating properly for several hours. Coogan left them again as they went for their maintenance debrief on the aircraft and both men commented on how unexpectedly pleasant and knowledgeable Coogan was. They had been warmed by his presence. It was no politician's act on his part; Coogan had genuine and unbounded admiration for his boys, and loved to be up at the sharp end with them. Coogan was a peacetime rarity, a fighting soldier who had climbed to the top of the greasy pole when there was no war on. Nelson and Davis had been together for five years, they were practically married; one of the qualities they had to have, before even being selected to fly SRs was the right psychological make-up, the ability to get on and work with other people. In Coogan they recognised a fellow, Nelson had been a former F-111 driver, and Davis had done tours in both B-52s and KC-135 tankers. Coogan, the old-time B-58 man kept himself current in almost anything he could, and had entertained them with snippets of information from the B-2 bomber, which he was fresh from checking out in.

The medic gave the two a short physical and then they

were dressed in their shiny orange S-1030 astronaut-style suits and helmets. Known laconically as 'silver tuxedos' the suits required three assistants apiece to get into, and provided life support should a decompression occur or should the crew have to eject at the aircraft's stratospheric operating altitude. Once they were kitted out the suits were tested for leaks and correct breathing, and when cleared, connected to the portable oxygen system. Grasping these, the two men waddled out to the waiting van, where they sat in reclining chairs. The suits weighed forty pounds, and were rather bulky, although comfortable to sit in, and were the reason that unlike other flight crews the 'crew dogs' did not perform their own preflight checks, but depended upon their mobile crew. When they arrived at the waiting black delta they clambered up the steps and were assisted into their seats by the accompanying PSD technicians, who got them comfortable and strapped them in. The big jet was slowly 'bleeding' fuel, the unique low-vapour-pressure hydro-carbon called JP-7, as its tanks were porous when unheated and unpressurised. It was another reason that the pre-flight sequences were planned, and 'hack' time important. Nelson sat at the front; his cockpit had reasonable visibility, nothing like that required for a fighter, but his four panels were sufficient for taxiing, take-off, landing and refuelling, which was all that was required. Davis, behind him, surrounded by his systems equipment had two small side panels only.

The J-58 engines were turned over by a directly-coupled bank of three Chrysler V-8 automobile engines. There was forty minutes to go, and they spent twenty going through their checks. Then Nelson released the brakes and with clearance to taxi the 107 foot long aircraft rolled out from its special 'shed'. Accompanied by a small fleet of ground crew and security vehicles it made its way to the holding point where they ran through the take-off checks and the ground crew removed tags and armed the ejection system. The Mildenhall runway was completely checked for obstructions, the aircraft was in Code One condition and with clearance to take-off it rolled out on to the centreline dead on 'hack' time. Nelson put the fuel to the two vast Pratt & Whitney J-58 turbo-ramjets and on full afterburner, propelled by 65,000 pounds of thrust the manta-ray-shaped aircraft accelerated down the runway. It took just on 4000 feet and 200 knots to become airborne, and Nelson rotated to a high 30 degree angle of attack, retracting the undercarriage. The steep angle of climb was to limit lower-altitude airspeed, as the SR had a specific never-exceed speed in KEAS knots equivalent airspeed in the thick air of low altitudes, and it was a cold morning. The ground crews watched as the black shape lanced upwards, riding on twin shafts of pure white heat, as long as the aircraft itself. Then they vanished into the murk of the English morning, and what the 'crew dogs' referred to as a 'no-kidding' mission was in operation.

The SR stayed subsonic to 25,000 feet, and some seven minutes after take-off made the first rendezvous with the Boeing KC-135Q. The routine for refuelling was as formalised as a dance ritual. It was called 'point parallel', and began with the tanker flying towards the receiving aircraft. The two were connected by an encrypted ranging device that measured distance and an encrypted ADF which gauged the bearings. The whole operation was done 'comm out', neither partner talked, which was why it had to be ritualised. Distance and bearing were monitored by the navigator of the Boeing and Davis, the RSO in the SR-71, both of whom guided their pilots. Levelling off at 25,000 feet the SR was some 45 miles behind the tanker, which was some 9 miles offset. When they were twenty miles apart the tanker began a 180-degree turn. As it rolled out 60 seconds later it was flying on the same heading as its receiver, and some three miles in front. Davis guided Nelson to within a mile of the tanker, at which point the pilot had a visual, and took over. The boom operator in the Boeing streamed a little fuel to give Nelson a better fix, and he slid up beneath the bigger aircraft, using the director lights under its belly, as well as his years of experience in the art. With the SR on station, the boom operator extended the boom and made contact with the SR's receptacle, some twelve feet behind Davis. The fuel – the very high flashpoint JP-7 to cope with the high temperatures of speed runs – began to gush into the seven fuel tanks. The SR-71 used up to 8,000 gallons per hour.

When the refuelling was complete the SR backed off from the tanker and the two aircraft separated. There was a pause while Nelson and Davis ran through their post-refuelling checklist, a dozen or so items including the closing of the fuel receptacle doors, and with that out of the way they accelerated again, climbing subsonically for some 8,000 feet before Nelson pushed over into a dive for a little over 3,000 feet, during which the SR went through the sound barrier. Intercepting the set KEAS shortly afterwards, with autopilot now engaged, the SR began to climb, maintaining its KEAS. The whole climb-dive-climb manoeuvre was known as a 'dipsy'. Steeply at first, and flattening out as the air became thinner the aircraft climbed to over 100,000 feet. At cruise altitude, they accelerated to near Mach 4, some 2,400 mph. At that speed the friction of even the thin air at such altitude produced temperatures in the region of 510 degrees Fahrenheit along the aircraft's titanium skin, causing the jet to stretch by some eleven inches. The Plexiglass windshield in front of Nelson heated up to 622 degrees, and some thirty yards behind him, the tailpipes of the turbo-ramjets responsible for it all burned white-hot at 1,200 degrees.

At cruise, the two men fell into a systems monitoring mode. For Davis, he had an extra responsibility this flight. He was listening to the pilot of another aircraft, and to his air traffic controllers. The Rhyolite satellite that sat in geosynchronous orbit 22,175 miles over Borneo had been listening since the Antonov taxied out from Vnukovo II, the VIP airport west of Moscow, and had re-transmitted the data to interested parties. They included Lt-Col Randy

Ellis in the SCF in Sunnyvale, California, General Coogan in Mildenhall, England, and Major Davis, in the RSO's seat in SR-71 number 17966. Over the Mediterranean, they began descent back down to 25,000 feet for a second refuelling from their next designated KC-135Q. Over Kenya, which the boomer in the tanker could see green and verdant below, but they could not, they topped off, and once free reaccelerated back up to altitude. Over the Indian Ocean, as they climbed they turned gently in a 35 degree bank, the reconnaissance aircraft was no aerobatic machine, to travel north.

Not far away, but much lower in the earth's atmosphere, the Antonov transport was on final approach. Davis was feeding the figures into his computer, and it was coming up with the right times. They were smack on target. Nelson had got his RSO into the sensitive area and now it was his aircraft. Although neither man could see the ground so far below them, they knew that they were exactly where they should be; the Northrop astro-inertial navigation system, peering at the stars from a small window behind the cockpit told them so.

The SR-71 could carry an array of interchangeable sensors, stowed in the interchangeable nose mission equipment bay bolted in front of Nelson, and in palletised, interchangeable reconnaissance equipment packs in the chines each side of the fuselage. The various cameras, side-looking airborne radar (SLAR) system, infra-red sensors, radar ferrets and other ELINT receivers meant that the intelligence take from any one mission could be considerable. On this particular flight, however, the most important sensors on board were the pair of 48 inch focal length technical objective cameras that pointed straight down, and slightly behind the aircraft. The photographs they took were imaged on ultra-thin, fine-grained Kodak film, which gave pictures of stunning clarity.

The transport landed, rolled out and went to ground control to taxi in. Davis heard the pilot talking, and the ground controller granting permission. He heard him talk on the 'phone, alerting the reception committee. The engines shut down and the ground crew wheeled the disembarkment steps into place. The doors opened, the guard of honour was in place. The men trooped down to meet their hosts. High above, invisible to the naked eye, the SR-71 streaked through the sky at over 2,000 mph.

Host and guest embraced. The sonic boom arrived at the ground, rattling windows, beating on ears. Everyone looked up. The cameras looked down.

As he touched down at Mildenhall Nelson streamed the big orange mesh parachute and held the nose high to add aerodynamic braking. He had flown a couple of slow circuits after descending from altitude in order to cool the airframe for the ground crew. Rolling at fifty-five knots he released the parachute, to be collected by the maintenance crew. It was standard procedures for the big aircraft to go straight to its shed on landing. The 'crew dogs' shut it down, and the ground crew rolled forward the crew access steps. Despite the hours inside the cockpit, where space was at a premium, they were not too stiff. Their 'silver tuxedos' and the special seats were remarkable for the comfort they offered. Clarence 'Kelly' Johnson, the designer of the SR had offered any of his employees fifty dollars if they could find *anything* simple about the aircraft, and as he said years later, he still had his money. The two airmen climbed into their van, leaving the ground crew to wait the half-hour or so until the aircraft had cooled sufficiently to be touched, its silver heat-reflective lined nose and chine bays emptied, and the intelligence take moved swiftly to data analysis for processing.

Nelson and Davis were finishing debriefing, getting ready to take a shower, change, eat a good meal when Coogan arrived.

'You did a wonderful job,' he said, grinning.

'Thank you, sir,' they chorused.

'I thought you might like to see what we sent you there for, and what you got.'

He took a freshly printed photograph from a folder and laid it on the table.

'A society photographer couldn't have done better than this,' Coogan crowed. It gave him intense satisfaction to see his system in perfect operation.

'Let me identify these sons of bitches for you. I know each and every damn one of them. Admiral Novikov, Navy. General Mikul'chik, Army. General Stefanovsky, KGB. Economic expert. Brigadier Malyshev, Spetsnaz. Their various aides. Here, Popov, Central Committee. Party Secretary Krilov's man. And on the other side. Shaikh Mansur, Speaker of the Majlis. Sayyed Mohammad. Hojat al-Islam Bokhara'i. Hojat al-Islam Beheshti.'

Coogan's finger moved unerringly across the crystal-clear image. It paused and tapped, several times, on one single figure.

'And here he is.'

Nelson peered at the representation of the man he had only recently flown over.

'That's the Khalif.'

'The mad mullah himself,' said Coogan. 'Khalif Hossein.'

Davis looked at the Khalif, who with head back, like all the others, seemed to be looking straight at the camera. He had the eye for detail of the RSO.

'He's smiling,' he said. 'It almost looks like he's smiling for the camera, doesn't it?'

PLESETSK, USSR

The Soviet technicians at Plesetsk – Randy Ellis' counterparts at the SCF in Sunnyvale California – noted, as was their job, that the Complementary Expendable Launch Vehicle, also known as the Titan 4, ordered by the

USAF because they had always had doubts about NASA's shuttle, that blasted off that morning worked perfectly. The 204 feet tall rocket cost $1 million per foot, and at that price, was expected to. It placed a KH-11 into a near-circular orbit slightly over 300 miles up, near-polar at 97 degrees. It was standard procedure, just as it was standard procedure for the Soviet technicians to take a keen interest in it.

They also noted that the Americans had taken advantage of their technological expertise in miniaturisation to allow the rocket to carry a small 'piggyback' satellite into orbit as well. This subsatellite had a similar inclination at 97 degrees as the bigger KH-11, but a quite different orbit, being highly elliptical. They watched as it sped over the Southwest Pacific basin between Argentina and New Zealand at a perigee of only 200 miles, travelling at some 17,000 mph, to swing further and further away from the earth and reach its apogee of 24,200 miles, at a point about half way between the heat of the Caspian Sea and the frozen wasteland of Novaya Zemlya. Because its movement, relative to the terrain below, slowed so considerably with the great increase in distance the satellite was able to 'hang' over the USSR for as long as eight hours.

Randy Ellis and his contemporaries at the SCF and NRO, and their Soviet counterparts were engaged in an on-going orbital game of hide-and-seek. There was practically nothing in the arena that went unheard or unseen by the two sets of adversaries, but from time to time each side could be caught napping, or even be fooled. Those hiding on either side tried to conceal the capabilities of their satellites as much as possible, by adding features that might go undetected, or by disguising them by virtue of their orbital characteristics to pass for a kind of satellite that they were not. The advantage normally went with those seeking, because like all other types of analyst, whether those looking at imagery at NPIC or SIGINT at NSA headquarters, they had categorised everything over the years to establish precise operational patterns, and anything that did not fit the pattern caused immediate suspicion.

The hiders had had successes, however. Radar ferrets known as Jumpseat had been given the same characteristics as the SDS relay satellites used by KH-11s, and Rhyolite geosynchronous SIGINT satellites had been successfully disguised as DSP-647 early warning spacecraft. The small piggyback satellite that settled into its highly elliptical orbit, 'hanging' over the USSR for hours on end was therefore judged by the Soviets who peered up at it to be a Jumpseat radar ferret, sent up to take precise measurements of their powerful phased-array ABM and space tracking radars by recording their microwave transmissions.

They were completely, fatally wrong.

NELLIS AFB, TONOPAH, NEVADA

The principal enemy of the combat aircraft was radar. It had not always been so, as the seasoned and true cartoon to be found in almost all aircraft design offices throughout the world testified. The humour of the drawing was to be found in the representation of the way each group within the team would have designed the aircraft. The aerodynamicists made one beautiful, smooth and flowing in line. The production team nailed together a few planks in the shape of an airplane. The maintenance crew's aircraft was a mass of access panels, with all the control runs on the outside.

The Electronic Warfare group's design was never on the cartoon, reflecting their hitherto lowly position in the hierarchy, the battles they had had to fight for each watt of power, each cubic foot of space and square inch of surface to drive and house their processing equipment and antennae.

If the EW group had been allowed to draw their sketch for the cartoon, it would have looked like a Stealthy aircraft.

The world had changed, absolute performance had been redefined and Low Probability of Intercept was king. It did not matter if a Stealthy aircraft could not go as fast, manoeuvre as violently, climb as high or carry as great a bomb load if its chance of being found was one hundred times less than its bigger, faster and more powerful relation. And if you couldn't find and intercept it *at all*, then the Stealthy aircraft could go and come back and bomb you for as long as its home arsenals held munitions. And those arsenals, as General Coogan had once reminded an uncaring President Cord, happened to be the productive capacity of the USA.

Any moving vehicle generated disturbances in the physical environment around it, which propagated through space as waves. It emitted infra red because of its heat. It made noise, and created vibrations. It absorbed and reflected natural light in different proportions. All of these disturbances were characteristic of the vehicle, they enabled an observer, a hostile one in the case of a military vehicle like a fighter or a bomber, to identify it from a distance. Because the disturbances were both unique and a method of identifying the vehicle, they were known as 'signatures'. They all had to be controlled to make a truly Stealthy aircraft, and none was more important than the radar signature, which was by far the most prominent, and the one that gave the hostile observer the most information at the greatest distance.

To the eye, only a very smooth object glinted in the light, because optical wavelengths were very short, and anything less was rough to a light wave. Because radar wavelengths were long, most synthetic surfaces were smooth, and would glint most efficiently when illuminated by the radar beam. It was this efficient reflection which accounted for the extreme range at which radar could detect targets, and which the Stealth designer had to reduce to make his aircraft less detectable.

The measure used to evaluate how visible an aircraft was to radar was known as the radar cross section, or RCS. The most important point about RCS was that a small, efficient reflector like a flat plate at two right angles, or normal, to the radar beam would reflect as much energy as a very large sphere, which was not an efficient reflector. Pre-Stealth combat aircraft tended to be full of such efficient reflectors. The best air-superiority fighter in the world, the F-15 Eagle had a side-on area of about 25 square metres, or the size of a very large house. Typical frontal-aspect RCS figures for fighters like the F-15 or Soviet MiG-29 Fulcrum were of the order of 100 square metres and for bombers like the B-52 or Soviet *Backfire* up to 1,000 square metres.

For Stealth to be possible, RCS had to be brought below 0.5 square metre, and the reasons such little attention had been paid to RCS in producing combat aircraft like the F-15, MiG-29 and certainly the venerable B-52 was that up until the 1970s in the USA, which led the field, the technology for producing such miniscule radar returns as measured by RCS was simply not available. There were a number of reasons for this. Stealth was not just use of special materials like antiradar paints and radar-absorbent structures, although they were a part of it, and without their use Stealth was not possible. It went much further than that, and began with the very configuration of the aircraft.

Only latest-generation computers were powerful enough to model the very complex interactions and reflections in three dimensions, over the very wide spectrum of conditions in which the aircraft would have to operate, mapping the radar image over its entire area, under a full range of wavelengths, and producing the kind of three dimensional compound – curvature typical of Stealthy airframes, the canted fins, curved and baffled ducts, flush inlets, high-aspect-ratio nozzles, flexible-skinned ailerons, concealed antennae and weapons bay.

The next problem facing the design team was that the Stealthy aircraft so produced was grossly unstable, so much so that it was quite unflyable by hand without electronic assistance. Fortunately, it was a problem that designers had become familiar with since the early sixties, when automatic flight control systems technology came of age, and such differing military aircraft as the AH-1 Cobra attack helicopter and the SR-71 reconnaissance aircraft were both unflyable without the use of their stability augmentation systems. The technology of 'fly-by-wire' with its use of multiple systems of rate sensors and accelerometers had advanced to the stage where aircraft no longer had to be naturally stable about their three axles, but could be totally unstable and still fly thanks to artificial stability.

The shape of these very unstable, low RCS aircraft tended towards one of two extremes because of their highly-blended configuration – they became either flying wings or lifting bodies. Very different to look at, the two were in fact different versions of the same thing, only differing in their aspect ratios.

The most talked about Stealth aircraft was the Advanced Technology Bomber, Northrop's B-2. In 1948 Northrop had produced a remarkable, and advanced prototype bomber that was tested by the air force until 1952. It was an all-wing aircraft the YB-49. Designed before the advent of nuclear weapons it was not put into production mainly due to an inability to carry the large nuclear weapons of the time. The concept of a flying wing came into its own once more with the arrival of Stealth, and the B-2 featured that configuration.

The B-2 was not a special case, however, but one of the first of a new breed of low-observable or Stealthy aircraft. After the C-17 transport, no US aircraft designed for operations close to an armed opponent would not reflect

LO technology in its design. In the pipeline the US armed services had such aircraft as the TAV or trans-atmospheric vehicle, the successor to the SR-71, capable of travelling from New York to Tokyo in just over thirty minutes under supersonic combustion ramjet power. The US Navy had the A-12, their Advanced Tactical Aircraft, the successor to the A-6 Intruder. The USAF was to choose between the YF-22 and YF-23 for their Advanced tactical Fighter.

These were all in the pipeline. However, alongside the B-2, the USAF had the Lockheed F-117A. It had fifty-six, operated by the 4450th Tactical Group, and flown from a complex of small hangars at their own base at the Tonopah Test Range in Nevada, under conditions of extreme secrecy.

Creating a truly Stealthy aircraft had been compared to a game of Dungeons and Dragons, in that success at one level, reducing the RCS, qualified the player, the designers, to tackle a new set of ogre-infested mazes. For the Stealthy aircraft, these were the other signatures.

The F-15 Eagle had a frontal-aspect RCS of about 100 square metres, as did its Soviet MiG counterpart. The F-117 was slightly smaller, some 20.5 metres long and 12.8 metres wide across its 67.5 degrees of swept wings. It weighed in at 20,500 kg and carried its four 900 kg weapons in twin internal bays. Its exterior surfaces were extensively 'faceted' to discourage the scattering of radar energy towards the transmitter location, the facets being separately constructed from advanced, Lockheed-developed radar-absorbent material, RAM, attached to a skeletal sub-frame. Its navigational/attack system was optimised for its role of covert precision strike and comprised a forward-looking infra red sensor, FLIR, and a boresighted laser designator coupled to a high precision inertial navigation system. The GEC Astronics flight control system enabled the pilot to fly it by wire. Sleek, swallow-tailed and radical, the entire aircraft was assembled with extreme care and precision to avoid RCS spikes caused by any surface discontinuities. It had an

RCS of 0.01 square metre, the area of a flat plate 1 cm square. It was the RCS of a medium-sized bird.

Next in importance after RCS were the thermal, or infra red IR signatures. IR mattered a lot, because it was the only spectrum outside the radar bands in which air-to-air or any other form of autonomous anti-aircraft weapon had been made to work. The weapon could recognise the thermal signature from the engines, the exhaust, and the very heat of the aircraft itself, and home in.

Once again, the Skunk Works team had defeated the ogres. The F-117 had two-dimensional exhaust nozzles fabricated from RCC – reinforced carbon – a member of the carbon fibre family originally produced for missile nose cones. Using dry thrust in the closed position, the 2-D nozzle effectively restricted the rear view of the engines to a very narrow angle, suppressing both radar and thermal signatures. The General Electric F-404 turbofan engines had integral hot/cold flow mixers, and were medium-bypass-ratio. In a high-threat environment cold air could be drawn in and mixed with the exhaust to defeat heat-seeking missiles.

There was more. Using the fuel as a heat sink in the manner of the SR-71, and special coatings to the airframe, the IR signature was tailored to emit at wavelengths which were absorbed by the atmosphere, thus defeating the infrared search and track systems – IRSTS – carried on all Soviet fighters.

The F-117 had laser radar and the Northrop astro-inertial navigation system used by the SR-71. It suppressed its own electronic noise with extensive use of fibre-optic cables, which caused not detectable emissions.

Creation of a Stealth aircraft did not depend upon the use of individual technologies, but on the skill, it was almost an art, with which they were all blended together to be effective against the very wide range of existing and conceivable threats opposed to it. Like their counterparts building the B-2 in Pico Rivera, the Lockheed engineers in the Burbank Skunk Works had exceeded themselves. The two aircraft had made all other fighters and bombers obsolete.

A week before the Titan 4 blasted off from Vandenberg with its real KH-11 and its false SDS/Jumpseat radar ferret satellites, the small wing of F-117s took off from Nellis. They flew to the *USS John F. Kennedy*, cruising some 200 miles off Washington. The carrier had transferred its own F-18 Hornets to shore, and on landing the F-117s were quickly taken inside the great hangars. It was not common for USAF aircraft to operate from Navy carriers, but it was sometimes done. Like all US tactical aircraft, the F-117 was possessed of an arrester hook. In the strike fighter's case, this was concealed in a housing under the flattened afterbody between the extensively-swept wings. Called the 'platypus', this held the slit-like exhausts of the engines.

The *Kennedy*, with her attendant ships, began steaming north east across the Atlantic.

DefCon III

Severe crisis. Does not indicate that war is likely

NATIONAL PHOTOGRAPHIC INTERPRETATION CENTER, WASHINGTON

'The data're Soviet,' said Ash. 'You'll have to dial that in.'

Jim Dalgetti, in the 'love seat' of the CRAY gave her a startled, odd look, but kept his thoughts to himself and began preparing the computer to digest the digital data that had been awaiting Ash in her computer bank when she returned to NSA.

There'll be hell to pay for all this before we're through, thought Ash.

Dalgetti worked quickly at the console, and once started, the CRAY moved swifter still.

A picture appeared, an overhead of a freighter in a coastal inlet. At the side the information as to time, date, altitude and orbit of the *Cosmos* appeared.

'There she is,' said Dalgetti. 'The SS *City of Flanders*. January 2 this year. There's your MiG in its box, and there the helicopter.'

'Where is she?'

The CRAY was able to recognise any place on earth, given some geographic features, and a coastline was easy for it.

'Georgia coastline,' said Dalgetti. 'Nineteen miles south of Savannah.'

'Thank you, Jim,' said Ash. 'Thank you very much.'

The CRAY gave her copies of what it had found, which she put in her file, and then she went to see Mrs Madani, who had left a message for her while she had been away.

'Mrs Amran,' the old aristocrat said with pleasure. 'Did you enjoy your holiday?'

'It was more of a working holiday,' said Ash. 'But it was productive.'

'Ah,' said Mrs Madani wisely. 'That is good. We too have been productive here. I have these for you.'

Pulling out a folder from her grey desk she spread three photographs on its surface.

'These go back a long way. Fifteen years.'

They were taken with a long lens by some forgotten intelligence cameraman, but he had known his craft and the images were clear.

'Manzarieh Park,' Ash said immediately.

'Well done, my dear.'

'My father liked to go to Mount Towchal. He would stroll through the park, among the oak and yew and cedar, and sometimes we would go with him. They have a training camp for murderers there now, at Niavaran, you know,' Ash said absently. She was staring at the photographs.

'They are *najis*,' said Mrs Madani contemptuously, using the Persian word for something impure, on no account to be touched.

'Yes ...,' said Ash.

The two men so close in conversation in the beautiful and old park, set on the gentle slopes of Mount Towchal were easy to recognise, even though they had been much younger then. Both in the garb of a mullah, from the *na'alayn* slippers on their feet to the black turbans on their heads that signified direct descent from the Prophet himself. The world would come to recognise the one as Khalif Hossein, ruler of Iran, but the good ol' boys in the country club would have been very surprised to see ol' Hank all dressed up like a raghead.

'Sultani and Hossein,' said Ash. 'Thank you, Mrs Madani. It must have taken you a very long time to find them.'

'My days can be long,' she said simply. 'I am happy to fill them with work that may hasten the time when we may go home.'

'We will,' promised Ash.

'You are *alem*, my dear,' she said, meaning one who was wise, a savant.

Ash left her and returned to Dalgetti, who had been waiting while the CRAY chewed on the rest of the data that Rykov had transmitted.

'I think it's got it,' said Dalgetti. 'Does that make sense to you?'

He gave her a slip of paper on which the CRAY had printed some numbers.

'14° 05′ × 64° 22′,' she read. 'Yes, that's it. They wouldn't have gone far.'

Bearing her prize with her she caught the Eastern flight to Jacksonville, to go to see Kowalski at Kings Bay, and by so doing saved her life. That evening a man rang quietly on her door bell, intending to kill her. There was no reply, and he slipped away into the night.

NSA HEADQUARTERS

'I have the smoking gun,' said Ash. She had come to MacDonald's office with a file and a large bag.

'We knew that Colonel Khosrow Parsa was in this country before the attack on the *Maine* took place, because we had his voice on tape. We were looking for evidence that the MiG and the MiL helicopter both came from Iran and were off-shipped over here.'

She took the photographs of the SS *City of Flanders* off the Georgia coast.

'The large box is the MiG, and in this image taken on a later orbit –' she produced an overhead of the freighter leaving '– the MiG is gone, but the MiL is still aboard. We assume it was trans-shipped on the high sea. Now. We wanted evidence that would tie the MiG to Sultani. Here is an overhead of Sultan Electronics' private airstrip on the morning of the attack on the *Maine*, and here is the image when seen through thermal imaging.'

Down the runway a brush had painted a long straight stroke that faded away some three-quarters along the strip. A thinner line traced the aircraft's progress out from the hangar, along the taxiway to the threshold.

'The CRAY informs me that the image we see there is the thermal signature of the R29B engine of the MiG 27.'

MacDonald nodded silently while Ash produced more of her evidence.

'Mrs Madani, bless her, has found three photographs fifteen years old. Sultani and Hossein.'

The photographs of the two men in Manzarieh Park joined the others on MacDonald's desk.

'I reasoned that once the MiG had made its attack on the *Maine* that not only would it be short on fuel by then but that they would want to bury the evidence anyway. That the fighter would simply be abandoned in the sea. So I asked the CRAY to find an area of water within one hundred miles of the wreck of the *Maine* that was abnormal, in terms of temperature and disturbance, microscopic air bubbles, dead fauna, oils, kerosene, hydraulic fluid and so forth. It had thermal data and multi-spectral analysis to go on and identified a point not far from the *Maine*. When it factored in time of ditching and local current and tide it came up with this. "14° 05′ × 64° 22′′′". I went to Kings Bay and Kowalski and I went out to the *Pigeon*. It's still off the wreck site. Kowalski went to the position the CRAY had given me in his Meerestechnik submarine, and this is what he found.'

Severely distorted and damaged, but clearly recognisable, its nose half-buried in the ocean floor, the photographs Kowalski had taken through the observation port of the small submarine depicted the MiG 27.

'Soviet markings,' said Ash. 'But –'

She reached in her bag and pulled out a bent alloy plate that had once been flat.

'This is a part of the cockpit that held the flight instruments. The submarine has moveable arms on it that can pick things up. On the plate are markings and instructions for the pilot. See.'

Ash displayed the plate for MacDonald to see.

'Arabic,' she said. 'It's not a Soviet fighter. It's an export model. Dalgetti tells me the serials on it match with the batch of MiG 27s sold to Iran.'

In the picture the MiG's canopy and pilot's seat were missing.

'They would have had a boat or ship standing by where they wanted the fighter dumped. All Khosrow had to do was eject a few hundred yards off and swim about for a minute or two until he was picked up. While I was at it, I had Dalgetti look for something else, closer to the wreck of the *Maine*. There's a flyspeck on the video film taken by "Nasir Khan". I had NPIC look at it. It's a Cessna 421 out of Port of Spain. Dalgetti gave us a position about eight miles north of the wreck site. The *Squab* went over and searched.'

She produced another photograph that showed a ruined twin resting on the sea bed. The gaping holes torn by the cannon shells were clearly visible.

'It clears up one little thing that was niggling at me. Sure it was useful to have the MiG 27 there to haul a great weight of depth charges to the killing ground in order to alarm the commander of the *Maine* enough to sit his craft on the bottom as a defensive measure, so that it would be intact for the removal of the missiles, but it was the helicopter that was the lethal instrument with its torpedo. A fighter jet can't drop a torpedo, it has to go in slowly, and at the correct angle, it's a delicate piece of equipment. So what was the real reason for the MiG? It was there so that if some passer-by stumbled on the scene of the crime, if they witnessed murder, then they were to be killed, to be silenced. The unfortunates in the 421 saw something they should not have, and they paid the price. Khosrow is an experienced air-to-air combat pilot, shooting down a passenger aircraft must have been lamb to the slaughter for him.'

'Right,' agreed MacDonald. 'Is there anything else?'

'There's more,' said Ash. 'I reasoned that in order for their plan to succeed, the Iranians had to convince us that it was the Soviets who had sunk the *Maine* and taken out the Trident missiles. They have succeeded in this endeavour; General Coogan, for example, is completely convinced of it. It has very largely been done through the efforts of their prime double-agent, Sultani, who has fed Coogan disinformation. How was Sultani found and caught? *By me.* It is my contention that I was steered to Sultani. Someone saw me arrive at Kings Bay and knew I knew Antonov. Therefore at the right moment "Mrs Nobles" the little old lady who was Commander Sanders' neighbour gently propelled me in his direction. A little later, we knew where to find the *Maine* itself – because "Shaikh Nasir Khan" *told me where to look*.

'Before I left I asked Jack Kowalski at Kings Bay to investigate both "Mrs Nobles" and "Shaikh Nasir Kahn". Both have vanished from sight. "Mrs Nobles" claimed to have a son down in Florida, in real estate. He can't be found. She claimed she had met Sultani with friends out at the country club. Nobody ever heard of her. She had a six month lease on the house. "Shaikh Nasir Khan" hired the big luxury yacht the *Jumping Jack*. A few days after I saw him he slipped away on an airliner, never to be seen again. *It all fits.*'

'Coogan will say it all smacks of conspiracy theory,' said MacDonald.

'Evidence is evidence.'

'Coogan is a true patriot, a genuine defender of freedom. He is coming to the end of his service career. The titanic death-struggle between the forces of the free world and godless communism that he has prepared for all his adult life has not materialised. Instead, an inspired economic history professor-turned president is proposing to have the mighty Soviet empire collapse under its own weight while we go back to simply being the world's foremost businessman and finest example of working democracy. It must do more than simply stick in his craw, it must be intolerable. Coogan is *longing* to demonstrate to the Soviets the efficiency of his air force and the indomitability of American will. Fortunately, we have enough here to put a stop to it. Let him bomb Iran instead. We have never been at war with the Soviets in our entire history, it would be disastrous to start now, and by mistake.'

MacDonald paused, fitting all the pieces together in his mind.

'Is there anything else?'

'One last thing. I went to Beirut. It is run, in as far as it is run, by Hizbollah, the Party of Allah, and has been for some time. Hizbollah is the creature of Khalif Hossein's brand of Shi'ia Islam, and has been ever since it was set up by Khomeini. Cord's assertion that he was able to make a deal with the militants to release the hostages because both he and they believed in God in their own way was always suspect, since the Shi'ite fundamentalists regard the "cross worshippers" as foremost among their enemies and obstacles to be overcome before their narrow brand of religion can hold sway over the world, and it is *inconceivable* that they would make a deal with a Christian American presidential candidate unless they were following the age-old tactic of *takieh* or dissimulation, in order to get Cord elected *because they wanted him elected*.'

MacDonald nodded in agreement.

'Harrison Taylor, Cord's chief of staff is dead,' he said. 'Died in a wreck minutes after resigning. Flattened by a dump truck. The driver claimed Taylor went through a stop light. The *word* is that Coogan had a file this thick, proving Taylor was a Soviet agent.'

'Like Sultani,' said Ash.

'Yes.'

275

'Something odd happened just before I left. I was in my house and the telephone rang, and it was Taylor. I'd never talked to him, but he asked if I'd be willing to write a policy document for President Cord, on Iran. He said he could send some stuff over, he'd have his aide, some guy called Riva, come by. I said I'd be happy to, only could it wait until I got back from holiday, as I was going right out of the door to catch the airplane, and he said okay. What was that about then?'

'I don't know. We probably can't know now. I'll try to set up a meeting with Coogan for tomorrow. Have all your evidence arranged.'

'It all smacks so much of overkill,' said Ash. 'I wish I knew what Khalif Hossein is planning to do with the Trident missiles, that it is so important to have us and the Soviets distracted like this.'

ELLSWORTH AFB, SOUTH DAKOTA

The cockpit of the Rockwell B-1B was a mixture of old and new, its instrumentation featuring both conventional dials with needles as well as the more modern vertical tape displays and the cathode ray tubes that dominated the work stations of the aircraft commander and co-pilot. The mix reflected the origins of the bomber, designed at a time when the technology was in flux. The B-1B was the 'penetrator' element of SAC, who had 100 of the sleek, swing-winged aircraft. Its successor, the ATB, Northrop's Stealthy B-2 was to take over its role once enough had been produced, and its cockpit was just about entirely 'all glass', all information being displayed on cathode ray tubes.

The differences between the two bombers, designed for

the same role penetrating the world's most sophisticated air defence system and delivering nuclear or conventional bombs to the targets selected, went further than cockpit design. The B-2 relied upon its design, its ultra-low signatures, to penetrate at altitude and attack its targets while remaining undetected. The B-1B, whilst incorporating Stealthy technology that gave it a frontal RCS of around ten square metres, as opposed to the 100 square metres of its prototype predecessor, the superficially similar B-1A cancelled by President Jimmy Carter – was not a genuinely Stealthy aircraft in the full sense of the word; it did not rely on Stealth as its primary means of survival when within the heavily-defended hostile airspace of the USSR, it relied upon its ability to fly at under 200 feet over the terrain at up to 600 knots, using its powerful avionics to fire accurate bursts of disinformation at any radar or detection system close enough to be a problem.

The 28th Bomb Wing operated two squadrons of B-1Bs, the 77th BS and the 37th BS, with sixteen aircraft each, flying out of Ellsworth. Three B-1Bs from the 77th had been chosen for the Smolensk mission, under the command of Lieutenant-Colonel James Hawkins. The number was deliberately small. Coogan had spelled it out at the briefing:

'This is a retaliatory operation. The Soviets stealthily sank one of our missile submarines. We are stealthily going to bomb their high-tech SDI capability back to the stone age. We are certainly able to do this if we throw in 100 B-1s along with the ten B-2s. We will also start the Third World War. This is a retaliatory strike. The Soviets will know something is going on, but by the time they have really realised what has happened we will be on our way home. More than anything else, this is a demonstration to them how we have the strength of will, the resolve and the ability to destroy any target they have with a very small force, and with impunity. Taking advantage of the fruits of our ET, we are going to use our high technology to rub their noses in their low-technology ordure.'

Some days before the allotted day of the strike Hawkins began planning the route that force Tango would take. In doing so he was able to take advantage of all the resources of SAC's Strategic Bombing Library, where the Smolensk SDI complex had long been a plum target. He set about preparing his route at a work station in the base. What he was doing was creating a map for his on-board computer to read, one that would exactly match the real terrain of the land all the way from the far-north Norwegian fjord of Skjerstad, across the bleak Malozemelskaya tundra, along the edge of the Urals to Smolensk itself, and then back out, heading north over the Pole.

This route, which when complete was known as the terrain database, was the key to the ability of the B-1s to penetrate Soviet airspace. The map was generated digitally, and required the storage of almost 400 million bits of data, which was why such a creation had not been possible before the days of data compression techniques and solid-state semiconductor memory. As the USSR was not in the business of providing detailed charts for the use of its enemies those hostile forces had to prepare their own. Doing this they began with information from the digital land mass survey of the US Defense Mapping Agency, which had put into digital form the information contained in the up-to twenty layers of data used to make a chart. This had the advantage that the new map could be 'decluttered' by editing out features a pilot was never likely to need. The map thus formed was only a basis, as it was simply not accurate enough to guarantee that a multi-million dollar strategic bomber travelling at 600 knots and 150 feet would not instead fly slap through some obstruction suddenly fifty feet above it. To make it sufficiently accurate, information from the great array of satellites owned by the USA was used. NASA's Earth Resources Technology Satellites had not just been put up there to help third-world countries with their resource management.

Hawkins' B-1 and the other two aircraft of force Tango would use the terrain database thus formed in a number of ways. The first was navigation. Continuous terrain-referenced navigation involved the use of radar altimeter returns, continuously compared to the stored terrain database. This provided a benchmark position for the inertial navigation system and satellite-based global positioning system indications. When combined in a Kalman filter, a software programme used by the on-board AiResearch central air data computer the position of the aircraft could be determined to within sixteen metres. The terrain database thus was responsible for map generation, navigation and terrain following. Once approaching the target it was used to provide high-resolution scene-matching correlation to provide terminal accuracy measured in metres. The B-1 might not be able to get its bomb into the proverbial pickle-barrel, but it could certainly hit the truck it was resting on.

At his work station, Hawkins was taking information from the base map network, which stored that information in solid-state semi-conductor memory. It held it in the form of ultra-violet-erasable EPROM, which stood for erasable-programmable-read-only memory. In creating his pixcel database Hawkins was transferring what he wanted in the form of electronically-erasable EEPROM, on to a cartridge that he would take with him to the aircraft to load into the terrain database system. In it he selected large-scale map areas of the route, and added limited-area large scale maps of the target area, plus waypoints, threats and all the information pertinent, gathered so untiringly by the circling Jumpseat radar ferrets and the infra red reconnaissance from the KH-11s. He viewed, selected, inserted large-scale map patches as required. Using the elevation data available he used the computer to plan the route to make maximum use of terrain masking for increased survivability. The winding route was also a product of the computer's calculations of engagement zones based on the type and location of the Soviet air defences near to the strike passage.

When it was done, he assembled with his co-pilot, Major Tom Mollis, and his defensive systems operator, Major Michael Carlucci and his offensive systems operator, Major John Rivera. They took the cassette to the base's CAE Singer simulator, where they were able to 'fly' the entire mission, the database prepared by Hawkins generating three-dimensional images of the terrain they would soon be flying over. In the simulator, the instructors were able to throw threats at the crew ranging from systems failure to attack by SAM missiles and MiG-29 fighters.

They survived. They left the USSR safe, having destroyed the target. When, with small pupils and sweat-stained flight suits they emerged into the Dakota sunlight their places were taken by the members of Tango Two. Following them would be the crew of Tango Three, and then, the teams making up Uniform One, Two and Three. The men of force Uniform were going to accompany their comrades across the Atlantic, but would only enter the USSR should one of the strike force encounter systems failure or other problems that would make them ineffective on the mission. In addition, the B-1s of force Uniform had another task of their own to perform from without the USSR.

As 'hack' time approached, Hawkins held the final briefing. The crews sat in arm-chair desks ready to take down any necessary information on their knee-boards. Hawkins began with the weather. It was good, which meant bad. Over much of the route there were snow showers, drizzle and low scud associated with a cold front. Over the target it was clear.

'There'll be some turbulence in the frontal zone,' said Hawkins. 'Barf bags issued on request.'

The men in the room smiled politely at their commander's little joke. They were all high-time veterans, at the pinnacle of their professions. Air-sick they did not get.

'We simply do not expect to be detected on our way in. However, from the moment we pop up short of the target the Soviets will know we are there. And once we've done the job, they're *certainly* going to know we're there.'

That got a better response, in the form of a number of grim smiles. With what the B-1s were carrying, the Reds would know, all right.

'Defences. The SDI complex is heavily defended. There is a dense zone all around it, in which are situated SAM 2s, 3s, 6s and 13s, as well as tracked ZSU-23/4 23 mm radar-guided anti-aircraft weaponry, 57mm flak and a variety of 14.5 to 23 mm cannon, optically aimed. The fighter jocks in their F-117s say that they can blast a path for us to get in and out, and we must believe that they can. However, it's just worth considering what might be fired at us. Without doubt the most dangerous threat is the SAM 6. They have two brigades defending the complex. Each brigade has five batteries and each battery twelve missiles. That's 120 missiles – about forty for each of us. The SAM 6 and 13 are effective – early versions of the 6 gave the Israelis a very bad time in the Yom Kippur war. You know it. 175 lb H.E. warhead on a telephone-pole sized missile. Can knock down an aircraft from 100 feet up to 35,000. Bad news. If the Soviets get any indication we're coming and have the radars warmed up they'll have a chance to fire them at us. We'd better hope the NRO's ferrets have given us the right information, and that the F-117 is as Stealthy as they claim. Remember, the SAM 6 and the 13 are smokeless, you can't see them coming, but your warning devices can. DSOs take note.

'The ZSUs are deadly, but inaccurate when dealing with targets travelling at over 300 knots. We'll be doing 480. Pilots. Immediately after delivery, get G on the airplane and break plane to defeat any missiles or aimed AA. At least 4G on the turn as you enter the egress path. DSOs again, any indication on radar warning receivers that you have SAMs, then let go with chaff and flares. Pilots. Immediately leaving the target, go to afterburner to pick up speed and get out of the hostile zone. Once clear, back to dry thrust. Too much AB and we could have fuel problems.

'Timing. We will go in in reverse order. Tango Three first, Two second and we'll go last. If any Uniform aircraft have to replace us they will take over the identity of the aircraft that has had to drop out. Spacing, exact thirty second intervals. The ordnance has fuse delay as you know, and is aimed downwards, but you still don't want to be in the area when the individual canisters get fired up in the air. 480 knots is eight miles a minute. Thirty second spacing is four miles. Simple.'

There was little else to say. The mission was as planned as any could be, the crews as ready as any on earth.

'This is a very special operation,' Hawkins said. 'We are sending a very specific message to the Soviets about the will of the free world to defend itself. Let's do it properly.'

The crews went out to suit up. They took real care with the fit of their flight suits, G suits, survival gear, torso harness. It was to be a very long flight, the discomfort of an ill-fitting piece of equipment could become a real problem if not eliminated from the start. Hawkins, preparing with the others allowed a stray thought to niggle at his mind as he fitted the layers of clothing. After all the effort and planning Coogan had put into the operation, he would have expected the fiery little general to have been present at the final briefing. He shrugged to himself and put the thought away. There was no accounting for the vagaries of the high command.

The vans were waiting to take the six crews out to the various aircraft, waiting and prepared in their barns. Hawkins, Mollis, Carlucci and Rivera dismounted inside the barn, where the ground crew was waiting. The big bomber, 147 feet long, and with its wings full spread to 136 feet loomed above them, dark in its low-visibility paint of grey and green. Ungainly on the ground, it became an object of beauty in its own element. The bomb doors were open, and the huge array of weaponry stored within the three bays visible.

The crew entered through the ventral entry hatch just behind the nose gear, climbing up into the crew cabin where Carlucci and Rivera had their stations. Between the two systems operators was the Central Integrated Test System console which monitored the status of key elements of the aircraft. Underneath the CITS was a tunnel through which Hawkins and Mollis crawled to get to the flight deck in front.

The flight deck contained the two work stations for the pilots, who sat in their blue and red Weber Aces II zero-zero ejection seats. Behind and to the left of the commander's seat was a small and cramped toilet. Behind the co-pilot was a seat and console where an instructor or check pilot could be carried. Unlike the regular crew, anyone occupying this position had no ejection seat and had to leave via a belly hatch in event of emergency. Strapped in, suited up, helmeted, General Coogan was waiting there.

Hawkins, the first through, stared at his superior officer in amazement.

'You ready to go, son?' said Coogan. 'I am.'

The two pilots emerged fully into the cabin, and Mollis, leaving the situation to his aircraft commander, began getting himself into his seat.

'You're coming with us?' Hawkins said, so taken aback he forgot to address Coogan as he should.

'When I was in B-58s we penetrated Soviet airspace a number of times. Never fired a shot, never dropped a bomb. Maybe they would have respected us more if we had. Maybe they wouldn't have sunk the *Maine*. Now we're finally going to do it, I'm not staying behind.'

Hawkins was horrified at the prospect of the chief of staff going on an operational mission.

'But, sir, you *must*.'

'Son,' Coogan said softly. ' "Must" is not a word used to five-star generals. Fire her up.'

The crew chief came crawling up the short tunnel under the CITS. He evinced no surprise at Coogan's presence, and Hawkins realised that naturally, Coogan had set it all up in advance. He checked that both pilots had attached the parachute risers from the ejection seat to the torso harness above each shoulder, had plugged in their G-suits to blow up the bladders, attached their survival kits to the seat of the torso harness. He ensured that they were attached to their seat belts, and gave them their helmets.

They plugged in radio leads and oxygen masks. Although the B-1 spent its operational life below 250 feet it had a ceiling of 49,000 feet, and on its way over the Atlantic would be flying at 35,000. They pulled on their nomex fire-proof gloves. Both men had the old-timer's trick of snipping out a fingertip on their left gloves, so to be able to monitor the colour of the nail bed, the quicker to detect and correct hypoxia.

The crew chief double-checked all fittings and removed the safety pins from the twin Aces ejection seats. They were now armed and could fire their occupants some hundreds of feet into the air to float safely down under the parachutes, all at the pull of a handle. With his tasks complete, the crew chief slapped both men on the shoulder, fraternally, and giving Coogan a quick salute crawled back down the tunnel. The pilots began going over the checklist of dozens and dozens of items. Soon the four General Electric F101-GE-102 turbofans were spooled up. In front of the cockpit the squadron ordnance crew who had loaded the vast quantity of weaponry into the bomber earlier in the day stood, wearing their noise-dampening earmuffs, holding up the long red ribbons that were attached to the safety pins that had rendered the bomb fuses and ejector charges inert. Now the big GBUs were armed and would explode when released from the bomber at the end of the designated arming delay.

The mission was radio-out. The crew chief guided Hawkins from the barn with illuminated paddle-boards.

When the bomber was on the ramp he climbed on to the back of the pick up truck that was to lead Tango One to the threshold. The other bombers were emerging from their barns, and they rolled purposefully in convoy, with their attendant vehicles, to the beginning of the long runway.

The bombers were carrying half-fuel at just about 100,000 lb. All six aircraft were due to rendezvous with their KC-135R tankers shortly after take off. They were still very heavy aircraft. Empty, the B-1B weighed 192,000 lb. With full internal armament, which all carried, they weighed a further 75,000 lb. The three aircraft of force Uniform were even heavier, as they carried external weapons as well.

The night was black. One after the other, the great bombers rolled down the runway, great white plumes of crackling fire extending back from the afterburning turbojets. They gained speed slowly at first, and then as they went faster, quicker and quicker. Wings fully spread, leading edge slats drooped, flaps deployed, the lift built up as the speed increased. Nosewheels lifted from the runway, the moustache-like vanes in front of the cockpit sensed the air and each aircraft rotated into its natural element, tucking up its undercarriage and accelerating into the night.

GEORGETOWN, WASHINGTON

Mahmoud Hojati was special. He had lived in America, but was imbued with the one true faith. He was a veteran of the war, and yet became a Volunteer for Martyrdom. Because of his unique skills, and his detailed experience of America, he was not wasted on mundane missions. He was not sent in a car or truck packed with explosives on a suicide run, he was saved for something that was special.

Although he had killed men as a soldier those who were to use him knew that killing individually, in cold blood, assassinating someone, called for different qualities, so they sent him to Niavaran, in Manzarieh Park, where there was a school of a special kind.

'Our aim here is to break you,' his instructor promised him. 'For you have been shaped by this earthly life for the purpose of performing ordinary deeds. We mean to put you back together again in a totally new form, so that you can serve your Creator and be fit for entry into Paradise.'

In the western special forces they had soldiers trained to be able to take on assassination missions. To help them select such men, those responsible employed psychotherapists and analysts, who found that the best soldiers for such tasks were men with good combat records, men with 'passive aggressive' personalities, who had a lot of drive, were well-disciplined, but who periodically experienced bursts of explosive energy when they could literally kill without remorse.

Had such a psychoanalyst been allowed to examine Mahmoud Hojati he would have found him to fit this psychological profile exactly.

Such men, when selected, were given further training in reducing the stress of killing. It involved a kind of 'Clockwork Orange' indoctrination that removed any qualms that might have remained about killing to order. With their heads secured in a special clamp, and their eyelids kept open by a special device, the men were forced to watch a series of gruesome films that grew steadily more horrible. The earliest and least unpleasant showed an African youth being crudely circumcised by members of his tribe. No anaesthetic was involved, and the 'knife' a shard of glass. Later films moved on to torture, and death.

The men at Niavaran had no time for such euphemisms as films. Mahmoud Hojati was teamed with another man, Jaafar Mahalati from Isfahan. The two became close. Their training involved the normal disciplines of special forces troops. Instead of watching films, they were taken on raids against suspected hideouts of anti-regime guerrillas. The men would then torture their captives in search of information. They took turns serving as one-man firing squads in Evin and Qasr prisons.

Mahmoud Hojati graduated from the school of assassins at Niavaran by strangling his companion, Jaafar Mahalati to death with his bare hands.

He was given a *ta'awidh*, a most powerful talisman, an armband made of leather, on which was inscribed a *sura* from the *Qur'an* protecting the faithful from the evil eye. A *ta'awidh* had to be worn under one's clothing, and carefully concealed from public gaze. Its owner always wore it when carrying out his mission to kill in the name of Allah.

Mahmoud Hojati was wearing it as he walked quietly up the hedge-lined lane that led to the doorway of the house in the smart district of Georgetown. The entrance to the house was concealed from view, he rang the doorbell. The door was opened by a slim, pretty woman in her thirties, blonde-haired and green-eyed. He smiled reassuringly.

'Mrs Amran?' he said. 'I called a little earlier. I've got the material from the White House for you. I'm Gulio Riva.'

'Oh, yes,' said Ash. 'Come in.'

TANGO FORCE

The B-1s of force Uniform launched their Boeing air launched cruise missiles or ALCMs at 02.10, fifty miles off the northern coastline of Norway. It was a version of the in-vogue military philosophy of 'shoot and penetrate'. Force Uniform shot, and force Tango penetrated. In wartime, each force would have done both. Once launched, the ALCMs were considered unstoppable. There was only one thing wrong. They should have left at 01.40. The operation was running half an hour late. It was fault of the USS *Kennedy*.

The carrier was a familiar visitor to the cold northern waters. When serving as a part of NATO, she operated in an ASW role. Because the Soviet coastline was either landlocked or blocked by thick ice for much of the year, the USSR had only two major submarine bases, Petropavlovsk on the Kamchatka Peninsula that bordered the Pacific, and Polyarnyy, north of Murmansk. Soviet submarines leaving Polyarnyy had to pass through the channel between Nordkapp, Norway, and Bear Island, south of Spitzbergen to get to their stations in the Atlantic. NATO always knew when they were leaving, because they had the floor of the shallow channel bugged. It was the Barrier SOSUS line, Sound Surveillance System. In wartime the *Kennedy* would have operated up there to sink the Soviet *Alfas* and *Typhoons* before they could get on station. She wouldn't sink anything, however, if she couldn't get her aircraft out of the hangar.

The forward hoist had jammed. It was unheard of but it happened. By the time it had been de-glitched and the F-117s were being flung into the air the operation was running half an hour late.

It didn't matter too much. The B-1s, coming over the Atlantic, and the B-2s coming over the pole, were informed via secure data link, and everyone slowed up. When the F-117s were in position everyone had adjusted. All it meant was that the two forces would leave the USSR as it was getting light, rather than in the dark.

Getting to Smolensk was the easy part. On the flight back out, the Soviets would have everything that would fly and carry a missile or cannon in the air vengeful and eager. But in the early 1980s, when the concept of emerging technology had been recognised the US knew it had a substantial lead over the USSR in computer technology, and had sought to widen it even more under DARPA's Strategic Computing Program. The fruits of ET were to be seen in the supercomputers in NSA and NPIC, and in the Stealthiness of the B-1B, the B-2, the F-117 and the KH-11 and its elliptically orbiting piggyback satellite, that both passed over Smolensk. The USA, in the person of its air force chief of staff, was betting that it worked, that the hordes of MiG 23s, 27s, 29s, SU-17s, 24s that would rise up from their bases like so many hornets would in fact be but Polish cavalry, stumbling about in the fog of battle. Stealth thickened the fog, but only for one side. Coogan, seated at his console in Tango One, could see like the Lord Himself.

The B-1s of Tango force remained with their tankers on the approach to Skjerstad fjord. The tankers' destination was the air base of Bodo, the destination of Gary Powers in his U-2 in May 1960. Powers never made it. He was shot down by a SAM over Sverdlovsk.

No one would be surprised at the presence of aircraft in the far-northern air. Bodo was much used by the USAF. Going the other way TU-95D Bears routinely ground out over the Norwegian Sea, going on over Greenland to the coast of Canada and the USA to ferret NATO radar and communications data, and SIGINT before landing in Cuba.

Force Uniform and its tankers were going home. Tango force's tankers were going to land at Bodo and replenish. In the fjord, the three B-1s took their last drink, and then unhooked. At 650 knots, they streaked over the ice and frozen tundra. Ahead and above them, unseen, were the F-117 strike fighters. Truly Stealthy aircraft, they did not have to fly at treetop height to survive. Ahead of them all, flying to a different target, were the Boeing ALCMs.

In Tango One, once over land the terrain-referenced navigation system was matching up with the INS and GPS. Their outputs were combined in the Kalman filter, and the position of the B-1 was where it was supposed to be. The two pilots were able to cross-check through use of the forward-looking infra red sensor (Flir) which was providing a head-up thermal image of the terrain ahead. Complementary all-round night vision was provided by flip-down flip-up image intensifying goggles. On their multi-function cathode ray tubes they could select data relating to navigation, terrain clearance, time to target, aircraft attitude and so on. In case the Defense Mapping Agency and the geosat satellites had missed anything, or the Soviets had put it up since, the B-1's covert, Westinghouse APQ-164 phased-array radar operated to detect unmapped obstacles. The radar was undetectable, with limited range, no sidelobes and only nanosecond dwell time as it scanned the terrain ahead. In this mode, one of thirteen, that ranged from high resolution ground mapping to ground moving target tracking, it used low pulse repetition in conjunction with frequency-hopping to ensure Stealthy operation.

The first waypoint came up, the tip of a scrub-shored lake. In the crew cabin, watching the headup Flir display presented on one of his multi-function cathode ray tubes, Rivera, the Offensive Systems Operator placed cross-hairs over the calculated position. There was a slight deviation, and he simply moved the cross-hairs to the correct location. With the navigation updated, the bomber was on the exact path to the target.

They were beginning to run into the turbulence associated with the front. Travelling at 600 knots life could be very unpleasant, almost intolerable, for the crew of a penetrating bomber in terrain-following nap-of-the-earth mode when passing through turbulent air. The B-1B was advanced, it had structural mode control that improved the ride-quality enormously through use of the moustache-like vanes on each side of the nose and the bottom rudder segment. The SMCS employed accelerometers to detect movement, and dampened it with the vanes and rudders. Even so, as the rapidity and force of the thrashing built up Hawkins went from 'hard' to 'soft' mode and the crew members were able to breathe once more without gasping.

In the B-2s, the air was like silk. They were at 35,000 feet, on autopilot. But for the fact that they were coming over the north pole the crew could have been conveying

290

passengers from London to New York for all the drama there was.

However, their 'master mode' switches were at 'Go to war'. Their flight controls were operating in 'stealthy' mode, all radio emitters were off and in the vast weapons' bays behind the cockpits the 18,000 kg of ordnance in their twin eight-round rotary dispensers were activated. The crews monitored their instruments and flew, unseen, towards Smolensk.

The advantage of having two types of offensive bombing systems, low-altitude and Stealth, was that the defensive systems necessary to detect them were by no means the same, and forced the Soviets to develop and maintain at enormous cost two sets of systems.

For the B-1s, very powerful radars were required. The power emitted by these systems was such that it was easily detected by the high-flying B-2s, and they were transmitting the information to the B-1s of Force Tango via satellite using secure, low-side-lobe, extremely high frequency link, thus constantly updating Hawkins and his two other bomber crews as to the threat ahead of them.

The B-2 had only one real enemy, which was very large, long-wavelength, early-warning radar. Versions of this, gigantic phased-arrays, populated in the northern reaches of the USSR, standing in the tundra like icons built to a forgotten god by men of a vanished age. They peered northwards, looking for bombers that might one day come.

Just as the B-2s were aiding their low-flying cousins, the B-1s had cleared the way for the B-2s. The Boeing ACLMs, air-launched cruise missiles, streaked over the bleakness of the tundra. After several hundred miles of flight since they had left their mother aircraft, the B-1s of Force Uniform, their accuracy could still be measured in feet. They proved it, by striking the great phased array radars, one after the other, dead centre.

The eyes that could see Stealth bombers were poked out, and the Soviets realised for the first time that they were under attack.

GEORGETOWN, WASHINGTON

'I've had the information in my briefcase for a while,' said Gulio Riva. 'Harrison Taylor gave it to me, then he had his terrible auto wreck, and you were away. I had to pass through Georgetown tonight and I thought I'll just give her a call on the telephone in my vehicle, see if she's home. I hope I'm not interrupting anything.'

'You aren't,' said Ash. 'A quiet evening in. Come into the living room here.'

The room was elegantly furnished. Riva looked around as he followed Ash in, as anyone would, but he was noting features that would aid him in his task. He saw with approval that the drapes over the windows were heavy silk, and drawn. The carpet was thick wool with underlay, and he knew that these Georgetown houses were solidly-built. He did not plan for Ash to make any noise when he killed her, but it was as well to be cautious.

Riva put his briefcase down on the low brass and plate-glass coffee table.

'Did Harrison Taylor say anything to you about it?'

'Not in detail.'

'It is the President who wants your views,' Riva said reverentially. He passed her a green file. As she took it, her subconscious sounded a warning. As she took a small step backwards she thought: he's too close. Europeans, westerners, Americans all stood a certain distance from one another, they allowed each person individual space around them, and it was considered bad manners not to, unless you were a part of a crowd, at a game, or on the subway. Those from the Middle East naturally stood close to one another. In conversation they would be close, to see what effect their words were having, to even smell the other person.

Gulio Riva, Mahmoud Hojati flexed his hands.

Watch the hands: that was the motto of the bullet catchers, the words of Major Ghaffari came into her mind. 'If you watch for the hands, you have that extra moment to save your charge.'

Ash had been given an extra second's grace. Her brain, trained, powerful, delivered the facts under the sudden pressure of her sympathetic nervous system: he is bigger, stronger, faster than I am, and trained to kill. If I run he will surely kill me, so I must damage him first.

Ash's small hands had long fingers, with shapely, oval nails that she painted with clear polish. Instead of stepping back again she stepped forward to meet her assassin as his hands came up. Her nails flashed, reaching for his eyes, with supreme reflexes his head went back and she felt the wetness of an eyelid. She missed the orb itself, but as Hojati sprang back blood had christened her nails, and ran down from the lid.

'*Bitch*,' Hojati grunted furiously. He came forward again, and Ash reached for a china dish of fine potpourri resting on a round Sheraton table. She flung it up into his face and while he was temporarily blinded made a dash for the door. Like a powerful animal, Hojati sprang the way his ears told him, and seized her by the arm. A hand grasped her face, tearing and squeezing cruelly, she bit down savagely on a finger and felt her teeth tear through the skin, he gasped with pain but did not let go. His other hand was around her throat, reaching for purchase, his head held away from her clawing nails.

As they staggered in lethal embrace over the carpet she knew that she would die now, as his strength was so much greater than hers. The realisation brought a memory into her mind, her mother's voice, advising her about men. 'They are stronger than we, but more vulnerable. Should one attack you, what he seeks to harm you with you may harm him with.'

As Hojati succeeded in grasping her by the throat she reached down between his legs, with him unaware. The eggs of his testicles slithered under her fingers until she pinned them with her nails and squeezed as hard as she could. Cloth tore and flesh ripped and Hojati snapped forward with enormous force, howling in ultimate agony. They smashed into the brass and plate-glass coffee table, which shattered under the force of the blow.

With incredible strength of will, Hojati's hands came up again, reaching for his victim. Thrashing in the ruins of the table Ash seized a long shard of glass, and struck.

She hit again and again until the screaming, and then the awful gurgling stopped. She stood, gasping amid the ruins of her living room, and blood dripped from her fingers.

TANGO FORCE

The route to the target was shown as a 'highway' track on Hawkins' Multi-Function Display. This information was drawn from the EEPROM cartridge he had so carefully prepared before the mission. In addition, he was able to update his computer with the latest information transmitted to him regarding Soviet radars by the incoming B-2s. They were through the front and the air was smooth as the attacking force swooped along its sinuous path, hiding among the folds of the central Russian uplands north of Smolensk. To the west the vast and languid Dnepr River drained the north European plain into the Black Sea, to the east, the other side of the uplands the Volga did the same. Ahead was the target.

The B-1s were accompanied by a total of twenty four F-117s, split into two flights of twelve, the first, commanded by Major Mike Connor, for the ground-attack role, armed with Maverick AGM-65 missiles, and the second, commanded by Major John Parke, which were armed with Advanced Medium Range Air to Air Missiles AMRAAM for the interceptor role. As the fighters were stealthy aircraft they were able to fly higher than the B-1s without fear of detection.

The F-117s were designed in a battlefield situation to be teamed with another, higher flying aircraft. This would normally be a TR-1, the successor to the famous U-2, flying at 75,000 feet well to the rear of the battle. The TR-1 was able to detect and locate targets by active or passive means and direct F-117s by datalink to the target area. For the attack on Smolensk, as the B-2s were penetrating into the battle area themselves, they were able to take on the TR-1's role.

In his cockpit, as they approached the Smolensk defences, Connor in the lead F-117 drew his information from a number of sources. Like the B-1s he had a large on-board database, as well as real-time intelligence from the B-2s. Information that he required could be displayed on his three large colour MFDs, which were a jump forward from the B-1's cathode ray tubes, being flat-panel liquid-crystal displays. To fight in his aircraft, Connor made use of his helmet-mounted display, which was the successor to the head-up display. The HMD made it possible to provide the pilot with such information as the bounds to the lethal envelope of his weapons, or direct his attention to a target that had been detected, while he had his head moving and 'out of the cockpit'.

Connor's HMD was known as 'Agile Eye', and made use of cathode ray tubes no bigger than his finger, and which presented its information to him as a hologram that was an integral part of his visor. As they began to come within range of the Smolensk defences, the constantly-changing map on his number one MFD began to indicate mushroom shapes on either side of the highway track in the distance. They were the lethal envelopes of the surface-to-air missiles ringing the SDI complex.

The great facility was split into two parts, the research establishment itself and the modern, fenced and guarded development where the 'brains', the USSR's top research scientists lived, in considerable comfort. Both parts were ringed by formidable defences. It was the job of the F-117s to blast a safe path through for the bombers. The colour-coded stores display on his number three MFD indicated that all his Maverick missiles were armed; the number two display gave a picture of the ground ahead as seen by his forward-looking infra red and laser rangefinders.

In front of his eyes, the basic information regarding heading, airspeed and basic weapon data was joined by a dotted arrow, which drew his attention to his first target. Connor had entered the mushroom, or volume of sky within which the SAM could destroy an aircraft. It was an SA-13 tracked unit of six infra red missiles with search/track radar, capable of firing on the move. Such a missile was the fighter's worst enemy. However, it was also an ideal target, electronically and thermally conspicuous, slow-moving and soft. Connor could 'see' it lit up like Christmas illuminations as it searched for him, or others like him. He travelled towards it, through its envelope, approaching at 500 feet and 480 knots. Behind it was a second unit, and Connor began programming two of his Maverick missiles for their targets. Once launched, the Maverick was virtually unstoppable, homing in automatically with video or IR sensor, requiring no command signals and putting out no electronic emissions. It could not be jammed, nor deceived.

The SA-13 was designed to detect a conventional fighter or bomber in time to identify it, slew and elevate the launcher, prepare the missile and fire as the target approached. The advantage was normally with the SAM system since its powerful radar, which Connor could 'see', waving to and fro like a veritable searchlight, was normally able to track an airborne target well before the target's own sensors could succeed in the more difficult task of finding the SAM system amid the clutter of objects on the ground. It was normally the fighter which had the missile fired at it, and had to take defensive action.

The SA-13 was slow and soft-skinned, without any defenses except its own missiles. Connor approached the bottom, the stem of the mushroom. Then he was clear.

They had seen him. He squeezed the trigger on his control and the first Maverick streaked away from the fighter from its forward missile bay, a lance of white fire in the night. Connor was inside the minimum range of the missile system. He weaved to the right to avoid flying over the wreckage. The night was lit by long streaks of flame as the missiles flew from the fighters. Fire erupted on the ground, it lit up the roof of the cockpit above Coogan's head, in the lead B-1.

High in space, a satellite 'hung' over Smolensk. Randy Ellis' Soviet counterparts had thought it a 'Jumpseat'-type radar ferret. It was not. Blue-green laser beams sprang from its body, and played on the buildings and structures of the SDI complex, twenty miles out, at 35,000 feet, Colonel Travis in the lead B-2 dropped his GBU-15 glide bombs. Through the camera in their noses the bombs were now slaved to their laser-designated targets. One after the other, the ten bombers released their loads before making a 180-degree turn for home.

The F-117s were quiet, it was first the noise of the exploding Maverick missiles that awoke the scientists and their families in the residential compound of the complex. Peering fearfully around their curtains, still dazed from sleep it was the shattering roar of the four GE F101 engines of Hawkins' B-1 on full afterburner overhead that told them that it was they themselves who were under attack.

The navigation of the B-1s had been perfect. They made their final run in as the F-117s ahead were clearing their exit path. At the initial point, still only 100 feet off the ground Hawkins pulled up into a 45-degree angle-of-attack, shortly afterwards turning 90-degree to port, while still climbing. At 5000 feet he rolled belly-up to maintain positive Gs and acquire the target visually. It was spread out ahead of him, the fenced complex with its houses and shops. Hawkins rolled back 180-degree, wings level, and began his bomb run. He watched his head-up display lining up the bomb fall line on the target. Hawkins was to cover the centre of the complex from end to end and the two following B-1s the areas to the left and to the right. The pipper at the bottom of the bomb fall line on the HUD crossed the ring-road of the complex and Hawkins began to release his vast load of weaponry.

The B-1s were carrying Avco Skeets. The Skeet was a 'smart' weapon, a terminally-guided submunition designed for use against tanks. The ones carried by the B-1s were a special version. Leaving the bomb bays the Skeet Delivery Vehicles, SDVs, each containing four 2.6 kgs Skeets deployed tail fins for stability as they descended to the target. At 600 feet over the residential compound they were slowed by their parachutes, power was supplied to the individual Skeets within, and their infra-red sensors cooled. At 100 feet the parachute was released and a peripheral rocket motor on each SDV ignited, forcing it to spin at 3000 rpm, shooting out pairs of spinning Skeets all along the length of the compound. As they were ejected a spring-loaded arm popped up, causing the Skeets to wobble, thus enlarging their search pattern.

When used against tanks once the target had been identified by the IR sensor the Skeet's warhead detonated to produce a 'self forging' fragment that turned a chunk of heavy metal such as depleted uranium into a streamlined projectile travelling at very high speed to penetrate the tank's armour by pure kinetic energy to deadly effect. The Skeets used against the residential compound were slightly different. They were programmed to recognise houses, or people. They contained thousands of heavy, depleted uranium pellets, just like enormous shotgun shells.

Spinning and wobbling, one hundred feet up they began to fire as they identified targets. Lines of rippling fire advanced up the complex, first in the centre, then the left, as the munitions of Tango Two found their mark, and then right.

As the complex began to burn, the first GBU-15s struck into the research facility itself. One after the other, the three B-1s pulled four and a half Gs in their turn, 90-degree out of plane with the target, back down to the nap of the earth, flying over the destruction wreaked by the F-117s on the exit path, and through its smoke.

The Skeet-aimed B-1s had achieved a Pk – a probability of kill – in their MOE of 1.00. Their mission had been 100 per cent successful, the best scientific talent in the USSR had been eliminated.

Now they had to get out again.

The Soviet western areas defence forces had been watching the Boeing E-3 flying in its holding pattern over the Baltic fifty miles west of Kaliningrad, an international airspace ever since it had hoved into view from across the Atlantic. They might have sent a Sukhoi Su-27 or a couple of MiG-29s up to look at it, but it was escorted by a number of F-14s from the USS *Kennedy*. When the first report of the giant phased-array radars being attacked came to them they went to maximum alert, and when the E-3 headed purposefully east towards the Russian coast at the moment the SDI complex at Smolensk was under attack they jumped.

The importance of the E-3 aircraft, known as Sentry, was that it was an AWACS aircraft, an airborne warning and control system, and as such one of the most valuable and potent pieces on the board. In a specific operation, such as the Smolensk raid, it was responsible for C³I – command, control, communications and intelligence, known in the jargon as C-cubed-I. The innocuous buzzphrase actually encompassed all the intangibles of military warfare, the parts without which bombers, tanks, artillery, troops and supplies were of no use. C³I was about knowing what your own forces were doing, making them do what you wanted, and knowing what the opposition was up to. Its inevitable opposite number was C^3I countermeasures, or C^3ICM, which was disruption of the enemy's C^3I.

The best AEW & C aircraft in the world, by a very large margin, was the Boeing E-3, and with its great array of electronics, powerful computers and numerous work stations and skilled operators it could handle both C^3I and C^3ICM. The importance of its radar system, the circular rotating saucer atop the fuselage, was that ground-based radars could only see as far as the horizon. The curvature of the earth hid low-flying targets like the B-1s. Putting radar on an aircraft at 35,000 feet meant that it could see over 200 miles away at ground level.

At his console in the lead B-1, heading out along the exit route Coogan assessed the threat and then sent a message via data link to Major John Parke's twelve F-1 interceptors accompanying them to leave. The flight of ground-attack F-19s that had wreaked such destruction to the defences of the SDI complex under the leadership of Mike Connor had already departed for the *Kennedy*. With his orders he sent a cryptic note: One better than Marianas.

The association between the intruding E-3 and the attack on Smolensk was clear, the AWACS aircraft could advise and defend the outgoing attacking force, which the Soviet command had guessed at an eight-to-ten strong flight B-1s. Only with the post-mortem would the importance of the ALCM attack on the phased-array radars become clear.

The Soviets had their own version of the E-3, a converted transport aircraft, an Ilyushin Il-76 known by the NATO designator of *Mainstay*. Given the path of the E-3 entering Soviet airspace and Smolensk itself, there seemed a good chance of being able to find the escaping force of B-1s if their *Mainstays* could be got into the area. Fortuitously, there were three within range, based at the base at Vilnius, some two hundred miles east of Kaliningrad. They were scrambled, along with a squadron of some thirty Su-27 *Flankers*, the USSR's best heavyweight fighter, and two squadrons of MiG-29 *Fulcrums*. In addition, the giant SA-5 missile complex at Kaunas was readied to launch against the E-3. The truly massive SA-5 had been built to defend the USSR against the Mach 3, 70,000 feet B-70 Valkyrie bomber, it had a range of 200 miles and could certainly knock down the E-3 if it got within range. The site at Kaunas was an enormous affair where the missiles were emplaced in concrete bunkers rivalling the V-2 sites of the Second World War. Forty of the great missiles were prepared, to be fired in a massive salvo to overwhelm the E-3s electronic defences.

Climbing through 22,000 feet, searching for the escaping B-1s the three *Mainstay* AWACS aircraft halted on the air defence radar screens, and their signature dwindled, and vanished. The operators stared in disbelief, for there was no warning, and no interceptors within range.

At Kaunas, the SA-5s were ready to launch. In a minute-long salvo that turned the dark streets of the town to day the forty huge missiles blasted from their fortified emplacements. The noise and glare brought the citizens from their houses, looking up at the sight of the rockets, with boosters and main stages filling the black sky with an enormous firework display.

As the last SA-5 left the site, the team of controllers at their consoles realised that someone else had taken command of their missiles. Their opposite numbers, high up in the E-3, using the vast amount of information gathered by the US intelligence machine had seized control of the missiles. The Soviet controllers found that they were completely excluded from contact by the precise frequency control and narrow jamming beams through which the Big Crow system poured millions of watts of radiated power via its electronically-steerable Rotman lens antenna.

They watched helplessly as the images of the missiles altered course, intercepting the images of the Su-27s climbing out of Vilnius. On the streets of Kaunas people gasped as the firework display reached its culmination, finishing as all good rocket flights should, with satisfying exploding balls of red and white flame that left fragments slowly falling and tumbling earthwards.

Then the MiG-29s began vanishing from the screens, struck by opponents they never saw.

THE USS JOHN F. KENNEDY

The catapult flung the F-117 of Mike Connor back into the air, he joined the rest of his flight, re-armed and refuelled, that sped towards the battle raging east of Kaliningrad. In place of the Maverick air-to-ground missiles that had proven so effective against the SAM sites of Smolensk the F-117 was carrying Hughes AIM-120 AMRAAM advanced medium range air-to-air missiles. The twenty two F-117s that included John Parke's flight from the B-1s that had accompanied the E-3 on its decoy mission had shot down a total of fifty four MiG-29s. Some, out of weaponry, streamed back to the *Kennedy*, while the remainder, with their missiles husbanded, continued to accompany the E-3 as it made its way back out of Soviet airspace. The Israeli Defence-Air Force had destroyed a total of eighty two Soviet-built, Syrian-flown fighters over the Bekaa valley in June 1982 for no loss. With Connor's flight being directed to the last remaining threat, the squadron of Su-27s approaching at maximum cruise from Tallinn, to the north, be felt there was a chance of the USAF beating that total.

The E-3 was capable of keeping track of over 200 aircraft at any one time. Twenty six Su-27s were approaching the twelve F-117s of Connor's flight. It might have seemed an unequal engagement, there were more of the Sukhois, which were bigger, capable of over Mach 2, the F-117 being subsonic, and were armed with a most powerful radar and both short-range AA-11 Archer missiles for dogfighting and medium-range AA-9 Alamos, as against the F-117's single-type AMRAAMs. It was indeed an unequal contest, but totally weighted on the side of the smaller aircraft, because the Su-27 pilots could not see the F-117 coming, nor could they cope with the AMRAAM missiles.

Connor could see the Su-27s. They were equipped with IRST, infra red search and track, which could not detect the emissions of the F-117s, and with their powerful radar, which also could not detect him, and for the same reason – because the F-19 was a Stealth fighter. The Su-27 was previous-generation technology, its missiles were semi-active radar homing, SARH, weapons, which homed in on radar energy transmitted by their launch aircraft and reflected by the target. The problem with SARH weapons was that the aircraft's radar had to illuminate the target continuously from launch until impact, just like a microwave frequency searchlight beam. While locked on and illuminating it could not see any other targets, and the pilot was blind and vulnerable to attack. And even before then, he had to find his target.

Connor could see the Su-27s doing just that. On his MFD they looked like great, waving searchlights.

The E-3 crew was directing the F-117s to their targets. Under ideal circumstances an AMRAAM-armed fighter like the F-117 was capable of a four-on-four attack. The men in the E-3 considered that they had it covered, they allotted Connor two lead Su-27s in the centre, and two stragglers to port. At a range of forty miles he 'initialised' his missiles' computers with the positions of the targets. At thirty miles, head-on, he launched, and then slowed the F-117 down, slowing the rate of closure and increasing the F-pole, the distance between himself and the target when the missiles hit and he was free to manoeuvre. Information

303

was fed from the fighter to the missiles via datalink. The F-117 tracked the targets and periodically transmitted their latest position to the missiles, allowing their on-board computers to extrapolate the target's track, predict its position at impact and determine the fastest and most efficient course to follow to reach that point.

The Su-27 pilots still did not know that they were under attack.

At fifteen miles range, with a closing velocity of over 3000 mph, the radar of the AMRAAM missiles locked on. The Su-27s had less than eighteen seconds to live.

The E-3 flew out of Soviet airspace, followed by its escorting F-117s. Scattered over the countryside behind them were the remains of Soviet state-of-the-art technology.

Far to the north, the B-1s blasted over the freezing tundra.

NARYAN-MAR, BOLSHEZEMELSKAYA TUNDRA, USSR

Vodka, the combat fighter pilot's natural belligerence and lack of belief in the views of his superiors, a misplaced faith in and understanding of the exact nature of *glasnost* and an alert and eavesdropping GRU agent had put Lt-Col. Sergei Polzunov where he was. *Rodina*, the Motherland could chastise her erring sons, while still not wasting their services. Sometimes, satisfyingly, the two could be combined. Sergei she sent to Naryan-Mar.

North of the Arctic circle, north of the game-filled *Taiga* pine forests, Naryan-Mar was the Soviet equivalent of Outaluck, Idaho, a place where the most excitement to be had was going to watch the Pechara river freeze over in winter. Sergei commanded a detachment of MiG-23 fighters of the Voyska PVO home defence interceptor force. He had some fourteen aircraft, of which at any one time between eight and ten were on line. Naryan-Mar was the posting that told a man he would stay at his current rank until he was ready to draw his pension. The pilots flew about ten hours a month to maintain proficiency and waited for the B-1s to come screaming over the Pole laden with nuclear hardware to announce the arrival of World War Three.

Which was exactly what Sergei considered they had done, and were doing. Not starting the last Big One, but either having entered, or being in the process of leaving the USSR via the polar route.

'Those dumbheads down at Kaliningrad don't have enough sense to pour piss from a boot,' he said contemptuously. It was three am, and he and his pilots were in full flight clothing, with the operational fighters being made ready in their hangars. All the crews were combat veterans from Afghanistan, all assigned to the dustbin of promotional hopes at Naryan-Mar, but still with professional pride in their job. They were *fighter jocks*, they knew how it was done. They were in their operations building, trying to make sense of the confused reports coming from the fighting far to the south.

'The *Yanquis* are playing them for suckers,' said Sergei. He was broad of face and shoulder, Slavic, creased, leathery, a veteran. 'The B-1s aren't escaping to the west, they're coming up here.'

He went to the huge chart that covered half of one wall, and made some quick, expert calculations.

'We know the time of the attack – here – and we say the B-1s are cruising at 500 knots. We know what routes an attacking force might pick, here, here, here. Gentlemen, by my calculations if we are on station in forty minutes time we may well catch some sharks escaping the net.'

He looked over the handful of tough, resourceful men.

'I don't have to tell you what that might do to our prospects of leaving here,' he said, and they all grinned savagely.

Nine MiG-23s were fit to take the air. Climbing out to take up station at fifteen thousand feet in the freezing air he called control.

'You're sure there's no one else up here,' he said. 'I shoot down a *Backfire* on a training run I can kiss my ass goodbye.'

'Who flies up here except you lot?' the man on the ground said laconically. 'If it's moving and in the air, shoot it.'

The J-band radar dish known as High Lark to NATO that was fitted to the MiG-23 had a search range of 53 miles. On a good day. Fresh from the factory. Settling into his holding pattern he reflected that all he was probably doing was burning of a few thousand gallons of the Motherland's kerosene; his chances of being in the right place at the right time were about as good as reaching for a handful of straw and getting pricked by the needle hidden in the stack.

His ETA for the bomber force came and went. Five, ten, twelve minutes overdue. And then, unbelievably, amazingly, a trace, a fast-moving trace on the radar scope. He thumbed his comm. button.

'I have them,' he yelled. 'Estimated speed 450 knots. Passing through search area Yellow, heading 348 degrees.'

As his fighters altered course like a pack of hunting dogs, Sergei Polzunov put the nose of his fighter down, accelerating to Mach 1.5, and began flipping switches in his cockpit. In a matter of a minute, as he closed on the three fleeing American bombers lights glowed. His two AA-7 'Apex' and four AA-8 'Aphid' missiles were armed, and only awaited his command.

TANGO FORCE

Michael Carlucci, the defensive systems operator at his work station behind the flight deck was the first to be aware of the fighters.

'Eight MiG 23s closing,' he reported unemotionally. 'Mach 1.1, altitude 800 feet, range forty three miles.'

Hawkins grunted. The defensive avionics suite aboard the B-1 was exceptionally powerful, with its 107 individual units distributed at strategic points around the airframe it could cope with threats from 360 degrees. He was certain Carlucci could use the AN/ALQ-161 and its numerous jamming chains to suitably confuse the approaching fighters. The light outside was brightening considerably, however, and the air was crystal clear at this latitude.

'I'd hate those guys to get a visual on us by some remote chance,' he said. 'The 23 has a good gun on it. You can't jam a fighter pilot's eye when he's got you in his gunsight. General?'

'Right,' said Coogan. 'They've come all this way to have a furball, so let's give them one.'

'You got that?' Hawkins asked the two in the back.

'We got it.'

Hawkins communicated with the two other members of Tango Force, and they prepared for the MiGs to attack. The forward bomb bays opened. The B-1s had not exhausted their bag of lethal technological tricks at Smolensk. Aboard the lead bomber, John Rivera, the offensive systems operator ejected a Loralei decoy from the countermeasures dispenser, as did his counterparts on the other two B-1s. The rocket motors of the three Loralei decoys fired up, and electronically linked to their mother ships they flew close alongside, the specially tailored propellant of their motors producing a high-fidelity infra red signature.

'Thirty miles,' said Carlucci. 'They've fired. Two AA-7s each. They have their radars illuminating us.'

The AA-7s were semi-active radar homing missiles, therefore. Carlucci and Rivera now knew which countermeasures to take. The AA-7 existed with infra red seeking capability also. The launching MiGs behind them, on the bomber's 'six' were now effectively blind as they used their radars to illuminate the targets for the missiles.

The Loralei decoys captured the interrogatory radar beam from the fighters, and reflected back disinformation. To their pilots, the B-1s appeared to be still flying straight and level at 150 feet, but it was the decoys they were looking at.

'We have them captured,' Carlucci informed his commander.

'Then let's go,' grunted Hawkins. In unison, the three B-1s pulled up in a steep, climbing turn that brought them out at 5000 feet, travelling the way they had come, back towards the approaching MiGs. The Loralei decoys continued to fly on, straight and level, pursued by the salvo of AA-7 missiles.

As the bombers rolled out of the turn and gained nose authority on the approaching fighters below the offensive systems operators deployed their ASRAAM weaponry. ASRAAM, advanced short range anti-aircraft missiles were AMRAAM's little brothers. ASRAAM was the successor to the phenomenally successful Sidewinder. Those carried in the forward bomb bays of the B-1s had been initialised through their standard computer interfaces before launch. They *knew* where their targets were. As they streaked away, three from each bomber, the focal-plane-array homing heads were assembling detailed images of their approaching targets. They locked on.

*

The blast as the proximity fuzed warhead of the ASRAAM missile exploded close by slammed the MiG sideways. Fragmentation sliced into its skin, tearing off compressor blades, piercing fuel tanks, chopping lines, and Sergei's cockpit filled with a mass of red lights. In the fraction of a second left to him before the ruptured fuel tanks around the glowing, ruined Tumansky engine exploded Sergei squeezed and heaved on the ejection lever on the seat, blasting himself clear as the fighter erupted into a ball of fire falling towards the tundra below. The MiGs had gone subsonic while launching their missiles. The airblast was still tremendous, and he was half-dazed as he hung in his swaying harness under his parachute, following his fighter down. Smoke trails from the rest of his flight filled the morning air. A handful of parachutes were drifting. In the distance three great, swept-wing bombers were turning, swooping for the nap of the earth, moving like sharks.

The tundra came up with a rush, and Sergei grunted and gasped as his boots slammed into the hard ground, and his parachute dragged him along. He managed to release himself, and staggered to his feet, allowing the canopy to blow away over the bleak landscape. On the wind came the fading roar of the bombers, going home.

SMOLENSK

Blackened rubble stretched all around. Where tall buildings had created canyons twisted, concrete-encrusted girders poked up at the sky. In the ruins priceless, cutting-edge-of-technology equipment lay crushed and shattered, overlain with the thick layer of dust that the rain had turned to mud. New was the straight line of wooden posts pounded into the scorched earth, the site of the formal flower-edged lawn in front of the destroyed headquarters building. Men stood tied to the posts. They stood in singlets and shorts, the decorations, medals and uniforms, the symbols of their power cut from them, lying in heaps on the ground. They were generals, commanders who had had responsibility for the safety of their country, and they had failed the motherland. Civilians were there too, those at the head of the Mikoyan and Sukhoi Bureaus, whose aircraft had failed so dismally. There too those who had designed the radars, the missiles that could not find the US aircraft that had done all this, created such destruction.

The soldiers from the motor rifle regiment stood preparing their weapons. There to watch and take heed were those who were to replace these men. There were those of the Central Committee. Secretary General Krilov was there. In among the crowd, unsure if at the last moment he might not be asked to step forward and have his western clothing slashed from him and be lashed to a post with the others, was Vladimir Rykov.

The thin veneer of *perestroika* was stripped away, and that deep, and enduring side of the Russian character that called for blood to be spilled for blood was exposed. The volley was crisp, the soldiers were aware of the need to demonstrate efficiency at such a time. The men sagged against their bindings at the posts, gouts of blood staining their singlets, spreading down over their stomachs, and the regiment's officers began moving swiftly down the long row, working with pistols to ensure all was done.

The crowd of important spectators began moving to the coaches and automobiles that had brought them there, a low muttering accompanying them. Rykov was suddenly aware of the presence of a KGB major at his elbow.

'Yes?' he said fearfully.

'Secretary General Krilov requests your presence,' the soldier said, expressionless. He escorted Rykov over to the shining Zil that waited with drawn curtains, engine purring.

Rykov got into the back with Krilov and the driver

began to drive out of the ruined SDI complex, moving with surprising speed and certainty considering the damage. The road, however, was intact.

Krilov extended a hand towards it. 'They didn't waste a bomb.'

He pointed left and right, to the destroyed buildings. 'Ten bombers alone did all this. A further three killed our finest scientific minds. Simply to demonstrate their overwhelming superiority in this area of sophisticated armaments the Americans shot down nearly a hundred of our fighters while leaving. Our own Special Defense Initiative, to use their expression, is in ruins. What news of theirs?'

'They are putting their space-based elements into place. It will take some while for it to be complete, however.'

'Cord has authorised it. After publicaly announcing its cancellation. I completely misread the man. As,' Krilov said grimly 'did you.'

Krilov stared straight ahead as the driver left the site, and picked up speed, following the motorcycle escort in the centre Chaika lane.

'The attack was a stroke of near genius,' he said softly. 'Cord has us thinking the wrong way, and he has tried to win the war at a stroke.'

He doesn't know about the submarine, thought Rykov. *He doesn't know it was meant to be a retaliatory strike.*

'I thought him an academic, a man elected by some strange whim of democratic chance, but he has proved himself a great leader, a man of action. Let us review the situation. The Americans are pressing on with their SDI programme. Ours lies in literal ruins. They have a small number of their very latest Stealthy bombers and fighters that have proven so effective. Give them *time*, and a combination of SDI, in a conventional war, and their high tech equipment, plus the strength of their rejuvenated economy will place us in such a position of inferiority that we will arrive at that doomed place you forecast in your monograph. What was it called? *The Contradictions Facing*

311

the USSR. A most droll title.

'But *time* is what they require. They do *not* have their SDI system formed sufficiently to affect a war. They have very small numbers of the Stealthy aircraft. *We* have huge amounts of less sophisticated equipment, and is it not said that "quantity assumes a quality all of its own"? I think that President Cord has been just *too* clever. I think that he has given us the opening that we needed to make our annexation of Saudi Arabia and the Gulf States totally successful. And let us see how Cord's rejuvenated economy fares *then*, without oil,' he added viciously.

'You agree?'

You don't disagree with the Secretary General, thought Rykov. You don't tell him the Americans think that we sank one of their ballistic missile submarines.

'I agree,' he said huskily.

'Then begin work,' said Krilov. 'The Americans forever boast of their free society. We will show them just how free it is.'

The limousine rolled across the concrete slabs of the airport, so constructed as to be easily repaired in time of war. The Ilyushin IL-62MK airliner stood waiting with its door open and Soloviev turbofans idling, ready to take Krilov back to Vnukovo II and Moscow.

Forgive me, Ashraf my sister, Rykov thought suddenly. I was meant to be the safety-catch, to prevent the weapon from going off by mistake. Now thousands will die. But I was afraid to be one of them.

WAYCROSS, GEORGIA

The big Grumman Ag-Cat biplane had been untied and its chocks removed. Its operator had rolled it back to the rig with the help of his big, black load man. The hose from the mixing rig was connected to the plumbing of the agricultural aircraft, and the Briggs and Stratton motor kept the liquid sulphur and fungicide swirling in the big 500-gallon rig, preventing it from settling into a granitic mass. Fuel was in the tanks, which had been drained for water. The 600 bhp Pratt and Whitney radial had been pulled through, and run for a while. It ticked softly as it cooled. The windshield was clean and polished. The farmer was waiting by his 130 acres of peanuts. The only thing missing was the pilot.

The operator, a good ol' boy who had flown the fields for years before his consumption of vodka affected his depth perception sufficiently for him to stay on the ground and organise rather than fly, and employ others to do so for him, paced anxiously in his blue Sears coverall. He hauled a pack of chew from his hip pocket and replenished his supply. The big Oldsmobile Ninety-Eight came rolling up the path through the pines, trailing red dust, and his wife drew up and got out.

'He ain't there,' she said, both affronted and worried. 'Mrs Howard, that lives next to him says he got in his car last night and drove off. She didn't give it any mind, but he ain't come back. *He's gone.*'

'Well dang.' The operator put his hand on the curved wingtip, making the big aircraft rock on its flotation tyres. 'He ain't never let us down before. Jimmy's one of the best pilots we ever done had.'

He peered hopefully down the red dirt road wishing to see the familiar old Cadillac rolling into view. All crop dusters wanted to drive Cadillacs.

'*Dang it*,' he said angrily. 'Where is that boy?'

THE PENTAGON

There could not have been a greater difference between the two. Ash had been kept waiting in an ante-room until Coogan had finished what he was doing. When an aide showed her in she moved stiffly, still in pain, while Coogan, twenty years her senior, was ebullient, his eyes glittering, his movements swift. He's *high*, she thought in amazement. Coogan looked sharply at her, and waved to a solid kitchen chair by his desk. Her hand had been stitched and was bound.

'Something happen to you?' he said.

If he doesn't know, I won't tell him, she thought. It will only weaken my position if he thinks Khalif Hossein is sending people to kill me. I would say it is because of what I know and he would think it was because I was plotting against Hossein, and that therefore all I have to say is worthless.

'A man attacked me last night. I'm bruised and sore.'

Coogan nodded, not unsympathetically.

'Washington's a bad town at night. Lots of muggings.'

He sat down behind his desk. The room was largely government-issue, suitable for a man of his rank; the kitchen chairs and a solid wood table by the wall testified to his background. He flipped open the file.

'All right,' he said. 'Let's go over this little thing.'

Ash half-choked. 'I don't call it little.'

Coogan ignored her protest. 'First off, you made use of Soviet data in preparing this. Where did you get them?'

'From a man called Rykov,' she said steadily. 'Vladimir Rykov.'

314

'I know Rykov,' Coogan said sharply. 'How did you get it from him?'

'He's my brother,' Ash said simply.

'Your *brother*. How can this be?'

'In the old days, before the arrival of Reza Shah, the one hundred or so leading families of Persia of which my family was one were divided into russophiles and anglophiles. My family had often belonged to the first category, and when the Russians began trying to separate Azarbaijan from Iran in the mid 1940s as a part of the manoeuvrings between the various factions my father, a young man, was married to the daughter of Ibrahimov, then chief of the Azarbaijani Communist Party in Baku. It was an arranged marriage, and to tell the truth neither party were too happy about it. They were even less so when it became apparent that it had been but part of the Persian technique of *ketman*, meaning secretiveness, and of *taqieh*, or dissimulation, by which Ahmad Qavam, known as the Old Fox, and the head of my family, who became Prime Minister, was able to defeat the Russians and by calling on US assistance ensure their removal from his country.

'The young Russian girl, Ibrahimov's daughter, unhappy, homesick and humiliated as thus being used as a pawn left with the rest of her countrymen. She was pregnant. My father, equally ill-used, never saw her again. He subsequently married my mother. Many, many years later, I, their daughter, exiled here in Washington saw the living ghost of my martyred father on the street of this town. I asked him who he was. He was Vladimir Rykov, my brother, whom I had never met. By strange chance, by the shuffling of genes, we had become the same, become analysts, working for different sides.'

Coogan shook his head. 'That's so strange it has to be true. How did you get through the polygraph to work for NSA?'

'Because they're stupid.' Ash said contemptuously. 'They ask you vulgar questions about sex, not whether you're related to a Russian.'

315

Coogan half-smiled. 'Yeah. I heard that. Okay, so that's how you got the data.' He tapped the file. 'A great piece of detective work. Proves the Iranians were responsible for the attack on the *Maine*.'

Ash was dumbfounded. 'You agree with me?'

'Sure. And do you want to know *why* they did it?'

Coogan opened a file of his own, and placed an image on the desk. Soviet high officials greeted by Iranian high officials stood on the airfield apron. All looked up.

'And this.'

More images. Convoys of trucks and flatbeds, heading south from the USSR into Iran.

'Military hardware. MiG-29s, -27s, T-82s, BMPs, weaponry and ordnance of all kinds.'

Coogan leaned forward, his eyes glittering.

'It's called *quid pro quo*, Mrs Amran. The Soviets are re-arming Iran. They have signed a defence agreement. The Iranians were never happy about stopping the war with Iraq. They're going to do it again and win. The price? Sinking the *Maine* and taking the blame if necessary.'

Ash stared at the photographs, her mind working hard.

'And the Trident missiles?'

'Are probably in the USSR.'

'They aren't. I'll tell you where they are. They're in a big building in the port of Khorramshahr. I had Jim Dalgetti go back over. We found crates. Crates going in, and they were the right size.'

Coogan shrugged. 'We'll take care of the details. The air force is good at that.'

What *is* it, she asked herself. He's high, he's immune to logic.

She tapped the image of Khalif Hossein welcoming the Soviets at the airport.

'How did you get this, General?'

'Sent an SR-71. They did a great job,' he said proudly.

'How did you know when to send it?'

'We had information.'

'From Sultani,' said Ash. Coogan didn't reply, and she

knew she was right.

'General,' she said softly, 'you have been led by the nose just as I was led, only not being one of them you cannot see it.'

Coogan smiled confidently, ignoring her. 'I'll keep the file, Mrs Amran. You won't be needing it, the USA has no further need of your advice. We'll take care of things.'

Ash got stiffly, slowly on to her feet. She turned the photograph of Khalif Hossein sideways, so that they could both see it.

'He sent you a message, General. You got the message and sent your fabulous aircraft with its brave, trained crew, you turned up on time, just as summoned, and took the picture he wanted you to take. The mullahs know you have to spell it out for the *Farangis*, they aren't very quick on the uptake.'

Beneath the rolled black turban eyes like a merlin's looked up to the invisible speeding speck in the sky, thin lips pulled back over the teeth in a savage, triumphant grimace.

'He's laughing at you, General.'

'Ash,' called MacDonald from his silver-grey Lincoln. She went over, and slid on to the soft leather seat.

'Fancy some supper?' he asked. 'I'm meeting my wife at the Metropolitan Club. They let the ladies in in the evening. I thought I'd make use of it while I can.'

'While you can?'

'You and I are both redundant,' MacDonald said cheerfully. 'I shall be moving on.'

'You too?' she said in surprise.

'The military have made a clean sweep,' he agreed.

'All my truths richocheted from the carapace of General Coogan like tennis balls bouncing from the armour of a tank,' she said. 'There was something burning joyfully within him that made him immune to all I said.'

'The US Air Force bombed the Soviet SDI complex at Smolensk flat. They destroyed anti-aircraft weaponry and attacking fighters like swatting flies. They lost no one. It is

317

probably the greatest triumph of military technology this century, it is the justification of Coogan's entire life.'

'I hoped we were in time to stop it.'

'Nothing was going to stop it,' MacDonald said. 'Have you been to the Met? The food is good. I can recommend the terrapin, if you're something of a gourmet.'

He looked across at her.

'We have no power to control events now,' he said gently. 'We may think about more civilised things. The dean of the faculty at Yale has kindly agreed to take me on immediately. I shall be lecturing in a week, and living in a very nice house not far from my old college of Calhoun. I shall visit Jonathan Edwards college from time to time, where a colleague is Master. The High Table there is good, it can hold a candle to your old *alma mater*, Oxford. What will you do, my dear?'

The Lincoln Continental rolled gently through the traffic. MacDonald was relaxed, the hideous pressure of his job was lifted from him, Ash realised he was glad.

'I must stay away, I suppose,' she said. 'Lest they send someone else to kill me.'

'You were meddling in politics, dear. Moore was right on that at least. I should have reprimanded you, but I valued your advice too much. And you are like a daughter to me. My wife and I never had children ... the technology was not available then, all the clever things they can do ...'

MacDonald pulled in just short of the club on the corner of H street and 17th.

'We have parking here,' he explained.

'You may stay with us at Yale for a while if you like. We would enjoy your company. And it would keep you away from Washington. I don't think it is a good idea for any of us to be near here for a while, do you?'

Ash looked at him.

'No?'

'No. You don't imagine the Soviets are going to let us bomb the peak of their technological effort back to the Stone Age and do nothing, do you?'

DefCon II

Severe Crisis. Attack Imminent

CORNELIA, MISSOURI

The long white *Coupe de Ville* ate up the miles effortlessly, burning gas at a gallon every fourteen miles the way it had been made to. Jimmy Tombs sat on the cream lattice-leather seat and enjoyed the cool of the air pumping out of the car's ducts. Back then, it had been the Cadillac engineers' boast that they had one litre of their mighty V-8 simply to drive the air-conditioning. The car belied its age, heading towards thirty years old. As a trained mechanic, Jimmy knew it was constructed like a tank, out of mild steel that was thick, with a great engine so understressed it had pulled the car near two hundred thousand miles and still hadn't been stripped down. Jimmy was going to be sorry to leave it behind.

Crop dusters liked Cadillacs, all the farmers knew that. It had been no trouble for Jimmy to buy one off another pilot, newly married and looking for a fuel-efficient VW. Crop dusters were transients too, everyone was used to the pilot arriving at the beginning of the season and working all the hours God sent when God sent the stinkbug and the armyworm and the fungus too. You went and showed him the fields and watched him spray, you liked it if he dragged the wheels just over your crop, maybe you met him occasionally in the bar and had a can and shot the shit, he went away when the season was over and you forgot about him until next year. You weren't sure exactly where he went, instructing kids to fly, wasn't that it? Yeah. Crop dusters made good instructors, they were popular with flight schools and students alike, because no one had such a feel for the air as they did, if you were talking stick-and-rudder, if you were talking taildragger, if you were talking about the sheer ability to bend an overloaded aircraft through the trees, to skim over the land at five feet, just to flat fly like an angel, you were talking about a crop duster.

In the winter, Jimmy went home to see his Mother, and to do what She wanted. When the war had been on his Mother had sent him off to fly. He had 1400 hours in Afghanistan, flying Su-25 *Frogfoot* ground attack aircraft, blowing Afghans into pulp. Since the war had stopped his Mother had kept Jimmy in the USA, to be there if She needed him. She did. The word had come through that evening, and Jimmy had packed a bag and got in his long white Cadillac and headed out of Waycross to pick up I-75 on his way to Missouri, never to return.

Nicolai Koltsov had one last task to perform for his Mother.

Jimmy Tombs, born Nicolai Koltsov thirty eight years before in Kalinin, rolled through the little city of Cornelia. To the north was Warrensburg and the University. East of Warrensburg Knob Noster and the State Park, which bordered the air force base. In the pleasant countryside north of Cornelia he looked for the sign that pointed down the dirt road. Chuck Rollins, it said. 'If it's Ag You Want, Come on In.' Jimmy took the road, the big tyres rumbling on the dirt. Ag operations are always down dirt roads, he thought.

He rolled out of the pines to find a long hangar set in front of a flat, mowed grass strip cut out of the trees. A large sign decorated the corrugated, white-painted side of the hangar. Chuck Rollins, it said. Ag Aircraft King. Whoever Chuck was, he might have been boastful, but he did not lie. Secured to rows of tie-downs were two or three dozen agricultural aircraft, from small red-and-white Pawnees, white Call-Airs, yellow Thrushes and Air Tractors, yellow-and-black Ag Cats. Jimmy parked his Cadillac by a couple of Chevrolet pick ups and went around to the front of the shop. The doors were rolled shut and he banged on the metal. A head poked out from the personnel door.

'We been waitin' on you,' it said. Chuck Rollins was like Jimmy, of medium height, small beer belly, powerful arms, legs and shoulders, going bald from wearing crash helmets.

'It's a long drive.'

'Yeah.'

They went inside. The shop was cool, lit by neon lamps hanging from chains on the roof. The hangar was equipped to maintain aircraft, with mobile tool chests, hoists, workshop, racks of spares. On the concrete floor stood five clean, needle-nosed agricultural aircraft. Three men were working on one, attaching a long rack under the wing.

'Jimmy's here, guys,' said Rollins. They were all so used to speaking American they did not revert to Russian.

The three came over, and they shook hands. Bruce, Joe and Harry. From Minsk, Kovrov and Belgorod. Rollins was a Muscovite.

'Bruce and Joe been flying Thrushes, so that's what they got. Me and Harry got the Air Tractors, and you got the Cat. We're using turbines for the extra load-carrying capacity and for the decreased radar signature. And they're quiet. Beer?'

'Please.'

Rollins handed Jimmy a chilled Michelob from a red and white cooler on the floor. He leaned against the green-painted unit along the wall and watched while Bruce and Joe manoeuvred the long, perforated cylinder under the wing of the Turbo Cat and began attaching it to the rack.

'It'll be like a full load,' said Rollins. 'Four of those weigh 3200 lb fully armed. We'll be light on fuel, of course.'

Jimmy looked at the 8 foot pod. Four pods gave four salvos of twenty-two 2.75 rockets. Tank-busters. Ship-gutters. Bomber-destroyers.

'Sure,' he said. 'We ain't going far.'

NSA HEADQUARTERS

The people of Washington were used to the blue and white airship that floated about the sky of the capital. In the daytime its sides carried giant logos advertising anything from beer to national airlines, and at night its light display could communicate information from a number of advertisers, one after the other, from the latest prices from the property developers across town to the best and cheapest drinks in town, Tommy's Bar, where there was Happy Hour from five to six and relays of young girls to shake their tits at you for just as long as you could still focus on them.

Folk were quite fond of the floating advertising platform. 'There goes thuh balloon' they'd say, inaccurately, as its soft hum came over the buildings. Advertisers liked it too, its rates were reasonable. Didn't really know how it made a profit.

It didn't. AerialAd, Inc. received a subsidy from Moscow.

At night, when it switched out its lights, you couldn't see it. In fact, being largely radar-transparent, it was a naturally Stealthy vehicle. So much so that it carried two transponders, so that Washington air traffic control would always know where it was if one should fail. Its shape was one of constant compound curves, and it lacked any large retro-reflectors. In addition, it had one or two features not incorporated by the ship's European designers, like non-metallic Kevlar propellers and RAM ducting and shrouding for the engines. Its RCS was thus reduced to a level that could give powerful military radars a difficult time, and which rendered it quite invisible to commercial surveillance systems.

At 2 am in the morning, it floated silently up wind of Fort Meade, allowing the air current to carry it towards the installation. It was at five thousand feet, flying above five-tenths broken cumulus. The lights of NSA Headquarters were visible through breaks in the cloud, and its position was verified by its on-board INS, and VORs. It was approaching the target.

Packed inside the gondola with the flight crew were twelve fit, trained young men. They could have joined such elite outfits as the British SAS or US Rangers, but they had received their instruction within the USSR. Their unit was *Spetsnaz*, and they wore the coveted blue-and-white striped T-shirts. That was underneath their black clothing, black parachutist's coverall, black paratrooper's boots, black crash helmet with attached night-vision light-intensifying goggles with integral power pack. They had black UT-15 parachutes and each a black supply canister that dropped with him.

The on-board computer had calculated wind speed and position, and when the drop point arrived a green light flashed on by the gondola door. With economical, slick, trained movements, the soldiers jumped, one after the other in a stick. The UT-15 parachute was unusual, based on a civilian competition model it sported controls down by the waist, rather than up by the ears. Its users were trained in both HAHO (High Altitude High Opening) and HALO (High Altitude Low Opening) techniques. The latter carried the risk of loss of control while at terminal velocity with a giant pack, and the problem of timing the low opening correctly, the former, on a high altitude, thirty-minute glide several miles to the target, the prospect of a highly-trained soldier arriving there with frost-bitten and inoperative hands if they were up by his ears, so the UT-15 had them down low. The soldiers could land on a mountain ledge twenty miles away from a HAHO drop;

the short float down into the clearing around the great NSA complex was approaching child's play for them. They landed within the facility's Cyclone fencing. All veterans of Afghanistan, they were under the command of Major Korchagin and his senior NCO, Sergeant-Major Mazurov, both of whom were veterans of the assault on the Darulaman Palace on Boxing Day 1979 which had formally announced the participation of the USSR in that war. They grouped and swiftly hid parachutes and supply canisters. Waiting in the clearing was a van, driven by a man in the uniform of the Federal Protective Service. His name was Halloran. He had worked for the FPS, guarding NSA Headquarters for six years. He took the troops to an annex of the huge operations building, which, by virtue of his position he had made available. NSA worked twenty-four hours a day, no one took any notice of the group of maintenance technicians with their clean overalls and yellow badges. Like all technicians, they had their specialised tool boxes and canisters of this or that with them.

The troops took over the annex that Halloran had provided for their use and waited for the day.

NATIONAL PHOTOGRAPHIC INTERPRETATION CENTER, WASHINGTON

Johnny Fowler worked the ten-till-six shift every day. While within NPIC during those hours he was responsible for the sound running of the air-conditioning of the building. It was a more important assignment than it might have seemed. Federal Building 213, situated in the run-down area near the old Washington Navy Yard had air-conditioners strapped to its side that were eighty feet long and nearly as high as the building itself. If they should fail to function not only would all the occupants of the building begin to sweat, but the fabulous array of supercomputers within, that scanned the incoming stream of information twenty-four hours a day, passing billions of bits of information into the data base would melt. In seconds.

It was for this reason that Johnny Fowler was a very important man in the building, and one who had access to the entire infrastructure of the environmental and power systems of the Center. No one questioned him that day, as he spent some time here, working at the access panels of the conditioners, there in the ducting, down in the basement where the emergency generators and fuel tanks were.

Equally, no one raised any questions when he left the building somewhat early. A man in his position did not have to punch time-clocks. Maybe he needed some spare parts, needed to fetch something not in the building.

Johnny Fowler had all he needed with him. Driving out of Washington on the truckless Parkway he took the turnoff for Savage Road, leading to NSA. In the distance the sky was dirty with smoke from a forest fire. A tiny aircraft swooped, painting a splash of white across the dirt. A fire-bomber.

Taking a quiet side-road into the woods Fowler took a full NBC-nuclear, biological and chemical-warfare suit from the trunk of his pick-up and dressed himself carefully. He sat in the driving seat, holding a submachine gun in his right hand, should he be disturbed. The drone of big radial engines became a shattering roar as the big yellow Canadair blasted overhead.

Johnny Fowler started his engine, and drove out on to Savage Road.

CORNELIA, MISSOURI

Like all children in the USSR Johnny Tombs, né Nicolai Koltsov had been taught how the Soviet Union single-handedly won the Great Patriotic War against the Germans. However, he had heard enough from his father, a tough old former Shturmovik driver to know that they had had a little help from their friends. All the Jeeps and Mack trucks were still around, for one thing. When he had been chosen for his undercover role he had stored the nugget of information away, and when he was actually in America, he read. All the little towns like Waycross had a smart public library, staffed by helpful middle-aged women; they could guide you to what you wanted. When he had read some, he knew why those in command over him allowed no foreign books into the USSR. All you needed were a few history books and biographies and the whole population would be demanding the vote. Democracy was an intoxicating, powerful drug.

It didn't mean that Nicolai loved his Mother any the less, or would not do what she wanted.

Because he was a combat fighter pilot, Johnny Tombs loved to read the experiences of those before him. He'd read the biographies of Bishop and Ball, Bader, Cunningham and Clostermann. He'd read Yeates' *Winged Victory* and Bolitho's *Combat Report*.

Waiting to go, he wished he'd left them all on the shelves.

Clostermann's account of waiting to go to attack the airfield in 1945, of going, and of just two coming back was haunting his mind. Airfields were among the hardest of targets to attack, everyone knew that. Clostermann's flight had had Tempests, state-of-the-art armoured fighters that did over 400 knots.

They hadn't had the punch carried by the five ag. aircraft sitting in a line on the shop floor, though.

It was coming up to time, to 'hack' time.

Johnny was sitting outside with Chuck Rollins, on the old creaking, metal swing-seat by the side of the hangar. The others were resting on the bunks inside.

'You know, I never thought we'd actually have to do it,' he said suddenly. 'I thought we'd be here for years, ready to be used, just like the rockets in their silos back home, just ready to be used, but never being fired.'

'Yeah. I know.'

Rollins tugged at a tuft of long grass and pulled out a stalk. He chewed on the juicy green flesh for a moment.

'I'm going to miss it,' he said. 'I like these people. They're like us, you know.'

'Yeah. Me, too. Fucking politicians.'

'Right. Fucking generals.'

'Fucking high-ups. Fucking *nachalstvo*.'

'Shoot the whole crew. Let guys like us get on with it.'

'Be nice, wouldn't it,' said Johnny Tombs, almost wistfully.

'It ain't gonna happen,' said Rollins. He checked his watch. From inside the hangar they heard the footsteps of the others, and the sound of the heavy pins being drawn, and the doors beginning to roll.

'Let's go,' he said. He looked at his companion solidly. 'We aren't doing it for the *nachalstvo*, not for the *vlasti*, General Secretary Krilov or the entire Politburo,' he said quietly. 'We do it for *rodina*, for the Motherland.'

As he heard the word, Nicolai Koltsov, Johnny Tombs felt a rush of emotion, felt the prickle of tears at the back of his eyes. It was so, he loved *rodina* the way a mother loved her little child, and the child blindly returning that love, unquestioningly, unreasoningly, unstintingly.

Johnny Tombs would lay down his life for his motherland, if She asked him to.

'It's funny, ain't it,' said Tombs finally, rising to his feet. 'They did the job with their Stealthy bombers and fighters. And here we are, we're Stealthy too. We've been here since they even thought of the word. Ain't no radar on earth ever spotted us.'

Rollins grinned. 'Maybe people are better than machines.'

They rolled their aircraft out, they got in, the way they had, season in season out, shifting about in the seats to get comfortable, the big doors left down to keep cool, sitting perched up, ag. planes were built like fighters, because the pilots had to have a good view. They tightened the webbing straps, ran through their check lists, the big three-bladed propellers began to turn, turbines whining, the air suddenly filled with shimmering heat from the big exhausts, with the pungent fragrance of burning kerosene.

Johnny Tombs was fourth in line in the big Turbo Cat. He'd never liked the bird as much as its radial-engined predecessor, when they'd reworked it and made it so long they'd done nothing for the visibility and on the ground you were practically blind. He waddled out behind the two Thrushes and Harry's Air Tractor, the prettiest of ag. planes, like an ugly duckling, fish-tailing it to peer around the great long nose and see where he was going. Nobody denied the Turbo Cat's ability to haul a load, though, nor that it was the best ag. plane in the world to have an accident in.

Johnny Tombs wondered morbidly how it handled 30mm flak.

Bruce was rolling, the tailwheel reluctantly coming up off the ground, slow to accelerate, then faster, the wheels bumping, the undercarriage legs coming in as the wings gained lift, and then he was off, the aircraft looking strange with the four great pods hung under the wings. Joe and Harry were on their way, the aircraft forming up with Bruce who had made a long, slow left turn at about eighty feet, the flight making a running rendezvous, and Johnny was going, the 750 shp Pratt & Whitney screaming at 100 per cent power. He leaned forward in his seat like all ag. pilots did, resting against the tension of his straps, the stick grasped lightly, forefinger loose, feet busy on the pedals as the rudder gained authority, the tyres rumbling, cool air gushing, and then she was flying, smooth in her own element, a swan.

He held the nose down to get airspeed and then low over the trees he cranked the aircraft round to formate on the flight. Rollins came up behind him, and they settled into a single file. Rollins put the nose down and they dropped down low over the road. The green of the State Park was ahead, and the other side, the air force base.

WHITEMAN AIR FORCE BASE, MISSOURI

Sergeant Billy Case was responsible for patrolling the east perimeter of the base. Case was approaching forty, a solid, thickset man who nearly had his twenty in. Airfield defence had been his speciality for most of his career. He had done two tours in Vietnam, had volunteered for the second, had defended Khe Sanh under General Keegan.

Whiteman was a very big air base indeed, which was one of the main reasons the B-2s were based there. To defend military aircraft in wartime, or time of danger, the concept of 'extending the perimeter' was used. Within the USA itself this was taken to be keeping the aircraft out of range of infantry-portable guided missiles of the anti-tank variety. The perimeter of Whiteman was sufficiently large, the air base occupying sufficient land for this to be quite feasible. In wartime, of course, there was the threat of attack from fighter aircraft, but even this was not taken to be a threat within the USA, but one which would apply more in the European, T-80s-rolling-across-the-Elbe scenario. The truth was, that although Whiteman had twelve batteries of Hawk missiles, a battalion of armoured cars and tracked multi-barrel 20mm and 30mm radar-guided anti-aircraft weapons the aerial threat was not taken seriously. Why should it be? Aside from the time a submarine-launched seaplane had dropped a few small bombs on a remote part of California in 1941 no city, base, port or hamlet in the continental USA had ever come under genuine aerial attack.

The saboteur, whether armed with missiles or plastic explosive was certainly given some mind, which was what Billy Case was doing in his Jeep with its mounted twin 0.5 machine guns. His patrol was the eastern edge, with its three Hawk batteries and five armoured cars/tracked AA. On the seat of the Jeep was a megaphone. Traffic on the public road that ran alongside the perimeter was forbidden to stop. Anyone doing so got a polite but firm reminder from the sergeant to put the pedal to the metal once more and move.

They were going to need a very big wrecker to shift this one. The old, old White eighteen-wheeler came dragging up the road belching filthy smoke from its stack and just plain died, there at the other side of the Cyclone fence. Two young guys clambered down from the cab, real cowboys, thought Case as he came bowling up in his Jeep. They had the long, tousled hair, the cut-off t-shirts displaying their big hands and powerful arms and strong shoulders, all the marks of country boys, used to heavy manual labour since young, they had the tanned faces, they'd picked a lot of tobacco in their time, heaved a lot of sacks. They had the hood of the White open by the time Case arrived, but by the age of it and the look of it, from the 'Maypop' tyres to the dented and scarred railroad container atop the flatbed it was going to take more than roadside tinkering to get it moving under its own steam.

The two boys waved as they saw the Jeep halt at the other

side of the fence.

'Okay, guys,' Case said through his loudspeaker. 'You stay where you are, I'm going to send a wrecker to get you clear. Ain't no one allowed to halt on this road.'

'Thanks, man,' one called. Case got back into the Jeep and called on the radio for his corporal to come and keep an eye on them. When he saw the Jeep coming he got in to drive up to his command post and call the wrecker. He left a few seconds before the corporal arrived, and saved his life.

Jim Croce wrote a song about truckers like them, he thought. He waved to Corporal King and accelerated up the perimeter road.

He looked in his mirror in time to see Corporal King and his Jeep roll over and over, losing all shape, blasted a hundred yards in a second like a toy hit by a fire hose. Twisting his head round he saw that the railroad container had changed shape. Two sides had fallen down to reveal a big four-barrelled gun mounted on an angled base. Spent cases sprayed into the air and smoke stained it. Case even knew what it was, in the frozen seconds as the White began moving, and behind him, two of the five anti-aircraft armoured cars flew into the air like toys. It was Case's job to know about such things, it was a Sea Zenith four-barrelled 25mm close-in weapons system, built to defend warships against missiles.

Case turned sharp left, heading away from the perimeter. As he did so, things began streaking over his head, and the three turning tracked vehicles vanished in white flame. Anti-tank, his mind told him, as he floored the throttle, reaching for his radio. Built to take out an M1 Abrams main battle tank. Chews up soft-skinned vehicles like that.

Pieces of metal, canvas, rubber and flesh were raining down from the sky. There was a gigantic explosion as the No.1 Hawk battery blew up.

'*Diversionary attack on the east perimeter*,' he shouted into his radio, but the channel was full of people screaming. In

333

his mirror the White went by in the smoke, accelerating towards the second Hawk battery.

His Jeep was hitting seventy as he headed into the centre of the air base, because there was only one thing worth attacking, and they were in the line of big hangars, there, over there.

There was an enormous roar as the commander fired the Hawks, one after the other on the flattest trajectory he had, over open sights, because the Hawk was an anti-aircraft weapon, and radar-guided, and the White was well within the minimum range. They missed, the Sea Zenith caught the fourth as it left the launcher and the emplacement vanished in a hell of white-hot rain.

The man sat quiet at the edge of the State Park, in his Nissan. He had a good view of the western perimeter of the air base. His windows were down, and he heard the soft whine of the turbines as they flashed overhead, just skimming the trees. He had his hand on the microphone of his CB-style radio.

Johnny Tombs cleared the tree line of the State Park with the other four aircraft echeloned on his left. As they put their noses down, and he saw the targets his stomach drew tight and a wave of pure nausea swept over him. It was always the same. Sweat drenched him, spurting up out of his skin, making his clenched toes slither within his boots. And yet his hand was steady, and his eye practised as he lined up the 30mm AA tracked vehicle the other side of the fence. He gave it a little deflection through the graticule. His loose forefinger tightened. Men were running like ants. The fence flashed below his wheels and he fired. A salvo of four rockets streaked from under his wings like flame and the target exploded, hurtling backwards, erupting as the ammunition destroyed it from within.

Like ballet dancers, the five ag. aircraft jinked left, and then right, twenty feet from the ground, three Gs on the turn, avoiding the flying debris, and then straightened out, leaving the screaming and the carnage behind, the air cool and smooth, five feet up, just like they were laying a swathe over the soybeans.

The hangars were small, a mile and a half away, like a row of agricultural barns.

Behind them, the two Hawk batteries were slewing as the radar sought to acquire the fleeing targets. In the State Park the man lifted the microphone of his radio to his lips.

Johnny Tombs was waiting. He had stopped breathing. He hated the missiles. He'd been there when the American Stingers started knocking down the *Hinds*. And the *Frogfoots*. His legs were shaking, beating a tattoo on the pedals, and he hunched up in his seat as the great hangars got closer. His thumb caressed the red button on the top of the stick, but waited.

The Hawks fired, erupting long plumes of white fire.

'*Missilesmissilesmissiles*,' the agent in the Nissan shouted into the microphone.

Elegant, like ballerinas again, the ag. aircraft popped up in a climbing right turn and at the top, at a hundred and fifty feet the thumbs squeezed. They were inverted, at the top of the barrel roll as the stream of flares poured out behind them.

From four. The dispenser on Harry's Air Tractor hung up. As the Hawks flew through the bright flares one caught the thermal signature of the exhaust as he pulled back on the stick, heading back towards the safety of the ground.

The blast shook them. Even Johnny Tombs felt it, his hands and feet dancing as he controlled the big biplane in the sudden turbulence. Four left, it meant an extra target.

The man in the Nissan accelerated out of the State Park. Cars were halted all along the road, as people stared dumbfounded at the military wreckage on the edge of the base. Four small dots receded across the field, becoming lost in the clutter of parked aircraft and buildings. Taking 23 north the Nissan driver heard the shocking thud of ordnance going off. In his mirror he saw fire and smoke rising high into the evening sky. His knuckles were white on the wheel.

'*Molodtsi* – well done, boys,' he muttered. Ahead a big tractor-trailer was pulled in to the side of the road. It was an old White with a railroad container on the flatbed, all stained with black smoke. Four country boys jumped down from the cab as the yellow sedan came up. They scrambled in and the driver pulled away, heading north across the Blackwater River. From the base there was still the noise of explosives going off, and a huge black pall of smoke was sweeping across the sky.

Johnny Tombs eased back on the stick to pop over an administration block. He saw tended green grass, flower beds, people frozen as they looked up at the flight of aircraft just overhead. The four were still in rough line abreast, about two hundred yards between them, matching the distance between targets. Rollins was slightly in the lead, the Air Tractor showing its clean lines, with the two Turbo Thrushes next, and the bulky Ag Cat trailing by a few lengths. They popped their noses back down and they were over the great sward of grass, criss-crossed by runways and taxiways. Tombs was low enough to see the markings on the VASI lights as he whipped over the threshold, and the thick black markings of the rubber on the runway. He had begun to breathe again, and it was all right, his first target was growing in the windshield, the hangar doors were rolled open, he could see the huge, bat-like shape of the bomber inside, festooned with all its striped umbilical connections, they must have been going to fly it later, men were running, on his left he caught the rhythmic gouts of flame from beneath Rollins' wings as his first salvo of twenty two rockets let go. The big grey bomber filled the reticule as Tombs squeezed the trigger, and suddenly the whole hangar erupted, the last rockets vanishing into the boiling fire. All four pilots were cranked round, thirty feet from the deck, pulling four Gs in a procedure turn that took them away from the destruction, and prepared them for their second pass. Tombs' vision was greying as he pulled out of the turn. No g-suit. He grunted as he dragged air back into his lungs, and counted the seconds before he could turn back in towards the remaining hangars. The other pilots were ahead of him, unconsciously increasing the power and speed.

From somewhere someone had got their anti-aircraft going, and the sky was lighting up with flashes and white smoke. A line of eight stitched its way suddenly across the sky in front of Tombs and he cranked the big Ag Cat back into the turn, holding near seventy degrees of bank, squinting back at the target through the green cockpit eyebrows at the top of the doors. All four hangars had been hit on the first pass and dense black smoke boiled up out of the huge holes punched in their sides.

Tombs was scared again, as the sky filled with flak and tracer, he unconsciously squeezed himself smaller in his seat. The Air Tractor in the lead fired again, followed by the two Thrushes of Bruce and Joe, bright in the rolling smoke. As Bruce squeezed the trigger and the pods belched flame the Thrush took a direct hit behind the cockpit, removing the entire empennage in a tangle of yellow and khaki alloy and tubing. For a whole second or more the aircraft kept flying, straight and level. Bruce squeezed the trigger again and the bird erupted in flame for a moment before vanishing into the boiling cauldron of the hangar exploding. Tombs fired again through the dense smoke, and scored his second direct hit. The smoke was dragging at his lungs, acrid and biting. There were two hangars left, and three aircraft. They went outbound once more, slipping like predatory fish in muddy water through the rolling black smoke.

Explosions and tracer were to Tombs' left and right, above and below him, striking huge chunks out of the concrete and earth. Things tore holes in his wings and sinister dazzling flashes danced by his cockpit. There was a ball of fire in the smoke as Joe took a direct hit, and then something burning, bouncing over the grass, setting it alight.

The Cat shuddered in the turn, all the holes blown in it and pieces knocked off it had reduced the lift, it was beginning not to want to fly. He eased the back pressure on the stick, Rollins was far ahead in the smoke, he fired once again. Parts of the panel in front of Tombs suddenly jumped out from their mountings, striking him in the face, and someone punched him hard on the shoulder, slamming him back in his seat. The inside of the cockpit was splashed with someone's blood.

The Cat was crabbing badly, and trying to drop its left wing. Rollins was lining up on the final, tenth hangar. He let go with his final salvo of eighteen rockets and as he passed to Tombs' left, travelling the other way, Tombs let go with his own. The Cat was shuddering, squinting back over his shoulder Tombs could see that the tenth hangar was still intact. They must have missed in the smoke.

He hurt. He wanted to leave, he was very tired. He hauled back on the stick in the ag. pilot's classic turn, the hammerhead. As the speed bled off he put in left rudder, and the Cat, almost motionless in the sky at one hundred and fifty feet swung cleanly around.

It was all in slow-motion. In the distance he could see the Thrush of Rollins skimming over the field to the south. Halted on the ramp near the hangar was a Jeep with a twin machine-gun mounting. A very determined man was firing at him through the smoke. He felt the shells striking the aircraft. The broad white expanse of the hangar roof was below him and he squeezed the trigger for the last time. The rockets knifed through the metal and flame billowed from the doors. There was an appalling screeching of tortured metal as the machine-gun found the propeller and engine. A blade flew off and the vibration threw Tombs around in the cockpit like a doll. There was little pressure on the stick as he tried to put it down. Pieces of aircraft flew past him, the ground was rolling over and over. It was still, and just the raw taste of blood in his mouth.

★

Rollins could never get over the speed of change in air battles. The strip in the pines was quiet. Some crows cawed caustically to each other, tumbling about in the sky as they headed for home. The sun was going down. He was drenched in sweat. The Air Tractor stood parked off the strip, leaving room for the others. The big Oldsmobile sedan stood waiting. On the back seat were five full changes of clothing. Rollins's hands were shaking so badly it took him ten minutes to get his flight suit and boots off and begin getting dressed. He opened the trunk, there was a red and white cooler there filled with beer. The boys would want a drink when they got in.

He was dressed in slacks and short-sleeved shirt, loafers on his feet and had dried his hair with a towel and combed it by the time it got dark. He took a tall bottle of Lone Star beer from the cooler and twisted off the cap. Bubbling and gold, he tilted the bottle into his mouth, sucking eagerly until it was all gone. He took another and put it between his legs as he sat in the driver's seat. He switched on the lights, and drove quietly out down the dirt road. It was dark, there was no one else coming home.

They had laid Johnny Tombs on the grass, his flying suit heavy with blood. The air was filled with the sound of burning, of hoses and sirens. They stared at Tombs in shock, in amazement. A white ambulance drew up alongside, its red lights twinkling round and round in the gloom. The sky was still light. As they lifted him on to the stretcher he saw a shape flitting through the smoke that still stained the air. It was like a bat, a flying wing. The missing B-2. A faint, rueful smile went over his face.

'Nine out of ten ain't bad,' he whispered.

OAKFIELD FARM, MARYLAND

The farm occupied some 1200 acres of Maryland's fine agricultural soil. An agribusiness, it had a small workforce and relied heavily on machinery – the big John Deere tractors and harvesters, an Ag Cat agricultural aircraft to put out herbicide, pesticide, fertiliser. It had its own ag strip in the middle of the land, with big new barns to house the equipment. The pilot, Levon Jones kept his hand in when not working in the Cat by flying the powerline patrol in the farm's Super Cub for the power company. Each weekend he flew in the little Piper, checking the lines, just fifty feet up. He was familiar with a winding route that took him north through Pennsylvania to Lake Erie itself.

If there was anything odd about the farm it was that it didn't hire any locals to work there. But if anyone mentioned it it was explained that Oakfield was just a part of a bigger organisation, and you know how it was with big organisations, they liked to have their own people do things, do them their way. People were happy with that.

With its high level of mechanisation the farm was run by just eight men, including Levon Jones. The bigger organisation which employed them was very big indeed. It employed Chuck Rollins and Johnny Tombs. It employed Johnny Fowler too. It had assets throughout the USA. It had owned Sultan Electronics. In Maryland it owned Oakfield Farm, and a mixed aviation operation that flew out of Washington County airport in Hagerstown. It owned the various aircraft there, the Lear Jet, the

Canadair, the Pilatus Britten-Norman Trislander commuter aircraft. It owned the airship that sold advertising over the capital. It was the USSR.

Levon Jones called them out at Hagerstown and they got the Trislander ready for him. The Trislander was a very solid, load-hauling, three-engine aircraft, built to operate in and out of short strips. It could take off in under 400 metres and land in just 260. On the day three of the workforce quietly drove into Washington and took the Eastern flight to Hamburg in Europe, before equally quietly sliding across the border into East Berlin, Levon Jones flew the Trislander from Hagerstown to the strip at the farm. The aircraft was built to carry eighteen. Twelve soldiers. Johnny Fowler. Four farm workers. Levon Jones. Eighteen.

When 'hack' time came, the four farm workers and Levon Jones were all strapped into their seats at the end of the strip. With them, firmly secured to the floor over the centre of gravity was a heavy, rectangular box. The humans were encased in full NBC suits. The box in the protective covering that had preserved it from corrosion since it had been covertly introduced into the USA some years before.

The three flat-six Lycomings were running. All take-off checks had been performed. The second hand slid past the sixty and Levon Jones pushed the levers to the firewall.

NSA HEADQUARTERS

The weather had been dry for some while, and there was a stiff breeze blowing. No one who noticed the forest fire burning away in the distance was particularly surprised that it had started. Every year it happened. The woods were full of dry tinder in the form of dead twigs and leaves, and there was always the thoughtless person ready to toss a beer bottle from a passing car, the glass soon to act as a magnifying lens, and …

The arrival of the big Canadair CL-215 water-bomber on the scene showed that someone was taking it seriously. To the north, Quebec Province was saved from devastation yearly by the team of CL-215s that worked there. The water-bomber was a floatplane, and took on its load of water, 5400 litres, five tons of it, in a single pass along any suitable strip of water, canal, river, lake or open sea near to the fire. It scooped it up in a ten second run and was back in the air in seconds, heading back to the fire. It was a truly effective fire-fighting vehicle, some of the people in NSA who saw the yellow and red bomber working in the distance recalled seeing the little documentary on the local news, there was an outfit over in Hagerstown who had bought it, they'd seen the Quebec ones in action and been impressed.

However, no one gave it much mind, the people who worked for NSA were top professionals, the cream of the nation's brains, cryptographers, codebreakers, linguists, analysts, engineers, scientists, mathematicians, they were all concerned with getting on with their work, not watching some pilot sweat dumping water on a fire. NSA had more Ph.D's per head of its work force than Harvard University. Quite a few had *been* at Harvard, of course.

By the time the CL-215 made its pass along the east Cyclone fence, flying upwind of the complex in the stiff breeze it was far too late for any of those very clever and educated people to do anything. Within the water-bomber was a separate spray tank holding some 100 gallons of a dark brown, viscous substance known by the name of VX. VX was a nerve gas. A few pounds of it killed 6000 sheep by accident thirty miles downwind of Dugway Proving Ground in 1968 when the Phantom fighter jet putting it out suffered from a trailing nozzle.

There was no accident about this pass. Within seconds people were falling like puppets on the streets of Fort Meade, cars drifting off track to crash into street lights and

342

store-fronts. In the annex to the Headquarters building Major Korchagin, the officer of the Spetsnaz team, watching from a window saw the bomber arrive and squeezed the command button on his radio transmitter. Within the bowels of the central air-conditioning the valves of the canisters brought with the troops snapped open and VX gas began to flood the building. Men and women of genius died at the desks, work-stations, in the laboratories and workshops.

Every man of the Spetsnaz team was in full NBC clothing, completely insulated from the outside environment. Under the command of Sergeant-Major Mazurov, six of the troops then went outside to the van which was waiting for them, and drove out through the main gate on to Savage Road. Three-quarters of a mile along it they detonated the charges that had been placed on four trees, bringing them crashing down, blocking any entry. Having set up their road-block they deployed with their AK-74 automatic rifles, RPK-74 machine guns and single US-built MK. 19 model 3 automatic grenade thrower, capable of providing efficient saturation coverage for up to 1600 yards. Thus equipped they were completely confident of beating off anyone who might arrive for the length of time necessary.

Inside the Headquarters building Korchagin and the remaining troops made their way down the corridor to the lobby, passing by the huge, shimmering mosaic of the Agency seal, the eagle grasping its skeleton key. The troops began dragging bodies out of the way to clear a path through the lobby from the glass doors of Gatehouse 1. The men and women had been felled as they walked or stood. Eyes remained open, faces slightly flushed, turning blue, expressions of surprise and alarm. Korchagin stood in the lobby, decorated with its oil paintings of past Directors of NSA, and pressed the button for a lift.

Levon Jones, from Leningrad brought the Trislander in over the felled trees and cut the power as the tyres kissed the tarmac of Savage Road. Johnny Fowler was waiting in his four-wheel-drive Chevrolet by the gate in the Cyclone fence, and Jones expertly turned the Trislander to face back down the road. The four soldiers inside unfastened the heavy box in its protective covering and took it out through the port door, loading it on to the bed of the pick-up. Fowler then drove in and to the headquarters building. Gunning the engine he drove up the twelve steps and into the lobby via Gatehouse 1. He halted by the waiting lift and the soldiers unloaded the box. Major Kamov went down into the basement where the greatest concentration of computing power in the world occupied city blocks stretching under the ground. They took the box out of the lift, and Korchagin, who was trained for the task armed the device. With this done they went back up in the lift, climbing on to the back of the pick up, which took them back out. The dead were everywhere.

Fowler drove down Savage Road in the gathering dusk. The Trislander was lined up for take-off by the trees of the road block. The soldiers got in swiftly and efficiently. The door was shut. They strapped themselves in and Jones put the fuel to the engines. He lifted off, climbing out in a shallow turn to keep away from the complex. Not far away a power line stalked north to Lake Erie. At fifty feet, Jones latched on to it. As night-time came, he flipped down the light-intensifying goggles on his NBC helmet. He knew the route. He had flown it hundreds of times.

Eight minutes had elapsed since the CL-215 made its pass along the eastern Cyclone fence.

The Lear Jet and the Boeing E-3A were some thirty miles apart, the Lear three thousand feet above the AWACs at 35,000. The Lear was out of Hagerstown, Maryland, the Boeing of NORAD – North American Air Defense – out of Offutt AFB, Nebraska. The crew of the Lear could 'see' the airborne warning and control system aircraft because its transponder, used to identify it to air traffic control radar was also registering on the Westinghouse radar of the Lear, more usually used for weather-avoidance. The

Boeing could 'see' the Lear, because that was its job – long range high- or low-level surveillance of all air vehicles. It was, for example, going to be able to track the fleeing Trislander on its way north and direct NORAD F-16s to it, which as it was flying at fifty feet commercial radars could not.

What the Boeing could not see was the AA-3 *Anab* air-to-air missile hanging under the Lear. The *Anab* missile, standard equipment for Su-15 and Yak-28 fighters normally employed I/J band semi-active radar to home in on its target. The one underneath the Lear had been modified to home in on the transponder of the Boeing. It made no difference if the pilot of the AWAC's aircraft switched off all electronic emissions, as his transponder had been subtly modified by the substitution of a small electrical relay to transmit under these circumstances. It had been but a matter of moments for the avionics technician in maintenance at Offutt AFB to make the substitution, using a part supplied him by Sultan Electronics. The USSR had Stealthy people in all kinds of places.

The *Anab* accelerated to Mach. 3 in seconds, it crossed the clear sky in under a minute. It took longer than that for the debris of the Boeing to reach the ground below.

CHARLTON ISLAND, JAMES BAY, CANADA

It was three hours from Lake Erie to Charlton Island in the Trislander, a long time for men to sit in full NBC clothing. The troops endured it with a certain stoic indifference. They had had to take far worse in their training. The AN-72 STOL transport had brought a full decontamination unit and set it up. When Levon Jones finally put the Trislander down on the rough strip on the unpopulated part of the island the troops were able to get out and walk to the unit. It took twenty minutes for full decontamination to be assured, and then they walked to the short take-off and landing transport in fresh clean clothes. There they relaxed in comfortable air line seats, and ate and drank. The food was good and the beer cold. The AN-72 climbed out over Hudson Bay on its long flight north over the Pole and home.

THE WHITE HOUSE

'You want to tell me what you see in this photograph?' asked Cord.

'We seem to have had this conversation before, sir,' said Coogan. 'The first EXCOM meeting.'

They were in the Oval Office. Facility had been made for Cord to present transparencies; the fan of a projector hummed as it sat on a table by the oak desk, and a screen was in place by one of the pair of long, ivory-brocade sofas. Coogan stood watching.

'That was a representation of the British Empire at the height of its overstretch,' said Cord. 'And you did pretty well, as I remember. Tell me what you see here.'

The image was an overhead oblique, of a town. There was Main Street, with its two shopping plazas. There was Winn-Dixie, Sears and J.C. Penney. There was the local bank, three filling stations, a tyre and muffler centre, the cinema. Sylvester Stallone displayed rippling muscles and a hundredweight of lethal ordnance on the poster outside. Coogan could see him through the glass provided by the president. On the road further out of town were three motels, and downtown itself, with a further cinema, a bookstore and hardware store. Over the railroad tracks there was a small centre with a 7-Eleven, a laundromat and a foodstore selling grits to the residents of niggertown around it. On the right side of the tracks there was a broad thoroughfare where the wealthy folk lived, and their new Chevrolets Hondas and Cadillacs were visible parked outside their smart houses, set in carefully tended yards. Moving back towards Winn-Dixie the high school was along the road from the Baptist Church and the offices of Ma Bell. The little town was surrounded by farmland, in the image a Case tractor was halted in mid-furrow, ploughing the rich dark soil.

'Well?'

'It's an American small town,' said Coogan. 'Completely typical.'

'Anything special about it?'

'It is empty. There are no people visible.'

Cord nodded. He thumbed his command and the next image appeared. It was a picture of war, of some great buildings that had received a direct hit. A huge crater occupied the centre of the photograph. There was rubble all around and on the fringes, trees blasted into matchwood, just blackened stumps showing.

'You know what this is,' said Cord. 'It's the National Security Agency and most of its employees. A small tactical nuclear weapon did that. Something like the warhead fitted to a *Kangaroo* air-to-ground Soviet missile. The kind of thing they can hang on bombers and fighters in their thousands. It's small change, General, compared to the real thing, the sort of things we and they tote around the oceans of the world in our ballistic missile submarines.'

Cord thumbed again, and the images kept coming. A newsman's picture, a tall building burning like a torch, the flames burning right through the roof into the sky.

'The National Photographic Interpretation Center,' said Cord, in the same, flat voice. 'The kerosene in the central heating tanks was pumped in a fine spray into the huge air conditioning system that cooled the computers. It filled the building in seconds. Then it was ignited. No one got out.'

Another picture. Ten blackened hangars. The debris of a

war zone.

'Whiteman Air Force Base. Home of the B-2.'

More hangars.

'Edwards AFB. Home of the F-117 Stealth fighter. Nine out of ten B-2s, forty-seven out of fifty-two F-117s. Quite a feat.'

'They were brave boys,' said Coogan. 'Five pilots attacked Whiteman, they lost three, one in hospital – critical but he'll live. Twenty attacked Edwards. They lost fourteen, two in hospital. They pressed home their attacks in the face of devastating fire. Crack pilots. As good as you'll find.'

Cord stared at Coogan. There had been frank admiration in the general's voice.

'You like war,' he said. It was a statement of fact, not a question.

'I'm a wartime soldier, Mr President,' Coogan said honestly. 'It doesn't mean I'm trying to start World War Three.'

Cord pressed his button once more and the original image of a small American town.

'What was it you said was wrong with this?'

'No people,' said Coogan. 'The place is deserted.'

'No,' Cord said quietly. 'Everyone is there. Men, women and children. Nigh on eight thousand, we'd say. They're all there, but they're inside, or otherwise out of sight. The farmer ploughing his field is probably just standing under a tree. Thermal imaging would spot him.'

Cord stared at Coogan. 'They're inside because they know the KH-11 is coming. That's the problem with satellites, isn't it? You know when they're going to be overhead. This "American" town is called Rome. Lots of little towns throughout the USA are called "Rome", "Paris", "London", and so forth. The Soviets decided to call this one Rome. It's in the Ukraine. It's a microcosm of American society. It turns out young men and women who can pass for American and they ship them over here. There are young married men and women who have young

348

children, and some of *those* come too. Some of those pilots you so much admire were brought up here. They passed, they passed for being what we are, American citizens.

'All the destruction that took place – NSA, NPIC, the bombers, the fighters, the AWAC's airplane – was just a small demonstration of the havoc the USSR is able to wreak within our nation should they ever choose to do so. Forget Stealth, forget SDI. While we've been pursuing excellence in conventional war the Soviets have been honing their skills in the war *they* intend to fight – an unconventional one. How do you suggest we defend ourselves against *this* kind of attack?'

Coogan stared at the simulacrum of America with loathing.

'We ought to bomb it flat,' he said.

'We aren't going to bomb anything. We and the Soviets have bloodied each other's noses mightily. It is time to call a halt. Do you know how the First World War started, general? It was because no-one cared enough to stop it. Some people – quite a few – actually wanted it. The German Crowned Prince summoned his people to what he described as a "frisch und frölich krieg" – a bright and jolly war. The Germans were paranoid – very like the Soviets today – they felt that they were being encircled by a ring of steel, that everyone was ganging up on them. It made them aggressive – like the Soviets – and frightened everyone else – like the Soviets. There were a lot of military arguments about railway timetables – that once you'd decided to go you couldn't just mobilise defensively, you had to attack all-out. The statesmen should have known better. Some did. Even the Kaiser, for all his braggadoccio and militarism – he attended to business at his desk in uniform, seated on a cavalry saddle – knew better. When his generals had forced him to give his assent, he said "You will regret having made me do this." He was weak, he should have said no.

'The First World War paved the way for the Second, it was like a great weight smashing down and crushing centuries of delicate patterns and habits and evolutionary trends in society, it left the way wide open for madmen like Adolf Hitler, for Lenin and then Stalin. The world would have been very different, and much better if the Kaiser had said "No". If the French hadn't been so eager to avenge 1870. If the Russians had had more sense. If the British had supported the Habsburgs the way they supported the Ottomans. The list of culprits is long … But it could all have been stopped if men had wanted it stopped.'

There was silence for a moment or two.

'I want it stopped,' said Cord. 'I want to talk to the Soviets before it all gets out of hand. They're paranoid again. We need to get back to making agreements, to slow, boring diplomacy, to doing deals and making trade. If we do that, in the end, we'll give them a disease that will finally make an end to wars.'

Coogan's throat was full of bile.

'And what would that be, sir?'

'Democracy,' said Cord simply. 'Welcomed by all ordinary people everywhere, whenever it has been offered. No democracy has ever fought another. And never will. The Russians, and the people of their empire had a very brief taste of it in 1917. They liked it, they found the flavour intoxicating. Lenin. Trotsky and the Red Army took it away again, but it was a joy only postponed, not cancelled. Our economy is starting to boom again. I intend to use some of its fruits to get *perestroika* moving again. It'll be cheap at the price, General. Now we know what happens when you try the other way.'

As Coogan left the Oval office for a brief moment he shared Cord's visionary idea; he saw elections, choice, the chance of ordinary people to select, have a say in how they were governed, he could see how democracy could finally free the Russian people, working like a solvent to loosen the adamantine cement of totalitarianism that held the Soviet Colossus together. It was like a shaft of sunlight playing in his mind, and then all the years of his

350

experience and training pushed the door closed, and shut it out.

A far more sinister picture emerged, one of a naive US administration allowing the Soviet leadership to buy all the consumer goods they needed to keep their population happy, buying at knock-down prices, buying on tick, on the never-never, giving them another chance to burrow into the sophisticated western technological base, plundering it at will to build up their military forces to new heights and strengths just when the West was weakening theirs. Coogan shuddered. It was a scheme worthy of Sun Tzu.

More than ever he was convinced that the election of Cord represented the greatest *coup* ever achieved by the Soviet Union's espionage forces. As an unwitting – for Coogan did not think Cord a traitor, only naive, academic, slightly unhinged – Agent of Influence he was unmatched.

He was going to need some more levers to get Cord back into line. He decided that while he was in the White House he would go and see Gulio Riva. The staffer had not been in touch, maybe he had some more information.

He made his way from the southeast corner of the West Wing where the Oval Office was into the central staff offices. On Riva's door was the name of a woman; tapping on it and going in he was confronted by its owner, a young woman in her thirties.

'Hi,' she said brightly. 'Good morning, ah, General, what can I do for you?'

'I was looking for Gulio Riva. Has he moved?'

The smile slid off the woman's face.

'Ah, yes, General, I guess you could say he has.'

'Where can I find him?'

'Find him. Um … let me get someone for you sir, I don't think that I'm cleared for this …'

She went out of the room and in a few moments a senior staffer appeared.

'General, good morning. I hear you're asking for Mr Riva.'

'That's right. I need to talk to him.'

351

'Yeah, quite a few of us would like to talk to him too. He's dead. We're keeping it under wraps; it would be very embarrassing if it got into the media.'

'What would? And how did he die?' Coogan asked, nonplussed.

'You recall the West German chancellor, Willy Brandt? He had a communist spy working for him. Brought him down when it came out. We don't want any repeat of that here. Gulio Riva was an Iranian undercover agent. An assassin, too.'

Coogan felt as though he had been hit by heavy flak.

'An assassin?'

'He tried to kill an NSA analyst. The head of the Iranian section. She managed to stab him to death after one big struggle. Brave woman. Name of Ashraf Amran.'

YALE UNIVERSITY, NEW HAVEN, CONNECTICUT

MacDonald had a comfortable house near Edgewood Park, within sight of the Maltby Lakes. The Yale bowl was not far off, and the cliff of West Rock visible in the distance. It was a university town, and Ash felt at home. She attended MacDonald's first lecture and he taught her the Whiffenpoof song. She went shopping with his wife and browsed in the magnificent library. A volume of the *Divan* in Farsi gave her great joy, and she spent hours re-reading the rhyming gazel couplets. Her mother had introduced Hafiz to her as a child, proud of the poet's Shirazi origins. She went to Trinity church on the green and prayed for the souls of the dead at NSA, NPIC, Whiteman and Edwards, together with those at Smolensk.

She came home and found Coogan waiting for her.

'He says he wants to see you,' MacDonald said

disapprovingly. 'You want we should call the cops and have him slung out? "Give him the old heave-ho," we could say, "and let us see him bounce twice".'

MacDonald was happy to be gone from NSA, he had shed years of stress. His wife had already commented that he was not much different from the undergraduates, and admitted to Ash that she was happy for it.

'Let's see what he's got to say first,' suggested Ash. 'General?'

'You may have been right and I wrong.' Coogan said quietly. 'But I have to know. I am a commander, a "great captain". Like those who went before me, I have to play a great chess game with the enemies of my country. There is bluff and counter-bluff, subterfuge and deceit. As a result of the Soviet strikes I am temporarily rendered blind and deaf, and furthermore have lost my most potent weapons. Because of the peculiar nature of the events leading to the strikes I cannot treat them as I otherwise would, as acts of war. I am fearful that I have been out-manoeuvred, and that the Soviets are planning to take advantage of my position, and of the position of the President, to make some major move in some strategically-important area of the world that will alter the balance of power leaving us impotent to oppose them.'

'Aren't those "the details"? I recall you said the Air Force could take care of that.'

'We can't. Even were all my technology operating as it was I still cannot know. The Soviets have made a deal with the Iranians. Arms have flooded into the country. You say that the missing Trident missiles are in a building in the port of Khorramshahr. I have to know if they are, and why they are. I have to know what the nature of the deal between the Soviets and Khalif Hossein is.'

'You need HUMINT.'

'Yes,' Coogan said quietly. 'I need a human agent, someone very knowledgeable, very up to date, very familiar with the wrinkles of the Iranian situation and psyche. I need a politician.'

'You need my husband, but he is in Evin prison.'

'No,' Coogan said intently. 'I need his wife.'

'Don't do it,' MacDonald cried in anguish. 'Coogan has blood on his hands. He kills all who come near him. He will kill you.'

'I want you to go to Khorramshahr for me, and to find the truth.'

KINGS BAY, GEORGIA

'I don't anticipate too much trouble getting in,' said Kowalski. 'It's not as though we were trying to penetrate Severomorsk or somewhere like that – though I've always felt it could be done. The Meerestechnik – the *Squab* – is a very small sonar target and very quiet – an ideal vehicle for covert operations of this type. Furthermore, the Iranian navy isn't up to much – even during the war with Iraq the best they could manage was shooting up unarmed oil tankers from speedboats. I doubt that they have the capacity for effective ASW, and submarines in general are much harder to detect and *much* harder to sink than most people imagine, and that includes the ASW forces of both this country and the USSR. We don't plan on being detected at all. To be honest I think your part of the operation is going to be tougher than mine.'

'I'll be in my element, just as you will be in yours,' said Ash.

'Yeah, I guess so. Even though I'm not expecting trouble I'm planning for it, it's the best policy. We're going to operate out of Kuwait. The Kuwaitis have been prime targets of the Iranian brand of fundamentalism since Khomeini's time, as I know you know, and are quite willing to help us. The *Squab* is there and I've had our DSRV, the deep-sea rescue vehicle, air-lifted out too. The

Tinosa which is a *Thresher* class SSN is standing by in Al-Kuwayt should we need assistance. Furthermore, we have a carrier group in the Gulf of Oman. I understand we won't be required to make any transmissions.'

'That's right. Obviously once I'm out I can be properly debriefed, but in case anything does happen once I've found out what I've gone in there for I'm going to send a "squirt" via satellite. I've got a one-time transmitter, the size of a credit-card. Type out the message, press the button and throw away after use. Developed by the boys in R & E at NSA, the Lord bless their souls.'

'Okay,' said Kowalski. 'We'll be flying out in the morning. The Air Force is laying on an executive Grumman GIII to take us out in style.'

'Nothing but the best for Coogan's heroes,' agreed Ash. 'You volunteered, Jack. Why?'

'I knew the boys on the *Maine* pretty well. If the Iranians sank her I want to be a small part of the operation to make them pay. And I'm the best, you know. There's not too many of us who have operational experience, but I do. You volunteered too, Mrs Amran,' he pointed out with a smile. 'Why?'

'Intellectual arrogance,' said Ash. 'To demonstrate that I have, as I have claimed, been right all along.'

Kowalski grinned. 'Ain't nothing like being the best,' he agreed.

He paused 'That all?' he asked curiously.

'No,' Ash said enigmatically. 'Not all.'

KHORRAMSHAHR

'Looks like the Soviets have got themselves a new warm-water port,' said Kowalski.

He had brought the little submarine up to periscope

depth. They were within the port itself. The voyage across the top of the Gulf from Kuwait had gone without incident, and they were on time. It was just past four in the morning, and Kowalski was viewing the port through the light-intensifying equipment. The ravages of the war years had been repaired, new quays, jetties and gantries poked out over the water. Roads, warehouses and oiling facilities had been rebuilt. A Soviet naval task force had taken up residence.

'We're going to have to be quiet-quiet,' Kowalski murmured. '*They* were not supposed to be here.'

The *Squab* had a crew of three. It was commanded by Kowalski, who sat like a pilot in his cockpit, 'flying' the little submarine, and was supported by sonarman first class Richard Davies, a boy from the backwoods with a brain for the twenty-first century, a graduate of all the Navy's electronic warfare schools who was putting in his time to have his Uncle send him to MIT when he left. He had been Number One on Kowalski's shortlist, and he had volunteered. Ash made up the complement, strapped into her seat at the back, where she could watch what the two submariners were doing.

Having come to periscope depth Kowalski was able to re-orient himself within the harbour, assisted by the Navstar system on board, which had received updated information from its satellite. They now knew where they were to within five metres. Seated by Davies at his console Ash saw their position indicated by cross-hairs on the VDU.

In his bucket seat Kowalski slid forward the throttle; inside the craft they heard the soft whine of the electrical motor as they gently accelerated up to two knots, and he put the joystick forward, so that they sank back completely beneath the surface. They left the rebuilt portion of the great port and navigated cautiously into the wrecked west quarter. The television camera mounted in the nose of the submarine gave a clear picture, using light intensification like the periscope. The port had taken a

356

terrible beating in the war with Iraq, and had been the scene of heavy fighting in the very early days, when defended by 1200 boys from Ahvas who marched in to die the death of martyrs. The three weeks of fighting that took place before the Iraqis occupied the ruins saw all killed under their leader, the lanky Gholum, known bizarrely as the 'John Wayne of the poor'. The Iranians retook the port two years later after more heavy fighting, and some of the results were still visible. Great blocks and shattered slabs of masonry and concrete, rusting hulks of ships drifted quietly by beneath and to the sides of the submarine, festooned with waving weed, the home of eel and crab, playground of fish.

'Okay.' said Kowalski quietly. 'This is the ruin of No. 3 dock. Here we are out of sight of the rest of the port. Nobody comes here, as it is wrecked, took a load of 155mm artillery rounds during the war, and it is believed that the hulk of the cargo vessel we see here still contains quantities of ordnance.

'We still aren't going to take any chances. We'll come up to periscope depth to transmit, and once we get the all clear you'll go out as we practised through the wet compartment. Take your time, do it as you were shown. When you leave the submarine and come to the surface look left, ten o'clock for the light. It's a short swim, the water is clean. The light will indicate your landing point, which is a sloping concrete slab, half in, half out of the water.'

'Right,' said Ash. She was wearing a swimming costume, had goggles up on her forehead in preparation for the swim, to protect her eyes against fuel-oil, had a pair of flippers and a pack inside a plastic waterproof cover, tied around her waist with cord.

'Once you have left we will remain here. We will lie on the bottom by the wreck. We will come up again to periscope depth at ten o'clock. You will be able to see the submarine by its lights when you are close. If for some reason you need us to surface tell us on the radio once

357

we're at periscope depth. If you need us to surface in an emergency, or at any other time than ten o'clock use your bell-ringer.'

Ash had been given a small device, which when dipped in the water was able to emit an acoustic signal to the submarine, summoning it.

'What will you do?' Ash said suddenly, anxiously. 'Will you be all right, waiting all that time?'

'Ma'am,' Davies said in his Southern way. 'Don't you worry 'bout us. All sailors love to goof off in government time.'

'We'll sleep some – in turns. Hot-bunk it,' Kowalski said with a smile. 'And we're going to eat some. We have real French lobster here, with mayonnaise and potato salad. That's a real favourite with submariners ever since Holbrook penetrated the straits and sank the *Messoudieh*. Then we got cold rare beef, we got rolls, we got fruit. There's something about a submarine that encourages the appetite – make me an SSBN commander and after sixty five days I'd weigh 250 pounds!'

'Then we gone read,' said Davies. 'We brought some light literature with us.'

'Dick's got a tome on electronics,' Kowalski said dryly. 'I have an H.G. Wells.'

'I want my Ph.D., same as you,' Davies grinned.

Ash understood the two men were calming her before her mission, and felt grateful.

'I'm ready, then,' she said. Kowalski brought the craft to periscope depth again. Ash had her radio activated, and brought the microphone to her lips.

'*Faqih*,' she said clearly, giving her call-sign. The response was almost immediate.

'All clear, *Faqih*,' said a man's voice, and Ash nodded to Kowalski.

'That's him.'

Ash pulled on her breathing apparatus, mouthpiece, pressure regulator, noseclip and bottle of air, and went forward into the diver lockout compartment.

'You're going to be fine,' he said reassuringly.

'See you tomorrow,' she said.

He shut the door. Through the glass he raised an interrogatory thumb and she nodded. She bit into the rubbery plastic of the regulator mouthpiece, breathed in the compressed air, settled her goggles and clip, and turned the cock. The port water began gushing in and she shivered, not entirely from the chill.

The water was up to her waist, aware of Kowalski's gaze through the glass of the door she leant nonchalantly against the side of the compartment. As the water came over her head and the pressure equalised she gave him a wave and spun the pressure wheel on the hatch. It moved freely, and the hatch swung slowly upwards under her urging. She gave a push with her flippered feet, and emerged from the submarine.

She broke surface, and pushed the goggles up on to her forehead, the better to see the light. Across the water, a red pin-point gleamed. Trudging with her flippers, she began to swim across the dock. The water was flat calm, swirled unfamiliarly around her neck. She had cut her long blonde hair short, and rinsed it black.

The light came closer, and her searching hands brushed against the slimy surface of the slab. She crawled on to it, and out of the water, and removed her flippers.

'Come,' said a voice. 'There is a place here where you can dress.'

It was Sayyed Saddam Kashk. He lit the way with a pencil-thin beam of a small torch. The artillery had thrown two great plates of concrete up to form a natural cave. Inside, Ash opened her waterproof parcel, and took out a towel, and military fatigues. She rubbed herself dry and dressed. She tugged on boots and slipped a small canvas pack on to her back. Kashk gave her a plastic pass which she clipped on, and she was a soldier in the IRGC. A sergeant, to give her some authority. The mullah was almost invisible in the dark, in his black clothing, but she could hear his breathing, smell his sweat. There was

something different about the fat man, and as he led the wa
out of the ruined quay she wondered what it was. Then sh
realised that he was not afraid. Wonders will never cease
she thought dryly. Her own heart was beating fast, and sh
could taste the metallic tang of adrenalin in her mouth.

They emerged from the ruins and on the road Kashk'
jeep was waiting. They got in and Kashk started the engine
Dawn was turning the distant sky the colour of a dove'
breast, the vehicle's lights cast yellow pools of light on to th
road. They emerged into the rebuilt part of the port an
Kashk stopped for a moment to replace the barrier that ha
blocked access to the ruins. As they drove in people wer
beginning to move.

'There is a mosque only quarter of a mile from th
guarded building,' he said. 'We will pray there, then wal
to it. I have access to the building that adjoins it. No on
may enter the guarded building, but I have devised a pla
for you get in.'

Good, thought Ash. Saddam's got himself organised
Her great fear had been that the mullah would allow hi
anxiety to affect his planning. It was going to work. /
modern mosque stood by the road, and soldiers and por
workers were entering in the grey light. They parked th
jeep close by the base of one of the tall minarets, and went i
to pray, taking off their boots and slippers, and laying then
with the others outside. As Ash bent to face Mecca, puttin
her forehead to the stone, it was cold. A tremor ran throug
her. The world of Khalif Hossein was chill, and filled with
treadmill of endless ritual, far exceeding the traditional fiv
daily prayers that symbolised the quintupal pillars of Islam

When they were finished they joined the other
streaming out to their work, and Kashk led the way dow
the dusty, rutted road. Water was visible down gap
between the buildings, from the overhead image As
carried in her mind she realised they were walking along th
access road behind the big wharfside warehouses. In th
light of day, the grey of warships was visible.

'The Russians steamed in yesterday,' Kashk muttered.

The building, slab-sided, windowless, ochre in colour was visible through heavy fencing and barbed-wire. It abutted on to another, and Kashk turned in to the guardhouse with confidence. He waved imperiously for the barrier to be lifted and having looked at their badges the IRGC soldier on duty complied. I have misjudged the fat man all this time, thought Ash. There is steel in him after all. Glancing to her left as they walked across the yellow dirt she saw soldiers and men with dogs patrolling the compound outside the building, visible through the heavy chain-link fencing.

They entered through a side door. The building was a warehouse, stacks of cartons and large boxes of various descriptions stood silently in rows. The floor was lit by neon lights hanging by chains from the roof. It was deserted, and Kashk led the way across to a set of wide steps that led up to a supervisory office in the corner, that looked over the whole. They climbed up, the big man puffing as he reached the top, and entered the office. Made from prefabricated panels, it contained desk, chairs, filing cabinets, a desktop computer, two phones and a section of aluminium ducting that ran along one junction of wall and ceiling to vanish into the wall that joined the two separate buildings.

'There,' said Kashk triumphantly, having closed the door. He pointed up to the ducting. 'The buildings are jointly air-conditioned. The passages that carry the air are of a whole. A small person, such as yourself, once inserted into the system, can make her way into the building next door. There are grilles, from which the air emerges. From one such grille you will be able to see into the great room next door.'

He pulled a folded piece of paper from his pocket and laid it flat on the desk. It was a ground-plan of a building.

'I have ascertained how the building is laid out. We are here,' he said, indicating the office with a broad forefinger. 'The duct travels along here, through these administrative offices, to emerge into the great room. It is said to be completely clean, and was prepared at great cost, so if your missiles are anywhere, it must be that they are there.'

Ash nodded, memorising the outline of the map.

'One must be *quiet*,' urged the mullah. 'Otherwise people will hear.'

'Right,' agreed Ash. She took off her boots and socks, her pack, and stripped to her swimsuit.

'I would volunteer,' said Kashk apologetically, 'but I would stick like a bung in a barrel. You are slim, and younger than I.'

They moved the desk so that it provided a platform beneath the duct. Kashk heaved himself up, the wood creaking under his weight, and taking a small screwdriver from the recesses of his robe began unfastening the access panel.

'I came earlier,' he said proudly. 'And made certain it would come off.'

'You're very organised, Saddam.'

He smiled. The panel came loose, and cold air gushed down over them. Ash got up on the desk, and grasping the lips of the duct pulled herself smoothly up into it. I haven't done that since working on the high bar at school, she thought. Behind her Kashk put the panel back loosely, to maintain the flow of air, and in near-darkness, she began to crawl forward. As she advanced down the tunnel it began to lighten, and she heard the wailing of religious music. Moving very slowly and carefully, she inched her way along until she arrived at a grille. Keeping her head back and away from the light she peered through. The music was coming from a small yellow transistor radio, several years old. Moving with fingers and toes, the slick synthetic material of her swimsuit sliding smoothly on the aluminium she edged on.

The ducting formed a T-junction to her left, which she ignored, remembering the simple layout of the map. She passed another grille, leading to an empty room, and then some minutes later, as the darkness brightened once again, she heard the clink of tool on metal, the murmur of voices.

Moving like a mouse, she arrived at the eighteen-inch-square grille, and was able to look down.

Each Trident D-5 missile was mounted on its own cradle. Each could be turned to gain access to its many parts. Towards the end of the room a number lay fully assembled, intact, shiny white and chequer-patterned, forty-four feet long, almost seven feet in diameter. Coming closer to her were several in an intermediate stage of preparation, exposing their complex internals. Underneath her viewpoint, several technicians in clean white overalls, wearing gloves, were working on three missiles broken down into component parts of nose cap, fairing, three motor stages, equipment section, warheads. The technicians were Iranian, and conversing sporadically in Farsi. Ash counted the missiles, there were six rows of four, twenty four missiles in all. They were all accounted for.

The journey back down the duct was arduous until she came to the place where she had entered the system, and tapping on the access panel saw the anxious face of Kashk looking up at her as he removed it. She slithered down, cold, with stiff muscles, and began tugging on her clothes.

'They're there,' she said laconically.

'You were right,' said Kashk. 'What will you do now?'

'Send a message.' She opened her pack and took out her transmitter. A grey plastic device not much bigger than a credit card, as thick as a box of matches, it had a keyboard on one side. Ash took a blunt spike from one edge, and began to type out her message. The transmitter would store it until she instructed it to pass it on, at which point it would expend its stored electrical energy in one 'squirt' of a fraction of a second, sending information in a tight beam, secure, super-high-frequency transmission. When she had finished, and was dressed once more like a soldier, she shrugged on her pack, and kept the transmitter in her pocket.

They went out, and the air was warm as the sun rose in

the sky. They walked out of the compound and back down the road to Kashk's jeep.

He drove across the sprawling base to an area of living-quarters, modern, constructed since the war, but in the traditional style of a number of rooms set around a central courtyard. Despite its antique layout, it was furnished with electricity and modern appliances. Kashk went to the kitchen to prepare some breakfast for them and Ash squatted in the courtyard with her pack. From it she took a gunmetal-grey rod about a foot long. Under the nimble prompting of her fingers, it turned into first a fan, then a lattice dish. Another small bundle became a tripod, she hooked the transmitter and dish together, and pressed the small red projecting button. The transmitter uttered an electronic squawk as it fired its information to the sky, and the deed was done. When Kashk emerged from the kitchen with bread, jam, fruit and coffee she was putting the pieces away in her pack.

Ash was very tired. She had not been able to sleep in the little submarine as it made its way across the head of the Gulf, and the events since leaving it had left her mentally exhausted. She went to the bedroom Kashk had put aside for her use, where she showered, and then lay down to rest. Kashk's quarters were befitting for one of his rank, well-furnished, and although there was no air-conditioning, she lay under the pleasant air of a moving ceiling fan.

Despite the comfort, and the relief of success, as she drifted to sleep she was uneasy, aware of something fundamentally wrong, but not knowing what it was. She slept for a long time.

When she awoke it was becoming dark. She lay in bed for some time, with her mind now clear, untrammelled by fear and fatigue, and she thought. At length she got up and showered again, then dressed. Pleasing odours were coming from the kitchen, where the fat mullah was cooking supper.

'Memories of home,' said Ash, sitting to watch. Chicken

364

pieces lay simmering in a rich brown sauce, and rice was fattening in a pan. 'When I was little, Nasir the cook bought two chickens from the poultry-man, they were in a basket with their legs tied, he bought the best ones, and took them out into the orchard, where he cut their throats. I was horrified. I called him all kinds of names. And in the evening the chicken was served, and it never occurred to me not to eat. He made fun of me, and asked if I was still sobbing over the poor birds. Everyone laughed.'

'I love to cook,' said Kashk, turning the meat. 'Were things different, I would be a restaurateur. I love to eat too,' he chuckled, patting his belly. 'It would be a better life than this ... I am not a good spy.'

'Better days will come again,' Ash promised. 'None of us will have to do these things forever.'

They ate, and Kashk's love of food had been translated into a fine dish.

When ten o'clock was near, Ash was at the water's edge, sitting on the slab, her breathing apparatus strapped on, dressed for the swim, her pack once more sealed up in its waterproof covering.

'Good luck,' said Kashk.

'Give my respect to your father,' said Ash. 'We will be meeting again soon.'

She pushed out into the ruined dock, her flippers trudging steadily and quietly, and when she was close, she saw the dim lights of the submarine, hanging like a great fish in the water.

Ash dripped water on to the bottom of the craft and the two men listened attentively.

'There has been one consistency in all this, from the very beginning,' she said, 'and that is that we have been led by the nose, directed where they wished us to be, when they wished us to be there, heard what we were supposed to hear, seen what we were supposed to see, and all along, thinking that we had discovered it all ourselves. It has been like a strange dance, in which all the moves have been choreographed. It went well here. Sayyed Saddam Kashk was organised and efficient. No one stopped us, it ran like clockwork. I saw all twenty four Trident D-5 missiles. I sent my message. I was efficiently transported back to the dock and sent off to my submarine. And Kashk was not afraid. Why? Kashk is not a brave man. He sweats with fear. He is a jolly man, who loves his food, and who is used as a courier by his father, the Grand Ayatollah, to keep his links with the west open against the day Khalif Hossein should be swallowed up in the ground.'

Ash picked up her flippers and pack, and stood up, ready to climb back into the chamber.

'I fear that I was brought here, conducted to the building, shown how to cunningly gain access and see what I was supposed to see in proper secret-agent manner. I have to go back now, and find out what I was not supposed to see.'

Sayyed Saddam Kashk slept the sleep of relief, of good food and a worrying task well done. Ash put the barrel of the Smith & Wesson .357 Magnum up against his head and switched on the light.

'You should have been afraid of *me*,' she hissed. Kashk came awake with a strangled cry of terror and found himself staring into two green eyes like chips of agate.

'I went back,' Ash whispered. 'Nobody was guarding the building, I cut through the fence, I went in as we did this morning, I crawled back down the air-conditioning duct and I broke through the grille into the great room where the missiles are. They're all fake. They are expensive props from a film, they are not the real thing. Where are the real missiles, Kashk?'

'I don't know,' sobbed the mullah. 'I swear, I only did what I was ordered to do. I did not know the missiles were not real. I was told to take you there, to let you see.'

'It had to be you,' said Ash. 'You were my link.'

'I am not brave, Ashraf,' he whispered. 'I did not wish to be tied to a post while they burned me to death.'

'We all have to be brave at least once,' said Ash. 'Now it is your time, and you can repay what you have done. Where are the Western technicians, the men who worked on the missiles?'

'You were close to them,' he said. 'They were kept in cells above the warehouse. But there is only one left, all the others are gone.'

'Well, then. Let us go and get him.'

When they stopped outside the warehouse Ash turned to Kashk in the jeep.

'Remember, Saddam, you serve me. Obey me and I will look after you. If you attempt to betray me I will shoot you with this giant gun. I am not a good shot but I could hardly fail to hit so large a target as you.'

Kashk bowed his head in submission. '*Aqa*,' he murmured, meaning Lord, or Master.

When they climbed the stairs one guard in fatigues sat dozing in a chair. There was a canteen visible, and behind a locked floor-to-ceiling gate a line of cell doors.

'On your feet,' Kashk commanded the soldier in bullying, peremptory tones. 'I am Sayyed Kashk, we have come to interrogate the prisoner.'

The bearded guard scrambled to his feet, half-asleep, ready to be cowed by the presence of the cleric. A bunch of keys were on his belt, and he hurried to open the gate.

'Quickly now,' said Kashk, cleverly continuing to keep him off-balance. The soldier scurried in front of them and unlocked a cell door a short way along the row. He threw back the door with a clang and pulled off a thin blanket covering a sleeping figure on a bank.

'Wake up,' he shouted. 'Authorities are here.'

Kashk waved a peremptory hand. 'You may leave.'

'Go with him, Saddam. Keep an eye on him.'

A thin, bearded European sat slowly up on the bunk and stared hostilely at Ash.

'So what do you want?' he asked. He was American.

'I am Ashraf Amran,' Ash said quietly. 'I work for the National Security Agency. You are Michael B. Logan, a guidance engineer who used to work for Lockheed.'

Logan's eyes widened in combined alarm and hope.

'What are you doing here?'

'It doesn't matter. Where are the Trident missiles?'

'On ships. Converted oil tankers.'

'And the other engineers?'

'On the ships. In case.'

'How did they get you to work on the missiles?'

'There was this one guy, he said he wouldn't do what they wanted, so they got all of us together and they tortured him to death in front of us. They took a whole day.' Logan's face stiffened in memory of the horror. 'After that we all did as they said.'

'What are they going to do with the missiles?'

'I don't know,' said Logan. 'But each and every missile is programmed for high-value Soviet targets.'

From along the hall she heard Kashk's voice calling in English.

'Ash, there is another guard here. More senior. He is suspicious.'

'We have to get out of here,' Ash said to Logan. She quickly pulled off her shirt and slipped her arms out of her swimming costume, rolling it down around her waist. Bare from there up she stepped out into the corridor and smiled invitingly. Another guard was arguing with Kashk by the gate.

'Hey, *jahel*,' she called. 'What's the fuss about?'

The two guards stared at her with eyes that goggled in their heads. Then, grinning foolishly, they came down the cell corridor, wide-eyed with sudden desire. Ash continued to smile, and reaching behind her pulled the Smith & Wesson out of her waistband. The lust died from their faces, replaced by sudden alarm and dismay. Ash waved the gun at the cell as Logan came out.

'Keep on going, boys. Straight inside.'

They stumbled into the cell and Ash turned the lock on them.

'Poor saps,' she muttered. 'Their women are wrapped up in *chadors* like Christmas turkeys. They get a look at a real woman it affects their brains.'

'I ain't seen a gal in a long time either,' Logan said dryly. 'I'm a tad weak at the knees myself. You're a good-looking lady.'

'Thank you,' Ash said, pulling her clothing back on. 'Now let's go.'

They hurried back down the stairs and out to the jeep.

'To the dock,' said Ash. Kashk drove quickly through the dark roads of the base. They arrived at the ruined west end and Ash pulled the barrier to one side, replacing it after the jeep went through.

'Are you coming with us?' said Ash, as Kashk drove to the dock.

He shook his head. 'I have an *alter-ego*, prepared for such a situation as this. I will become Colonel Morteza Ghaffari, of IRGC intelligence, and make my way to Shiraz, where I will be under the protection of my family. Also, I cannot swim, so could not get to your submarine, and have a great fear of enclosed spaces, and so would have to be shot by your great gun for endangering you all.'

Ash smiled in the dark. 'Take care, then,' she said, 'for I shall have need of you again.'

'Your servant will be waiting,' Kashk assured her.

Ash and Logan scrambled down among the ruins of the dock to the water's edge. Above, they heard Kashk's jeep driving away, and as the sound of the engine disappeared they could hear an uproar in the distance, from whence they had come.

'Damn. The guards have raised the alarm.'

Ash dipped her bell-ringer into the water, and pressed the command to summon the submarine to the surface. While they were waiting for it she tugged on a flipper and sealed up her pack once more in its waterproof wrapping. Then she gave the other flipper to Logan and they got half into the water. In the distance, men's voices were shouting, engines revving. In the middle of the dock there was a gurgle, and as they began to swim out, a red pin-point of light leading them home.

'I've brought a guest,' said Ash, as she swam the last few yards.

Kowalski eyed Logan as he cocked an ear to the uproar in the distance.

'At least he's thin,' he commented. 'We have enough reserve buoyancy for him.'

Ash realised that Kashk would have been left to float in the dock like a whale.

'I take it the hunt is up,' Kowalski said dryly. 'Get in and let us leave.'

Ash and Logan scrambled and slithered inside, and strapped themselves into their seats as Kowalski shut the hatch. Davies, bespectacled, shaven and alert was at his console.

'Good morning to you both,' he said cheerfully.

'Hallo, Dick. It's good to see you, it is. This is Michael Logan, who was a prisoner, now a free man.'

'Hatch shut and clipped,' Kowalski intoned ritually. He dropped the short distance to the deck and climbed into his commander's chair. There he reached for the rocker switches on his left panel and blew tanks. The submarine sank rapidly under the surface. He levelled off at thirty feet and pushed the throttle forward. They began to make their way out of Khorramshar, cruising silently at three knots. By the time they had cleared the port itself and were making their way down the channel to the sea the light filtering through the ports was changing from black to a deep blue-green.

Kowalski, Ash and Logan had all relaxed slightly after the tension of conning their way silently and invisibly out into the channel. Davies remained hunched at his panel, his headphones on, head cocked to one side.

'What is it, Dick?' Kowalski said quietly.

'Not sure, sir. But I think there's something out there. I can hear something. Very faint.'

'There's bound to be a lot of activity,' said Kowalski. 'There's a whole battle group back there.'

'There may be a picket at the head of the channel.'

'Then we must tip-toe softly by. Please no one drop anything. No noise.'

Kowalski had the *Squab* close to the bottom of the channel. His speed through the water of 1½ knots on the electric motors was increased considerably by the flow of the waters of the *Kārùn* River making their way from the Zagros Mountains to the sea. After another fifteen minutes Kowalski spoke again.

'We're past *Kh-e Bahmanshir*. We have deep water. Next stop Kuwait.'

The words were no sooner out of his mouth than the hull of the submarine reverberated as though lashed by a metal whip. Ash and Logan flinched and Davies' face contorted as the noise slammed through his headphones.

'Sonar,' said Kowalski. He gave the Squab full power. 'What're they doing, Dick?'

'Dangdangdang,' Davies cursed. 'They just got lucky, sir. They're jumping about up there like some Sunday fisherman done foul-hooked a perch. They're trying to get under way.'

The violence of the sonar lashing was diminishing as they made distance on the surface vessel above them.

'They're coming, sir.'

Kowalski cut the power and made a 90-degree gliding turn to take them off-track and down on to the bottom. They touched the silted floor at 230 feet. Above, an express train was thundering towards them.

'Speed twenty-nine knots, captain. It's a "Krivak"-class frigate.'

'Accounts for the fast reaction.' Kowalski said calmly. 'It's got gas turbines. More to the point, it's got twelve-barrelled RBU rocket-launchers for use against people like us. Stand by to feel what a fly goes through when you slap it with the swatter.'

'They're firing.'

Even without sonar, they could hear the crash of the rocket boosters striking the water as the Soviet frigate sought to blanket the area of sea into which the *Squab* had escaped with lethal ordnance.

'Warning time,' said Davies.

'Just time,' said Kowalski. 'We just lie here and say nuff'n, like Br'er Rabbit.'

The RBU depth bombs began to explode. They seemed above the submarine, but marching towards them with each 'click-brr-roomp-whoosh' becoming louder and louder.

'Brace yourselves,' warned Kowalski.

A giant bellowed beside them and slammed the submarine sideways. A second later an enormous concussion burst directly overhead. Glass shattered and gauges broke. The sonar in front of Davies went dead. In the pitch dark Ash felt the interior of the submarine momentarily illuminated by a greenish glow, like a lightning flash, and felt her hand, braced against the side of the hull smacked hard as it pushed inwards under the force of the explosion. The straps bit into her flesh and her head whipped to and fro as though she were trapped in a head-on automobile wreck. Through the singing in her ears she could hear the tinkling and slithering of glass and objects moving into different positions within the hull.

There was silence, and then the barbed-wire of the frigate's sonar began lashing on the hull as it came back for another attack.

B-2 NO. 0006

In the right hand seat of the B-2 Coogan saw the dawn as the north African coastline came up. The bomber was cruising at 580 knots, level at 55,000 feet. It was quiet in the cockpit, Colonel Travis in the captain's chair monitored the instruments and the progress of the flight. From time to time Coogan would talk about things that interested him; Travis had the good subordinate's quality of replying, but not initiating conversation.

Coogan had been quiet for some while, pensive.

'We should have won in Vietnam,' he said.

'Too right, sir.'

'The politicians wouldn't let us do the job. It made us rather bitter, didn't it? Sometimes got to a man. I recall one man in my wing, he had some badges put on his helmet. First one said Bomb Saigon Now. Second said Bomb Hanoi Now. Third, Bomb Disneyworld Now. Fourth and last, Bomb Everything. He didn't make it. SA-2 took him out over Laos two short of his 100 mission hosedown. Never got the Last Mission Parade.'

Soon it would be time to get ready, shift in their seats, get down to their combat altitude. Begin the bomb run.

'You could bomb Saigon, Hanoi or the Kremlin itself in this aircraft and no one be able to stop you,' Coogan said with satisfaction. 'Any threat to the USA at all, we can take it out.'

THE USS *SQUAB*

It was quiet. Ash lay on the single bunk, Kowalski sprawled at ease in his chair, which he had tipped backwards. They were showered with white fibres from the lining of the hull, with paint flakes and dust from the ventilation system. Although they had brushed themselves down as best they could it was still in their hair and on their clothing. Aft, Davies and Logan murmured quietly as they worked over the submarine's electricals, wiring diagrams, instruction books and tools spread about them. The interior was dimly lit by the emergency lighting that Davies had managed to bring to life in the aftermath of the attack, working by the illumination of a pencil-flashlight

held in his teeth. In the gloom the work light that the two
engineers had rigged over the damaged propulsion system
glowed brightly.

Kowalski nibbled thoughtfully on a lobster claw. He
seemed unruffled by the violence of the attack.

'How long have we got?' Ash asked softly. The two men
had been working for several hours.

'We have air for another six hours. More, maybe if we
stay quiet, don't use it up.'

'And then?'

'If it comes to it, we don our escape lungs. Here.'

Kowalski delved in a locker by his chair and drew out a
pack.

'Pressure regulator, mouthpiece, nose clamp, and this
bottle of compressed air. A fifteen minute supply.'

'We go out like I did?'

'That's it. But we'd rather not float up to the surface,
especially seeing as we're still in the river's flow. There are
too many nasty tales of crews escaping from bottomed
submarines close to shore and being carried out to sea by
malign currents to die. So we'll stay with the *Squab* as long
as we can.'

'Still I'm glad we've got a diver's compartment.'

'The final victory of John P. Lake over John Holland.
Lake thought a submarine should be able to infiltrate
special troops into enemy territory in a clandestine
manner, and designed his boats with it in mind. The
American Admiralty were horrified at such ungentlemanly
ideas about waging war, and went for Holland's boat,
which set the style for submarine development thereafter.
Except that now all modern submarines have diver
lock-out compartments for special forces, Green Berets,
SAS and SBS, *Spetsnaz*. Even an SSBN can deploy a
special team and their little boats and funny gadgets if
need be.'

'Think they can mend it?' Ash murmured. 'That
depth-charging was awful.'

'Submarines are tough,' said Kowalski. 'And young

Dick back there made a radio-controlled model airship out of stuff he got in his mama's kitchen when he was twelve. He'll fix it. Especially with a rocket scientist to help him.'

They rested quiet for a little while longer.

'It's good to be home,' Ash said unexpectedly.

'Home?'

'It's Persian water that's flowing over me.'

'Ah ...' said Kowalski in understanding. 'You're a first-generation refugee. The USA isn't home, it's a friendly land of exile. My grandparents were the same, fled from Kiev after the Revolution. They never felt American, they felt Russian. Even when they were old, they would talk of *rodina*, the motherland, and tears would start in their eyes. You know what they brought with them from Russia? Their most treasured possession?'

'What?'

'A box of Russian soil. Soil.'

'I have no need of soil,' said Ash. 'I shall be going home.'

As she spoke, something touched the submarine. It stroked the hull with a gentle electronic hand, and made it ring, very softly, very quietly.

'Sonar,' whispered Kowalski.

'Those Russian sons of whores are coming to finish us off.' Ash cried in indignant fury.

Davies, sonarman first class came up the submarine, his shoes crunching on the broken glass and debris, picking his way carefully through the loose items strewn about the deck, he beamed at Ash in the dim light.

'Ma'am,' he said. 'It sure is a pleasure to meet someone as tone-deaf as you.'

The noise came again, softly stroking the craft as it lay on the bottom.

'What we heard from the Krivak was a dual-dome Soviet anti-submarine sonar. Rather crude and basic, appears to the target to be approximately B in tone, with some retarded half-notes as it dies away. What you hear now –' he paused to enjoy the sound again '– is pure, it is

F-sharp. The note becomes chromatic as it dies away, with some accidental grace-notes. It is the sound of a BQS-6 spherical bow transducer. It is the *Tinosa*.'

KHORRAMSHAHR

A man, and two machines sat waiting patiently. The man sat high in a minaret above the mosque, a *muezzin* in black, crouched like a resting crow. One machine sat on the roof of the building within which Ash had crawled along air-conditioning ducts. It stared with an unblinking eye at the sky. The second machine sat alone in a room inside the building. It had travelled half the oceans of the world, in its time, resting atop a Trident II D-5 inter-continental ballistic missile alongside four of its comrades. It was a thermonuclear warhead, and it had formerly been carried inside the *Maine*. The *muezzin* was connected to the two machines by electrical cable; they would wait forever, he would wait for as long as it took.

Spread out beneath the *muezzin* in his tower was the port, with its Soviet ships and crews, *Shaytan's* playthings and his disciples. The receptor on the roof stared into the blaze of the sun high in the sky, but was not blinded by it, and it was not what it sought to see.

It did not see the satellite that had once orbited over Smolensk but it saw the laser beam that shot out from it like some slim, immensely-long finger. The satellite knew where the building was because it had been told via secure data-link, and asked to point it out to another machine. No one had known that the receptor would be waiting to see it first. The laser designator was what it had been waiting for. It alerted its master, sitting high in his minaret.

As the light glowed on the little console before him, the

muezzin's heart was filled with purest joy. He stood, a switch of command in his hand, and his beautiful, trained voice flowed out, as sweet as a bird, calling those present to prayer, as sweet as a passing nightingale. He squeezed the trigger of the switch in his hand and the electrical impulse travelled down the cable into the room where the warhead waited for its summons.

Inside the casing, the shaped blocks of Uranium 235 fitted in their housings, protected by the elaborate control equipment that prevented detonation from fragmentation, fire, impact, electrical charge or anything other than the explosive device within the warhead that would compress them into one single compact block that exceeded the critical mass of U-235.

The electrical pulse arrived at the explosive, and ignited it. The eruption slammed the blocks together. They became one, and the *muezzin* entered paradise.

DefCon I

**'Cocked Pistol'.
State of readiness for war**

RIYADH, SAUDI ARABIA

A small team manned the flight control centre at the airport, a few miles north of the city. There were no flights after eleven at night, so Nasir al-Hoss and his crew were just watchmen, a part of the nation's military defences, keeping an eye on the radar screens.

Not long after midnight Nasir became aware of a distinct feeling of nausea, and of a desire to evacuate his bowels. Arranging for a colleague to cover for him he hurried to the lavatory. There was a line of cubicles, and from the sounds emerging he realised that others too had been stricken. Breaking into a run he managed to reach the bowl in time.

His vomiting and dysentery lasted a long time. When he weakly emerged, with sweat bathing his entire body, he bent at the faucet and drank. Almost immediately, he was afflicted by an even more powerful bout of spasms. At two-thirty in the morning, the entire team of watchmen was laid low. No one was there in the control-room to realise that the radar system had failed.

The Antonov An-12 turboprop transports were flying at 15,000 feet. They had taken off from Krasnovodsk on the Caspian Sea, and over-flown Iran on their way across the Gulf and into Saudi Arabia. Each aircraft carried a hundred *Spetsnaz* paratroopers. There were sixty aircraft in all, each designated for a target, each man certain of his task. Soviet military doctrine called it *Desant*, it was the single concept of putting troops behind enemy lines to wreak havoc out of all proportion to their numbers. *Spetsnaz* forces were always under the direct command of the 2nd Chief Directorate of Soviet military intelligence, the GRU, and attached to different organs of the state. Represented among the teams entering Saudi airspace were men from the Army, GRU Central apparatus Strategic and KGB. Fifth column intelligence-gathering and intelligence and sabotage agents were already in place. It was the fifth-columnists, men from the Asian republics of the USSR, Muslim themselves, fluent in Arabic, who were paving the way for their airborne colleagues. The water-supplies were already spiked with the *shigella* bacteria that had so severely afflicted Nasir al-Hoss and his colleagues; electronic warning and reconnaissance equipment, radar; early warning and air defence equipment was being incapacitated.

The airborne teams had targets. Some were designated for the capture of the key airfields and industrial centres, others for the destruction of troops within garrison, destruction of logistic installations and transport systems, seizure of key areas of terrain to ensure the swift advance of the Iranian forces, the capture of key prisoners and documents for intelligence.

The hundred men in Major Anatoly Korchagin's Antonov were attached to Department 8 of the KGB, which while strictly an intelligence-gathering and counter-intelligence organisation had *Spetsnaz* units. They were trained and designated for the task of assassinating senior military and political figures.

Like all elite fighting units throughout history, the Soviet special forces desired and were permitted a certain freedom of choice in the tools of their trade. As a side-arm, Korchagin favoured the well-made, efficient little Polish wz/63 machine-pistol, which offered the advantages of single-handed operation combined with remarkable fire power. For his principal close-quarter weapon he used a combat shotgun. Shotguns were the favoured weapon of most special forces for urban fighting, not least because of their awesome close-range performance – a 450 grain 12-bore slug would convert a small rock into dust from a few yards – and variety of ordnance that could be fired. Korchagin used the best, the Franchi SPAS-16, and his webbing held a variety of grenades and pre-loaded box magazines for the gas-operated semi-automatic weapon. For speed of action and freedom of movement on this specific mission he had restricted his own weapons to these two, but his unit was heavily armed, and for any firefight exceeding the fifty yards or so in which his shotgun reigned supreme he could call upon the services of any number of AKM assault rifles, not to mention 30mm AGS-17 '*Plamya*' (Flame) automatic grenade launchers, RPK-74 light machine guns and 12.7 × 108mm NSV heavy machine guns for sustained fire, and RPG-7D rocket-launchers.

All the troops wore Iranian IRGC uniforms. The world was not to know of Soviet involvement until it was much too late. Fifteen miles from Riyadh the Antonovs designated for that city went to flight idle and glided silently towards the capital. The troops formed up ready for launch. They were using standard UT-15 parachutes and infra-red goggles. The An-12 could deliver its men in a stick in under a minute through its upward-folding rear ramp-doors.

The air was cold, the light was green. At a steady trot, the troops ran forward to fall into the night.

They were using HAHO – High Altitude High Opening – to glide unseen and unheard into the heart of the city. As Korchagin hung from his harness and looked at the capital ahead through his goggles he saw it lit up with splashes of garish light. All the targets were under infra-red illumination – invisible to the naked eye – directed from neighbouring buildings by the fifth-columnists already in place. The parachuting troops were all as familiar with the topography of Riyadh as the most knowledgeable Saudi street-vendor, and as they glided in and oriented themselves they began to steer for their individual targets.

Korchagin's destination was *Qasr al Murabba*, the cubic palace that was home to King Fahd and the Saud monarchy. Gliding in from the east he could see it clear through his goggles, lit from the Post Office building – itself to the east of the palace, so as not to blind the incoming soldiers. Much thought and practice had gone into the mission. All the soldiers were combat veterans from Afghanistan, some, like Korchagin himself, having taken part in the assault on the Darulaman Palace of President Hafizullah Amin on Boxing Day, 1979.

To his left he could see the Water Tower, an elegant striped mushroom, symbol of the oasis city's dependence on deep wells. At one hundred feet the grounds of the palace filled his vision. He steered for the broad terrace in front of the south aspect. He could see no guards. However, their presence would not go unnoticed for long. It did not matter. The successful attack on the Darulaman Palace that had signalled the beginning of the war in Afghanistan was to be the model. No one in *Qasr al Murabba* was to remain alive. Korchagin as a young Lieutenant had been in the group that had shot President Amin in his top-floor private bar, where he had been celebrating the feast.

Some two hundred men had been given the responsibility for clearing the palace. Of these half were designated to secure the perimeter and the other half to secure the palace and kill everyone inside. Like Korchagin each of the various team leaders was wearing a small transmitter, and each of his team earphones that picked up the homing signal when they faced the source, thus ensuring that the groups could assemble with speed upon landing.

The night was still, and Korchagin hit the stone terrace with a thump, but remained standing, and was able to shuck off his parachute and harness without being dragged over the ground. From inside the courtyard and on the terrace came the multiple thudding of the paratroops landing. Retaining his infra red goggles for the moment he could see the teams assembling. His squad of ten under the command of the Sergeant Major, Mazurov. Mazurov was tough, a disciplinarian, his troopers considered him *sukhar*, without human emotion, but he was a first-class soldier. He had the team at Korchagin's back in seconds. There was still no reaction from anyone in the palace, and as the teams streamed out to secure the perimeter Korchagin led his into the palace, discarding his goggles as he went.

Night lights were on. They all knew the layout of the palace perfectly, they had practised in a mock-up that had been built for them, the building taken apart and laid out floor by floor. They slipped quietly down the corridor on the stylised carpet and encountered their first occupant, a night-watchman, dozing by a wall. The great hand of Malyarov, their Arabic-speaking corporal from Kirghiz wrapped itself around his mouth and muffled his cries, leaving only agonised and terrified eyes visible as Mazurov swiftly worked on him. When Malyarov released his grip and posed his short, sharp questions the information poured forth like water from a tap.

The King was in his royal suite, there were no reports of illness, of dysentery. Korchagin had thought that likely. Ordinary folk drank the local water, despite its high mineral content and harsh flavour, but those of more sophisticated palate, like those who dwelled in the palace, would only consume bottled imported water.

Malyarov looked questioningly at his commander, and Korchagin nodded. The corporal hit the prisoner with one Kung Fu blow, and he died. *Spetsnaz* troops spent what their western opposite numbers considered an inordinate amount of time practising martial arts, but it did make for easy silent killing.

As they hurried on, and made for the stairs, the quicker to reach the royal quarters a Saudi guardsman poked his head over the top. Immediately, Korchagin fired the grenade he had fitted to the Franchi; it bounced off the roof and as it exploded, he followed it up with a tear gas grenade, slapping it smoothly into the cup with his left hand and firing with his right. They sprinted up the broad stairway, pulling down their gas masks, the screaming of injured men and gunfire in their ears. At the top they cleared the corridors of anything living with a sustained burst of fire from the AKMs, and ran over the corpses. Korchagin's squad continued to make for the royal suite while behind them the second squad began classic room-clearing, kicking down the doors and lobbing in grenades, shooting anything that still lived after the explosions.

Korchagin's men ran into stiff resistance from a group of Saudi guardsmen who had erected a makeshift barricade outside the twin doors, high, decorated and carved, to the royal chamber. Glotov and Keldysh went down to accurately-aimed M-16 fire, and most felt the sting of grenade splinters in their flesh. At very close quarters Korchagin's Franchi was lethal, its unique muzzle choke spreading the shot in an oval pattern. He paused to slap another box magazine into the gun and was a few paces behind Mazurov and Malyarov as they crashed through the doors, pouring AKM fire through the smoke of the battle. As they entered the luxurious suite, with its modern furniture and accoutrements in stately surroundings they spun around like dolls, their grenades left unthrown in their hands, hit by a full magazine of automatic fire. Korchagin slammed against the wall with the rest of the squad as the grenades went off, then hurtled into the room, his shotgun pumping lead. He glimpsed a figure firing from a bathroom doorway, a big man, incongruous in white nightshirt and black flak-jacket, and saw red splashes stain the snowy material as his slugs tore home. He rolled behind a heavy wardrobe, slamming in another magazine. Grenades tumbled over his head, tearing holes in the wall, Galtov went down to a final burst from the big man, who was firing one-handed from by the bath, where he had been blown by the blast, and Korchagin fired twice.

With his ears singing he walked through the smoke as what remained of his squad checked the rest of the suite for occupants. The big man lay sprawled on the floor, the white of his robe turned to red. A gold-plated Heckler & Koch MP5 rested in one paw, a gift from the manufacturers to a monarch, but its owner had used it as the manufacturers had intended. The House of Saud was not an effete monarchy.

King Fahd was dead, a man in the illustrious mould of his fighting ancestor, Ibn Saud. Korchagin turned away. The palace was filled with the steady crump of grenades, the rattle of gunfire and screams of the dying. He made his way outside, into the courtyard, where the radio transmitters had been set up for the second wave of An-12s. In the dim light of the approaching dawn great parachutes appeared, suspending pallets of supplies beneath them. Under automated control, they had been dropped five miles away from the Antonovs, and glided in following the radio beacons. The loads were heavy, containing ammunition, mortars, anti-tank rockets, barbed wire and other materials to fortify the palace, they descended fast, but beneath them were two telescopic poles some four metres long; as the poles struck the ground of the courtyard they triggered a retro rocket pack that ensured a soft landing.

As his men made the palace secure a flight of MiG-27 ground attack fighters came screaming over the city in the dawn light. Their bomb racks were empty, and in the distance smoke was staining the sky. They wore Iranian markings.

Korchagin waved an ironic hand in greeting.

'*Molodsti*,' he murmured dryly. 'Well done, boys. *Molodsti*.'

THE WHITE HOUSE

The Critical Intelligence Communications network, or CRITICOM was the means by which vital information could be transmitted to the President and a handful of other top officials within minutes of its being known to intelligence. The necessity for such a fast-reaction system had become obvious as far back as December 7, 1941, when some intelligence officers had had indications of a Japanese strike against Pearl Harbor, but had been unable to communicate their information in time. As a system, it was efficient, only the speed required to initiate a CRITIC leading to the occasional error of interpretation, as when an Air Force analyst, tracing a Soviet bomber to a landing on Lake Baikal excitedly informed the President that the USSR had a new generation of such aircraft capable of operating from water, quite forgetting that it was winter, and what happened to water that far north when it was.

It had been the boast of NSA, who operated the system, that they could get a CRITIC on to the desk of the President within ten minutes of initiation. As what remained of NSA was radio-active dust drifting in the upper atmosphere the task had been taken on by its *alter-ego*, British GCHQ, and it was a measure of the co-operation between the two agencies that once initiated, the British had the CRITIC – to Cord's bedside, not desk – within eight minutes.

There were a number of intelligence indications that mandated the president being informed, day or night. The detonation of a thermonuclear device within a port

388

housing a Soviet battle group most definitely qualified for inclusion on that list.

Cord was informed shortly after three fifteen in the morning, and was able to dress and shave while waiting for further news. At seven, in the bright light of day he was informed that the Air Force chief of staff was waiting to see him.

'Send General Coogan in,' he commanded.

When the door opened it was not Coogan who entered, but his deputy, General Marshal. With him was MacDonald.

'I thought I was told General Coogan wanted to see me,' said Cord.

'General Coogan is dead, sir,' said Marshal. 'I am chief of staff in his place.'

'Dead? How did he die?'

'Radiation sickness.'

Cord stared at Marshal in absolute horror.

'Coogan dropped a nuclear weapon on Khorramshahr?' he whispered.

'No, sir,' Marshal said stolidly. 'Air Force intelligence received confirmation that the Trident II D-5 intercontinental ballistic missiles from the *Maine* were completing refurbishment in a large building in the port of Khorramshahr. General Coogan took the decision that the missiles should be destroyed before they could be either deployed or used.'

'So he *bombed* them? And they went off?' Cord asked in amazement.

'No, sir. All US strategic weapons incorporate elaborate control equipment to ensure that the nuclear devices they incorporate can only be detonated on command. Some of our weapons have survived all kinds of accident without causing an unwanted nuclear blast. Furthermore, the explosion at the port of Khorramshahr equates in kilotonnage to one single warhead. Twenty four missiles of seven warheads each would have caused an immeasurably greater blast. General Coogan decided to destroy the missiles by means of GBU glide-bombs using laser designation to ensure terminal accuracy measured in feet, the bombs to be delivered by the Air Force's sole B-2 ATB bomber to ensure stealth.'

The presidency was said to age a man at double the normal rate, and MacDonald, watching and listening in silence, could almost see it happening to Cord before his eyes.

'The B-2 was piloted by Colonel Travis, with General Coogan as his co-pilot.'

'The chief of staff went on an operational mission?' whispered Cord.

'General Coogan was not under the control of his subordinates,' Marshal said uncomfortably.

'I'll say,' breathed Cord.

'We have received a report from the British Royal Air Force base at Akrotiri in Cyprus. The B-2 landed there not long ago. It did so on autopilot, programmed by its dying crew. All the bombs carried by the aircraft were still within its bomb bay.'

'So how did the nuclear blast take place …'

'There is one more thing which may explain what has happened, sir. General Coogan wrote something on his kneepad as he was dying. He said, "Tell them Ashraf Amran was right." '

'Who is Ashraf Amran?'

'Ash was head of the Iranian section at NSA when I was deputy-director there, Mr President,' said MacDonald. 'She believed that the Iranians had planned and executed an elaborate operation to sink and capture the *Maine* and her nuclear missiles, and that furthermore, they had done so in such a manner as to make us think that the Soviet Union was responsible. She produced considerable evidence to support her case, which was rejected by General Coogan.'

'Where is she now? Let me talk to her.'

'General Coogan sent her into Khorramshahr by means of a submarine, to find the missiles,' Marshal said apologetically.

'So where is she?'

'British GCHQ, which has been operating for us in the SIGINT role since the destruction of NSA, reported that early in the morning the Soviet ASW forces attacked a submarine that had left the port of Khorramshahr. It is believed to be the *Squab*, the submarine carrying Mrs Amran. GCHQ report that the Soviet forces believed that they had sunk it.'

'Is there a chance that she could still be alive?'

'It is possible, sir. The Navy has a rescue mission in progress.'

'If she is still alive I must see her as soon as possible. Organise the fastest jet you have to pull her out of there if the Navy bring her back.'

'Yes, sir.'

'Let's hope she's alive,' Cord said sombrely. 'I've had State on the line before you arrived. The Soviets aren't talking to us. They've clammed up completely. It does not look good. They are going to do something. We went to DefCon II at four thirty-eight this morning.'

AL KUWAYT

The *Tinosa* did not remain surfaced for long. As Ash and the other occupants of the *Squab* left naval personnel swarmed over her, removing the DSRV. Once it was detached the *Tinosa* would revert to her function as hunter of other submarines, and other surface vessels. Following the invasion of Saudi Arabia the USA had gone to DefCon I. A small motorcade was waiting for them, and took them swiftly from the docks to the international airport. As they arrived, a long, sinister blue-black aircraft was taxiing in, lower, sleeker and even at rest faster than the fat white passenger jets that lay immobile on their ramp areas in the middle of a war zone.

'What's that?' Ash asked Major Hawkins, the USAF officer who was responsible for getting them from the *Tinosa* to the airport. 'Looks like some version of an SR.'

'SR-71B,' Hawkins said proudly. 'The president wants you back home as fast as possible and that's what'll do it. SR-71 with raised second cockpit for training duties. That's where you'll be.'

'If I'm to see the president I need to shower and change into some clean clothes. I'm smelly and dirty.'

'You have time,' said Hawkins. 'There's a shower off the office here. I'll have one of the girls lend you some clothes. But for the flight you'll be suited up. You shower while they're turning the SR around, and then we'll have the PSD boys get you into your S-1030.'

Ash was separated from Kowalski, Harris and Logan, and given over to the care of an efficient and kindly female USAF Captain. Through the window of the office, as she clutched her borrowed spongebag on her way to the shower, she could see vehicles surrounding the long reconnaissance aircraft, and two orange-suited figures clambering down the crew access steps into a van.

The shower was pure joy, and with her Islamic heritage she understood why Paradise to a Muslim was always associated with sweet, running water. When she was clean and dry she dressed in T-shirt and pants and socks, and draped herself in her benefactor's long cotton dressing gown. She was then escorted to a room at ground level which had been appropriated by men from the Physiological Support Division. The pilot and reconnaissance systems officer of the SR were there, still suited in orange, but without their helmets.

'Ma'am,' said Colonel Nelson, shaking her hand. 'I sure am glad you're alive. The president told me you were the most valuable person in the world right at this minute. I'm Bob Nelson, I fly that big thing out there and this is Brad Davis, who runs all the systems. I get him to where he wants to go and he does the work.'

'Pleased to meet you, Mrs Amran,' said Davis. 'How you could go down into the sea in one of those things is beyond me!'

'I guess they say that about you,' Ash smiled.

While the two PSD technicians were getting Ash into her suit Hawkins came in.

'I've been talking to British GCHQ. They've been listening to the Iranians. Somehow they know Mrs Amran is alive, and here. They spotted the SR coming in on their radar at Bushehr just across the Gulf – what *else* goes at Mach 3 plus at 100,000 feet? They're pulling an entire *wing* of MiG 29s out of the fighting with the Saudis. They're on the ground refuelling at Masjed Soleyman and are to launch a major strike on Al Kuwayt. The *Coral Sea* is heading up a battle group coming up the Gulf, and she's got her Hornets and F-14s in the air. I guess we need to get you out of here as fast as we can, Colonel.'

He looked across at Ash, now inside her suit, with a mixture of awe and alarm.

'Just what is it you know, Mrs Amran?'

'I think that's only for the president to know right now, right Mrs Amran?' said Nelson.

'Why don't you call me Ash. Everyone does. If I'm to go at Mach 3 plus and 100,000 feet I think we'd better all be Ash, Bob and Brad. I'd feel happier.'

The two airmen, the 'crew dogs' grinned pleasantly. Ash recalled reading that SR crews were selected for their ability to get along with people. A fighter pilot could be mean, those who flew SRs had to be team players.

'Well, Ash, if you're ready, we'll get out to the bird. We have to run through a few things before we can go, so with all those MiGs on the way the sooner the better, I'd say.'

Fully suited and helmeted, Ash's outfit was tested for leaks and correct breathing then clutching her orange box containing the portable oxygen system like Nelson and Davis she waddled through into the van that took them out to the SR-71B.

She sat high up on the SR training aircraft. Nelson was

below and in front of her, and Davis in his electronics-packed compartment somewhere below her feet. She had an acceptable view ahead and to the side, it felt not unlike peering out of the hatch of the *Squab*.

'You'll find the suit and seat real comfortable,' said the PSD sergeant responsible for strapping her in. He connected her up to the aircraft's own oxygen source and removed the portable supply. 'Open this hatch here and there's some food tubes. You can warm them up by holding them up to the window.'

Holding them to the window? thought Ash.

'You'll want to stay ahead of your liquids,' the sergeant advised. 'These here are Gatorade, these water, you can drink them by pushing the nozzle through the adaptor here on your helmet. Best of luck, ma'am.'

The cockpit canopy swung down, and she heard it lock. In her ears she could hear Nelson and Davis working through their checklists. In her cockpit, dials swung to life, lights illuminated, switches clicked and levers moved. The great engines fired into life and the aircraft began to move, following and surrounded by a small armada of ground vehicles.

'The MiGs are crossing the coast,' Davis said calmly. 'The F-14s are engaging.'

As they rolled on to the runway itself Ash saw a flight of grey aircraft swinging across the far end of the airfield; as adrenalin pumped in alarm she heard Nelson's comforting voice.

'Hornets,' he said. 'They're friendly.'

She heard him communicate with the flight leader and then the SR-71 began to move, pressing her inexorably back into the seat. The nose rotated like a lift setting off for the 98th floor and they lanced into the sky. They climbed out over the rippled grey water of the Gulf, studded with oil terminals and rigs. She looked out to her left and dimly could see the darkness of home in the distance.

'We're going to take on fuel and then we can hurry along,' said Nelson.

A fat grey and white tanker was approaching in her windshield. They were overtaking it. She saw a thin white spray of fuel trail from the v-winged boom. It passed over her head and the movement of the two aircraft stabilised. Twin-tailed Hornet fighters were around them in the sky, as she watched they all scattered from formation. White fire streaked from beneath wings as missiles accelerated to terminal velocity.

'The MiG 29s have arrived,' Davis said laconically. 'I'm making us hard to see.'

The hazy air was lit with flickers and flashes of light as things she could not see exploded. Then they were free of the tanker, clear, she could hear Nelson and Davis running swiftly and efficiently through some items that concerned them, and then they were accelerating up. Like a roller-coaster, the big aircraft nosed over and the Gulf came up at her. On the dial that said KIAS two needles moved, one like a barber's-pole went past Mach 1 and she grunted as the SR flattened out of its dive and recommenced climbing. Then the cockpit moved with tremendous force to the side, her faceshield smacked into the canopy and the seatbelts bit into her through the suit.

As quickly as her helmet hit one side of the cockpit it slammed into the other. The aircraft appeared to be trying to tumble in mid air. A missile. One of the MiGs.

Nelson was talking. 'Just an unstart,' he said calmly, and as he did so, the violence ceased, the nose swinging back to the left, and then the right as the autopilot corrected its own over-correction. They were climbing smoothly once more.

'Just had to capture the inlet,' said Nelson. 'When it goes out on you it makes the bird try to swap ends. And gets your eyeballs hitting the limit switches, right?'

Ash heard the genial chuckle in his voice and forced herself to match it.

'It felt like they were playing table-tennis,' she said.

'GCHQ says we got a smart one. Colonel Parsa and two wingmen are climbing to 75,000.'

Khosrow, thought Ash. I went to such trouble to find you, and you are going to such trouble to kill me.

She could hear the noise of the 'fuzzbuster' going off, warning of incoming missiles.

'Chaff,' said Davis. 'Let's move ourselves.'

Ash looked out to left and right, but could see nothing but the steadily darkening deep blue sky. Was this how modern warfare was – just symbols and diagrams on cathode-ray tubes, real-life arcade games that snuffed out your life like a candle if you lost.

'Parsa's still got two X-10s left. He's getting a good firing resolution on us.'

'We got the altitude now,' Nelson said calmly. 'I'd say we're ahead of him.'

The SR had levelled off, and at a hundred per cent, with full afterburner the barber's pole was moving around the dial.

'We can out-run an X-10.'

'Parsa's going down. He's out of fuel. He hung in that long to try.'

The sky was the deepest blue.

'We're going home, Ash.'

Exhaustion swept over her, her head nodded inside the big helmet and she slept.

BALTIMORE

It was a summer morning. The girls were in their light, colourful cottons, because it was what they wore, even if on the other side of the world a new war had started. The Arabs were always fighting one another. At least with President Cord you knew the US wouldn't get dragged in, there'd be no more Vietnams.

The sun streamed in through the window as Sue

Roberts took the call. It was long-distance, overseas, you could tell by the quality of the sound. She thumbed the switch for Eddie Lavasani. It was Eddie's old countrymen who were in the tanks going to Riyadh. That was funny, Sue thought, as she waited for him to pick up the 'phone. You never thought of Eddie as Iranian. He'd become an American, one of us.

'Call for you, Eddie.'

'Who is it, honey?'

'He says he has a message from a Mr Khalif.'

There was silence at the other end.

'Eddie? Shall I put him through?'

'Yes,' Lavasani said slowly, heavily. 'Put him through.'

Sue transferred the call, and before she cut herself off she heard the voice from so far away, grinding, a foreign language.

When Eddie Lavasani came out of his office he was pale, sweating, he looked ill.

'Eddie?' she said in alarm. 'Are you all right. Was it bad news?'

'Yes,' Lavasani said wearily, unhappily. 'Bad news. I have to go out, Sue.'

'Oh ... when will you be back? The clients ...'

'Back?' Lavasani looked at her blankly for a moment, then the ghost of a smile went across his face. 'Not for a while. I won't be back for a while.'

He went out, leaving the secretary wondering frantically who would deal with Fawcett, Hamilton and Levine when they came. Lavasani went out to the parking lot and drove home in his Dodge. He put the car into the garage, and closing the door transferred an infantry-portable *Stinger* ground-to-air anti-aircraft missile from its place of concealment into the back of the station-wagon. When it was covered up he took a small aeronautical enthusiast's radio, and tuned it to the approach frequency of Andrews Air Force base, outside Washington. With this done he got back in and drove out to the Washington-Baltimore Parkway. It was repaired, although they were still pulling up the charred stumps of the trees. You could see where NSA had been.

LOCKHEED SR-71B 17958

Ash must have made noises of awakening, for as she opened her eyes and blinked in the sunlight in the cockpit she heard Nelson's friendly voice.

'Good morning, Ash. Sleep well?'

'I did,' she said. 'I was so tired, I never thought I'd doze off inside a space-suit. Where are we?'

'About forty-two minutes out from Andrews AFB.'

'Have you heard any news since I fell asleep?'

'Yeah,' Nelson said sombrely. 'Things are getting out of hand. The Soviets used a nuclear depth charge and took out the *Coral Sea's* battle group in the Gulf. Whole damn thing. Two of our attack subs have sunk the *Kiev* and the *Leonid Brezhnev*.'

Ash remembered the captain of the *Tinosa* saying, 'Operating a submarine against a carrier is easy ... the carrier's ASW protection is often like Swiss cheese.'

She prayed that Cord would hold on until she got there. Sinking the two carriers would be considered 'lateral escalation'. In the gaming world it would also be considered 'signalling'. The problem was always that the enemy might not recognise the signal, or the lateralness of the escalation and take it for simple ratchet-effect raising-the-ante escalation into full-blown war. At which point possession of MIRVs automatically gave the side that struck first the advantage.

She was thirsty, and hungry. She stuck a tube through the adaptor on her helmet and drank some water. Rummaging in the food locker she found a tube of roast beef and mashed potato with gravy. It didn't seem very appetising cold, and the PSD sergeant's advice about holding it to the windshield came into her head. She reached forward to put her gloved hand on it and the heat burned through. The friction of the air, thin as it was, was making the whole aircraft hot. She held the tube against the window and in a minute it was heated through. She ate it with pleasure.

The SR began letting down; they had taken on their last load of fuel and the Delaware coastline was visible on the horizon. The deep blue of the sky began to change through duck-egg to a clear summer's day.

'We're cleared for a straight-in at Andrews,' Nelson said as they came over Chesapeake Bay. Ash had heard him talking with the men on the ground. 'They got a motorcade waiting.'

To her right Ash could see the Naval Academy at Annapolis, in the distance, Baltimore. As they came over the Patuxent river she could see the cars and trucks moving on 301, and the runways of the great air base spread out ahead.

'Home, sweet home,' said Davis, who could only see out of the side, but could pick the distance to go from the navigation equipment in his compartment. He sounded relieved.

'*Jesus –*' The blasphemy was uttered a fraction of a second after they heard the Sanders AN/ALQ-156(V) missile detection system go off for the second time in the flight.

'*Missile incoming.*'

The nose of the SR went down and the big jet was pulling unusual g-forces as Nelson cut across the path of the ground-to-air missile, leaving a great swath of heat behind as he gave a huge blast of afterburner through the J-58 turbo-ramjets. Chaff and flares spewed from the Tracor dispensers and Davis played a symphony on his electronics as he stole the rangegate from the missile.

The nose was back in level flight and Nelson was reacquiring the centreline as though nothing had happened.

'We're clear,' he said. 'I'm going to put her down, we don't need to give the bastard a second shot at us by going around.'

They came over the threshold and Nelson flared to a perfect landing. The chute deployed and he held the nose high. Then they were rolling, and at a taxiway a pick up with an illuminated sign that said 'Follow Me' was waiting.

'They're going to hurry me off,' said Ash. 'So I'll thank you now.'

She had listened to the two 'crew dogs' enough to acquire a little of the jargon.

'That was a no-kidding mission,' she said, and they laughed delightedly.

Men were waiting, two PSD crew removed Ash from her harness and oxygen supply, they took off the big helmet for her, and unsnapped the sealed gloves from the wrists of the suit, which they left her in. She waddled down the crew access steps and into the waiting presidential Cadillac. There was Colonel Frost, whom she remembered as Sultani's intelligence interrogator, and two secret servicemen. They were in convoy with two other cars and motorcyle outriders. As they emerged on to Pennsylvania Avenue Ash saw a long white Cadillac broadside across the road, a Dodge station wagon half buried in one fender. Three big black men were beating a man into pulp at the side of the road. She caught a glimpse of his bloody face.

'Stop the car,' she said. 'Get that man,' she ordered the secret servicemen.

The sight of the Ingram guns that sprouted from the bodyguard's fists, and the trained-attack-dog demeanour of the men was enough to halt the killing.

'We done saw this mothahfockah shoot at the big black plane,' one black panted triumphantly. 'We done chase him, 'n we caught him.'

'Bring him here,' Ash commanded. 'Put the others in your car there. I want them.'

The man was hustled into the Cadillac, where blood slid down his face and spattered on to the thick carpet.

'I know you,' said Ash. She had pulled the face from her photographic memory, and matched it with a name. 'You're Lavasani. Why did you try to kill me?'

They crossed the Anacostia river, with the Capitol building in the distance.

'I was ordered to,' gasped Lavasani. 'Hossein has my wife and children. I had no choice ...'

He began to weep, tears mingling with the blood. Ash sat back in her seat, and composed her mind. As in all crises, the president would have called upon the advisers he felt happy with, and they were often men who did not know anything about the problem. They would all be very powerful men, however, and the situation they now found themselves in the most stressful they had ever endured. Under such conditions nothing was harder than doing nothing. The threat to their psychological integrity was such that *action* became imperative, they would want to treat her as a messenger, a bearer of information to be accepted or not, and dismissed once given, in order that they make decisions, and order actions. Ash could not allow that to happen, she was going to have to take command of these powerful men, to have them listen to her, to make the decisions, issue the orders herself.

The Cadillac sped around the Capitol and up Pennsylvania Avenue at speed, with the motorcycle cops on their Kawasakis clearing the way. The gates were open, and they entered the grounds of the White House.

1600 PENNSYLVANIA AVENUE.
THE WHITE HOUSE

The motorcade stopped outside the West wing, home of all the Presidential staff offices. Ash turned to Lavasani.

'We are going to see the President and his closest advisers,' she said quietly. 'When we meet them I want you to tell them why you were instructed to kill me.'

'But my family –' Lavasani protested. 'It was always made clear to me they would die if I ever said anything.'

'I am Ashraf Amran,' she said, with steel in her voice. 'I promise you that your family will come to no harm, and that I will restore them to you.'

Lavasani looked at her wonderingly.

'If you let me down, not only will they die, but I will hand you back to the black men and let them finish what they began. You understand?'

'Yes,' Lavasani whispered.

'Then let us go to them.'

Frost took Ash and Lavasani, accompanied by the secret servicemen, into the West wing. Here were many famous rooms and offices – the Roosevelt and Cabinet Rooms, the Oval Office, all richly and historically furnished – but the President would not be in any of them. He was in a totally functional room, furnished with the best intelligence the highest technology could gather, sunk deep under the great mansion, hardened against nuclear attack. The Situation Room.

The Situation Room was from where the President and the members of the National Security Council handled national crises. It was linked to the National Military Command Center in the Pentagon, where the Joint Chiefs presided over the nation's primary war room. In case of a nuclear strike taking out the two principal command centres – known as 'decapitation' – in crisis situations selected cabinet officers and government officials were removed to alternate command posts across the nation. There was the Alternate Military Command center in southern Pennsylvania, and 'special facilities' at Mount Weather in northern Virginia, in Massachussetts and in Texas. The Vice-President went aloft in one of four identical Boeing 747s filled with communications equipment. The aircraft was the National Emergency Airborne Command Post, NEACP, which the military pronounced Kneecap. Others simply called it the Doomsday Plane.

The President in the Situation Room represented the National Command Authority. Should he be killed or disabled the NCA did not follow the Constitution's line of succession, but followed a route dictated by military doctrine, passing first to the Secretary of Defense, and then, if necessary, to the deputy Secretary of Defense. If nuclear catastrophe followed nuclear catastrophe it passed to the Secretary of the Army, then the Navy, the Air Force, and reached its final destination with an Air Force brigadier general in the last 'Looking Glass' NEACP 747 flying over Armageddon.

When they came out of the lift and through the big double doors Ash saw printed on one corner of the great presentation screen behind Cord: Defense Condition I. At the sight of 'Cocked Pistol' her stomach churned. Khalif Hossein's planning had been meticulous, almost faultless. The USA and USSR were on the brink of war, and there was so very little time left.

'Mrs Amran,' said Cord. 'We are so pleased that you are here and safe.'

'Thank you, Mr President. Luck and skilful sailors and airmen are largely responsible for that.'

She was still wearing her big orange suit, her 'silver tuxedo'; it was cumbersome, but she had no change of clothing; it would not be appropriate to brief the President and the members of EXCOM in t-shirt and pants, she thought. Besides, there was no time.

'Attempts were made to kill me both flying out of Al Kuwayt and on approach to Andrews Air Force Base. The first involved a wing of MiG 29 fighters, the second a shoulder-launched ground-to-air missile. The man from whose shoulder the missile was launched is here. He is, if you like, my credentials for what I am about to tell you.'

She turned to Lavasani.

'My name is Lavasani,' he began, very quietly.

'Speak up,' Cord ordered.

'Lavasani,' he said, louder. 'I am a former officer in the Iranian Imperial Guards. When the Shah, my master fell I fled to this land with my family. I found employment. One day, about eighteen months ago, I came home to find my wife and sons not there. Waiting for me was a man, an emissary from Khalif Hossein. He told me that my family had been kidnapped, and were on their way to Iran. They would be kept safe, and I would receive communication from them, proof that they were alive. If I told anyone what had happened, they would be killed. I was required to be available at any time for clandestine activity. My martial skills were put back in practice, I received instruction in the use of *Stinger* missiles, and was given one to keep ready. Until today I received no instruction to do anything. I received a call at work from the man who controls me. He ordered me to go to Andrews AFB and listen for an SR-71 approaching. I was to shoot it down. I asked the man why I should shoot it down. He was over-wrought, in the middle of battle, he screamed that there was one aboard who knew, who could reveal the plan, who would prevent the dawn of the age of Allah over the world. Then he calmed himself, and reminded me that he would kill my family if I was recalcitrant. I made my way home, collected the missile, and drove to the base.

404

Through the skill of the crew and the hand of God the missile missed. Some patriotic black men saw me do it, after a short car chase they caught me. I was only rescued by Mrs Amran and her guards. She is the one they said knew, and would prevent the age of Allah.'

'Thank you,' said Ash. 'Take him, now, and treat his injuries. No harm should come to him, we none of us know what we might do if our families were under threat, and I have promised him he shall be reunited with his.'

Frost took Lavasani out, and Cord looked at Ash. The other members of the EXCOM team were clustered around the long table.

'The dawn of the age of Allah?' Cord said, eyebrows raised.

'Yes. Has Dr MacDonald briefed you on the background to this?'

'Yes, he has.'

'Very well. I was taken to Khorramshahr because I believed that the Trident missiles from the sunk *Maine* were there. Through the machinations of my agent there I was able to see the missiles, from a distance, in a great assembly hall, being worked on by technicians. Once outside, I transmitted the information to General Coogan, who had sent me. Being tired, I slept during the day. Before sleeping, I was uneasy, aware that I had not thought the whole through. When I awoke it was clear in my mind. I went back to the place I had seen the missiles, and it was empty of people, I was able to climb down and examine the missiles. They were but expensive props. My agent had been suborned, through fear, like Lavasani. I had been brought there to see what they wanted me to see, just as General Coogan had been shown what they wanted him to be shown. My agent and I rescued one nuclear technician being held a prisoner, a man called Logan. He told me where the missiles were. Most had been fitted into surplus oil tankers, and sent to sea.

'General Coogan arrived, as they expected him to, to bomb the building in Khorramshahr. They exploded one warhead, destroying the Soviet battle group at anchor. I believe they hoped to catch the B-2 bomber, in order to show it to the Soviets, but it was of little matter, since Soviet SIGINT would be able to tell the mission had taken place, and would have seen it at Akrotiri anyway.'

Ash paused, and looked around the silent, but powerful men around the table.

'I am sure we have all been players in political-military simulations or wargames, if you like. At blue versus red, Sam versus Ivan, NCA – National Command Authority – level, what is the most difficult thing to get to happen?'

'To cross the nuclear threshold,' said Davidson, the Secretary of Defense. 'People won't do it, not unless they're made to.'

'That's right, sir. They won't. People have consciences, they try to play by the rules. When nuclear war became the new kind of war we still tried to stick with the old rules. The nuclear threshold is the place the rules end, because beyond it there are no rules. In a *game*, to get players to launch, to make the first strike, Control has to rig the game, to make it outrageous. I have played in many games where in the hot washup afterwards blue or red players complain to Control, saying "you made us do that. If you'd left us alone we would have negotiated a peace".'

Ash paused, to give her words effect.

'Khalif Hossein is Control. He has rigged the game. He has exploded the first warhead, he has made us cross the nuclear threshold. The Soviets have responded in kind. *We are across the threshold*. There are no rules that we know of now. The pressure is on, and the world reduced to a box in which the walls inexorably close in on us, reducing our options to a tiny and dreadfully dangerous few. You gentlemen have been discussing options, such as Selected, Limited and Regional Attacks. *With nuclear weapons*.'

Ash looked around them, and saw that she was right.

'The Soviets are doing the same thing. If both of us have *time*, we will pull back, begin the long negotiations – "jaw, jaw, not war, war." It's always been so. I've read the histories. The Berlin blockade, the Cuban missile crisis, the *Pueblo* – the initial response was to get tough, even throw a demonstration nuke, but always, the government officials, through days of searing pressure, managed to reject the early emotional reactions, the desire to *do* something, and produce good, well-thought-out decisions and policies. The Truman administration rejected the idea of putting an armed train through to Berlin because if the Soviets interfered with it it was war, and settled on the airlift. It broke the blockade, we succeeded, there was no war. President Kennedy's administration thought about destroying large areas of Cuba. They had the time to think it through and came to a better, more successful policy. It is always the same, it can be done, and the men in this room are as good as their fathers were, they can do it too, *but you have to have time.*'

Ash looked up, and pointed at the huge world situation board with its silent threat; Defense Condition I.

'Gentlemen, we are not going to get the time. Very soon, that board is going to light up with the evidence of a nuclear strike against the USSR. It will look like a Limited Attack launched from a number of our SSBNs. It will in fact be from the missile-carrying oil tankers. With the events that have taken place since General Coogan's bomber destroyed the SDI complex at Smolensk, the steady escalation up the ladder, do you think the Soviets won't retaliate in kind? Or *greater* than kind? And what will we do then? Won't *we* retaliate? There will be Major Attack on both sides, gentlemen, and the age of Allah will have been born in the radio-active glow of the remains of Western civilisation.

'Without their knowledge, the USA and the Soviet Union have been drawn into a dreadful partnership, a grisly reel in which the steps lead to a culmination of killing. The Germans have a word for it; it is a *Totentanz*, it is the Dance of Death.'

She turned to Cord. 'Mr President, in all the crises between the USA and the Soviet Union, whatever the differences between the President and the General Secretary, they have always been partners, whatever their mutual enmities or differing viewpoints they have always worked together to avoid nuclear disaster. You and General Secretary Krilov are 'kings', however much you both wish to outwit the other for the gain of your nations, you are both more sensitive to each other's position and problems than anyone else concerned. You both know that you are partners in this – game – in which the prize is avoidance of nuclear war. Despite the steady escalation, even because of it, General Secretary Krilov will be anxious to communicate privately with you.'

'We have had no success in using the hot line teleprinter,' said Cord. 'We're considering using a form of back-channel. Secretary of State Davis is attempting to communicate with former Soviet Ambassador Gorshkov.'

'I think that may be too late, sir. I may be able to help you. I will need to communicate with Moscow via satellite, using SHF. I will also need to set up a line to the Satellite Control Facility to advise them on the use of the SDI stations once the missiles are launched.'

'Now hold on,' expostulated the Secretary of State. 'Aren't you moving out of your league some here?'

Ash turned to him, a small, resolute figure in an overly-large orange suit that rustled when she moved.

'Mr Secretary, I was out-ranked and told I was wrong by General Moore, who is now dead. I was outranked and told I was wrong by General Coogan who is also dead. Both would be alive had they listened to me. If I am outranked once more in this room, if you believe that you gentlemen can handle this situation in the very short space of time left to us, then we will *all* die.'

There was silence as Ash stared at the group of powerful politicians, and then Cord smiled, breaking the tension.

'That puts you in your place, Charlie,' he said amiably. 'Mrs Amran, if you will arrange for me to talk to General Secretary Krilov I shall be most grateful. I think you'll find all you need at the terminals over there.'

Ash was shown to a terminal, and an anxious operator hovered over her.

'I have a link through to a computer in Moscow. I arranged it with equipment given to me when I was at NSA. It's secure. In *emergency*, I can arrange it so that I can speak direct on the telephone. I'm going to do that. I hope that my party is in. When I've talked to him, I'm going to want to talk to the top operator at the SCF. When the missiles fire they're going to be dancing, and I'll need their Fred Astaire.'

'I'll set it up,' promised the operator.

Ash's fingers tapped lightly and deftly over the keyboard.

'It's through,' she said, and reached for the telephone by her side.

She could hear the distinctive Russian tone on the line, and then there was an electronic burp as the receiver was lifted.

'Rykov.'

'Vladimir. It is Ash.'

'Ash ...'

Her brother's weariness and fear came clear.

'Ash, I let you down. I never told Krilov.'

'I know. You knew what happens to the bearer of bad tidings.'

'Yes ...'

'You have to go to him now, Vladimir.'

While she was speaking, Ash was tapping out co-ordinates and information on to her VDU.

'The USA and the USSR are being duped into nuclear war by Khalif Hossein, who seeks to find the Prophet's Paradise in a world of ruin. Very shortly what will appear to be a Limited Nuclear Attack will appear on your defence screens. I am transmitting the order of battle to you. *It is not a US attack*. Only the original Trident missiles acquired from the *Maine* have nuclear warheads. The short-range missiles are Iran-Cs. The long-range missiles other than Tridents are Long March missiles

409

acquired from the PRC. We are going to try to take out the Tridents with our SDI battle stations. We don't have enough capacity to knock out all the missiles. Take your IBM disk with you so that you can put the information into your defence computers. I'm speaking to you from the Situation Room in the White House. President Cord is here with me. When you have told General Secretary Krilov what you know, both what I told you in Paris, and what I have told you now, ask him to call President Cord here. They have to talk.'

'I'll do it,' Rykov said steadily. 'I have the information.'

'Good luck.'

Ash turned to her assistant as Rykov rang off. 'Have you got the SCF?'

'They're on the line.' He handed her a 'phone.

'Hullo?'

'Hi. Colonel Randy Ellis here.'

'Hullo, Randy. This is Ash Amran. Any time now you can expect what will look like a US Limited Nuclear Attack on the Soviet Union to appear on your screens. It isn't, but for the moment that's beside the point. I am transmitting the order of battle to you. The missiles that have to be taken out will appear from here, and here. They are genuine Trident II D-5s and *must* be taken out. All others can be ignored as they are there only to simulate attack, and to provoke a Soviet counter-attack. Do you have that?'

When Randy Ellis spoke, his voice was steady.

'Yeah, we have that. It sounds like there's some story behind all this. You'll have to tell me about it afterwards.'

'I will, afterwards.'

'Well, better get on with it,' Ellis said jauntily. 'We ain' never used this stuff in anger before. Guess we're about to find out if it works. See if the taxpayers got value for their money.'

They kept the line open. Ash sat back in her seat, and found that Cord had been behind her, listening and watching.

'How do you know which missiles will be which?'

'Logan told me. He's a guidance engineer for the D-5 rogramme. He set up the co-ordinates for each MIRV. I'm utting them here for you, so that you have them when you alk to Krilov.'

They waited, as the screens remained blank. Then a elephone rang, and a young woman on the White House taff stood up anxiously.

'Mr President. I have General Secretary Krilov on the ne from Moscow.'

RODINA I. USSR NATIONAL COMMAND CENTRE, MOSCOW

The Soviet leadership did not consider the Kremlin in the ame way as the Americans did their White House. The eneral Secretary did not live there, unlike the President, referring his dacha or luxury apartment, and the Soviets ad not constructed their own version of the Situation .oom there. Their system of numerous alternative ommand centres scattered over the nation was similar to at of the USA, however, and the principal one lay a fast il ride from the Kremlin's Borovitsky gate up Gorki treet, across the Triumphalnaja ring-road and on past the Dynamo' sports complex to hit the M10 to Leningrad. ust short of the Moscow Beltway was Rodina I, a vast nderground command post some seven hundred feet cross, and over five hundred feet under the earth, rotected by one hundred feet of reinforced concrete and our hundred of earth fill. It had a railroad spur to bring upplies, and was equipped for occupation of up to a year. eneral Secretary Krilov and his high command had been ere ever since the news of the thermonuclear warhead xploding within Khorramshahr had been flashed to them y the Soviet version of CRITICOM.

Rodina I was obsolete. It had been designed and built in the early 1970s, when American guidance systems for their ballistic missiles could not guarantee a direct hit. What was in a Trident II D-5 could place 300 kilotons of force 500 feet over Krilov's head, and for all the concrete and earth, he might just as well be standing in the landscaped grounds above when it went off, for all the good it would do him.

Krilov was not above ground when Rykov made his way to him, he was in the post's Command room, which was very similar to the White House Situation Room in appearance and function. It was from there that he called President Cord. As he did so, Rykov opened a separate line to Ash. Both leaders signified their assent to the move and Ash realised that the two 'kings' were working together to try to stave off the impending catastrophe. The open line between her and Rykov represented a form of 'back-channel', a way for them to transmit and receive information without recognition of formality.

With the huge situation screens in both great rooms blank of ballistic missiles, but with furious fighting in both Saudi Arabia and the Gulf, and with both sides having struck vicious blows the initial sparring between President and General Secretary was slow, as Krilov paused to confer with his commanders. Ash and Rykov murmured to each other in Farsi, so as to be able to say whatever they wished, without fear of reprisal.

'Does Krilov believe what we are saying?' said Ash.

'I think Krilov has accepted the involvement of the Iranians. He seemed to believe me. He understands that I feared to tell him before. Some of the others are suspicious, they feel it is a trick, a way to get in a first strike without retaliation. The information you have sent shows that the missiles are targeted to take out our military capability – the *Backfire* and *Blackjack* strategic bomber fields. The land-based missile silos, the command centres, our C^{3}I. The military is pointing out that the US SSN probably have the capability to take out most of our

412

SSBNs, and the missiles that we can launch will be sufficiently few in number to be taken care of by your SDI capability. It is, they say, a way to win the war at a stroke. They are urging retaliation the minute we have information that the attack has been launched.'

'Which is what Khalif Hossein is counting on. Use the information we've sent. The missiles won't all have the same flight characteristics. You must have your computers analyse them. The short-range rockets are Iran-Cs. The long-range and Long March rockets and up to twenty-four genuine Trident D-5s. The Iran-Cs and the Long Marches have conventional warheads, they'll make a big bang all right, but they aren't nuclear. We're arranging for our SDI to take out the real Tridents with our space-based Brilliant Pebbles interceptors.'

'I'll get them to prepare to analyse the flight characteristics of the missiles.'

'Okay,' said Ash. 'I'll still be here.'

While she waited, and while Cord strove to convince Krilov, the telephone rang again for Ash. It was Randy Ellis from the SCR. When Rykov came back on to the line she spoke urgently.

'Vladimir, we have a problem. I've just been talking to the people commanding the SDI system. What we have in place is just sufficient to cope with the missiles. Our problem is that we don't have our Phase One complete. The full proposal calls for 100,000 interceptors and we don't have anything like that up there yet. In short, there's a gap, a window, in our coverage and two of the missiles are going to go straight through it.'

'Where are they aimed?'

'They're aimed at you,' Ash said steadily. 'They're to take out Moscow.'

Rykov hissed. 'Once they realise it they'll order the Major Attack Option. The lot. The whole thing, Ash.'

'Listen. The Tridents are fitted with MARV. The warheads are in manoeuvreable re-entry vehicles specifically designed to outwit anti-ballistic missiles. You have ABM systems around Moscow. We're sending you the programme that's written into the D-5 MARV – what it'll do to escape an ABM. Your men can make the requisite fire control adjustments to the *Galosh* missiles.'

'Get it coming, Ash. I'll patch it through.'

It took time. Both 'kings' sat huddled with their closest advisers, the line open but dormant. At her console Ash heard people gasp, saw Cord bound to his feet.

In Rodina I Rykov watched as Krilov strode grim-faced to the telephone. He raised his eyes to the slowly-lengthening lights of death rising on the presentation screen in front of him.

'So, Mr President,' said Krilov. 'It has begun.'

THE SITUATION ROOM, THE
WHITE HOUSE

Secretary of State Davis was staring intently at the presentation screen.

'The attack is almost exactly half of what you predicted,' he said sharply to Ash.

On the line from Moscow, Rykov's voice was worried in her ear.

'Ash … where are the Tridents attacking Moscow? We can't see them.'

'It's a Limited Attack,' said Ash. She was as familiar as Davis with the way nuclear war might be handled. Both had participated in the Political-Military simulations at the National Defense University and other power centres.

'It's a Limited Attack,' she repeated. 'It's designed to get Moscow to retaliate. They'll have timed their launches. There's no point in taking out Krilov until he's initiated an escalation. What we'll see in a few minutes is a *second* decapitating attack designed to keep the escalation going

414

all the way to Major Attack by both sides, designed to destroy all centres of military and political command, along with all major cities. And bring about the age of Allah.'

Davis nodded rapidly. 'Sure. The next attack will decapitate their command by hitting the major command posts, beginning with Krilov in Rodina I, and take out their C³I. Command will pass to some Major-Generals scattered over the nation, who filled with grief and fury will press every damn button they have.'

Ash noted that Cord had been keeping tabs on the situation in the room even while talking to Krilov.

'Mr General Secretary,' he said quickly. 'Our latest intelligence here is that you may expect a *second* attack within a few minutes.'

Cord explained to Krilov what Ash's theory was.

In the cold of space, groups of intelligent machines had spent their lives waiting for this moment. Far, far out, at 60,000 miles, a quarter of the way to the moon old American spacecraft known as Vela Hotel stared down at the earth, watching for the double flash that registered a thermonuclear explosion. Closer in and geosynchronous a second group watched for the give-away blasts of heat that indicated a missile attack had been launched. It was this group that had detected the strike and provided the information to the commanders waiting in the Situation Room. They were the three DSP-647 satellites that orbited over the Equator at all times; one DSP East parked over the Indian Ocean, and two, known collectively as DSP-West over the Atlantic and Pacific, and it was these two that had sounded the alarm.

Closer to earth were clusters of small interceptors sitting within environmentally-controlled platforms. The system was known as Brilliant Pebbles; it was the first operational space-based BMD, ballistic missile defense, system in place. Wild and wonderful technology had been mooted for the 'Star Wars' missile defence, from directed-energy weapons based on lasers and particle beams to homing-and-kill weapons like the HOE, Homing Overlay Experiment, rocket that took out its target by means of a great flail of weighted and rotating spokes some 15 feet in diameter. The Brilliant Pebbles system used kinetic energy kill like the HOE rocket without any flail. The pebbles, the interceptors were only some three by one feet big, embodying incredible feats of miniaturisation and precision. They would need it. The task of colliding with a Trident D-5 ICBM blasting into the stratosphere at full boost was roughly equivalent to being able to knock down a wasp on the wing using a rifle and standing a mile away.

Solar cells covering the outside of the platforms provided housekeeping power to maintain the pebbles in a state of readiness at all times. When Randy Ellis talked to them from the SCF they listened, and knew which of the yellow/white/pink/blue/ultraviolet signatures of the blasting rockets to ignore, and which to acquire. Ellis sent the command to eject, and fire. Once launched, the interceptors received tracking information direct from the Boost Surveillance and Tracking System, BSTS, in orbit until acquiring their targets directly using their high-resolution, multi-spectral Livermore sensors.

It was essential that the pebbles be launched early enough to take out the Tridents in their initial exoatmospheric phase before the missile bus in each distributed its passengers, the MARV warheads and penetration aids. Each phase of missile flight required a different Surveillance, Acquisition, Tracking and Kill Assessment, and the killing part of each SATKA got more difficult the further the flight was allowed to go, and one single missile became many targets. Because of Ash's warning, the American BMD had been alerted, and the pebbles streaked to their targets. Plumes of fire burst from shining, conical thruster nozzles as the interceptors made last-second adjustments to their tracks. In the SCF Randy Ellis's video screen saw the tiny flare it was tracking suddenly expand to turn the whole display white, one-tenth of a second after impact. He looked up to see the other screens burst into light, one after the other. Slowly, the picture changed to show clouds of debris spreading into space, all that remained of the incoming missiles. There was a brief, muffled cheer. The great presentation screen was still filled with light, falling down on the USSR like deadly rain.

'Our SDI has destroyed the genuine ballistic missiles,' Cord said steadily to Krilov. 'What remains are the impostors. They have conventional warheads. Your targets may expect explosions, but they will not be nuclear.'

'I have issued orders that if even one warhead is nuclear we shall retaliate with a Limited Attack. In this event I expect you not to continue the escalation.'

'I understand,' said Cord. He motioned to Ash, who had read the situation, and was already talking to Randy Ellis.

'If we've done our sums wrong the Soviets are going to respond with a Limited Attack of their own. Better get your pebbles ready.'

'Okay.'

All watched as the rockets arced in towards their targets. From time to time, everyone looked curiously, fearfully at Ash, still sitting in her 'silver tuxedo' flight suit. All depended upon her, whether she had made the right calculations.

The first Iran-C rocket hit half a mile from the hardened ICBM silo, one of the many grouped on the plain outside Ostrov. The another, and another. Then the big Long March rockets.

'We're waiting,' Rykov said fearfully.

'Vela Hotel says no nukes,' Ellis said to Ash.

'The 'phones are ringing,' said Rykov. 'Yes, they were shaken ... but not nuclear.'

Again, there was a muffled cheer, cut short as the presentation screen lit up for a second time with another attack.

'Good girl,' Davis said shortly. 'You got it on the money.'

There were still no Tridents.

'They'll have planned to wait last of all to knock out

417

Krilov,' said Ash.

So it proved. A few minutes later the final two missiles arced up, their destination Moscow.

'Now we just have to hope the Soviet ABMs do their stuff.'

The Soviet Union had a limited deployment of *Galosh* surface-to-air missiles around Moscow, providing a thin area defence. The *Galosh* was a 65 by 8 foot multi-stage solid-fuel missile with a range of several hundred miles and a one to two megaton warhead. It was designed to be brought sufficiently close to an incoming missile or warhead of the MIRV or MARV type by the phased-array Missile Site Radar so that it could destroy it with its own warhead by means of an X-ray kill. Outside the atmosphere the X-ray effect of the ABM's nuclear warhead was able to destroy a target at several miles range by evaporating the surface layer of its heat shield at such high velocity that the shock waves brought about damage to the warhead's own mechanical structure.

As the Tridents entered the stratosphere on their course to Moscow, the batteries of *Galosh* missiles began firing, the great weapons blasting into the sky with such noise that they brought the citizens on to the streets.

Past the apogee of their flight, the Tridents came apart to release their fourteen independently manoeuvreable warheads. ABM and SLBM, attacker and attacked twisted and turned towards each other in technological ballet. Then the *Galosh* warheads exploded and the dance of death ended. On the presentation screen the plot halted.

'It's over,' Rykov whispered. On her other telephone Ash could hear the wild cheering from the SCF. All over the Situation Room men and women stood in attitudes of relief, slowly collapsing on to chairs. The Secretary of State shed tears that ran in rivulets down his cheeks.

Two people in the room realised that all was not finished. Ash and Cord. Ash sat quietly at the console, and gently put the receiver back into its cradle. Cord still held the 'phone that connected him to his counterpart in Moscow.

'Congratulations, General Secretary,' said Cord.

'Thank you,' said Krilov. His voice had a slight tremor in it, the realisation of the imminence of death, the approach of the most sophisticated and powerful weapon on earth, aimed directly at him. Cord was presidential; listening, concentrating.

'The Iranian forces will not continue fighting in Saudi Arabia, Andrei,' Cord said, using Krilov's first name. 'That just leaves your forces. We have just been to the brink of mutual destruction. It is not worth repeating simply for an increase in strategic leverage.'

'I was told it was the only way out. Our problems are … great.'

'There are alternatives,' said Cord. 'The USA and USSR could co-operate. You and I trust each other now. We could make arrangements, do business together. Let us agree to meet.'

'Very well,' said Krilov slowly.

'Your forces will leave Saudi Arabia.'

'We will withdraw.'

'Secretary of State Davis will begin making the arrangements for us to meet.'

'I shall look forward to it,' said Krilov.

When Cord put down the 'phone the cheering broke out again anew, recognition of Cord's statesmanship. The office of the Presidency was said to make its occupants grow in stature, and all in the room recognised that they had seen it happen before their eyes. Ash sat quiet in her big orange flight suit, waiting for the din to die down.

Cord began to prepare to leave the great underground bunker, his acolytes gathering around him for the return to the world of sunlight and of peace. As he began to walk out Ash called to him.

'Mr President.'

Cord looked across at her and beamed. 'Come,' he said. 'Come with me.'

Ash remained sitting in her seat.

'Mr President,' she said. 'It's not all over. Khalif Hossein

419

fired eighteen Tridents. He's got six left.'

'He can't start a war now,' said Ash. 'But six Tridents have thirty warheads, less one for Khorramshahr, and each is big enough to devastate the largest city in the land. I would say Hossein is able to wreak terrible havoc here, should he so choose.'

Cord had recovered fast from the most unwelcome news.

'Our SDI system works,' he said. 'It just shot down the incoming missiles. He fired them, we shot them down. He tries it again, we'll do it again.'

'That's conventional warfare. I had something more underhand in mind. We have an open society. A freighter, quietly off-loading crates in some tranquil inlet. Trucks, indistinguishable from any others, rolling along our highways, and into the biggest cities in the land. Timed to explode all together …'

'How do we stop him?'

'We execute him, of course,' said Ash.

'How? A bomber strike? We invade? Delta Force?'

Ash smiled. 'No. I'll handle it for you.'

'What will you need?'

'I'd like aid for my country. A new Marshall Plan to restore the fortunes of Persia. She is devastated after so many years of war and terror.'

Cord looked at Ash in puzzlement.

'I meant to kill Hossein. What will you need? I'll place our best soldiers and equipment at your disposal.'

'I won't need that. We'll do it the old-fashioned way. It's worked since the beginning of time.'

'THE ABODE OF THE SNAKES'. JAMARAN, IRAN

The village was walled, fortified, featureless. Renowned for the poisonous adders that made it their home it had been shunned by the upper reaches of Tehrani society in the days of the Shah. They had preferred to cluster about their monarch's winter palace in neighbouring Niavaran, on the pleasing slopes of snow-capped Towchal. The bleakness of Jamaran appealed only to the chill personality of Grand Ayatollah Khomeini, who made it his home. All other villagers were swiftly encouraged to donate their homes to him as *sahm-e-Imam*, or the Imam's share, with suitable compensation in the next world. The Revo- lutionary Guards turned the village into a fortress, defended by a £4 million Siemens electronic security system, Soviet ZSU multi-barrel anti-aircraft guns and 1200 hand-picked IRGC troops. The Ayatollah spent what remained of his life there; when Khalif Hossein ruled, he inherited it.

The guards at the gate bowed when they saw *A'alam Ayatollah al-Odhma Sayyed* Kazem Kashk, for all knew the foremost Grand Ayatollah of Shi'ia Islam. Khalif Hossein ruled Iran, but *A'alam* Kazem Kashk ruled the mullahs throughout the land who instructed the faithful every Friday. With the old man was his son, the fat Sayyed Saddam Kashk, and a small woman in full *purdah*, wearing the *chador* and *hijab*. She stood respectfully, subserviently, behind the two men.

'Take me to Khalif Hossein,' the A'alam commanded, and men hurried to do his bidding.

They were shown to the Khalif who sat cross-legged, alone, on a coarse rug in a small room, a *hojrah* within the *hosseinieh*, the House of Hussein, the place where believers gathered to mourn the martyred Imam Hussein.

'Leave us,' said A'alam Kashk to the guards, and they went out through the curtained door. Khalif Hossein sat staring broodingly at his feet, and made no sign that he had recognised that his visitors were present.

'Islam is a way of life,' said Kashk. He had sat opposite Hossein, with his son by his side. The woman stood quietly by the wall, at the back of the room.

'Islam knows that human men and women are weak, it has found ways to help them, to support them in this world as they prepare for the next. It does not terrorise them. Islam does not ask that young girls who do not wear the *hijab* have acid thrown in their faces, nor that men and women who have fled in fear be seized and brought back, to be tied to posts and burned with blazing faggots until dead. Islam has no quarrel with the Christians, or the other People of the Book. Let them care for their people in their way, and we will care for ours. Talk of *jihad* by the City of Faith against the City of War, *jihad* throughout the world, is a notion from the past, from a time when our faith was not mature. We do not seek to destroy the People of the Book so that we may return our faith to its embryonic beginnings.'

There was silence in the small room, only the sound of *Sayyed* Saddam Kashk's breathing. He was nervous. His father was calm as he delivered judgement.

'But this is what you sought. You called yourself Khalif, and sought to seem as great as the twelve Imams. I am *marja-e-taqleed*, and I decree that you hold no rank in Islam, you are but Mr Hossein. You are *mufsed fel-Ardh*, a corrupter of the earth, you have the devil inside, *Nafs-e-ammarah*. You thought only of bloodshed and violence, you sought power over the world; power is like a hungry dragon demanding more and more flesh. What you did was *ja'er*, evil, illegitimate. You talked of the People of the Book as people of *Shaytan*, when it was you who were *muharib an al-Allah*, waging war on Allah. I declare that you are *murtad*, a heretic, and may be the object of *qital* for all true believers.'

Hossein finally raised his eyes, and they were filled with amazement.

'*Qital*? You would have me hunted down like a dog?'

'You shall be killed to fulfil the will of Allah.'

Hossein raised himself to his feet. Fury emanated from his seamed, hawk-like face.

'It is you, your fat son and this woman who stands before me saying naught that will not leave here alive,' he promised.

'We shall,' said the woman, from behind her *hijab*.

'You shall?' mocked Hossein. 'And who makes so bold a claim?'

'I am Ashraf, the wife of Afsar, whom you have locked away in Evin prison,' she said, stepping closer to him.

'There are many who oppose me who are in Evin prison,' boasted Hossein. 'And many more to come. I am not finished, not with you, nor with the cross-worshippers and other followers of the City of War.'

'Do you not know me?' she said. 'If you saw my face, you would know.'

She was close to him as she pulled off the *hijab*, and let it fall to the stone floor.

'Do you not recognise the daughter of *Sayyed* Qavam, whom you had murdered at the Refah schoolhouse? Did they not strangle him on your command?'

There was a thud that echoed in the small room as Ash's fist hit Hossein's chest. In the moment of his dying he stared in disbelief at the handle of the dagger that protruded from his body.

'Go to your maker,' said Ash, and he fell to the ground.

DefCon V

Lowest level of alert. Peace

TEHRAN

The airport lights gleamed on the shining paint of Boeing
747 Air Force One, at rest on the ramp, but not on the
drab camouflage of the C-58 Galaxy transport rolling
slowly down the taxiway. The President was on his way to
Moscow, and was stopping in Iran to honour the new,
democratically-elected government. That government in
its turn was returning six items of property owned by the
USA. The weights-and-balances had been done and
checked, the loadmaster had overseen the securing of the
great missiles on their pallets and the giant transport
aircraft was on its way home.

In the great banqueting-hall of the palace the
chandeliers glittered with light. Silver cutlery rested on
snowy linen; wine glasses stood alongside those for water.
The Persians had long enjoyed wine, now those who
would fill their days with ritual from morning until night
were gone, for those who wished, it was available. The
hum of noise from the guests died away as the
newly-elected Prime Minister appeared with President
Cord. She wore a long, flowing cream silk dress. Hidden
by its length her feet were in soft and comfortable shoes.
She glowed with health and achievement; her opponents
had sought to make capital of the distracting effects of her
pregnancy during the election campaign; she had given the
serene riposte that her new life symbolised the new life
beginning for the nation, and in the result, the people had
agreed with her. Cord's visit was just in time, her
confinement was due the following week.

Faces from the past were in the hall; the exiles had come home. Familiar figures stood at the top table, Nelson, Davis, Kowalski, sonarman first-class Richard Davies, Michael B. Logan and Hamish MacDonald were there. So was Johnny Tombs, otherwise known as Nikolai Kotstov. He was going home in Air Force One, a symbol of reconciliation. On the breasts of the men rested Orders of Hosain with Swords and Diamonds, and they wore the accoutrements of *Chevaliers* of the *Legion d'Honneur*. Among the guests Mrs Madani and Eddie Lavasani and his wife waited for the Prime Minister to speak. She was practical, she kept her greeting short, people were hungry and thirsty, if she stood for too long her feet would swell.

'We welcome President Cord and his colleagues. We rejoice that our country is once again open to friends and visitors from the rest of the world, and that our American friends and allies have chosen to honour us by their presence here today. As a nation we have been closer to the American people for the past hundred years or more than any other. Ours has been a beautiful friendship that brought immense benefits to both sides, one born and nurtured by shared dreams and personal experiences. Our recent estrangement caused much unhappiness and suffering. Now it is ended. As our poet Hafiz said:

"I break the cord of your friendship
So that when it is knotted again, I come closer to you." '

The applause filled the hall as the Prime Minister and her guest of honour took their seats. As the crisp-coated waiters began moving among the tables and starched napkins were spread Ash felt her baby begin a tattoo of pleasure. He always waits until I have relaxed, she thought fondly. She beamed at Afsar, sitting by the First Lady.

The Galaxy rotated some 8500 feet along the runway and climbed out into the dark night, going home.

THE SNOW BEES

Peter Cunningham

Patrick Drake is ambitious. He's a high flyer who wants to get to the top of the corporate ladder – fast. And a business trip to sort out a fiasco of a French vineyard looks just like the fast track to promotion.

It isn't. He reports back to head office and then he's fired.

From muck-raking in a molehill of missing money, he steps on a minefield of murderous activity. In a tightening web of terrorism and violence he finds himself facing the naked savagery of the international cocaine trade. Fighting to clear his name – and to save his life – he unravels a threat of fear and fanaticism that runs from South Africa to Spain, from Ireland to the United States. And at any moment he may feel the fatal sting . . .

'Ripping' *Oxford Times*
'Gripping' *Standard*

0 7474 0137 3   Thriller

CONTROLLING INTEREST

Bernard Bannerman

'The body of a woman solicitor was discovered by staff
arriving yesterday morning at the Holborn offices of the
prestigious London solicitors, Mather's. Katrina Pankhurst
32, had been shot. Police are investigating.'

A murder on the premises is bad news for a law firm. It
discourages clients. It also discourages recruits which is
damaging to a firm like Mather's with a reputation, a lot
of clients, but very few partners. But, as Dave Woolf, one
time lawyer, part-time boozer and (almost) full-time private
eye realizes, a thorough professional would prefer a murder
to a leak any day of the week.

Also by Bernard Bannerman in Sphere Books:
THE LAST WEDNESDAY

0 7474 0383 X   Crime

CHOPPER 5: RENEGADE MIAs

Jack Hawkins

MEN OF THE FIRST AIR CAV

They were the cowboys of the sky – the U.S. helicopter gunship soldiers who believed in what they fought for and laid their lives on the line.

NO TERMS FOR TRAITORS

As the Viet Cong move in on the Special Forces camp near Dong Tre, the First Air Cav lays down awesome firepower, blasting the enemy from the hills. In the heat of battle, Brody spots something that turns his guts to ice – a Viet Cong squad led by a couple of American GIs.

Brody and his men have their orders: track down the killers and waste them. Outnumbered, they attack the enemy camp and fight hand to hand until the First Air Cav explodes on the scene, turning the bright green hills of Dong Tre into a Viet Cong bloodbath. And when the smoke clears, there's no place to hide for the

RENEGADE MIAs

Also by Jack Hawkins in the CHOPPER series
in Sphere Books:
BOOK 1: BLOOD TRAILS
BOOK 2: TUNNEL WARRIORS
BOOK 3: JUNGLE SWEEP
BOOK 4: RED RIVER

0 7474 0478 X   War Fiction

All Sphere Books are available at your local bookshop or newsagent, or can be ordered from the following address: Sphere Books, Cash Sales Department, P.O. Box 11, Falmouth, Cornwall TR10 9EN.

Please sent cheque or postal order (no currency), and allow 60p for postage and packing for the first book plus 25p for the second book and 15p for each additional book ordered up to a maximum charge of £1.90 in U.K.

B.F.P.O. customers please allow 60p for the first book, 25p for the second book plus 15p per copy for the next 7 books, thereafter 9p per book

Overseas customers, including Eire, please allow £1.25 for postage and packing for the first book, 75p for the second book and 28p for each subsequent title ordered.